Kni

MW01673589

The Country Gentleman

SALZWASSER
VERLAG

Knightley William Horlock

The Country Gentleman

Reprint of the original, first published in 1865.

1st Edition 2022 | ISBN: 978-3-75259-004-3

Verlag (Publisher): Salzwasser Verlag GmbH, Zeilweg 44, 60439 Frankfurt, Deutschland
Vertretungsberechtigt (Authorized to represent): E. Roepke, Zeilweg 44, 60439 Frankfurt, Deutschland
Druck (Print): Books on Demand GmbH, In de Tarpen 42, 22848 Norderstedt, Deutschland

THE

COUNTRY GENTLEMAN.

BY "SCRUTATOR,"

THIRD EDITION.

LONDON

THE COUNTRY GENTLEMAN.

CHAPTER I.

It was a calm, serene day in the first week of August, some thirty years ago, when, seated in a large garden chair in the pleasure grounds of Woodborough Park, two beautiful girls were enjoying the delightful shade of a fine old cedar, by whose thick and wide-spreading branches the scorching rays of the meridian sun were excluded. It was noon; not a leaf of shrub or tree, by which this sylvan retreat was surrounded, fluttered; not a breeze stirred sufficient to agitate the stately poplars, which raised their tall, spiral heads from the margin of a small lake lying at a short distance beyond the garden, and on whose smooth, silvery surface, not a zephyr played with its silken wing —not even a fish rose to cause a momentary circling ripple on the glassy bosom of its glittering waters. Above, around, beneath them all Nature seemed lulled to sleep, save that at intervals the hoarse cooing of the Cushat dove, echoing through the beech grove above the lake, broke in upon the stillness which reigned around.

Before these two fair daughters of Eve, who, of nearly the same age, had scarcely reached their seventeenth birthday, lay reclining on the nicely-kept lawn, supporting himself carelessly on one arm, his handsome face turned towards them, the form of a youth, who had just attained his twenty-first year.

"Well, Edmund," said Agnes Gerard, "so you are come home for the holidays at last; we thought you did not intend to honour us at all with your presence this autumn."

"Vacation, you ought to have said, Agnes; that is the correct term, as used by Oxford men; I am no longer a boy," with a contemptuous cast of his upper lip.

"Then what are you, pray?" asked Agnes, unable to suppress a laugh at his ill-concealed annoyance; "are you a *hobble-de-hoy*, neither man nor boy? eh, Edmund?" and another and louder laugh burst forth from the lips of the playful girl; on which Edmund, springing up, said, "I shall not remain here another moment, Lady Agnes Gerard, to be thus insulted;" and, with a haughty look at his fair tormenter, which excited more merriment and a still haughtier mien, he turned abruptly away into a walk which led towards the house.

"Really, Edith," said Agnes, "it is too absurd in that silly boy giving himself these airs. I shall not submit to such pettishness."

"I think you provoked it, Agnes," was the reply, "for no one likes to be laughed at, and we must not forget Edmund's kind, generous disposition, ever so ready to do anything he thinks will afford us pleasure."

"Papa spoils him, Edith, by too great indulgence. No one can do anything right but Edmund, in his opinion; and now you may depend I shall be lectured for hurting Mr. Edmund's feelings, merely because he chooses to be in a bad humour. He was to have taken us a drive in the pony carriage this afternoon; but now, I conclude, we must have John instead."

"Oh, no, I think not," Edith said; "Edmund will not forget his promise; and I shall tell him you did not intend seriously to offend him."

"You can do as you please, Edith; but I small make no concession to this petulant boy, who ought to ask our pardon for leaving us in such an impertinent manner; and, as I see the gardener coming this way, I shall desire him to tell John to get ready to accompany us on horseback, in place of Master Edmund driving us; so come, Edith, and let us prepare for our excursion."

Whilst the two girls are thus occupied in making their toilet, we will take this opportunity of relating something more of their families and themselves, with a short account of Edmund also.

Agnes Gerard was the only surviving child of the Earl of Woodborough—the child of his old age, as he had married late in life—her mother having died when she was only two years old; and it is almost unnecessary to add that, having been in consequence greatly indulged by her father from infancy up to the present time, she had now obtained complete ascendancy over him, and her will had become law to the whole household, not excepting Mrs. Errington, her highly-respected and talented governess, who had in vain attempted to curb her wayward, haughty temper when young; but her youthful charge invariably appealing to her father on any differences arising between them, he generally decided in favour of his child.

Agnes, notwithstanding, had become exceedingly attached to Mrs. Errington, who was a most kind-hearted, affectionate person, loving her with almost parental love; and being a lady by birth and education, the widow of a naval officer, in reduced circumstances, the Earl had entrusted her also with the superintendence of his domestic arrangements.

Agnes had now nearly completed her education. She was tall for her years, very graceful in her deportment, her features classically regular, with dark blue eyes and luxuriant chestnut hair, and her form beautifully defined, lacking only the development of mature growth to constitute its perfection of mould. Her mind and manners had also been formed by Mrs. Errington to comport with her high position; for, although one of that neglected, ill-paid class, a governess, Mrs. Errington was a person of superior intellect, and extremely lady-like; and being the daughter of a clergyman of old family, she had always mixed in good society. The Earl had exercised great discretion in selecting such a person to fill that most important situation, all-important to the future welfare of his only child; and being satisfied, after a twelvemonth's probation, with Mrs. Errington's many excellent qualities, she was considered and treated on all occasions as one of the family. She was not mewed up and confined in the school-room, like a nun in a convent, as too many unfortunate governesses are, without the opportunity of speaking to another human being, save the children under their care, or the nursery-maid. The Earl possessed too much good sense and feeling not to perceive that it was necessary for his daughter's future welfare, if not with any regard for her own comfort, that Mrs. Errington should still continue to mix in the best society—to observe continually the manners and courtesies of high life, to enable her to impart what was desirable to her youthful pupil. There was consequently no dinner party, however large or aristocratic, at which Mrs. Errington was not present: and when at first expressing her reluctance to appear on such occasions, she was courteously told by the Earl that she must always consider herself one of the family, and that so far from his desiring her to absent herself upon these occasions, he only regretted he had not greater opportunities for her to mix more frequently in society; and it must be confessed Mrs. Errington well deserved the Earl's confidence, since, irrespective of her religious and moral character, she was a person who would not pass unobserved, even among the most distinguished of England's aristocratic matrons and daughters.

In addition to her annual stipend, the Earl insisted on making her a handsome allowance to meet the extra expenses of dress, &c., and to enable her to appear as she ought amongst his guests.

The general treatment of governesses is both unjust to them and unjust to their youthful charges; although I am constrained to admit, from the pushing propensity so characteristic of the present age, when so few are satisfied with their own lot in life, that a great many young women are forced by their mistaken parents into the position of governesses, who have no pretensions to fill such responsible situations; and save from the fact of being sent to a miscalled seminary for young ladies, where they have acquired a smattering of the French, Italian, and German languages, in other respects not better as to family than upper servants; in short, I have known instances in which the children of servants have been educated for this profession, and numbers from the lower classes—daughters of small tradesmen, petty-farmers, village carpenters—are brought up to earn a wretched subsistence in this arduous calling, for which they are wholly unfitted. For admitting they possess good natural talents, and have acquired a sufficient knowledge of the general elements of education to impart instruction to others, yet from their thorough ignorance of the common customs and usages in genteel society, they are obviously incompetent to teach the daughters of gentlemen that refinement of ideas and manners, that easy gracefulness of carriage, so necessary to shine in that sphere for which they are intended.

If, however, such persons are entrusted by parents with the governance of their children, they should at least afford them an opportunity of mixing in society, and observing themselves the manners and customs of the world, of which they must be profoundly ignorant. Unfortunately, there are too many highly accomplished ladies of good birth and education, who have once moved in the best circles, reduced by adverse circumstances to seek such situations, and who are justly entitled to every attention.

Edith was the only child of Colonel Maxwell, a gentleman of old family, and good landed property, residing at Morton Grange, about three miles distant from Woodborough Park, where he had lived since the death of his father, some ten years previously, having then retired from the army, although still allowed to retain his rank. Mrs. Maxwell was his junior by some few years, yet in the prime of life, and still handsome, lady-like, and agreeable, and fondly attached to her daughter, who had been brought up under her own careful tuition, with the assistance of masters to finish her education.

Edith, however, had not been spoiled by too much indulgence; for her father being of the *martinet* school, kept her under rather strict discipline. In stature, Edith, like her friend Agnes, exceeded the medium height of women; she was slightly although elegantly formed, with large and lustrous hazel eyes, fringed with long lashes almost sweeping her cheeks. Her features, if not so classically formed as those of Lady Agnes, possessed even greater attraction, from being illumined by the most winning, bewitching smiles, which increased the fascination of the beholder the longer he dwelt upon them; and if her eyes betrayed the gentle emotions of a heart kind and feeling almost to a fault, her fine forehead betokened also deep intellect.

We are all sensible of the divine beauty of form; it is this which first attracts our attention: we gaze upon and admire it as the masterpiece of creation; but there is a far greater loveliness of mind, which lies not in the secret of outward proportions, and this beauty belonged to Edith.

The beauty of Lady Agnes, like that of a handsome gaudy picture, attracted at first sight general attention, but there was nothing beyond to engage a deeper interest. Her features, although faultless, wanted animation, and there was a half-witching, half-scornful expression about her beautiful mouth, which seemed to command rather than invite admiration. Edith differed entirely from her young companion in features, feeling, and ideas, being of most gentle and affectionate disposition, without a particle of vanity in her composition.

Of Edmund Knightley, we may briefly relate that he was the second son of an old English squire of that name, living at Wychwood Court, in the same neighbourhood, and godson of the Earl, who had taken such a fancy to the boy, that he felt more happy at Woodborough than in his father's house, where his elder brother exercised a galling dominion over him, on account of Edmund having been left a fine place and good landed property by an uncle (on the mother's side), Mr. Pemberton, who, dying without children, made Edmund his heir.

The Earl and Mr. Knightley being old friends as well as neighbours, had hoped that their friendship would be still further cemented by the union of their children; and the Earl perceived, with great inward delight, the partiality of his godson for his daughter, which had become now too evident to be mistaken. Edmund was a fine manly youth, clever and intelligent, of high, generous feelings and steady character, and the Earl loved him already as his own son; and next to Agnes, who held the supreme authority at Woodborough, Edmund's influence was recognised by the whole household, none of whom dared dispute his will, although that will was never exercised except in the most gentle manner, so that he became an especial favourite with all. When at home (for Woodborough seemed his home) during the holidays and vacations, Master Edmund was everything with the out-door establishment. The head keeper waited in the servants' hall to know if he intended going out shooting, the groom to have his orders about the horses, the bailiff about the farm; in short, Edmund had become the Earl's prime minister in all such matters, and he well deserved his godfather's confidence, possessing good sound sense and discretion. He was, moreover, a capital marksman, superior horseman, and clever at all athletic games, as well as an apt scholar. By this description we do not intend to claim for Edmund perfection of character. A young man may possess all the good qualities we have assigned to him, and yet fall far short of being a model for imitation.

The Earl, as to years, now fast approaching the limits of the age allotted to man, in form and stature represented a baron of the olden time, with a frame well proportioned, although considerably above the general standard. In manners he was exceedingly courteous, and held in great esteem by his neighbours and friends for his genuine kindness of heart and affability. Having, since the death of the Countess (to whom he had been too deeply attached to form a second marriage) given up the world with his town-house, his chief amusement was derived from agricultural pursuits; and his once expensive establishment had been reduced in order to provide more amply for his daughter, as the greater portion of his landed property went with the title to the next male heir.

St. Austin's, the place left Edmund by his uncle (now under trustees during his minority), lay about eight miles from Woodborough, and to this the Earl looked forward as his daughter's future home; and a more beautiful locality could scarcely have been found. The place, as its name denotes, belonged formerly to a monastery, the ruins of which were still standing in the grounds below the present structure, which had been erected by Mr. Pemberton's grandfather on higher ground. The house itself was a handsome edifice, sufficiently spacious for a gentleman of large property. There were two entrance halls, one on the western side, the carriage approach, and the other or inner hall (containing a fine oak staircase leading to the principal bed-rooms), the door of which opened to the lawn and flower-garden. On the ground floor were the usual apartments; saloon, drawing and dining rooms, of large and lofty dimensions, with a fine library of books. The site had been chosen with great taste, being protected on the north side by a finely-timbered hill, and surrounded by the most beautiful scenery, diversified with woodlands and water—three large lakes lying in succession down the valley, by the side of which the lower drive extended nearly two miles, before reaching the lodge gates.

These fine pieces of water, covered with swans and wild fowl, abounded also in fish, and being visible from the lawn and drawing-room windows, particularly attracted the attention of visitors, with the old abbey ruins, some half mile distant, the large oriel window still standing, forming a vista through which the eye was directed to the distant heath-clad hills. Below the house, and on both sides of the lakes, lay the large deer park, studded with magnificent oak and elm trees, beneath which, clustered in irregular groups, and adding greatly to the natural picturesque beauty of the scenery, reposed the deer, flapping their ears, and tossing their still soft velvety antlers to keep off the flies during the heat of a summer's day.

No public roads or pathways passed by, or within a mile of this secluded retreat, which, embosomed amongst the hills, lay in almost silent though majestic repose—like the Happy Valley—undisturbed by the rattling of public vehicles or the noisy clamour of men. Not even the ploughboy's whistle could be heard, no arable land being visible in this lower domain. The stillness which breathed around was, however, broken in the early spring months by the hoarse voices of a large colony of rooks, and the woods resounded with the shrill notes of the blackbird and thrush.

A rookery is generally considered as almost a necessary appendage to an old English family place; and it was once remarked by a country squire, the view from whose house had been obstructed by a new gaudy-looking structure, built by a rich parvenu who had lately purchased a few acres of land for this purpose—"Thank God, these fellows cannot build trees!" It is the misfortune, however, that they can *buy*, if they cannot build fine trees. Well would it be for this country, did the old Jewish law prevail here, which prevented landed property being alienated from its rightful possessor for a period exceeding fifty years, or beyond the year of jubilee, when it was obliged to be restored to him or his family. Under our one-sided jurisdiction, and that miscalled court of equity, aided and assisted by a set of voracious harpies—the just reward of whose nefarious acts and deeds would be a gallows as high as Haman's—country gentlemen are robbed and plundered of their old family estates, and consigned almost to beggary; and the money-made man, with his ill-gotten pelf, stalks through the halls of many an old ancestral home, where even the pictures from the walls seem to bid defiance to his insolent intrusion.

The rookery at St Austin's extended far and wide, containing many thousand birds, whose evening flight, on their return home, darkened all beneath them when, after a few circular evolutions above the house, they descended from a rapid whirl, with compressed wings, like so many black darts sent hurtling through the air from the skies above, falling into their resting-place among the trees; and during the building season, these black barons of the wood were seen strutting about the lawn, with almost imperial dignity, like lords of the place whose authority none might dispute. In fact, they had never been molested for many years, and old Mr. Pemberton left directions in his will, that they should never be ejected from their possessions by gun, or any other means. To my ear the cawing of a large body of rooks, diversified with the occasional shrill notes of the jackdaws, which attach themselves to the flock, and join in the chorus, like terriers with a pack of fox-hounds, if not quite musical, produces a most soothing effect; and their movements during the nesting season are not only entertaining, but highly interesting. It is amusing to observe the bowing and talking of the male bird to the lady bird of his choice, equalling in politeness of manner that of a gentleman in a ball room on his introduction to a partner: then after this ceremony, their flying away together in search of a site for their future house—the consultation held between them as to the eligibility of the spot—their search together after some large sticks for a foundation for their nest—the care with which these are fitted in their proper places—the rapidity with which smaller sticks are then added to the structure—then the collection of roots and grass as a lining, which puts the finishing stroke to their labour. Yet in this community of birds, private property is duly respected; since I have often noticed the purloining of sticks from their neighbour's nest, by an idle pair of young birds, immediately punished with the entire demolition of their own, by a party of some ten or twenty others, all pouncing down at once, and tearing it to pieces.

Whatever the opinion of sceptics, there must be a language among animals and birds, and an instinct separated only by a very thin partition from the reasoning faculties of man. The feelings of the dog are shown by barks and whines, expressive of joy at his master's return, with other outward signs—by growls at a stranger's intrusion; and what emotions of love or anger are shot forth from his dark hazel eyes, and expressed by that vehicle of a dog's feelings, his wagging tail! Their notice of passing events is also wonderful. I knew a dog which regularly attended church every Sunday, with a gentleman's servants. The carriage was ordered usually every day in the week, weather permitting, for the ladies to take their accustomed drive, yet Bob never followed it; it was only on the Sabbath that he accompanied it to church, and took his seat in the servants' pew, where he conducted himself with as much propriety as many professing Christians.

Bob was a character; a strange one for a dog—possessing an idiosyncrasy of disposition like his betters. His master kept his town and country house, being as much or rather more of a citizen than a country gentleman. Bob was the same, he liked change of scene, and when tired of the country, he would set out alone upon his eight mile walk into the City, where he remained some few days, perhaps longer, as it suited his fancy, and then returned to his country house again. Master Robert, as he was called, was as well known upon the road as in the City, and when assailed by larger dogs (he was a terrier), his mode of defence consisted, not in barking and biting them through the foreleg, as other little dogs do; but in sitting upon his haunches in a begging position, which so astonished strange dogs, that they passed him by without further interrogations. Bob possessed a meek disposition, seldom showing fight, but his greatest enemy was a large cock turkey, by whose gobbles and sharp beak he was terribly alarmed. The bird grew exceedingly red in the face on seeing Bob in his defensive attitude; he longed to put in a blow; but Bob shoved out his foot at every feint of his opponent to get in. The turkey moved round to find an opening for a dig with his beak. Bob moved too on his haunches, presenting the same unbroken front, and thus foiled the turkey, who at last retired from the ring.

From this digression on rooks and dogs, we will return to the young owner of the rookery.

CHAPTER II.

WE left Edmund in rather a pet with Lady Agnes for calling him a *hobble-de-hoy*. Now if there is one epithet more galling to a young member of the University of Oxford, although perhaps still in his teens, it is being called a *boy*. But Edmund, was more hurt than annoyed by Agnes laughing at him. It showed a recklessness on her part for the feelings of others, and Edith would not join in this provoking merriment at his expense. He did not regard so much the expression used by Agnes, but it was her manner and look which pained him deeply; for Edmund loved her with all the intensity of a first passion. We must call it passion, since his affection was not founded on esteem and admiration of her good qualities, but on her personal charms and beauty.

On returning to the house, he, however, went directly to his own room, and having prepared himself accordingly, walked down to the stable-yard with the intention of driving the pony carriage round to the hall door, which was his usual custom when taking the ladies for a little excursion of this kind. His annoyance and surprise may be imagined, therefore, when he found John, the under coachman, occupying his place in the little carriage, who informed him of the orders received from Lady Agnes. Without saying a word, Edmund turned round, and walked away from the stables towards the upper drive leading to the farm.

Lady Agnes, with Mrs. Errington and Edith, was already waiting in the hall when the carriage was brought round, and Mrs. Errington, knowing Edmund's promise to drive them said, "My dear Agnes, where is Edmund?"

"Indeed I don't know," she replied; "but as he is not here I shall not wait for him."

"He engaged to be our charioteer this afternoon, my dear, and we must not be so uncourteous as to go without him; perhaps he is with the Earl."

"No, ma'am," replied the footman; "I saw Mr. Edmund going towards the stables, only ten minutes ago."

"Then ask John where he is," said Mrs. Errington.

John's answer was, that Mr. Edmund, on finding he was ordered to attend the carriage, had left the yard without speaking a word, and had gone towards the farm.

Mrs. Errington, from this reply, coupled with Edith's look when her eye rested on her pupil's face for an explanation, surmising the truth, prudently forbore making any remark, and the three ladies entered the carriage in silence, ominous of a disagreeable drive, which it proved to all, since in such close proximity to a servant the ladies could converse only on commonplace subjects. Lady Agnes was also in a bad humour, and vexed with herself for ridiculing Edmund, yet resolved not to admit even to Edith that she had done wrong to him who was ever doing little acts of kindness to her. In this frame of mind everything that evening went wrong with Lady Agnes—the ponies went wrong—they took the wrong road, and in recovering the right one they nearly turned the party out. Lady Agnes could not go to Mr. Knightley's place (their intended destination) without Edmund, and she did not know where to go besides. Mrs. Errington was indifferent where they went, and Edith also.

"Then," said Agnes, in a pet, "we had better go home again." Meanwhile Edmund had been walking very fast for so warm a day, of which he appeared to be unaware, when at a sudden turn of the road he met the Earl returning from the farm.

"Why, Edmund!" he exclaimed, in surprise, "where are you going in such haste? I thought you were to have taken the ladies a drive this afternoon."

"So thought I, dear uncle"—the familiar name by which he had addressed the Earl since childhood—"but Lady Agnes willed otherwise by ordering John to attend her and driving herself."

"Some little misunderstanding between you, I fear," remarked the Earl.

"Of no moment," replied Edmund, "we shall be friends again at dinner-time, I hope."

"But, my dear boy, with your usual candour, you must tell me how it originated."

Notwithstanding his disinclination to say more, Edmund was compelled by cross-questions to state what had occurred.

"A very foolish affair altogether, dear uncle, you must admit," when he had told the cause of their difference, "and I was particularly silly to be annoyed by Agnes laughing at me, but I did not quite like being ridiculed before Edith."

"It was highly improper in Agnes doing so," replied the Earl, "and I shall give her a severe reprimand for her conduct."

"Let me entreat you, my dear Lord, not to say one word to her on the subject, or it will assuredly widen the breach between us, which may now be readily healed. A hint or even look of displeasure from you will convince her directly that I have mentioned that which I ought to have concealed."

"Well, well, Edmund, perhaps you are right; I will not allude to it at all."

During the whole evening Lady Agnes maintained her hauteur of manner towards Edmund, of which, apparently regardless, he directed his chief attentions to Edith, talking in his usual light, cheerful tone, as if entirely oblivious of the little *fracas* on the lawn. Agnes pouted with her pretty lip, and a quick ireful glance shot from her flashing eye, as it occasionally rested on her two young companions. Instead of sending Edmund, as she intended, *to Coventry*, it appeared that she herself had been excluded from all conversation that evening, for, replying to her father's and Mrs. Errington's questions in monosyllables, they ceased addressing her, and she was, therefore, left to her own unpleasant reflections, and the amusement of tormenting her pet spaniel; the evening having turned out too wet to admit of the young ladies taking their usual walk after dinner—at this season of the year the most pleasant time of the day being the evening.

The next morning little improvement was perceptible in Lady Agnes, over whose fair brow a cloud still lingered, threatening stormy weather. Edith was out of favour, also, for taking Edmund's part against her, although poor Edith pleaded wholly guiltless to the charge.

Soon after breakfast, Captain Duncombe, eldest son of Mrs. Duncombe, a widow lady who had taken a lease of St. Austin's during Edmund's minority, rode over to speak to the Earl (who was one of Edmund's trustees) about some repairs to the house, and having an eye to a little business on his own account with

Lady Agnes, he had resolved to spend the greatest part of the day at Woodborough, although aware of the Earl's dislike to himself.

The Captain was a gay, dashing young officer, very good-looking and agreeable, now in his twenty-fifth year, but reported as going much too fast for his means, and, from his expensive habits, occasioning great anxiety to his mother, who had two other sons and two daughters to provide for. The Earl, knowing his propensities and immoral course of life, suspecting, also, his intentions towards his daughter, and wholly disapproving his visits, was unable, however, to prevent them, although he was never invited to dine at Woodborough. On this occasion, the Captain, receiving more than usual encouragement from Lady Agnes, who considered it a good opportunity for annoying Edmund, sat chatting with her, regardless of the Earl's frowns, until luncheon was announced; whilst partaking of which, as a matter of course, he suggested to Lady Agnes that a row over the lake would be a most delightful recreation on such a sultry day.

"Oh yes," she exclaimed, catching at the idea, "it will be quite refreshing; don't you think so, Edith?" appealing to her friend, who gave a ready assent.

"I had rather you did not go on the water this afternoon, my dear Agnes," the Earl remarked; "you have a slight cold already"

"Oh, nothing at all, dear papa, and I have set my mind upon this little excursion over the lake, which we shall enjoy so much this sultry day."

"Well, my dear, if you must go, Thomas must go with you to row the boat, as Edmund has strained his wrist this morning."

To this proposition Lady Agnes perceived by her father's manner it would be useless to raise any objection, for there were some occasions on which he was very decided, and she saw by his look this was one when remonstrance would prove unavailing.

Now, Thomas, the footman, was a fine athletic young man, fond of all rural games and sports, and a great favourite with Edmund, who often took him out shooting and fishing, and he was also a good oarsman. Thomas, therefore, prepared with alacrity to obey the Earl's orders, having a preference for out-of-door work of any kind to loitering within doors, since, there being another under him, he had little to do.

The party were soon seated in the large four-oared boat, used also for fishing; Lady Agnes and the Captain occupying the stern, with Edmund and Edith further forward, nearly at the head of the boat, Thomas pulling in the centre. The lake, which lay just below the lawn, extended over some thirty acres, being very deep in the middle, but shallow all round the shore, and of an oblong shape. There was scarcely a ripple on the surface of the water, across which they were propelled by the vigorous arms of the stalwart footman, who appeared too intent on his occupation to notice very particularly the attentions and soft *sotto voce* speeches of the Captain to his young mistress. Thomas, however, did notice sometimes a little heightened colour on the cheeks of Lady Agnes, and it displeased him. Edmund, also, observing the same, sat almost silent by Edith.

They had been about an hour on the water, when Agnes desired Thomas to pull to the upper end or head of the lake, which was flanked by a small plantation of trees and evergreens, with some pretty meandering walks—just such a sylvan retreat for lovers as they would desire. Thomas, guessing how the case stood between his favourite, Edmund, and Lady Agnes, and that the Captain might take advantage of their little difference, was considering how he might best circumvent his manœuvres, when a sudden thought struck him, on which he acted without further reflection. They were now in about six feet water, the Captain lolling over the side of the boat, then going at a fair rate, when by catching a crab, as it is termed, with one oar—that is, suddenly checking the oar on one side—Thomas capsised the Captain by the unexpected jerk, sending him headlong into the lake; but, contrary to his expectations, his young lady was dragged overboard with him. Before, however, he could spring to her assistance, Edmund, forgetful of his wrist, had seized her in his arms, and was half swimming, half wading with her to the bank, the water scarcely rising up to his chin; but the Captain, being a much shorter man, and unable to swim, kept bobbing up and down, screaming for help, which Thomas, thinking he had now received a pretty good ducking, at last tendered with the end of the oar. But Thomas reckoned without his host, for, in attempting to pull him in, he was himself capsised by the Captain, the boat turning completely over, and poor Edith with a scream sent also into the water.

Thomas tore himself violently from the Captain's grasp, to rescue Edith, whom he immediately caught up in his powerful arms, and while she clung round his neck in her fright, the Captain held on to his jacket behind, until he found his feet on *terra firma*. Lady Agnes, recovered from her terror, was still standing on the bank, and could not restrain a hearty girlish laugh on beholding the Captain towed on shore in this ridiculous manner; and the moment Edith was landed the two girls ran off as fast as their wet clothes would permit them for the house, in great merriment at the Captain's expense, and rather pleased than otherwise with their adventure.

Mrs. Errington, however, seeing no fun in it, sent them both to bed, and there kept them between the blankets until the half-hour bell rang for dinner. Captain Duncombe, exceedingly disgusted with himself for the poor figure he had made in his aquatic exploit, marched directly to the stables, and, mounting his horse, rode off home. At the dinner-table the young ladies looked much the better for their cold bath; but the Earl and Thomas looked very serious. Lady Agnes, however, having recovered her good humour, which she was now freely exhibiting at the Captain's ludicrous performances in the water; and the Earl, seeing this little incident had turned in his favour, joined also in the laugh.

CHAPTER III.

LEST it may be imagined by any romantic young reader of these pages, that, as a necessary sequel to the little incident recorded in the last chapter, Lady Agnes should become all at once desperately in love with Edmund for preserving her from drowning, or that Edith should feel impelled by similar feelings to bestow her heart's affections on Thomas the footman, I beg to state that such was not the result of the adventure, although both the young ladies expressed themselves very grateful for the services rendered them; and Lady Agnes never after reflected on the young Oxonian for being a *hobble-de-hoy*.

The ungallant Captain, as he was henceforth denominated, fell down to zero in the young ladies' opinion, and Agnes, who was beginning to think she was half in love with him, suddenly changed her mind, offering to hand him over to Edith, which gracious offer was politely declined by her young friend declaring her resolution not to fall in love with any gentleman just at present; for although girls of seventeen, as a general rule, consider it a reflection on their budding charms not to have one beau at least to their share, by or before that period, yet Edith had been deterred from the indulgence of such a phantasy or flight of the imagination, by her papa's denunciation of such childish follies, and pooh-poohing the idea of a girl falling in love with any man, until first approved of by her parents. From these premonitory hints, Edith, being a prudent girl, and an affectionate daughter, had not as yet allowed love to enter into her youthful calculations, although there were two young gentlemen in the neighbourhood, who apparently required only a little encouragement to throw themselves at her feet; one of these being Edmund's elder brother, and the other the son of Mr. Shuttleworth, a retired cotton-spinner, reported to be worth two or three millions, who had, within the last three years, purchased the place and property of Mr. Egerton, a late country squire of that neighbourhood, who had been dragged down to ruin, and his property torn from him by nefarious law proceedings.

For two years the millionaire had been set at naught, or valued at his true price, by the country gentlemen, but had at last become on visiting terms with Colonel Maxwell and one or two other families, about a twelvemonth previous to the commencement of my tale. Mr. Zacharia Alphonso Augustus John Shuttleworth, the hopeful heir of the Shuttleworth family, a pink-and-white faced young gentleman, in his twenty-second year, resembling his mamma in rather a Dutch-built style of figure, after being sent at an early age to Eton, then to Oxford, and lastly on the Continent to spend a year or two in travel with a private tutor, returned home, having been modelled into something like a gentleman as to external appearance and the cut of his coat; but for all this pummelling, lecturing, and tutoring, the commonest labourer would never mistake him for a gentleman. The quiet, easy deportment of true gentility was wanting, as well as its characteristics of mind, heart, and feeling.

His first Christian name having been abbreviated when a boy by his father to Zack, was now, at his mother's desire, to give place to the second, Alphonso; and her domestics were ordered henceforth to call him by no other, on pain of instant dismissal from her service. Mr. Alphonso Shuttleworth, therefore, as we must perforce call him hereafter, having dined twice at Morton Grange, with his papa and mamma, cast a longing eye on the sylph-like form and bewitching face of the beautiful Edith. In short, he was quite enchanted by her grace and loveliness, and under some pretence or other, he had driven over there two or three times since, when, finding her at home, his passion had been fanned into a raging flame, which pervaded his whole mind and body like a devouring element; so that he disregarded the golden image of Mammon he had been taught to worship, setting up Edith as the idol of his heart, whom he resolved to marry if she had not a shilling in the world. He never for a moment doubted that his father's enormous wealth would immediately procure for him this coveted possession, and he had deluded himself into the belief that his handsome face (for such he thought it, and his mamma also) had already made a most forcible impression on the young lady's heart.

Alas! for Edith; how unconscious was she, poor girl, of raising such a storm in the breast of the young cotton-lord. But fortunately for her neither Alphonso nor his papa had yet set foot in the Hall of Woodborough, neither could old Squire Knightley be prevailed upon to leave his card at Hardington, since that place had been reft from his old friend Egerton, and transferred into the hands of Mr. Shuttleworth; so that Alphonso was obliged, patiently or impatiently, to await the return of Edith to her father's house before any further progress could be made in his suit; although the aforesaid youth made a most serious mistake in supposing himself the sort of person any young lady could fall in love with. Women do not, generally, fancy pink-cheeked young men, with smooth chins like their own, and figures the shape of a bale of cotton, with long, soft, straight, light hair. They believe there is neither sentiment nor spirit in men of this description. They look too much like the dolls girls have thrown aside in the nursery; and Alphonso might have sighed himself as thin as a thread-paper without obtaining the love of such a girl as Edith Maxwell. In fact, Alphonso's papa was a much better-looking man than his son, although not so finely polished; possessing rather large though not coarsely vulgar features, and his eye betokening great activity of mind. He was a sharp, shrewd, intelligent man of business, and having practised some few years as a solicitor, he was up to all the quirks and quibbles of the law.

Mr. Shuttleworth, having been employed solely by business men, that is, tradesmen, in Manchester, was thereby let into their secrets of rapid money-making by speculation; and having made two or three ventures himself in that line, which proved successful beyond his expectations, he was induced to embark more largely in such enterprises, so that in a very short time—marvellously short to the uninitiated—he was reported the richest man on 'Change. It is an old and true saying, that "money makes money;" but there is another equally true in the present state of monetary transactions, that "money can be made without money," a solution of which mystery will be best explained by a term well known to business men—paper-flying, or bill discounting cases being continually brought under public notice where tradesmen have made their thousands and tens of thousands with scarcely any capital whatever. There are facilities and accommodations afforded to men in business, by bankers and others, on the bare security of their names only, which a gentleman of good landed property might apply for in vain, except through the usual ruinous process of lawyers, law, mortgage, &c. The most iniquitous transactions in this money-making age are almost daily exposed, and until the public safety is protected by some new parliamentary enactment, roguery will ride rampant and rough-shod through the land. Even the lowest radical papers are compelled to cry out against the wholesale adulterations of every article sold for consumption, or the use of man.

On being put in possession of Hardington, the first act of the millionaire was to pull down the old time-honoured house—whose thickly-built walls had withstood the wintry blasts for three past centuries, and would have stood unmoved for a century to come—and erect a fine Italian-looking edifice on higher ground, the front being decorated with a portico of that order of architecture called the composite, and the interior finished off in the most expensive manner. On one side, the drawing, dining, and breakfast rooms, all connected by lofty folding doors, formed a range of apartments more than a hundred feet in length. The same floor also contained a large hall, splendid library, billiard room, with lady's boudoir, and hot and cold baths. The dome over the grand staircase was enlivened by gaudy paintings, of various devices, and a range of columns decorated the corridor leading to the bed-rooms.

The offices, over which were several good bed-rooms, besides sleeping apartments for the servants, were on a corresponding scale. A large conservatory, ornamented by pilasters, and connected with the breakfast-room, extended on the south side, crowded with plants and exotics of the most rare description. The kitchen-garden contained forcing houses, pineries, &c.; in short, the place was replete with every luxury of the nineteenth century. The drawing-room espceially presented the appearance of a large upholsterer's show-room, being crammed with every expensive article of furniture the genius of the upholsterer could invent. The retinue of servants corresponded with the house—the footmen of the loftiest stature to be procured—expensive articles these, which are paid for by their inches—appareled in gorgeous liveries—with carriages and horses on a par with those of any nobleman's establishment.

Mrs. Shuttleworth, as to form, bore a very striking resemblance to a turtle, being of about the same dimensions from her shoulders downwards, with a short, thick neck, on which was stuck a little, round head, with full, vermilion-coloured cheeks, and light grey eyes; as, however, she had supplied her husband on first starting with materials for greasing his spinning-wheels—being a tallow-chandler's only child, and possessing a large fortune—she carried matters with a very high hand over the household.

Mr. Shuttleworth, through his immense money power, had become a terror to the country squires, by purchasing every acre of land he could lay his hands upon—even very small farms, surrounded by another gentleman's property—outbidding every one else, more for the purpose of extending his influence, than as a fair investment, since the land so purchased would not return him two per cent.; and his round, fat squab of a wife was no less an aversion to the squires' dames, by cutting them all out with her gaudy equipages.

An instance of this man's extreme assurance in such matters occurred the morning after the two young ladies' plunge in the lake, when a letter was addressed by him to the Earl, proposing to purchase St. Austin's for his eldest son, who, on marrying, would require some place of his own.

"Here, Edmund," said the Earl, handing him the letter, "is something which concerns you more than myself—cool and impudent."

Edmund, having read the contents with a flushed face and angry brow, returned the letter in silence.

"Well, my boy," asked the earl, "what answer shall I return?"

"It requires none, in my opinion, dear uncle, and I should treat such an impertinent proposal as it deserves."

"Then do with it as you please, my dear boy—here it is," again placing it in his hands.

B 2

Edmund rose from the table, and going to the fire-place tore the letter to pieces, and throwing them into the grate, resumed his seat, without another remark.

The Earl, regarding him with an approving smile, said, "You have acted properly, in thus treating with cool disdain the impertinent proposition of this upstart cotton-spinner, who appears to think that every feeling must be sacrificed to money. But who can the lady be, whom this mighty Alphonso delights to honour, as about to be raised to the second place in the empire? Is it you, Edith, who are to be thus distinguished?" asked the Earl, with an inquiring glance.

"Indeed, no," she replied, quickly recovering from her slight confusion, and now returning the Earl's gaze with a steady eye

"The Colonel patronises this Mr. Shuttleworth," continued the Earl, "having, I am told, invited his family to dinner, at Morton Grange, several times, and has accepted his hospitality in return; so it may be resolved between the high contracting powers—the papas on both sides—to form a nearer alliance. What say you, Edith, to becoming Mrs. Alphonso Shuttleworth?"

"Never, my lord, with my consent," replied Edith, indignantly; "his father's treatment of poor Mr. Egerton, which Lucy told me of, I can never forget."

"I hope," added Edmund, "you will always adhere to that resolution, and not be persuaded by either father or mother to accept that low-minded cub, young Shuttleworth; for in that case, Edith, we should seldom meet again, since, as the friend of John Egerton, I never can or will hold intercourse with one of that man's family, who, trampling his feelings under foot, robbed him of his property and his home."

"I am rejoiced to hear you express such warm, manly feelings in defence of your ill-used friend, my dear Edmund," said the Earl, "and I certainly think Colonel Maxwell will ere long discover his mistake, in recognising a man of such ideas and principles so entirely at variance with gentleman-like conduct."

CHAPTER IV.

THERE is one other family of whom I must take notice in this early stage of my tale, that of Mr. Knightley. Descended from a long line of ancestors, who had possessed Wychwood Court for many generations, Mr. Knightley was now in his fiftieth year, rather tall and thin, standing about five feet eleven, and possessing a fine intelligent cast of features, little impaired by the hand of Time; in appearance and manners the personification of a highly bred and highly polished English gentleman. Being endowed with great natural abilities, clever, and well informed on general subjects, well versed in literature and the laws of his country, he had been selected to fill the office of chairman at the quarter-sessions; discharging his duties to the satisfaction of his brother magistrates, with equal courtesy and discretion. He held, in addition, another very responsible and arduous post—that of master of the fox-hounds, which had been kept in his family for more than a century.

Of Mrs. Knightley we need only say, she was a lady of very old family also, exceedingly pleasing in manners, and still retaining the elegant figure, if not the beauty, of her early life. Of their second son, Edmund, we have already taken notice; of their eldest, Reginald, it may be said that he inherited the good looks, without all the good qualities of his parents, being haughty and imperious in temper, and of a selfish disposition; yet possessing the polish and courteous demeanour of his father, and from his remarkably handsome features, and affability, he was quite a spoilt pet with the ladies of the county; and with his sister Emmeline, now in her nineteenth year, one of the most gentle, kind-hearted beings in existence, we will close this short sketch of the Knightley family.

At Woodborough, after the clearing up of the storm, calm weather succeeded, and Lady Agnes continued on the most friendly terms with Edmund; but she received his little attentions—presents of flowers and fruit—with a complacency which would have been destructive to the hopes of a more experienced lover. To her they had become matter of course offerings, and the smile with which they were received was considered by the young lady as a sufficient remuneration to the donor. Edmund, however, seemed to view everything connected with her conduct through a magnifying glass. The slightest tint on her cheek appeared to him a deep blush. The most trifling agitation was construed into embarrassment from another cause, and her gracious reception of his services tantamount to a reception of himself as her accredited lover; and this optical as well as mental delusion continued with Edmund, varied by occasional risings and fallings of the heart, according with the temperature of the weather, or rather the temperature of Lady Agnes's mind, until the expiration of his vacation; when a tear standing in her eye on leave-taking, sent him off in high spirits to Oxford, fully impressed with the idea that on the termination of his studies Lady Agnes would become his wife.

A fortnight after his return to Alma Mater, Edmund sent her a present of some choice and beautifully-bound books, the reception of which she acknowledged by a very affectionate letter, containing many expressions of kind feeling towards him —how dull they were without him, &c. &c.—and concluding by subscribing herself his most affectionate friend; which Edmund, by a wide stretch of imagination, converted into so many terms of undying love.

To an under-graduate of Oxford (the term signifying a young man who has not taken his degree), who is debarred from ladies' society, the form of his loved one is cherished more fondly and continuously than it might be in the turmoil of the busy scenes of life. A reading man, studying for his examination, is almost like a monk shut up in his cell. Early in the morning he is summoned by the tinkling of the little bell to chapel, from whence he returns to his solitary breakfast; that being dispatched, his books are laid on the table, over which he continues poring the greater part of the day, varied by a lecture or two with his tutor, until the dinner-hour; after which a friend or two may join him at his wine. During the spring or summer months, he takes his constitutional walk or ride in the evening, after which his studies are resumed until a late hour at night. This is the every-day life of a reading man at college; and, as a relief from this monotonous perusal of Latin and Greek authors, we need scarcely say how refreshing and exhilarating are the contents of a letter penned by the hand of a beautiful and dearly-loved girl, the object of his first and most pure affections.

Such was the case with Edmund now, although he had previously enjoyed many months of relaxation from deep study, when he had joined in the festivities of college life without being led into dissipation, and the too common vices indulged by non-reading men, from which highly moral and religious principles had preserved him uncontaminated; and, we may add, the love of Agnes acted also as one of the strongest repellents against any illicit desires. There are seasons of temptation, especially to the young and sanguine, when the best may be led astray, and forget their duty to their Creator; but in this hour of trial, the love of woman, if not the love of God, will save man from pollution. When oblivious or regardless of that eye which beholds the secret work ngs of the heart —of that omnipresent Spirit ever hovering around him, the imaginary form of a dearly-loved object stands in his path, like his guardian angel to turn him from evil. Let the worldly-wise and the libertine scoff and jeer at boys' and girls' love, if they will. Let parents preach on prudent matches, which they in their youthful days never thought of. But, in defiance of jeers and scoffings—of ridicule and expediency—I maintain that youth's first pure love of woman has rescued, when no other power could avail, many a man's soul from perdition. To the young I say—Love, love as early as you may some dear, sweet-tempered, pure, chaste girl—love her with all your heart and mind—with one sole, undivided affection, and that love will save your soul from destruction. But, above all, love the God of love; reverence his laws and commandments, and rest assured those commandments were not written by the hand of a hard taskmaster, but dictated by a sincere love to man, by whose obedience to those precepts his truest happiness will be secured on earth, with a foreshadowing of that which awaits him in heaven.

The love of Agnes proved an additional incitement to Edmund to keep himself unspotted from that little world in which he had been now living for more than two years.

After Edmund's departure from Woodborough, Edith returned home, to the great joy of Alphonso, who had made almost daily inquiries of the old woman who kept the lodge gates, as to when Miss Edith might be expected.

"Lauks now," said Mrs. Kirkman, the gatekeeper, to Mrs. Green, the under-gardener's wife; "there that young Halfonser, as they calls him, is always a-pulling up here in his fine curricle to know when Miss Edith's a-coming home. What's that to him, I should like to know?"

"A good deal, perhaps, Mrs. Kirkman; the young gentleman wants a wife, I suppose, to help spend his money for him."

"He won't get Miss Edith, though, Mary Green; she's much too good for the like of him."

"Don't make too sure of that, Mrs. Kirkman; gentlefolk be as fond of money as we poor souls, and I'd bet a new shilling-piece that if the old cotton-spinner comes down handsome, the Colonel wouldn't hang back."

"I thinks other guess, Mary; the Colonel's too proud of his family to let Miss Edith be married to a cotton-spinner's son, howsomever rich he may be; and then, such a plain, common-looking young man as that Halfonser. Why, Mary, you wouldn't let un change places with your John?"

"No, Mrs. Kirkman, that I wouldn't; our John's a more genteeler young man than he, for all his money; and they *do* say it warn't come by in an honest fashion like."

"Then I do say, Mary, and houlds to it, that he aint a fit man for our sweet young missus—dear heart! so gentle and so good! There, she do come and sit in that chair for an hour at a time, axing questions, and talking just like Betsey White; and bless her pretty little face! allays a-bringing summut for I or the old man—half a pound o' tea one time, a gown at another, flannel to keep us warm in the winter—money almost every week, to get the old man some more comforts when he comes home from work; and only two days agone, seeing our flitch o' bacon were handy gone, Farmer Tomkins, a-going to market, hollers out at the gate, 'Here, dame Kirkman,' says he, 'I got a present for ye; help to pull it out;' and down he bundles another great side o' bacon; ''tis for yerself and the ould man, to hang up in the kitchen and look at, if ye don't like to eat it.' 'Lauks, Mr. Tomkins,' says I, 'you be werry kind to us poor old folk.' ''Tain't my doing,' says he, 'and I sha'n't tell ye, dame, who sent it, although ye may guess. It com'd from a young lady, who see'd the flitch agin the wall were cut very short t'other day;' and, with a laugh, and whisk of his whip, Farmer Tomkins were gone. There, Mary Green, what do ye think of that?"

"I think's a good deal on it, Mrs. Kirkman, and Miss Edith's a dear, sweet young lady, and there's one young gentleman I should like to see her married to; but they say he's bespoke for her leddyship at the Park yonder."

"I knows who you do mean, Mary, Master Edmund; ah! he's a nice young man, and the only one hereabouts likely to make a good husband; but lauks, look yonder, if there bain't that Halfonser a-driving up the road, as fast as the mail coach." And the old woman had scarcely time to put on her bonnet when "Gate" was called out, and on its being opened he drove through.

The gate had not been closed a minute, before another voice was heard shouting, "Holloa! Dame Kirkman, open Sesame;" and young Squire Knightley appeared on horseback.

"Who has just passed through?" he asked quickly.

"Mr. Halfonser."

"Hang his impudence?" muttered Reginald, impatiently, not waiting to hear the other name; and setting spurs to his horse, he went away at full speed on the turf beside the drive, making the dry ground rattle like a board under his horse's feet.

"Oh, dear! oh dear!" cried the old gate-keeper; "that young Squire Knightley 'll be the death of Mr. Halfonser—look! look! he's a-frightened the curricle hosses, and they be a-running away, too, over the Park. Oh! my gracious, Mary, look! look! if there bain't Halfonser sent a-spinning hup in the air like a shuttlecock; and that hard-hearted young squire a-riding on, as if nothing war the matter."

Truly enough, such was the case; for Reginald, rattling by the curricle at full speed, set off Mr. Alphonso's high-bred horses, which bolted, defying all his powers to check them; until, from a sudden jerk over a large mole-hill, he was capsised out of the vehicle; but the groom kept his seat, until the horses stopped of themselves at the second gate. Alphonso picked himself up, a great deal more frightened than hurt, having descended from his pirouette in the air, as all falling bodies do, with his heaviest part downwards, and finding no bones broken he began to be exceedingly irate with the person who had caused his overthrow.

"Who is that insolent blackguard," he demanded of his servant, as he came puffing and fuming from his walk up to the carriage, "who set my horses off?"

"Young Squire Knightley, sir," the man replied.

"He's a blackguard notwithstanding, George, and deserves a good caning for his impertinence in galloping by me in that manner."

"You'd better not call him names, sir, or talk about caning, unless you wants to get a good horse-whipping first, and be shot arterwards. He can do both pretty well, sir, and it doan't take much to set his young blood a-biling up."

"Well, George, turn the carriage, I shall go home."

"What for, sir?" asked George; "you bain't damaged at all, as I can see—just a bit of dust on your back, which I'll brush off with my handkerchief."

"I feel rather sore, and out of humour, George, and had better not present myself before the ladies now."

"Dang it all, sir, I'd go on, if I had my arm broke, or the young squire will make a pretty joke of you before the young lady, for turning tail and running away. We shan't never hear the last on it; face 'em out, sir—face 'em out at once—you neddn't stop no longer than's agreeable."

Thus pressed, Alphonso felt compelled to proceed, and was soon after ushered into the drawing-room, where he found Reginald Knightley talking and laughing with Edith and Mrs. Maxwell, at what he surmised to be his mishap, as they ceased speaking on his name being announced.

Alphonso felt rather a warm sensation about his face and ears, as Reginald surveyed him with a proud, disdainful look on his approaching Edith, who was sitting with him on the sofa, evidently with the intention of offering his hand; but his heart failed him at this moment, from seeing no corresponding movement on her part, or even a smile of welcome. This increased his confusion, and he drew back with a bow; Reginald continuing his conversation with her, in a gay, lively tone, as before.

After sitting some ten minutes longer, Reginald rose, saying to Mrs. Maxwell, "I wish to see Edith's pony, which she tells me is pronounced incurable, and turned out to grass, if you will allow her to walk with me so far, for he will come to no one but herself?"

"Oh, certainly," was the reply; and as the young lady left the room to put on her bonnet, Reginald, politely opening the door for her, added, with a laugh, "Don't be long at your toilet, Edith—I will wait in the hall."

These words suggesting unpleasant reflections to Alphonso's mind, he proved anything but an entertaining visitor to Mrs. Maxwell, who felt relieved by his departure; soon after which Reginald again entered the drawing-room, whilst Edith ran upstairs to take off her bonnet.

"Really, my dear Mrs. Maxwell," he said, "I cannot conceive how you can patronise that cub."

"Why?" she replied; "he is very passable, although not quite so handsome or so agreeable as Reginald Knightley; but as he has now become one of us——"

"Pardon me, my dear madam, for interrupting you, but Heaven forbid he should ever become one of us—as well might a cart-horse start for the St. Leger, as that fellow presume to rank amongst thorough-bred gentlemen.

"Well, Reginald, he is very well in his way."

"True, my dear madam, but *his* ways are not *our* ways; and that fellow's groom looks more like a gentleman than his master."

"Well, poor fellow, he cannot help his appearance; but the Colonel thought it better to be on good terms with the neighbours, and therefore called on Mr. Shuttleworth."

At this moment the Colonel entered the room, and after the usual salutation said, "So, Reginald, you set off Mr. Shuttleworth's horses, and upset the young gentleman, I hear, by riding so furiously past his curricle?"

"I was not before aware, sir," replied Reginald, with a contemptuous curl of his lip, "that my pace was to be regulated by that of Mr. Alphonso Shuttleworth."

"Oh! certainly not, Reginald, but he is a young hand with the reins."

"Then he should let a better man handle them. I suppose, if he comes out with the hounds, I shall be compelled to pull up that he may take his fence before me."

"Come, come, Reginald, that is carrying matters a little too far; but I know you have a prejudice against this young man and his father."

"Which I feel convinced, Colonel," with a low bow, "will never be overcome; but the fact is, my dear sir, I took advantage of your elastic turf to give my horse a breather before regular hunting, not expecting to knock over a cub in my gallop; or make a *shuttlecock* out of a Shuttleworth."

"Well, well, Reginald, you can be very bitter sometimes, but don't be too hard on this young fellow and his father."

"I shall be as hard upon them, Colonel, as they have been on my friend Egerton, and woe betide the old fox or cub if they ever cross my path; and now for my mission, which is to ask you, Mrs. Maxwell, and Edith to partake of our last haunch of venison on this day week."

"We have no engagement for that day, I believe, my dear?" appealing to Mrs. Maxwell, "and therefore we shall have great pleasure in accepting your invitation."

"I am rejoiced to hear it, Colonel, as the Earl and Agnes honour us on that occasion, with a few other friends; and now, having other calls on hand, I must make my *congé* to the ladies and yourself."

Reginald Knightley, although not a marrying man, that is, not intending to enter into that state, without finding a wife with sufficient fortune to support his present style of living, resolved from that day to checkmate Mr. Alphonso's attentions to Edith, of which he had before been informed, more for the purpose of keeping him at a respectful distance, than of endeavouring to engage the young lady's affections; and this he thought might be easily effected, by the friendly intercourse which had from childhood subsisted between them, without endangering her happiness or compromising his honour. Reginald liked Edith better than any girl in that neighbourhood, in fact he had a very great regard for her; and could not bear the thought of her being transplanted into a family with whom he felt it impossible to hold any intercourse. He knew also that young Shuttleworth possessed a low, mean, selfish disposition, with vulgar ideas and vulgar habits, which would render any girl of a refined mind miserable if married to him.

He did not, however, attribute to Edith such bad taste as to accept willingly such a person as Alphonso—that he believed impossible; but he feared her father's influence over her might be exerted, as the Colonel appeared evidently resolved to patronise the young cotton-lord—with what views he could not understand, except in reference to his daughter. Reginald, therefore, intended to step forward boldly, and dispute every inch of ground with his detested rival, and determined if necessary to explain his motives to Edith.

CHAPTER V

CAPTAIN DUNCOMBE had become on very intimate terms with Alphonso—not on account of any similarity of ideas or tastes, but from prudential motives; intending to draw upon the young man's purse, when an opportunity occurred for this manœuvre to be put in execution. Moreover, there was always a feast of good things at Hardington, and some rare bins of wine, with the flavour of which the Captain was so exceedingly pleased, that he patronised the cotton-spinner and his family circle very frequently, where, truth to speak, he received a cordial welcome. Mrs. Shuttleworth was as much taken with his gay, sprightly humour, and as much amused by his stories (of which he possessed a great fund), as her son and heir; and he had rendered himself so agreeable, that the lady of the mansion told him "he would always find his knife and fork ready, whenever he liked to drop in and take pot-luck."

The Captain had been taking his "pot-luck" there a few evenings after Alphonso's misadventure at Morton Grange; and when the lady had retired to her drawing-room (the lord of the mansion being from home), Alphonso began, with their second bottle of claret, to relate his ill-treatment, so he termed it, by Reginald Knightley.

"Well," remarked his friend, "there was nothing to catch hold of on that occasion; he had as much right to be galloping on the turf, as you to be driving on the carriage road."

"But I heard him laugh as my horses swerved aside, and I believe he did it on purpose, to make them run away."

"Nothing more likely; but still this is no *casus belli*, you can't call him out for it; but as both visit at the Grange, you can soon find an opportunity for quarrelling with him; for he is a confounded, overbearing, insolent puppy, and I will be your second, my boy, which is more than I would be for any except a very particular friend."

"Thank you, Duncombe," was the short reply, in a tone which clearly implied, "No thanks to you for the offer."

"This Reginald Knightley seems on good terms with the Maxwells," he continued, after a slight pause; "paying his *devoirs* to the young lady, I suppose."

"I suppose not," said the Captain, "for the Colonel is a close-fisted old chap, and won't fork out very freely for his daughter during his lifetime, and Reginald knows when he is well off. He has now his five hundred a year, to find himself in clothes and horseflesh, and on marrying, the old squire may allow him a thousand more; but this won't maintain a wife and children in the style he now lives at his father's house. You may take my word for it, then, young Knightley won't marry any girl without lots of money down, and that he won't get from the Colonel."

"She's a deuced pretty girl, that Edith Maxwell," remarked Alphonso; "don't you think so, Duncombe? quite a clipper!"

"By gad, sir, there's no mistake about it; but pass the bottle, old fellow, you have helped yourself twice to my once, and that's not fair with such wine as this."

"Beg pardon, Duncombe, but we'll have another fresh bottle," pulling the bell, on which the butler entered with coffee.

"Take that stuff away," said Alphonso, "and bring more claret."

"Tea is ordered in the drawing-room, sir," replied the man, "of which I was desired to inform you."

"Then the old woman may keep all the cat-lap to herself, Mr. Sharpnose; but you bring us another bottle of claret, and say we are coming when that's finished."

The butler obeyed, soon returning with the wine.

"Now, Duncombe, you shall have the first buss at it," Alphonso said, beginning to feel excited; "and I should like uncommonly to get the first buss at that girl's lips."

"You don't say so, do you? Well, you're not perhaps singular in that wish," replied the Captain; "I should fancy it very much myself, for she is the prettiest girl I have seen yet in the whole county, and will make a splendid woman when she comes to maturity."

"Then why don't you make up to her yourself, Duncombe?"

"I can't afford to marry, without plenty of the current coin down on the board. You can; that's just the difference between us; but with a tenth part of your governor's money, I would put in a bidding for her to-morrow."

"Well, Duncombe, I've a deuced good mind to have a shy at her myself, and I daresay our two governors could soon come to terms, if she suited me."

"Confound your impudence," thought Duncombe. But he merely said, "Oh, of course," with a sneer, which Alphonso did not observe. "But you must be quick about it, for there is Welford of Elmhurst, with lots of tin, and that fool Addleby, of Addleby Hall, both on the look-out for wives. Welford is a conceited coxcomb, and thinks no woman in the county good enough to suit his fastidious taste; but he may alter his opinion when he sees Edith Maxwell. By the way, Shuttleworth," continued the Captain, "you ought to have had your stud of hunters all in trim by this time, fit to go."

"The governor don't wish me to keep hunters, that's the truth," was the reply; "I don't intend to hunt."

"Not hunt!" exclaimed the Captain, in well-feigned astonishment; "not hunt! then what the deuce are you going to do with yourself through the winter months? Going to Margate or Ramsgate, I conclude. You can't live in London this time of year, and if you go to Leamington, Cheltenham, or even to Brighton, you will be expected to hunt there, or be set down as a regular spoony. Here, you *must* hunt—every man in the county does, down to the chimney-sweep on his jackass. Go to bed and to sleep like a dormouse for the winter if you like—shut yourself up in the library as a book-worm; but for a young fellow like you to be driving a pair of horses about the roads in a curricle, when every gentleman is out hunting—by gad, sir, the thing is perfectly ridiculous, and you'll be the laughing-stock of the whole neighbourhood. By gad, sir, every girl in the village would turn up her nose at you, let alone the young ladies of the county. Don't look at one of them if you don't hunt. Ours is, *par excellence*, a fox-hunting county; half the fellows who go out with the hounds hate hunting for the hunting only; they go to the covert side to meet their friends and neighbours. It is a grand re-union—a sort of general club-house gathering, *sub Jove frigido*—they are expected to be there, it is the fashion of the neighbourhood; you *must* hunt here, or tell your governor to sell his place again, and go elsewhere."

"Well, but the huntsman has not left his card upon the governor yet, which makes him feel sore on the subject."

"It would surprise me wonderfully if he had. Will Laing don't visit at gentlemen's houses, although he is a great man in the field."

"I meant Mr. Knightley," Alphonso said.

"He is the master of the hounds, my young novice, not the huntsman; but why is that to prevent your hunting? The master of the hounds is a mere master of the ceremonies in the field. It is not necessary you should know him personally to hunt with his hounds, not a whit more than you should know the manager of a theatre, the stewards of the races, or the committee of a hunt ball. The hunting field is open to all alike who conduct themselves with propriety—noblemen, gentlemen, professional men, farmers, tinkers, and tailors, the latter generally preponderating as to numbers."

"Where do all the tailors come from, then?" asked Alphonso, very innocently.

"Can't say, my boy; but when you first come out there will be one from Hardington."

"What, Jones? he don't keep a pony."

"He keeps a goose, though, as well as another old gentleman I could mention—however, *n'importe—you'll* be a confounded tailor if you don't come out"—(and aside, "a d—d tailor if you do")—"but now as to horseflesh; you must get at least half a dozen hunters directly, and short time enough to put them in trim, having only a month to do it. Every man shows on the first of November—a regular thing, an established custom."

"Show where, Duncombe?"

"In the field, to be sure, on horseback at the place of meeting;" (and aside—"I'll be bound you show off deuced soon.")

"The governor won't stand half a dozen more horses,' replied Alphonso.

"The governor be hanged! he *must* stand it, or shut up shop here, and go back to Manchester. When you are at Rome, you must do as the people of Rome do."

"I have been at Rome, Duncombe."

"Every cockney goes there now-a-days; but what did you see there?"

"Oh! St. Peter's Church, the Coliseum, and lots of other things—I don't recollect what."

"Well; now you are in *Huntingshire*, you must go and see the hounds, and as you haven't any nags yet, I'll tell you what I'll do. I will let you have a couple of mine. I can't spare more—well-seasoned hunters, know their business, carry you like a bird across country—and you shall have them at cost price, just to set you going. They have had their regular sweats, hard as nails in condition, splendid animals to look at, heads and tails well up; all alive ho, and right as a trivet"—(so they were, each having only three legs to stand upon!). "I keep six myself, but I can soon pick up two more, and you shall have these two as a particular favour."

"Thank you, Duncombe, I feel greatly obliged by your kind offer, but I must ask the governor about them first."

"Put them in the stable first, and ask your governor how he likes them afterwards. Why, what did you do at Oxford? Ask the governor about everything you meant to do?"

"No, not, exactly; but he wouldn't let me keep hunters there—said I must read for a double first—so kept me a private tutor instead."

"Well, but what did you do on your own account?"

"Pulled in a four-oared boat."

"Very slow."

"Gave champagne breakfasts."

"Rather fast."

"And drove tandem with a hired team."

"Very snobbish; but what became of all the Latin and Greek you had to swallow?"

"Well, Duncombe, I read deuced hard for a double first,

being crammed all the long vacation into the bargain, and——"

"Got plucked at last," added the Captain; "just as I thought. That comes of following your governor's advice. He thought to make a great man of you in the Latin and Greek line, and made a fool of himself, and you too. Now, if he had set you spinning away with your couple of hunters and covert hack, champagne breakfasts, wine parties, and hot suppers, doing the thing in style, as a young fellow with lots of tin ought to do, he might have made something like a sportsman and a gentleman of you by this time. Men would have spoken of young Shuttleworth as a fine, dashing, good sort of fellow. What do they say of you now? That you were a spoony at college, knew nobody worth knowing, except Sally Jones and Polly Brown, whom everybody knew to their cost; went for a double first, without knowing Xenophon from Sophocles, and got plucked as a matter of course. Now we must begin *de novo*, strike out a new line, cut a swell with your ten hunters, and a spicy drag to the place of meeting, and you will get on in the county, and be thought something of. If you don't go out hunting, you may as well go to the d—l at once. So now we will go for a cup of cat-lap to the old woman."

"Let us have another bottle first, Duncombe."

"Not a drop more now, my boy; but we can finish off with a jug of mulled claret and a grilled bone in your own room, after your mamma is gone to roost."

On entering the drawing-room, Mamma Shuttleworth was observed reclining in her arm-chair, fast locked in the arms of Morpheus, and snoring loudly.

"Hark to Juno, hark! cry," screeched the Captain, considerably elated by the last bottle of claret, and uttering a scream, which bundled the old lady out of her chair like a bale of cotton.

"Mercy on us!" she exclaimed. "What's the matter? Is the house on fire?"

"Only your bedroom chimney," replied the Captain.

"Oh, my gracious!" cried the old lady, who had a great dread of fire, beginning to roll out of the room as fast as her short legs could carry her.

"Stop, mother," said Alphonso; "it's only the Captain's gammon; there is nothing the matter."

"Oh! but I am sure I heard some one screaming."

"Just the Captain spoke a little loud, mother, to rouse you

out of your nap; that's all, honour bright; so sit down again in your easy chair."

"Ah! Captain, you're always cutting your jokes; but 'twas your fault I was caught napping, sitting so long over your wine. I can't think what you men can find to talk about."

"Why, my dear madam, I was giving your son a little insight into country life, of which he is marvellously ignorant, and some very necessary advice how to become a popular country gentleman."

"That's very kind of you, Captain."

"It was intended so, I assure you."

"Then, what is he to do?"

"He must keep a stud of hunters to begin with, as every gentleman in the country does, who can afford it."

"Oh, dear, dear! I'm so afraid of Alphonso hunting; he'll be sure to meet with some fearful accident, break his arm or his leg, or something dreadful."

"That's all stuff and nonsense, my dear madam, begging your pardon; old ladies' fancies; people that hunt don't break their arms and legs oftener than other people who don't hunt; but if you want your son and heir there to be set down as a molly coddle, don't let him hunt, that's all. His father made a fool of him at college, and you will make a fool of him at home, so there's an end of the business." On which the Captain gave vent to his spleen by stamping on the tail of a large, sleek Angola cat, lying on the hearth-rug before the fire, causing pussy to speak out pretty loudly.

"My goodness! what ails Tomasina to-night," exclaimed her mistress, "twirling and twisting her tail about in that fashion?"

"Got the cramp, I suppose, like myself, from eating too many filberts," replied the Captain. "Egad, Al— no, hang it, Shuttleworth, junior, I should like just a liqueur glass of pure cognac to settle matters."

"Better have a cup of tea, Captain dear," suggested the lady.

"No, I thank you; I never take tea except at breakfast, or coffee either."

"Well, Alphonso, will you ring the bell, and order what the Captain wants?"

"I wish to goodness, madam, you would call your son by some other than that outlandish name; it sounds so ridiculous that I cannot pronounce it: Augustus, if you like, that's bad enough; but Gus would do for short, or even Zack for Zachariah."

"Oh, Captain, I cannot bear them short nick names, Jack, and Tom, and Joe, they sound so vulgar; and then, I can't abide Jim and Bill."

"To the latter, I confess a particular objection," replied the Captain, "as they are generally deuced disagreeable fellows, when they pay one a visit about Christmas time. Now, George Brown, Harry Jones, or any fellow with a common name, may get plucked at Oxford half a dozen times if he likes, and he is soon forgotten in a crowd of such other names; but an Alphonso, or Cicero, or any out-of-the-way name, will be remembered with his plucking to the end of his days. 'Who's your friend?' asked a gentleman of me the other day, when your son had been speaking to me. 'Shuttleworth,' was my reply. 'Not Alphonso, eh? the fellow whom every one of that day remembers to have been plucked for his great go at Oxford!' Personally your son is unknown; but the name of Alphonso strikes every Oxford man directly, as connected with that unlucky go; so, in plain terms, my dear madam, if you don't cut the name, I must cut the connection; instead of Zack call him Jack at once, the last name instead of the first; Jack Shuttleworth will do, it sounds sporting—Jacks are generally good fellows."

"Well, Captain, but I never heard anything about this before."

"And never would hear it," he added, "to your dying day, from anybody except Tom Duncombe. People who come to eat your good dinners, and drink your wine, don't say unpalatable things to your face, although they say deuced disagreeable things behind your back; but I have noticed many a sneer at the name of Alphonso, which meant, 'That will stick in his path through life.' I wish the lad well, and therefore boldly tell you the truth."

"Then, Captain, I will call him John for the future; and now, as it is past eleven, I must wish you good night."

It is unnecessary to state the reasons—there were more than one or two—why Captain Duncombe appeared to take such an especial interest in Alphonso as to inflict this lecture on his mamma, with whom he generally contrived to have the best of the argument; for Mrs. Shuttleworth, from his high connections on the mother's side, and his general acquaintance with the county families around them, always gave way to his opinion on social questions; irrespective of which, the old lady had taken a great fancy to him, from his handsome person, agreeable manners, and lively good-humour. The Captain knew also the fashions, forms, ceremonies, and etiquette observed in the higher circles, and gave her many useful hints on such subjects, so that he might say or do almost what he pleased at Hardington.

Now, the Captain was too good a judge to make a market of Alphonso in his first deal with the two hunters. They were both old and stale on their legs, but just the animals to suit a novice; they knew their business well, and *would* go with the hounds; and one, named Mameluke, pulled hard to be where he ought to be—a trifle too hard for a timid rider; in short, it was little use pulling against him, but let alone, he went pleasantly enough. The bargain was concluded that night over the grilled bone and jug of mulled claret, and the two horses were to become Alphonso's property, for one hundred and eighty guineas, if approved of the next day; and it is almost needless to state that Alphonso, deeming it imperative upon him to hunt, and being greatly pleased with the form and condition of the horses, gave the Captain his draft for the amount claimed, without hesitation, and Marmion and Mameluke were transferred to his own stables.

Now, Alphonso, having the hunters, was in the predicament of the boy who first purchased a bird, and then felt obliged to buy a book to keep it by. He had not the most remote idea of riding over a fence, and was therefore under the necessity of applying to the Captain for instruction, who, after a few preliminary lessons as to mounting and dismounting, holding the reins, seat in saddle, &c. &c., took him out on Marmion, the oldest and steadiest of the two (it being now the first week in October), for a short trial across country.

"Now, Jack," cried the Captain, as they approached a flight of hurdles across a clover field, "this is soft falling if you are capsized; so, harden your heart, sit down firmly in your saddle, stick tight with your knees and thighs, lean a little backward, as you see me do, give Marmion his head, and come along."

At the first charge, Alphonso got his discharge from the pigskin, being thrown forward, like a trapped frog, with arms and legs extended, on to his horse's neck, around which he clung with instinctive tenacity, much to the disgust of Marmion, who, not being accustomed to such hugging from his former riders, threw up his head, which, coming in contact with Alphonso's olfactory organ, or nasal projection, sent him back to his seat with a bloody nose.

"Well done, Jack," shouted the Captain, "ably recovered."

"I call it very badly done, Duncombe, to get a bloody nose the first go."

"Save the lancet, Jack—you wanted bleeding uncommonly; save you from an apoplectic attack."

"Gad, I don't much fancy this sort of thing."

"Well, nobody quite likes having his claret spilt; but it's a good beginning, bleeding and physicking for training, which every man wants as much as his horse, to ride well to hounds! now you'll follow my advice, perhaps, the next time, by leaning well back when your horse rises at his fence, which would have saved you that noser; but young, obstinate fellows always think they know better than their teachers."

"Indeed, Duncombe, I did not despise your advice, but somehow or other I could not sit back, being suddenly jerked out of the saddle."

"Well, never mind; riding don't come quite so natural to men as whooping to owls, but practice makes perfect; turn about, and at it again, now the claret tap is stopped."

This time Alphonso fared better, having one leg only thrown out of his stirrup—it was an *all but*, but he did not fall.

"That's your game, Jack; I see you don't mean falling; you'll do, my boy, presently."

And after a few more jerkings and jumpings over the hurdles, Alphonso began to like the fun, and the Captain, patting him on the back, thought they had better leave "well alone" for that day, and go home to luncheon.

Alphonso related his adventures with great glee to his mamma, who, being kept in the dark as to his bloody nose, began to think her darling would turn out a hero in the hunting-field, and eclipse the whole country by his wonderful exploits in horsemanship. Shuttleworth senior, although a non-hunting man, and averse, at first, to his son's joining in the pursuit of the fox, was obliged at last to yield to Duncombe's arguments.

"Your son must hunt, sir," remarked the Captain; "and if you object to his meeting Mr. Knightley's hounds, he can hunt with the Marquis of Dunkerton's pack, which generally meet within moderate distances. I know Dunkerton well, and will introduce your son to him, that is, provided he hunts, not otherwise."

"Very well, Duncombe, then I suppose he must hunt."

"No doubt about it, my good sir; so let him do the thing

well, and I will give him all the necessary instruction before the regular season commences."

Matters being thus arranged, the Captain obtained an order to purchase three more hunters, which was done without delay, and greatly to his own satisfaction, Duncombe pocketing by the deal a hundred and fifty guineas, the allowance made to him by his friend Dickens, the horse-dealer, for sticking them into the cotton-lord at a very stiff price.

We may here remark that the Marquis of Dunkerton hunted the country adjoining Mr. Knightley's, and we may also add, that the greatest contrast was perceptible between the two masters: the Marquis, who also kept race-horses, and betted heavily on turf events, being most imperious and abusive in the field, whilst Mr. Knightley's conduct was remarkable for courtesy and forbearance towards those who might unwittingly interfere with his sport.

CHAPTER VI.

THE fox-hunting community being now in tolerable jumping order, we may jump over the intervening space of time (not a very wide leap) to the first day of November, when the opening of the campaign was fixed for Wychwood Court, the seat of the master, where breakfast was provided on a large scale for the expected company.

One of the most conspicuous personages on this occasion was old Squire White, a tall, stout, robust man; as to age, approaching his sixty-fifth year, but still hale and hearty. Abel White was one of the old school of fox-hunters, fond of the sport, and, it must be admitted, rather fond of good port wine, which most people would suspect, from his jolly rubicund face. Mr. White had lived a bachelor's life, having been once the owner of very large landed property in the county, of which, somehow—nobody could tell how—he had contrived gradually to dispossess himself, without any ostensible cause. He had lived well all his life, although not extravagantly; kept his four hunters, with a moderate establishment of servants; gave, in his turn, good, plain bachelor dinners, with port, sherry, and madeira—the two latter seldom tasted by himself—but at this rate, people said, he had never lived up to half his income; still that income was now reduced to about seven hundred per annum, this small property, with the old Elizabethan house at Westwood, having been strictly entailed by his grandfather's will. He was on visiting terms, however, with every family in the county, and a most welcome guest at every dinner-table, from his jovial good humour, and almost inexhaustible fund of anecdotes.

Mr. Welford, of Elmhurst, who had been bequeathed a very large fortune, amassed in trade by a rich uncle, presented a most striking contrast to old Squire White, both as to bodily frame and appearance—Welford being slightly formed, of thin and prepossessing features, and, as to dress, a dandy of the first water. Here were presented the two opposite specimens of Old and Young England. The large, full red coat, broad-brimmed hat, loose cravat, huge waistcoat, woollen cloth continuations, and mahogany-topped boots, with the strap over the knee, in opposition to the swallow-tailed scarlet, the white buckskins, and the highly-polished jack-boot, just then coming into fashion, which has always struck me as more appropriate to the leg of a French postilion than to that of an English fox-hunter.

Welford had now reached his thirty-fifth year, and in reply to the question often asked by his friends, why he did not marry, coolly remarked, "that he had not yet seen any woman at all adapted to his taste;" thereby insinuating that he had only to ask, to have any young lady he might condescend to admire; for which, and his conceited, foppish manners, he was anathematised by old Squire White as an insolent, upstart puppy, giving himself more airs than the greatest nobleman in the land.

There was another rich bachelor also present on this occasion, Addleby, of Addleby Hall, who bore the rather appropriate nick-name of Addlehead, from his eccentricities. Still, to those mammas who cared little whether their daughters married a man or a mopstick, provided he had money, Addleby presented the prospect of a good investment in the matrimonial line, with a fine old place, and his ten thousand a-year; although, as the old squire said, "he exhibited the devil's own temper when put out of his way, which could only be excused by the bee in his bonnet."

The only other person I shall now stop to notice out of this goodly company—amounting in all, with red, black, blue, and green coats, to about three hundred horsemen—is Will Lane, the huntsman, who was born at Wychwood, and had lived from boyhood in the Knightley family. Will, from hard work, and his entrance on his second half century, began to look very badgery about the head; but being of a thin, spare frame, he still exhibited the greatest activity in the field, and rode as well up to his hounds as in the first season of his appointment to the post of huntsman. Will was what is called a character, *i. e.*, he possessed certain idiosyncrasies or peculiarities of disposition, speech, and action; but he was a great favourite with the whole fox-hunting community, and most highly esteemed by his master for his strict integrity and the zealous discharge of his duties in the kennel and the field.

"Well, Will," asked the old squire, "what do you think about a scent to-day?"

"I'm a-thinking, sir," he replied, "that there's a feeling in the *hair*, which will make your old mare's tail shake; although I'm rather dubious about giving any decided opinion on scent, which, as you knows, squire, is rayther a ticklish subject."

"There's the young cotton-lord come out to see how we do things, Will," continued the old squire; "that's him talking with Captain Duncombe, on the big brown horse—he must be blooded to-day."

"Oh, in course, squire, if I catches him up at the finish, but I'm a thinking he don't look a likely one to be there if we have much to do."

A full hour having been consumed in the preliminary business of the day, breakfasting and partaking the master's good cheer, the order was given to "move off," and Will Lane trotted away with his pack, when a brace of foxes were quickly on foot, which were rattled about at a spanking rate for ten minutes, when the old dog rode away in full view of the ladies, a large number of whom had driven over to grace the opening meet of the season.

A shrill view holloa from Charley, the first whipper-in, brought the hounds tearing out of the covert, when, settling down on the scent, they went away like a flash of lightning.

"Come along," cried Duncombe to his *protégé* Alphonso; "he's away."

"Who's away?" asked the novice.

"The fox, to be sure, you spoony!" muttered the Captain; "come on, I say, and give your horse his head; we have got a capital start—there go the darlings, right before us!" and setting spurs to his horse's side, the Captain went down the hill on his thorough-bred, as if he was riding for the Derby. Alphonso, greatly against his inclination, was obliged to follow, for Mameluke, maddened by the clatter of the cavalcade behind him, pulled enough to tear his rider's arms off, for go he would, although not possessing sufficient speed to overtake his late owner. Now, riding fast down hill tries a man's pluck far more than riding across country; and the perspiration broke out over Alphonso's face (who was also sadly out of condition from insufficient training and too good living) before he reached the bottom of it; in fact, as the Captain observed when looking back, "Jack was in an awful funk, with a very wishy-washy kind of seat, and holding hard on by the reins," at which he was still tugging with might and main.

"I'm a-thinking, Captain," remarked Will Lane, who had passed Alphonso coming down the hill, "that young friend of yours will be doing mischief to himself or somebody else afore he goes much farther."

"Not unlikely, Will, for he is a confounded tailor on horseback, and sits like a bale of cotton; but we can't stop for repairs now."

This was said as they were approaching the Park palings, which with a ha-ha they both cleared.

"Now, then," cried the Captain, looking back as they were rising the hill, "if young Shuttleworth can sit *that*, he will sit anything—Mameluke will have it, and by Jove, sir, he's over, neck and crop, somehow—hanging round his horse's neck. No matter—he has done it in a fashion of his own, and here he comes up the hill, all right again in the pig-skin."

To say that Alphonso enjoyed the fun, or saw anybody or anything save his horse's ears and the fences before him, would be an absurdity. Mameluke *would* go where the hounds went, and his rider, finding it hopeless to pull against him, gave up the attempt in despair, still holding on by the reins, and clinging to his horse with fearful tenacity. Once or twice, he thought of throwing himself out of the saddle, but that he knew, at the pace he was going, must be attended with a serious fall; and now, having reached the Captain, he was cheered on by him, and restored to a little more complacency of mind.

"Well done, Jack, you're a trump, and no mistake—beat the whole field, by jingo! Come along, my boy, we have got it all to ourselves, and you shall have the brush."

"I say, Duncombe," he asked, "when will it be over? I'm tired to death already, and can't sit much longer on horseback."

"Then tumble off, and you'll be killed at once, Jack, by some of those hundred fine fellows behind riding over you."

"Oh dear! oh dear!" muttered Alphonso, as he was torn through a rasping bullfincher, "I wish I had taken father's advice, and never bought a hunter."

Forty minutes without a check, on a warm, sultry day, with a burning scent, brought the old fox's career to an untimely end in the middle of a large grass field; and Alphonso, now completely exhausted also by his unwonted exertions and the heat of the weather, reeling out of his saddle, fell fainting on the ground.

"Halloa, Jack!" cried the Captain, "what's the matter?" But no answer being returned by his prostrate friend, Duncombe, leaving his horse, ran to his assistance, and by the aid of his pocket companion, containing a pretty stiff mixture of cognac and water, the prostrate hero was revived, and able to stand again, before Reginald Knightley and a few others came up.

"You are all right now, my boy," the Captain said, "but finish the flask, whilst I get the brush for you, and tip Will not to say anything about the fainting fit; but, by Jove, it *is* hot work, and no wonder a fellow who is not used to it felt a little squeamish."

Reginald's surprise and annoyance on beholding Alphonso the third in at the finish may be readily imagined; but having ridden in his wake for the last two miles, unable to catch Mameluke, he saw very clearly that the young cotton-spinner was indebted to the judgment of the old hunter, not his own, for the place he had been enabled to hold.

"Well Knightley," exclaimed Duncombe, "a good beginning this—splendid thing—never went faster—and a glorious wind-up—nothing could be better."

"I am glad to find you are pleased," was the short and formal reply, uttered in a sneering tone peculiar to Reginald, who, without further remark, addressed the huntsman.

"Is master near at hand, sir?" asked Will in return.

"Not more than a field or two behind, and you had better not throw the fox to the hounds before he comes up. But where's the brush, Will? I want that for a lady."

"Very sorry, sir," said Will, touching his cap, "but the Captain claimed it, as being first up."

"For that young cub, of course, to whom he has sold his old horse," added Reginald.

"Very likely, sir, but I was a-thinking that young gentle-man ought to be blooded."

"That young eotton-spinning blaekguard shall never be blooded to our hounds, Will Lane," replied Reginald, in a sharp, savage tone of voice, with whieh he turned on his heel and walked away.

The master having now reaehed the spot, the fox was thrown to the hounds, and after half an hour's respite, to allow stragglers to fall in, the order of mareh was again issued for drawing a fresh covert. Our noviee, however, having had more than suffieient for one day, and glad of the opportunity to eseape further punishment, no sooner found himself on the turnpike road than he gradually fell baek into the rear rank of the cavaleade, and at a sharp angle, when hid from the Captain's view, who was talking with other men, he turned his horse and trotted away home, burning to relate his wonderful adventures to his mamma, and exhibit the trophy he had won.

Great was the disgust of Mamma Shuttleworth when her hopeful son, rushing into the drawing-room, poked the brush into her faee, exelaiming :—"There, mother, I have beaten all the field this morning, young Knightley and the whole lot, and won the brush."

"Lauks, Alphonso, do take that nasty stinking thing away! Is that all you got by going out hunting?"

"Yes, mother, and something worth earning too, whieh the best riders can only get by beating a hundred and fifty others; do you eall that nothing?—jumping over hedges and ditehes and park palings, and riding five or six miles straight aeross country, without being thrown from my horse, and leaving everybody behind me exeept Tom Duncombe and the hunts-man. Why, mother, my name will be up all over the eountry, as the best rider in Huntingshire; and Duneombe says he will introduee me to the Marquis of Dunkerton the day after to-morrow, when we are going out with his hounds."

"Well, my dear boy, I am glad to find you get on so well; but pray take that nasty fox's tail out of the room—my goodness, how it smells!—and well wash your hands, my dear, before you come down."

CHAPTER VII.

About half-past four that same afternoon, the Captain (who had become so domesticated at Hardington as to have an apartment there assigned to his especial use, to which a part of his very extensive wardrobe had been removed) returned from hunting, rather disgusted with Alphonso for giving him the slip, and on finding that unhappy wight snugly ensconced in an easy chair by the fire-side, he began to let loose at him for sneaking off before the day was half over.

"You're a nice man for a small party, Mr. Jack, to turn your back upon your friend, just when I was singing your praises to half a score of fellows; and you may imagine my annoyance when asked afterwards, 'Where's your friend, Duncombe?—lost a shoe, I conclude'—and some such other remarks not very agreeable to hear."

"Really, Duncombe, I beg your pardon for leaving you so abruptly; but the fact is, I was so thoroughly done by the heat, and my arms so cramped by pulling at Mameluke, that I could not have ridden over another fence; so I thought it best to let well alone, and go home at once."

"Well, Jack, perhaps you acted wisely this time; but I had intended introducing you to a few men worth knowing, so you are the loser. Now ring the bell for a glass of sherry and a biscuit, since the contents of my flask went down your throat."

"You must say nothing about that to the governor, Duncombe, or you know the consequences."

"I am not such a fool, Jack, as to blab out of school, so now (after tossing off a couple of glasses of sherry) let us go to the stables to see our nags."

"Oh! never mind them, Duncombe; they are sure to be taken care of."

"I am far from thinking that a sure thing, Jack, in such an establishment as yours, where there are more masters than men—so come along."

Now the Captain was a very particular man about his horses—quite as particular in seeing them well-cared for and dressed, as his own precious person; and he could not afford to lose a good hunter when he had made him; it would be so much lost time, and income too; for the latter depended very much on the former—the Captain being a sort of gentleman horse-dealer.

"By Jove, sir!" exclaimed Duncombe, as they passed through a side door into the stable-yard, "just as I thought! that ruffian of yours has got Saladin tied up outside the stable door, without a rag upon his back, and, by all that's wonderful, he is brushing the dirt off with the besom! Halloa!" shouted the Captain, unable to restrain his anger one moment longer—"halloa, you d——d ragamuffin, drop that besom and take my horse into the stable, or, by Jove, sir, I'll double thong you! Do you hear, you oaf?" exclaimed the Captain, as the man continued scrubbing away, his horse's fore-leg being strapped up to prevent his kicking.

No answer being returned, Duncombe rushed up, and seizing the besom from the helper's hand, threw it across the yard, exclaiming in great passion, "If you ever dare touch a horse of mine again with that article, I'll knock your head off with it."

"Then clean un yerself," replied the man; "I won't have no further hand with un."

"Get out of my way, you insolent blackguard," cried the Captain, "or I'll cut you to ribbons;" and taking his horse into the stable, he threw the cloth over his back, and went into the saddle-room.

"Why, what are you going to do?" asked Alphonso, in amazement.

"Going to do, sir? Do you think I will stay here another minute, to be insulted by that ruffian of yours to my face?"

"Oh! pray don't go, Duncombe. You promised to dine with us, you know; and I'll make it all right with Thomas—he shall beg your pardon directly."

"He shall leave this stable, sir," replied Duncombe, fiercely, "and your service this moment, or I'll never put foot in your house again, as long as my name is Duncombe. Do you think a gentleman is to put up with insolence like this from a servant?"

"I am really very sorry," replied Alphonso, "for what has happened; and if you insist on Thomas being discharged, he shall leave."

Thomas, on hearing this alternative, being in nowise disposed to quit such comfortable quarters, now came up very submissively, to beg the Captain's pardon, saying, "It was Mr. Morgan's orders (the head groom) that the horses should have the dirt first brushed off outside the stable door."

"Hang Mr. Morgan!" exclaimed the Captain; "he shall

not be my master, if he is yours; and if he does not know better the management of hunters, he has no business in a hunting stable. I told you not to take my horse outside the door—how dare you disobey my orders?"

"I'll never do it again, Captain, if you'll pass it over this once," said Thomas, very humbly.

"And you will never use the besom again, will you?" asked the Captain, "like an ostler at a public-house dressing a cart-horse."

"No, sir, I never won't, if you'll forgive me this time."

"Very well," muttered the Captain, not relishing the idea of losing his dinner; "I shall come down again at eight o'clock to see how my horse is done up for the night;" with which he walked leisurely out of the stable, as if he were the master of it, not Alphonso Shuttleworth; but before regaining the house he had recovered his temper.

"I say, Morgan," remarked Thomas to his superior, when they were alone, "that ere Captain comes it pretty strong for a wisitor."

"I wouldn't have knocked under to such as him, Tom, if I had been in your place," was the reply.

"Well, I think you would, Mr. Morgan, for I turned it over in my mind. There is old master and young master, very well in their way—easy, good sort of people—never finds fault; then you see good sittivations aren't to be had this time o' year just for axing—and above all, I should be uncommon sorry to leave a very particular friend of mine, a fine portly old gentleman what stands in the corner of the cellar, with the three hexes marked on him; so putting this and that together, Mr. Morgan, I thought it best to knock under to the Captain, for in these matters he's master's master, who, 'tween you and I and the wall, just knows an oss from a helephant, and that's all."

Pending this short dialogue the Captain had ascended to his room to prepare his toilet for dinner; and it must be admitted, few could surpass him in this business, his wardrobe being supplied by the first artist of his class in London. Duncombe possessed the art of dressing well, and looking well when dressed; in short, he was a model for a tailor to fit. Scores of men never look well in the best cut coat; but the Captain's tailor declared he would rather make him a suit for nothing than receive double the price from other gentlemen. The Captain did credit to his tailor, and procured him many excellent customers; and on the other hand, the tailor gave long credit to the Captain, by never sending in his bill under five years; and he might have dispensed with this unnecessary trouble, since he never got his money.

After dinner the Captain expatiated on Alphonso's performances in the field, which had far surpassed his expectations.

"He will do, sir, now," he said, addressing his host; "your son has made a most successful *début*, and won his spurs gallantly. Fifty men asked me who that young dare-devil was on the chestnut horse. 'Jack Shuttleworth, of Hardington,' was my reply. 'Never heard of him before,' remarked one; 'Seems a good sort of fellow,' said another; 'Of course he'll become a member of the club?' added a third; so you see, sir, I was not very far wrong when I told you fox-hunting would make a man of him, that is, if you wish him to become known and popular in the county."

"Well, Duncombe, I dare say you are right; but my only fear was that he would never ride well enough to follow the hounds."

"Beat every man out to-day, sir, save your humble servant and Will Lane; and the day after to-morrow, I purpose introducing him to the Marquis."

"I'm sure John ought to be very much obliged to you, Captain, for taking all this trouble about him," added Mrs. Shuttleworth; "only I hope you won't make him do too much—he's not so strong as you are, and he was always a poor sickly child."

"Well, my dear madam, I do not dispute your word, but to look at him now, he's just the subject for an insurance office, and bids fair to live till he's a hundred."

"But, Captain dear, it must be dreadful dangerous riding over hedges and ditches to follow those dogs, and after all to bring home nothing but a nasty, dirty, stinking fox's tail."

"Well, but I suppose you wouldn't dress a fox," retorted the Captain, "if Jack could bring one home."

"Dress a fox for dinner, Captain! Whoever heard of such a thing? I'm sure Mr. Antoine, our French cook, wouldn't allow it to be brought into the kitchen."

"Perhaps not, my dear madam; a dish of fricasseed frogs is much more in his line than a roasted fox. These French cooks never trouble themselves about plain roast and boiled; but they will hash up one of your old shoes with their sauces and seasonings, spices and what-nots, &c., that you would not know it from a maintenon cutlet. My man, when we were in Paris last summer, saw one of these *artistes*, as they call themselves, making gravy for a fowl he was condescending to roast; and this was the process he adopted: after drawing, he washed the inside, as well as his hands, in a small basin of water, and this, with its contents, was transferred to the saucepan for gravy, with sundry other little piquant materials to make it palatable."

"La! Captain, what a nasty, filthy man! It makes one sick to think of such things."

"What won't poison will fatten, my dear," remarked Papa Shuttleworth; "and there's another old saying, that every person eats a peck of dirt before he dies."

"He need not be a long-lived man to do that," added Duncombe; "for my belief is, with this confounded French cookery, most men eat a sack at least before they reach their fortieth year: but kickshaws, patties, and all that sort of thing, don't suit my palate, after knowing how they are concocted; so just hand me some of those walnuts, Jack; for, according to the vulgar old saying, 'An apple and a nut you may eat after a slut.' "

On the withdrawal of Mamma Shuttleworth, the three gentlemen drew their chairs round the fireside, settling themselves down for a cosy half hour or so with a fresh bottle of claret.

"I think, Duncombe," said Shuttleworth senior, "you know something of Rushmead Farm, belonging to Mr. Perrin?"

"Well; and I have good cause to remember it, having been nearly drowned in that confounded dyke, dignified by the name of a brook, where, from the boggy nature of the ground, my horse floundered in head-foremost; and, but for the farmer's team coming to my rescue, he had been food for the hounds within half an hour."

"Perhaps you know Mr. Perrin also, Duncombe?"

"Yes; and a very good sort of man he is; but having sons now grown up, he wishes to sell his farm to set them up in business also. The soil is good, although requiring draining; and it is said that, being surrounded by his land, the first offer has been already made to Colonel Maxwell, which is, of course, fair enough."

"Oh! certainly," remarked Shuttleworth; "but my agent tells me the Colonel is not very flush of cash, and rather partial to what he has."

"Your agent is not far out; but he does not know, perhaps, what I know about this little farm, which, although measuring only one hundred acres, is worth about £20,000."

"How so?" inquired Mr. Shuttleworth, pricking up his ears at the sound of a bargain as a hunter does at the horn.

"A mine of wealth lies under these dirty acres," continued the Captain; "black diamonds, sir—so a friend of mine assures me, a clever geologist, who walked with me over the farm, for I thought it would be just the place to suit me—a nice snug little hunting-box—although I fear it will go too high for my finances."

"Well," added Mr. Shuttleworth, "I might be tempted to make a bidding, if the property is put up to auction—not otherwise, of course."

Nothing more was said upon the subject that evening; but Mr. Shuttleworth had already resolved in his own mind to set his agent to work out more about this farm, and endeavour, if possible, to ascertain the price asked by the owner of it.

The *auri sacra fames* is well described by the Latin poet. It is an accursed hunger, never satisfied—*quo plus habet eo plus cupit.* There are no limits to its craving appetite. Mr. Shuttleworth thought only of money, and making money—how, or by what means, he cared not; and that night his dreams were about Rushmead Farm, and the bed of black diamonds underneath it.

But of what was the Captain thinking that same night when he retired to his own room?

"Ha! ha!" he muttered, as he stood surveying himself in a large mirror, "you won't beat me in this respect, Master Jack; and I rather suspect no girl would hesitate a second between the two. Yet that confounded money knocks down the best-looking fellow in the world, without a blow, when papas interfere; but I think now these two governors—the Colonel and the cotton-lord—are sure to fall out about this farm, when it will be my turn to fall in."

Now, the Captain had lately taken it into his royal consideration, that Huntingshire was a very good county for a sportsman to live in, possessing many recommendations to a man in his circumstances and rather peculiar calling as a gentleman horse-dealer; and, after weighing the pros and cons deliberately over, the Captain had come to the conclusion that the best thing he could do was to marry Edith Maxwell, and establish his head-quarters at Morton Grange. He had become of late a great favourite with the Colonel and Mrs. Maxwell, and was always welcomed by the young lady with a cheerful smile, so that he indulged the idea — not a very unnatural one

— that, with his handsome person and agreeable conversation, he could easily win any young girl's affections by a little extra flattery and attention.

Moreover, Edith was a girl any man might feel proud of; and being an only child, she would, of course, succeed to all her father's and mother's property. The greatest obstacle likely to stand in his path was his *protégé* Jack, with his father's cotton bags of money; and therefore, as he termed it, to set the two governors by the ears, he had hatched up this story about Mr. Perrin's farm, rightly conjecturing this would prove a *casus belli* between the haughty Colonel and the money-making cotton-man.

Young Knightley, he believed, would not marry any one except a woman of large fortune. Welford was too great an ass, and Addleby too great an idiot, to cause him the least uneasiness; so the Captain had already settled the thing—that Edith was sure to fall in love with him, and the Colonel to consent to their marriage without hesitation.

"I hate housekeeping," he soliloquised; "so the old pair of birds will take this trouble off my hands. During the summer I will take my wife to the different races, where I can pick up crumbs enough to pay our expenses, and then return for the hunting season to Morton Grange, and do, as heretofore, a snug little business in the horse-dealing line."

Having thrown his fly, the Captain awaited with the patience of an angler to see it taken by the greedy old trout for whom it was prepared, entertaining no doubt as to the final result. Mr. Shuttleworth had already exhibited unmistakable signs of being attracted to the lure; but, with his extreme caution, no further allusion was made to the little farm during Duncombe's stay at Hardington; yet the next day a secret consultation was held with his agent, and directions given him to sound farmer Perrin as to price, and advance upon the Colonel's offer a thousand pounds or two, when he could ascertain what that was; and, to avoid collision with his neighbour, the agent was to buy it ostensibly on his own account.

CHAPTER VIII.

THAT same evening the Shuttleworths had issued invitations for a dinner party on rather a large scale; including the Maxwells, Mrs. Duncombe and her daughters, Welford, Addleby, Major Hamilton Townsend, a retired officer of dragoons, who had lately come to reside in the village of Hardington, with his wife and a large family of young children, the Rev. John Sherrard, the vicar of the parish, and a few others from the neighbouring watering place of Waterton; the number of guests exceeding twenty.

This was, to use the Captain's expression, "the first throw off of the Shuttlecocks" to gain a footing in the county, by a gorgeous display of their plate and furniture. The dinner consisted of every delicacy of the season, irrespective of the manufactured dishes of Monsieur Antoine. The wines were the best that could be bought, and, from the servants being thoroughly practised in the parts they had to perform, nothing was *out* of place that was placed on the table, but there was a stiffness and rigidity throughout the entertainment which none could dispel or soften down. The host and hostess were *out of place.* A large dinner party, out of their own sphere of life, was to them a new and perplexing affair. They were too nervous and anxious to feel comfortable themselves, and their uneasiness appeared to have imparted itself to their guests — and, save for the Major, who cared only for a good dinner, and plenty of good wine, conversation would have come to a dead stop. The Major rattled away with his stories and anecdotes, commenting also upon all the viands placed on the table.

"Splendid turbot that, ma'am," addressing Mrs. Shuttleworth, on whose left hand he was sitting; "had his twin brother for dinner yesterday sent me by Dunkerton; with a short note—have it here, somewhere," fumbling in his pocket amongst a lot of other letters; "left it at home, I suppose. These were his words, however: — 'Dear Ham,—Large spread yesterday—opening day. My fool of a fishmonger sent me down two of a sort, which don't agree at table or elsewhere — so you are the gainer. Fish won't keep this weather, which is good for nothing but scent. He will serve your brats for a week. Yours ever, Dunkerton.' The weight of this fish, ma'am, was over forty pounds—obliged to boil him in the brewing copper, and bring him to table on the tea-tray."

"My gracious! Major, what a monster he must have been! I never heard the like."

"Oh! nothing at all, ma'am, to what I have seen at Torbay. Had a haul there last summer of one hundred turbots at once, none under five, and several over forty pounds in weight."

"La, Major, what a sight! but I suppose fish was cheap there: we gave three guineas for ours."

"All went to London, ma'am, where the best of everything goes; my friend, to whom the place belongs, and the whole manor besides, couldn't get one of these fish for a dinner party he had that day, although landed in sight of the Abbey windows; but was obliged to send to Exeter for his dish of fish."

"How very provoking, Major; what's the use of living near the sea if you can't buy cheap fish, and plenty of it too?"

"All done by contract, ma'am, with London dealers; London spoils every country place now for cheap living. I was staying with Lord Ballyroan in Ireland, last May—went to see a run of salmon; and, by gad, ma'am, out of one pool the men took three hundred at one haul, and not a fish under ten pounds—splendid fellows!—made one's mouth water to look at them—but not a fin could we get—cars in waiting—off they went to Dublin and London."

The Colonel, sitting opposite, opened his eyes very wide at this large take of salmon, and could not resist asking in what river it happened.

"The Boyne, Maxwell," was the reply; "saw it with my own eyes."

"I don't doubt your word, Townsend; but you must admit it was rather an extraordinary draught."

"And which," added Duncombe to his neighbour, "I shall not swallow, if the Colonel does."

"Rare Hermitage this, Shuttleworth," tossing off a glass; "Dunkerton can't beat it."

"Glad to find you approve of it, Major; suppose you try it again."

"With pleasure, sir;" and down went another.

On the appearance of the second course, consisting of wild ducks and pheasants, the Major indulged in a long shot at the former, by recounting a midnight adventure of his own on the Hampshire coast, in search of wild fowl.

"Paddled out on the mud, Maxwell, in snow shoes; heavy work, with a duck-gun weighing twenty-five pounds on my shoulder—as dark as pitch; floundered about for an hour at least; heard a loud flapping over my head—fired at random, and down they came about my ears, sir, like hail; picked up a score, sir, besides those that were winged and escaped on the sand. My companion nearly drowned; went out too far, found the tide coming in, couldn't run for it, so what do you think he did, Maxwell?—sharp-witted fellow at a pinch—paddled back as far as he could, until the waves overtook him, then stuck the barrel of his large duck-gun in the mud, and held on by the butt-end. A near thing with him, poor fellow; the water rose up to his chin, and he gave himself up for lost—luckily for him it rose no higher; and he told me afterwards he never made himself so tall in his life, obliged to stand on tip-toe all the while, with his teeth chattering like castanets from fright and cold."

"Why didn't he swim for it?" asked the Captain.

"Couldn't get his feet out of his wooden shoes, Duncombe; nailed to his board, sir, like a fatting goose."

"Like what, Major?" asked Mrs. Shuttleworth.

"A fatting goose, ma'am; poultrymen nail the feet of the geese to boards to prevent them running about when they are penned for fatting."

"La! how horrid, Major; you men are so cruel."

"Not more than your sex, I believe," replied the Major; "what do you think of the girl skinning living eels?"

"I don't believe a word of it, Major; just a made-up story."

"Then you won't believe what I have seen myself in Paris, market women cutting off the hind legs of frogs, the only saleable part, it is said, and letting the fore legs carry away the body. In two or three months the legs grow again."

"Mercy me, Major, what horrid cruel wretches! but our countrywomen wouldn't do such things."

"No saying, ma'am; young ladies even are very cruelly disposed sometimes; cut men's hearts into ribbons, without caring a pin about the pain they inflict."

"They can take care of themselves, as I tell our John never to fall in love till he has found out that the lady won't say no."

"He will be clever to find out that," said the Major, "without first asking the question."

"Our Alphonso aint bad-looking, Major, and, with what we can give him, not likely to be refused by any sensible girl;" casting a glance at Edith Maxwell, who was sitting by his side, which, by the way, the said young lady did not observe; but her worthy son, catching his mother's remark, although uttered in a lower key, turned as red about the gills as an excited turkey-cock; wishing his mamma had been in London, or anywhere else, save where she was.

Alphonso had, on his mother preparing to pair off her guests when dinner was announced, anticipated her intentions with regard to Edith, by immediately offering her his arm, without observance of ceremony or etiquette, and nearly overturning his friend Duncombe in his eagerness to clutch the prize, which when obtained he scarcely knew what to do with. Alphonso was not a lady's man, having never mixed until very lately in ladies' society; and, when seated at table by the side of this beautiful girl, he felt tongue-tied in her presence, of which the Captain took advantage, having placed himself on her other side, by carrying on an animated conversation with her during the greater part of the dinner-hour, greatly to the annoyance of his own partner and Alphonso also.

The Major, by his stories and adventures by sea and land—mostly of home manufacture—had brought the assembled guests into something like sociable humour, some laughing at, others commenting on, his Munchausen-like exploits, until even Alphonso's tongue became loosened, and he had ventured on some remarks to his fair neighbour, about what he had seen in his late travels on the Continent, when his mother's allusion to Edith upset him altogether, and feeling himself so confused by the betrayal of his own thoughts in his burning cheeks, he scarcely dared look at her again. The Major's quick eye, detecting his confusion, was fixed steadfastly upon his face; and there was also that spiteful old spinster, Miss Hibbard, from Waterton, sitting opposite, enjoying his misery, by a malicious smile, which said as plainly as words: "Ah! young gentleman, I see what you are up to."

Alas! for poor Alphonso. He never felt or looked so sheepish before; and Duncombe noticed him too by saying, "You look rather warm this evening, Shuttleworth; suppose we try a glass of hock together?"

Refusal was out of the question, yet Alphonso at that moment felt savage enough to kill his friend, but he dared not offend him, having foolishly trusted Duncombe with his secret *penchant* for Edith, only a month before, when rather elated by a few extra glasses of wine. At last, to his great relief, Mrs. Shuttleworth rose from table, and he never felt more delighted than when he saw the ladies retreating, rejoicing even more at losing his dinner partner, than he had rejoiced at first on obtaining her arm; for he dreaded lest she might have suspected his true intentions towards her, and might perhaps treat him as a silly stupid boy for his *gaucherie* and lack of conversation.

The all-engrossing topic amongst the gentlemen that evening was the projected line of railway from Manchester to Liverpool.

"Wonderful invention this steam power, Colonel," Mr. Shuttleworth remarked. "Gigantic enterprise, sir, which will bring Manchester and Liverpool within four hours' drive of each other; the greatest discovery in scientific knowledge ever yet made; travelling at the rate of sixty miles an hour! The full development of the arts and sciences, of manufacturing and engineering appliances, has been reserved for the nineteenth century. This is the age of genius, sir; who would in times past have thought of using boiling water as a propelling power—a large tea-kettle, sir, as an instrument of locomotion?"

"It was thought of, however, sir," said Mr. Sherrard; "and the discovery of steam power made two hundred years ago by a clever Frenchman named Solomon de Caus, not less celebrated as an architect and painter than as an engineer; and this unfortunate man, on explaining his invention to Cardinal Richelieu, was considered mad, and confined in the Bicêtre, where he became, by long imprisonment, *actually mad*, and thus perished with his secret; so you see a confirmation of the old saying—'There is nothing new under the sun;' and although we may in some few respects exceed the generations that have passed away, it is quite clear to me that in many other respects they have surpassed us. What are our cities, as to their architecture, beauty, or extent, when compared with those mighty cities of old—Babylon and Nineveh? Why, London and Paris are mere market towns. We read in the book of the prophet Jonah that Nineveh was an exceeding great city of three days' journey. And who has not read of the mighty Babylon in ancient history, its lofty and massive walls, its palaces and hanging gardens, and the magnificent temple of Belus or Baal—the riches of which, and the value of its sacred vessels were reckoned at twenty millions of our money?—and as to architecture, sir, we are even in this all-enlightened century, as you suppose it to be, mere copyists."

"That's right, my worthy pastor," exclaimed Addleby. "You and I, although we were born in the last century, are not quite such fools as people take us to be; and four posters or the mail go quite fast enough for old-fashioned people."

"I hope and expect, Mr. Addleby," replied Mr. Shuttleworth, "that within ten years there will not be such a thing as a mail coach left in England?"

"These steam-engine fellows shall never pass through my lands," said Addleby.

"You will find more difficulty, sir, in breaking through the Act of Parliament obtained by this railway company than they will in breaking through your land, although you will of course receive the full value for what they require; private interests are not, in these times, permitted to interrupt those grand schemes which are undertaken for the benefit of the people."

"Benefit of the people, indeed!" replied Addleby, now becoming excited, for he was a staunch Tory, Church and State man in politics. "What do these companies care about the people? They are neither more nor less than a combination of knaves, banded together for the sole purpose of enriching themselves at the expense of the public. This is the fact, sir, and in my opinion there is, in this all-enlightened age, a greater preponderance of gulls and fools than has ever existed in any other age since the creation of the world. Schemes, and projects, and plans are set forth by some half-dozen artful rogues under the name of companies, in which people are ensnared, like fish in a net, by the promise of heavy interest for their money. I hate the very name of a company, sir; and this railway company I will oppose by every means in my power."

"Well, Addleby," interposed the Captain, fearing a collision between him and Mr. Shuttleworth, "it don't signify much whether you oppose it or not, for, like a hard-mouthed runaway horse, this confounded company *will* go ahead, notwithstanding all our efforts to hold it back; but I hope and trust they won't cut through our vale country, or I shall vote them a nuisance as well as yourself; and now I propose an adjournment to the drawing-room, if our host has no objection, or the ladies will think we are all getting tipsy, and not fit for their society.

On entering the drawing-room, the Captain's sisters, two fashionable-looking girls, pretty rather than handsome, one in her twenty-second and the other in her nineteenth year, were seated at the piano, finishing a duet often rehearsed in private for public exhibition, and more accomplished musicians, both in vocal and instrumental talent, could not be found throughout the county of Huntingshire, and the ease and elegance with which each played her part could not fail to elicit the applause of the most indifferent listener. Welford was by their side in a moment, being himself excessively fond of music, and on the conclusion of their song paid them the highest compliments. He hoped they would favour him with something else—anything they pleased—it could not fail to be attractive, with such sweet, well-modulated voices as theirs—he felt quite enraptured —he had never heard such perfect harmony!

The young ladies expressed their appreciation of Welford's compliments, they were of course mere compliments—they did not profess to be scientific performers—they knew very little of music—but they would sing another duet with pleasure, provided he would in return favour them with a song—they had heard Mr. Welford possessed a very fine voice.

"Quite the reverse, I assure you," that gentleman replied; "but I will cheerfully comply with your terms, for the pleasure of hearing you again."

After a flourish of fingers over the piano—a continuation of which, with sundry abrupt jerks and stops, threatening destruction to the strings of the instrument, and not inappropriately, therefore, denominated execution—an Italian bravura was commenced with its *Io's and Dio's*, with which, as it progressed, every person in the room appeared to be in raptures, although, save and except the two performers and Mrs. Maxwell and her daughter Edith, not another person knew the Italian language from Hebrew. With the termination of the song, and the applause following their performance, the two sisters retired from the piano, and Mr. Welford, according to promise, seated himself on the music stool, running his fingers over the keys in very artistic style; but his compass of voice being infinitely inferior to either of the young ladies, after hearing his first stanza, little attention was paid to him by the company, and conversation was resumed throughout the room, much to his annoyance.

"I say, Duncombe," remarked Major Townsend, "put a cap on that fellow's head, and a shawl round his shoulders, and he would pass for a woman. Egad, sir! his note is not higher than a hedge-sparrow's. I detest *he*-pianists, even among professionals; but there is something extremely *molly-coddlish* and effeminate to my mind in a gentleman sitting down to play his own accompaniment on the piano. Welford is a specimen of the nineteenth century man; a pink and white dollish face, silky and shoppy in manner, like a linendraper's apprentice;

and as to dress, the very quintessence of foppishness. Yet that fellow has the impudence to say there is no woman good enough for him in the whole county. Egad, sir, no girl of sense would marry such a monkey-legged chap as that."

"Money is everything now-a-days, Townsend, with women as well as with men, and Welford may have a duke's daughter if he likes; it is my belief no girl in this room or in the county would refuse him; she would be silly to do so, with his fine place and splendid fortune."

"Well, Duncombe, that may be your opinion, it certainly is not mine; and I will bet a cool hundred that Miss Maxwell would refuse him point blank, and another moneyed man into the bargain, whom I noticed at dinner trying to make himself over agreeable, and who signally failed, if I am any judge of a girl's physiognomy, or else she had got some cotton in her ear to bar other cottony speeches out; but there, you see, he is trying it on again, asking her to sing, I suppose, which she won't do, it appears, at his solicitation."

"Perhaps she may at mine, though," thought the Captain, as he turned away to make the inquiry; but Edith Maxwell declined to sing at all that evening. Her mamma objected to her doing so at present before company—her voice was not sufficiently matured to sing in public.

The fact was, Mrs. Maxwell did not choose her daughter should sing that evening, for reasons she did not think it necessary to give any one; so the Captain contented himself by sitting and talking with her instead, to the visible mortification of Alphonso the Little, as he then appeared, from his utter inability to squeeze in a word. The Captain possessed the faculty, natural to some gifted individuals, of rendering himself most agreeable to ladies. His face was sufficiently handsome and manly to attract their attention, his smile very winning, his address most insinuating, and his conversation lively and agreeable; he made pretty little speeches, and paid pretty little compliments, without gross flattery, and all those little attentions which are a sure passport to a lady's favour. Many men attempt the same things without success, because there is a constraint or apparent condescension in their mode of speaking or manner, which women, with their quick perception, immediately detect. Duncombe, therefore, had become a great favourite with the fair sex, from antiquated dowagers to misses in their teens. Even aunts patronised him; he was so respectful, so courteous, so much the gentleman. We must not be surprised, then, at Edith being pleased with him. She preferred his society to that of every other person in the room. She liked him very much as a companion to talk with—not flirt with—Edith was no flirt; and had necessity been laid upon her—stern necessity, from which there could be no appeal—to select one from this party as her companion for life, we have a shrewd suspicion her choice would have fallen on the Captain. But I do not say that a thought had as yet entered her mind about marrying him. Edith had not indulged any serious ideas about marriage; she had not troubled herself about it; for up to this period of life, although just seventeen, strange as it may appear to other precocious young ladies, she had not fancied herself in love with any one.

Now our friend Alphonso, who not only as to the outline of his figure, but also in regard to innate propensities, resembled very much the fat boy as represented in the Pickwick Papers, having been grievously disappointed in his project of getting Edith alone into a snug corner, where he might feast his eyes upon her beauty without interruption, as the fat boy did on his Christmas pie, felt exceedingly annoyed by his Mentor, Duncombe, so coolly taking the game out of his hands when he had begun to flatter himself with the idea of playing a winning card; for Alphonso, disgusted with his own sheepish behaviour during dinner-time, and now bottle-valiant from drinking an extra quantity of wine, had made up his mind for a desperate conflict that evening with poor Edith, not with hard blows, but soft words and soft looks; and here was the Captain seated by her side, doing exactly what he had intended doing himself, only in a far more agreeable manner, and Edith's cheerful smile and beaming eye betokening the pleasure she felt in his society.

To portray Alphonso's rage as that of an exasperated tiger, or a lady bear robbed of her cubs, would be a very faint similitude; he could have stabbed Duncombe to the heart there and then, and torn his body into infinitesimally small pieces through one of his father's cotton mills; but as he glared upon him in his fury, the Captain returned his savage look with one of such thorough pity that Alphonso sprang from the sofa, and retreated quickly to the other end of the room, for he felt almost tempted to stain his mamma's best satin damask with the Captain's blood.

CHAPTER IX.

THE same individual man undergoes so great a metamorphosis between the hours of nine at night, after a good dinner and plenty of wine, and nine o'clock the next morning, that you would scarcely recognise him as the same character. Many an old fox-hunter who has ridden hard in his time still rides very hard when seated in his arm-chair after dinner, which requires only a little wider stretch of an already excited imagination to become converted into a saddle, comfortably ensconced in which, he fancies himself again charging gates, post, rails, and double fences, as in the days of his manhood's prime. But what a contrast does he present the next morning, creeping leisurely along to the covert side, with nerve barely sufficient to ride over a mole-hill!

Such was the case with Shuttleworth junior. With the fumes of wine, his other fumes had also evaporated, and he descended to the breakfast-room, the morning after his papa's grand dinner-party, looking the picture of meekness and submission. There sat his enemy (whom he had killed twice over in his dreams of the past night) by the side of his mamma, quite alive, and as cheerful as ever, who on his entering said, in his usual manner, "Well, Jack, my boy, how do you feel this morning?"

"Pretty well, thank you, Duncombe," was the meek reply, as he quietly took his seat at the lower end of the table.

After breakfast they took their usual stroll together down to the stables, when Alphonso, thinking the Captain's silence on the events of the preceding evening seemed something like a desire to evade any recurrence to an unpleasant matter, in which he had not acted as he ought to have done, put in a feeler, by saying, "I didn't think, Duncombe, you would have treated a fellow as you did me last night, after what passed between us a month ago, when you advised me to put up for Edith Maxwell."

"I never advised you to do anything of the kind; the question originated with yourself, Master Jack; you said you had a great mind to 'put up for her,' as you call it, or words to that purport, but it does not follow that, because Mr. Shuttleworth junior considers himself entitled to 'put up' for Miss Maxwell, other gentlemen are to be put down. By your violent eagerness to seize upon that young lady when dinner was announced, you very nearly put me down, sir, into her mother's lap; and if there is one thing I abhor more than all others, it is *gaucherie*, or awkwardness, in the presence of ladies. Although not through his own fault, a man making an apology for a thing of this kind looks like an ass; and I felt, when barely saved from being plumped down like a lubberly boy into Mrs. Maxwell's lap, by your excessive rudeness, just inclined to send you spinning across to the other side of the room, Master Jack, which I rather fancy I could do at any time without any vast amount of trouble; but if you have the least doubt on the subject we can have a trial with the gloves, which are hanging up in your room, just to determine the controversy."

"I did not intend to offend, much less to upset you, Duncombe, last night, and was not aware, until you told me, of pushing you so rudely aside, for which I now make every apology."

"Very well, Jack, it is all right again now; but although I don't care for a little rough-and-ready play or fun amongst men, I don't intend to be made a fool of before women; and to punish you for your rudeness last night, I paid rather more attention to Miss Maxwell than I might otherwise have done."

"Perhaps you have altered your mind, Duncombe, and mean to cut me out altogether, as you did last night, from trying to render myself agreeable to her."

"I always select the prettiest girl in the room to chat with, or flirt with, Jack; this is a failing to which I confess myself very liable—but—yes, then follows the saving clause."

"And what's that, Duncombe?"

"That being tolerably well off as a bachelor I don't contemplate matrimony without a full equivalent, or rather more, with a wife, to compensate for my loss of liberty. And now we may as well throw our legs over our horses' backs, and give them a canter to open their pipes for to-morrow, when we shall have something to do to keep clear of the crowd of horsemen who generally patronise the Marquis at his favourite meet, Scurry gorse. You have not yet tried your new nag, which I named Dickens, after his late owner, and although said to be quiet with the hounds, I won't answer for him, therefore keep clear of the pack, or the Marquis may proffer you a little advice on riding to hounds."

"How very kind of him!" replied Alphonso; "he must be a very good-tempered sort of fellow."

"I hope you may find him so, Jack; but his lordship's temper won't stand hounds being ridden over, so mind what you are about to-morrow."

We may here, by the way, relate that Duncombe had first become acquainted with the Marquis of Dunkerton from being in the same regiment with him for three years, and that on his lordship's leaving thc army their acquaintance was still kept up by meeting constantly in the betting ring, at races, and also at the covert side during the hunting season.

The Captain was a clever hand at book-making on turf events, and often let the Marquis in for a good thing, from being well known to the first trainers and jockeys; and in return for little favours of this kind, which had proved most profitable investments to his lordship on several occasions, the Captain received invitations now and then to spend a few days at Dunkerton Park, to shoot or hunt with the Marquis, who was not only a sportsman in the widest acceptation of the term, but tolerably well acquainted with every other game besides wild game—from billiards downwards, not even disdaining a shy at snuff-boxes.

Duncombe had opened the campaign against the poor pheasants on the first of October at Dunkerton Park, and in the evening, *inter alia*, Shuttleworth, the cotton-spinner, was brought up on the board.

"Do you know that confounded fellow?" asked the Marquis, "who, report goes, is killing every fox which gets into his coverts."

"Yes, Dunkerton, I made a point of calling upon him, just to enlighten him on this subject—for living between the two hunts he would have done us an infinity of mischief—and, I am happy to say, my remonstrances have proved effectual. He promised me to discharge every one of his keepers if the hounds again drew his coverts blank."

"Bravo! Duncombe; this cotton man, then, cannot bc a very bad sort of fellow, notwithstanding all that is said against him. But what of his son?"

"Cubbish, my Lord, decidedly, and rather snobbish; but inclined to disperse the dross quite as fast as Shuttleworth *père* has collected it, when he has the power. I shall try to make something of him."

"Or, rather," added the Marquis, with a laugh, "something *out* of him, Duncombe—eh?"

"Well, between ourselves, I don't intend to turn bear-leader for nothing, and he must pay for my piping; but the old one may be turned to some account, too, by your lordship, as he has more loose cash than he can find investments for."

"Does he bet or play, Duncombe?"

"Neither, I am sorry to say; but the game he is now playing is to get on in the county, to become a country gentleman, magistrate, and deputy-lieutenant—having purchased already every strip of land he could lay hold upon near Hardington. But the old squires vote shy of him. To the Knightleys he is odious from buying Egerton's property. The Maxwells, however, have exchanged cards and dinners with him, for the Colonel dreads his money power, lest he may buy two or three small portions of land intermixed with the Morton Grange estates."

"Maxwell has an only daughter, too," added the Marquis, "and a very pretty one."

"But the Colonel is too proud of his child and his name to wish her to change it for Shuttleworth," rejoined the Captain; "and I believe will make it a condition that his son-in-law, whoever he may be, shall take his daughter's maiden name, instead of her assuming his. But we are now running wide of our line. Shuttleworth senior is an ambitious man. He has made more money than he wants, and now wants preferment, having got an idea into his head that he is to be the founder of a great family. All these money-made fellows pretend to despise honours and titles, running down the aristocracy because the grapes are sour; yet at heart they are as greedy of honours as of money-bags. Shuttleworth aims first at being made a magistrate for the county, then deputy-lieutenant, then member of Parliament, and so on in quick succession until he can get squeezed into the House of Lords. He knows all these things can be done—have been done—and will be done again and again, by money and money's power—interest. He is prepared to pay for his promotion, as every snob must in the army—so, my Lord, you being Lord-Lieutenant, may make something of the old fox, whilst I handle the cub."

"Well, Duncombe, it might be done perhaps, although at present I don't see my way at all clearly. Of course, I could not call upon him, neither would the Marchioness visit the cotton-spinner's wife, or receive her here—that is quite out of the question."

"Undoubtedly; but with your permission I could introduce

the young Shuttlecock to you when regular hunting begins, for my patronage is conditional on his hunting—and your lordship might ask him to a shooting party, or something of that sort, and I will manage afterwards about his father."

"Very well, Duncombe, you may introduce the cub to me when you like; that will save the foxes, and we can talk about the papa at some future time."

A month had now elapsed since this conversation; Duncombe, meanwhile, puzzling his head how to effect an introduction between the Marquis and Mr. Shuttleworth, when his mention of the railway project the previous evening suggested itself to the Captain as a *modus operandi*, or means to carry out his object; and with this view he again broached the subject after dinner the next day, by asking what per-centage this railway would be likely to pay.

"On whose account do you make the inquiry, Duncombe?"

"On my own, sir—I have a few spare hundreds idle at my banker's, but cannot afford to risk the money in an idle scheme."

"This is no idle scheme, Duncombe, or my name would not be down as one of the directors. It is a sure thing, and the original shareholders will get cent. per cent. for their money if they wish to sell, even in six months, when we get our bill passed. Our plans and calculations have been made by the most scientific engineers and cleverest men of business, and there can be no doubt as to the issue. You will have to pay only by easy instalments, until the line is opened for traffic, and I will give you an undertaking on paper, to relieve you of the shares you take at my suggestion, any time within twelve months, or twelve years if you like, at cost price. Our line will pass through some part of the Marquis of Dunkerton's property, and if he does not oppose us, I will let him into a good thing or two. You understand—twig—eh?"

"Just so, sir," replied the Captain; "I will sound the Marquis on this subject the first fitting opportunity; but he won't listen to politics, statistics, or money matters in the hunting field."

The next day, their hunters being sent forward, the Captain drove up to the place of meeting with his *protégé* in his mail-phaeton, drawn by a pair of well-bred horses, the turn-out under Duncombe's direction being quite the thing, neither overdone nor underdone, and though stylish and neat, without that superfluity of hieroglyphics on the panels of the carriage, meant to represent family arms—or that gorgeous display of plate on the harness by which a *novus homo* thinks to attract the public eye, as demonstrative of his importance.

The Marquis had already arrived, and was sitting on his hunter, surrounded by the pack selected for that day's work, talking to Sir Digby Colville, a young baronet of good family, and a great friend of the Marquis, who had been invited down by him to stay as long as he found it agreeable at Dunkerton. Sir Digby Colville was not a person to pass unobserved, even in the greatest crowd, at the most fashionable re-union in London, being of commanding stature, with remarkably handsome features, and particularly aristocratic in appearance and manners.

"What a pity it is," observed the Dowager Lady Grumbleton to another anxious mamma of three grown up daughters, with one of whom he had been dancing the preceding season at Almacks, "what a pity it is that Sir Digby is so poor!"

"Poor!" exclaimed the Countess of C—— in surprise, "he has been represented to me as having his clear ten thousand a-year at least."

"His father was reported to have had that income in Irish property, my dear," replied the Dowager Lady Grumbleton; "but we all know that these Irish properties of ten thousand a-year mean about a third of that sum, collectable from moor-land and potato-field farmers, which, in unfavourable seasons, is not collectable at all. Poor fellow! he is very good-looking certainly—very agreeable, quite one of us in appearance and manners, my dear," with a sarcastic smile; "but as a moneyed investment by no means a desirable *parti* for one of your daughters; in short, I am told, on reliable authority, that his present income does not exceed one thousand a-year."

This short dialogue may suffice to show the position of Sir Digby Colville at the close of the last London season, who gladly availed himself of his friend Dunkerton's invitation to spend a few weeks with him in the country. The Baronet kept his cab horse and park hack when in town, and possessed also three or four clever Irish hunters, well bred, and equal to carry his weight (over fourteen stone) with the fastest fox-hounds, which, having had their usual summer's run in the park at his old family place in the Emerald Isle, had now arrived at Dunkerton in anticipation of a few good days with the Marquis, when they might be turned to a good account. Sir Digby, now in his thirtieth year, having sown his wild oats during his father's lifetime, had, upon succeeding to the title and estates three years previously, found it necessary to turn over a new leaf, and commence on its blank page a short ledger account of his incomings and outgoings; in fact, he found it imperative upon him to look to his P's and Q's for the future, for with his father's incumbrances on the property, in which he had been a participator to pay his own debts also, the income on which he could rely barely amounted to one thousand per annum. He had, however, acquired sufficient worldly wisdom to understand the wide distinction between being poor and appearing poor; and he knew that by appearing poor he might become a really poor man for the residue of his days.

A poor gentleman, to make his way in the world by any means, has great difficulty, for almost every man is against him; all ask the question, what is he fit for, not being brought up to any business or profession? The trade will have nothing to say to him; he does not write well enough even for a lawyer's copying clerk, and if he did, they could not insult a gentleman by offering him such a low salary; all ears are closed against him, unless, through some influential friend, he may find that of a leading man in office open to assist him in some subordinate situation; failing that, he must work for his bread by hand or head—rob or starve.

A poor lord or baronet stands in a more awkward predicament, without superior talents and interest in high places to advance him. Sir Digby Colville had not passed through London life without being convinced of this fact; and he had also discovered another, that from his neglected education he was unfitted for any official appointment, could he have procured it. But he was fully appreciated by the fair sex, even dowager duchesses patronising him. To the ladies, therefore, he looked for assistance and advancement; he had a title, with a handsome person, to bestow on any young lady who possessed an equivalent in money.

Sir Digby, unlike Irishmen generally, had become a tolerably prudent man; yet he was not strictly of Irish blood, his mother having been a Scotchwoman. Three months of the year, during the height of the season, were spent by him in London, where, from his good connections, he had obtained an *entrée* into the first society; and as a set-off against his extra expenditure at that time, he was compelled to economise for the remaining nine, either at his old place, or by visiting his friends. On the first of August he made it a rule to leave

London for grouse-shooting, which meant simply to keep a watch over an English party to whom he had let moors with a limitation as to the number of birds to be killed annually.

These gentlemen were also boarded by him during the season at so much per head weekly, their host always presiding at the dinner-table ; the second course, of grouse or game, being conditionally supplied by themselves; so that the Baronet realised more by letting his shootings and furnished apartments to single men than by the letting of his moor-land to bad-paying tenants. Being also a good judge of horses, he always picked up every autumn three or four well-bred, young, weight-carrying hunters, with which he set sail, about the end of October, for some friend's house in England, where he had only to provide provender for them and his groom, the cost of which the sale of one of his stud proved generally sufficient to cover ; buying at about thirty pounds, and sometimes selling for three hundred ; for one horse, which cost him only thirty-five pounds, having actually pocketed five hundred ; and the horse was said to be worth all the money, possessing great speed with immense power.

In short, the Baronet had become a first-rate manager in all these matters, and being a very agreeable, entertaining companion, his society was rather eagerly sought after ; he had also the good sense to keep his own counsel, so that few knew his true circumstances, and none suspected him of being on the look-out for a rich wife, the general impression amongst his friends and acquaintances being that Sir Digby Colville was not a marrying man.

This little digression anent the Baronet has led us somewhat wide of the scene with the Marquis of Dunkerton's fox-hounds, to which, on now returning, we find the Captain, after emerging from sundry wrappers and a large top garment, and alighting from Alphonso's drag, approaching *on foot ;* for that day, riding *a kicker*, he knew this was his only safe mode of approach to the royal presence of the master when surrounded by his spangled favourites.

"Ah ! Duncombe," exclaimed the Marquis, appreciating his caution, "how do ? Glad to see you out with us again. You had a good thing, I am told, with Knightley on the first."

"Pretty well, my Lord ; your hounds are in splendid condition, never saw them look quite so well before ; old Chorister seems in tip-top trim," as he patted the old hound's head ; when, laying his hand on the neck of the Marquis's horse, he said, "A word for your ear only, Dunkerton," to whom, on bending his head, the Captain whispered, "I've brought the cub out; shall I introduce him now, or some other time?"

"Now," was the reply, "and as we shoot to-morrow, bring him over, with your guns, and dine; the Marchioness is from home."

Alphonso was accordingly produced, presented in due form, and complimented by the Marquis on becoming a fox-hunter; in return for which our hero expressed his approval of the pack by remarking, "Your Lordship has a splendid lot of dogs out to-day."

"Pretty fair," was the reply; "but you must see the ladies."

"Shall feel proud, my Lord, to have the honour of an introduction to your Lordship's family," replied Alphonso, very innocently.

"What a muff!" muttered Sir Digby. "Come, Dunkerton, let us be moving; we shall lose the best part of the day in coffee-housing this fine morning. Who's your new friend?" as they walked their horses away.

"A young cotton-spinner, Digby, whose father has lately purchased a large tract of land and wood in my hunt; and, therefore, to save the foxes, I must patronise the cub; one of the privileges peculiar to the master of fox-hounds being that he must know every man in his own country who owns a hedge-row."

Meanwhile Duncombe had mounted his hunter, keeping with Alphonso at a respectful distance behind the hounds, until they were lost to sight by being buried in the thick gorse covert. For a few moments nothing was heard save the shrill voice of the noble huntsman; and then a half-stifled note of old Chorister from beneath the tangled covert, which begins to wave and shake.

"Have at him, old boy!" cries the master; and in a few seconds more the forms of the spangled pack are seen leaping and jumping here and there, hurrying to join their old leader. A screech from Dick at the farther end is heard.

"Away!" screams the noble huntsman. "By gad, he's off!" and with a few short, thrilling blasts of the horn, which set the whole field of two hundred horsemen in motion, the Marquis bounds away at the head of the cavalcade. Alphonso is torn along by his impatient steed right through the throng, knocking against one here, another there, with shouts ringing in his ear: "Hey, you tailor! where are you going to?" "Holloa, you sir on the brown horse, you have nearly broken my leg!" But our hero, regardless of reproof, held on his course. A gate is before him, which an obsequious farmer is trying to open for the Marquis. Dickens will have it; knocking the farmer off his horse, and sending the rails flying, as he bursts through the timber in his furious career.

The hounds are straining away across the next field; in another minute he is alongside of Bill, the first whipper-in. Crash goes Dickens through a stiff blackthorn hedge, with his hind legs in the off ditch, which caused Alphonso a bloody nose, from the horse throwing back his head.

"Never mind, Jack," cried a familiar voice, "pick him up, and come along."

Jack would willingly have declined the invitation, but Dickens *would* go along; besides which, his rider, thinking his honour at stake, to keep his place with the hounds of the Marquis, as he had with Mr. Knightley's, pocketed the affront of the bloody nose, and again set forward at full speed, crashing and rasping through all opposing fences—his horse being what is called a rusher—until he found himself going slap through the pack—which had come to a sudden check from the fox being headed by a ploughman, amidst a volley of anathemas hurled at his head by the enraged Marquis; of which, apparently wholly unconscious, Alphonso kept on his career until he was brought to anchor in a deep brook below, by his horse swerving at the brink, thereby sending his master flying over his head into the stream.

"He'll be drowned, my Lord," exclaimed one gentleman, more compassionate than the others.

"He may be drowned, and be d——d," replied the Marquis, "for all I care; a confounded snob! but, hark! there's a halloa forward." And away he went with the hounds, which were quickly on the line again, leaving our hero to his fate, which, however, was not to be drowned that day; for he was soon seen crawling up the bank, which satisfied the Captain, without going down to his assistance, that no damage had been sustained by his friend, save a ducking; and, as the hounds were going in a different direction, he was left to catch his horse as he could.

CHAPTER X.

It took Alphonso much longer time to catch his horse than it did me to write my last long chapter. He went, churning the water in his boots, over several fields, until he found his runaway steed in the hands of a stout farmer, by whom he had been captured whilst attempting to walk through one of his gates, a little too stiff to be broken, and hitched by his bridle to the post. It is almost superfluous to add that, after tendering the farmer a sovereign for catching the runaway, our hero felt in no humour to continue the chase that day, with the shouts and execrations of the Marquis still ringing in his ears; and he accordingly inquired the nearest road home, which he reached, exceedingly disgusted with the figure he had cut, by having his handkerchief bound round his head *al Turco,* in place of his best beaver, which, ere that time, the eels had nestled in at the bottom of the brook.

Having had a good run, and killing their fox at the end of it, the Marquis had forgotten all about Alphonso's riding through his pack, fortunately without injuring a hound; and Duncombe returned by dinner-time to Hardington, also in high spirits, and began rallying Alphonso on his Quixotic exploits.

"Egad, Jack, you astonished the Marquis not a little by going slap-bang through his pack, and then performing that pirouette into the brook."

"The Marquis astonished me a great deal more by using such abusive language," replied Alphonso, in a sulky tone; "I won't stand that from any man."

"Then you must sit it, like other fellows. Why, sir, he has anathematised me up hill and down dale for riding *with* his hounds, when he could'nt catch me, not for riding *over* them, as you did, smashing two couples of his favourites right and left. Egad, sir! that was enough to make any huntsman savage; but he is all right again now, and asked me to bring you over to-morrow, to shoot and dine with him."

"Did he indeed, Duncombe?"

"Yes, to be sure he did; so now I'll tell you what to do. That devil you bought of Dickens is a rushing, tearing brute, and wants a riding-master on his back, so you offer him to the Marquis for his whipper-in, to ride during the season, and he will make a hunter of him. This will please the Marquis and save your neck, my boy, for he will kill you; but he won't attempt running away with Bill after one or two trials; and at the end of the season he will be worth a mint of money—very nearly thorough-bred—and up to fifteen stone; that's the way to do business, Jack; so now let us go for dinner, as I feel uncommonly peckish."

The invitation to shoot and dine with the Marquis the next day put Alphonso into good spirits, as well as his papa and mamma, for the remainder of the evening.

"Well, really, Captain dear," exclaimed the latter, "our John ought to feel so much obliged to you for introducing him to the Marquis; and I begin to think this hunting will make a man of him at last; but, my gracious! what a figure he came home, and so out of temper, I couldn't think what had happened!"

"Just a dip in the brook, my dear madam—save a shower-bath—do him all the good in the world. Cold water is the finest thing ever invented for all sorts of complaints; cure a runaway horse, won't it, Jack? stop him at least, for a time. I have heard it spoken of also as a certain remedy in heart complaints," with a meaning look at his friend Jack. "There is an uncommon nice-looking piece of water at Morton Grange, in which Thomas, the footman, tried the experiment of seeing how much he could swallow without being choked."

"La, what a silly man, Captain!" Mrs. Shuttleworth said. "What made him do that?"

"Why, they say the lady's maid made him do it. Thomas must needs fall desperately in love with this young person, who is nearly as pretty as her young mistress; but Arabella Tomkins not favouring his suit, seeing that she preferred a handsome farmer, Thomas declared his intention of drowning himself, at which all the domestics raised such a laugh that the excited footman rushed out of the servants' hall in a frenzy, without his hat, exclaiming—

"'I'll do it! I'll do it!'

"'No, you won't,' said Harry, the groom; 'I knows you aint got the pluck to do it, so I'll go and see fair play.'

"'Oh! Harry,' cried the cook, 'do ye stop him,' as Thomas was seen running towards the pond. 'Oh, dear! I'll go myself,' and away bundled the cook in full chase, followed by the scullion girl and housemaid, all three screaming 'Murder!' but, ere they could overtake him, Thomas had plunged into the water up to his neck, not caring to go farther, where he stood like a hunted stag at bay, with the women screaming on the bank. How long this farce might have lasted it would be difficult to say, or to what further lengths or depths Mr. Thomas might have gone, had not the Colonel, hearing the cries of the women, reached the place, who, on learning the cause of all this outcry, threatened his delinquent servant with instant dismissal, and a situation in the county gaol or lunatic asylum, for attempting self-destruction, unless he immediately came out.

"It would seem," continued the Captain, "that the household at Morton Grange is composed of very inflammable matter, inasmuch as a fortnight after this little incident had occurred the cook was found going off into hysterics, sobbing and crying, 'Oh, I've done it! I've done it!'

"'Done what?' asked the scullion girl.

"'Oh! that bottle in Thomas's pantry,' replied the cook, sinking back in a chair.

"'Mercy on us!' exclaimed Mary, rushing into the pantry, where a bottle stood on the table labelled 'Poison;' 'if she hasn't been drinking the boot-top stuff!' And up ran Mary, without hesitation, to the drawing-room, consternation depicted in her face, telling her mistress the cook had just poisoned herself by swallowing half a bottle of oxalic acid.

"'Confound the woman!' muttered the Colonel, springing up from his chair. 'Another love affair, I conclude. These servants of mine will drive me distracted. Where's Thomas?'

"'Gone with my young lady to Woodborough,' replied Mary.

"'Then run to the stable-yard, and tell William to go instantly for the doctor, and send the butler to me directly.'

"'He's holding the cook, sir, who's gone off into strikes.'

"'Hang the fool!' exclaimed the Colonel, impatiently; 'there, get away;' and he stalked hastily into his own room; and, after mixing up a large tumbler of prepared chalk-and-water, he descended to the kitchen, where he found every female domestic of his establishment gathered round the cook, wringing their hands, with loud lamentations at her untimely fate.

"'Oh, poor thing! she'll die; nothing can save her;' 'Oh, lauks, how dreadful!' &c.

"'Hold your chatter!' shouted the excited Colonel; 'and you, Markham, make that fool of a woman drink this tumbler of mixture. Down with it, you idiot!' cried the Colonel, as the cook cast an imploring look towards her master's face.

"'It is your only chance; drink it, or die;' and down it

went, for cooky had now been awakened to her awful position; and the doctor, arriving soon after, followed the Colonel's draught with emetics and other poison neutralisers, which saved, as Bill termed it, 'the crowner's 'quest' that time; and as there appears to be a good deal of *low* fever about Morton Grange, I advise Jack to keep aloof from it."

"Well, I'm sure, Miss Edith is a love of a girl, and I wish our John would take a fancy to her."

"Don't talk such nonsense, mother, pray," interposed Alphonso, blushing up to his ears.

"I call it the most sensible thing you could do, John," replied his mamma; "and, as I tell papa, I want a daughter-in-law to keep me company in this large house. Why, lauks! there is room enough in it, and to spare, for three good families; and that range of rooms, at the end of the long gallery, just the thing for a nursery."

"There, mother, that will do," said Alphonso, becoming impatient of further remarks on this tender subject.

The shooting party at the Marquis's came off the next day without any incident occurring worthy of note, save that our hero mistook the head of one of the beaters for a woodcock, but by bobbing his own, and shutting his eyes at the moment of pulling the trigger, the charge went over the man's hat, without inflicting any serious wounds, two or three stray shots only lodging in his thick cranium, to heal which, in place of lip-salve, Alphonso proffered a golden ointment as a sovereign remedy in such slight cases.

The Marchioness being from home, there was only a small male party at dinner that evening; after which Alphonso, when *plenus Bacchi*, said, "I regret, my Lord, exceedingly having caused such confusion amongst your dogs yesterday, but the fact was, my Lord, the brute I was riding ran away with me; and if your lordship will do me the favour to accept that horse for one of your servants, he is quite at your service. He cost me two hundred guineas, and Duncombe says he will make a splendid hunter, being only five years old."

"I am much obliged by your polite offer, Mr. Shuttleworth, but I cannot think of depriving you of so valuable a horse. My whipper-in, Bill, shall, however, try what he can do with him for you, if you like to send him over to our stables; and when steady with hounds, he shall be returned."

"As you please, my Lord, but I don't care about riding him again, and hope your lordship will keep him, if he suits."

"I wish Mr. Shuttleworth would make me that offer, Dunkerton," added Sir Digby Colville; "that brown horse will be worth three hundred, with a month's careful handling across country."

"So much the better for Mr. Shuttleworth, then, Colville, for I think Bill a likely fellow to cure him of his runaway propensity."

"Cool fellow that!" interposed Duncombe. "What do you think he did the other day?"

"Rode at a plough-team, perhaps, if in his line," said the Marquis.

"No; but I saw him going down-hill full gallop, over rough ground, with the reins loose about his horse's neck, the handle of his open pocket-knife between his teeth, both hands being occupied in tying a lash on to his whip; and, to make the act more daring, the horse he rode was a speedy cutter, with very shaky fore-legs."

"Well, sir," remarked Sir Digby, "Tom Smith's riding for a fall is milk-and-water to Bill's audacity; but I suppose his neck is insured from everything but a halter."

Later in the evening, cards being introduced, Alphonso found himself facing his friend, the Captain, and Sir Digby opposite the Marquis, at a quiet game of whist, just to pass the time. The five-shilling points seemed rather high to our hero, who had never gone beyond one under the parental tree; but, of course a Marquis would not play for such a trifling sum—he could not expect it in aristocratic circles; and as his partner, the Captain, swept off the winnings from the two first rubbers, Alphonso thought it very good fun.

"You are in luck to-night, Duncombe," remarked the Marquis; "I can't afford to lose much more money."

"Oh! never mind, my Lord, luck will change over to your side now, for fortune is a very fickle dame. What say you to golden, instead of silver points?—it will save my carrying home all these small coins jingling in my pocket. I shall be accused of robbing the toll-keeper."

"As you please," replied the Marquis, with a laugh; "guinea points, if you like."

The third rubber fell to the Captain, who, on collecting the sovereigns, said, "Ah! these yellow boys are much prettier things to handle; but whist-playing is dry, thirsty work; will your Lordship favour us with a tankard of mullet claret?"

"Pull the bell, Duncombe," was the reply; and on the

butler entering, the tankard, brandy, and champagne were ordered to be placed on a side table, near them.

The game continued; and as the wine and spirits went down, other false spirits arose, which tempted Alphonso to exhibit his contempt for money by offering to treble the stakes when the luck had gone over to the other side. The tankard and brandy-bottle had been replenished three times, when the Captain, thinking enough had been done for one sitting, rose from the table, exclaiming, "By Jove! Jack, it is past one o'clock; we must be trudging."

"Oh! never mind the time, Duncombe; George will sit up for us till five in the morning."

"Very likely; but you seem to forget the Marquis hunts again to-morrow. So now, you settle your reckoning with Sir Digby, and I will do the same with my Lord."

On squaring accounts, Alphonso and the Captain were down on the debtor side to the amount of one hundred and fifty each, so deep had they been playing; when the Captain said—

"Well, my Lord, the tables are turned in good earnest against us; and as I have not my cheque-book, I must beg the favour of pen and paper to write you a draft on my bankers."

This being readily supplied, Alphonso availed himself also of the same mode of discharging his obligation to the Baronet. A smile passed over the features of the Marquis on reading Duncombe's autography, which was immediately transferred to his pocket without any remark; and their carriage being in waiting, the Captain and his chum shook hands with the Marquis, who said he hoped to see them out the next day with his hounds.

"Doubtful, my Lord—can't promise;" but in an *aside* as he was leaving the room, "that cub has had brandy-and-water enough to keep him in bed till twelve o'clock to-morrow. Good night, my Lord."

After they were gone, Sir Digby said, "That youngster bleeds freely, Dunkerton; I suppose it's all right with this slip of paper he has given me? How do you stand with the Captain?"

"Thus," replied the Marquis, handing him Duncombe's cheque, on which was written—

"Messrs. Knockemoff & Co.

"Please pay the Marquis of Dunkerton one hundred and fifty bob.

"J. DUNCOMBE."

"Egad! Dunkerton," remarked his friend, "this is the most curious little document, in the shape of a draft, which has ever come under my inspection; but I suppose you know your man, and the Messrs. Knockemoff, his bankers?"

"I have never heard of any such firm," was the reply; "but Duncombe told me, before sitting down to cards, that if he lost he could not pay—so throw the paper into the fire."

"Well, Dunkerton, in that case you must, of course, share my profits; that is, if *£ s. d.* come out of the paper I hold—perhaps that is a hoax, too."

"Oh, no, Digby, you will find that right enough when you take it into Waterton the day after to-morrow."

"Why not to-morrow?"

"We hunt to-morrow; and to present his draft so soon would show distrust of the man, or too much eagerness for his money; so now I must say good night."

The following morning Alphonso awoke about ten o'clock with a splitting headache, and great craving for soda-water, three bottles of which he had already emptied when Duncombe entered his room.

"Why, Jack! in bed still! when do you mean to turn out?"

"Can't say exactly, Duncombe, feel very queer this morning; sitting up so late does not suit my book, and that mulled wine has given me a terrible headache."

"Well, you did not spare the liquids, Jack; a quart of spiced wine, with a pint and a half of brandy to your own share, was not much amiss to finish off with, after a bottle of champagne, ditto claret, ditto port, at and after dinner, besides liqueurs. You drew upon the Marquis's cellar pretty well for the first set to."

"And I have an idea," replied Alphonso, "that his Lordship drew pretty heavily on my pocket."

"You made a fool of yourself and me, too, Master Jack, in that matter, by insisting at last on five-guinea points, and fifty the rubber."

"Did I? by Jove! Duncombe. 'Pon honour?"

"Yes, you did, you arrant donkey, when you could not tell the queen of hearts from the knave of diamonds; and if it had not been for the Marquis stopping you, you would have made it fifty-guinea points, and five hundred the rubber. This may suit your bankers' book, my fine fellow, but it don't suit mine; and your foolery last night has put me on the wrong side of the ledger."

"I am sorry for it, Duncombe; but you shall not suffer for my folly. I'll make it good to you in a day or two; but I must not draw too heavily just now, or the governor will stop the supplies. Of course you won't say anything about card-playing last night?"

"Certainly not, Jack; so now I must say good-bye for the present, having business to attend to at home."

CHAPTER XI.

CAPTAIN DUNCOMBE was well received at Morton Grange, for there is a kind of brotherhood amongst military men which draws them together. He was also a good listener, apparently never tired of hearing the Colonel's often-told tales and exploits, and always treating his host with the most deferential respect; in fact, the Captain became as great a favourite with the master as with the mistress of the house. Neither were his visits, as we have stated, irksome to the young lady; and as St. Austin's lay only three miles distant from Morton Grange, the latter was made the half-way house between that and Hardington, where he called generally two or three times a-week to retail any scraps of news he might chance to pick up in the hunting field, or elsewhere. Elderly gentlemen, as well as old ladies, although they may appear to disregard it, are not averse to a little scandal about their neighbours, and the Colonel enjoyed a bit of gossip over his wine, with which he was supplied by the Captain.

"Grand affair, that dinner party at Hardington," he remarked, two evenings after, when *tête-à-tête* with the Colonel, sipping his claret; "but the report is that Shuttleworth is going a deal too fast for his money, verifying the old adage of 'light come, light go.' The building and finishing of that new house has cost him a mint of money; and then look at his plate, absurdly magnificent for a man in his position—at least thirty thousand pounds sunk there. A friend of his, I met there last week from Manchester, said to me with a shrug of his shoulders, 'Our host has had luck on his side hitherto, but a fall in the cotton market, which we are now expecting, will play old gooseberry with his paper currency.'"

"I understood, Duncombe, that he had realised his money, and ceased business altogether."

"Oh, no, my dear sir, not so; he has lots of paper afloat still, and an agent in Manchester who transacts business for him; so that some fine day a crash may take place at Hardington, for these speculating fellows, with so many irons in the fire, generally burn their fingers at last."

"Why, Edmund Knightley told me he offered to buy St. Austin's of his trustees, for his eldest son."

"A mere flash in the pan, Colonel; there was no charge in that barrel; just a little puff, to show his consequence, and make people believe the report of his immense wealth. This Manchester friend of his told me he had not paid for his plate yet, at least, not more than half of it. 'Come, come,' I said, 'that won't do,' wishing to fish out the truth. 'But it will, and must do,' he replied, 'and I think I ought to know, as I am his jeweller, and came over to get the rest of my money.' 'Which of course he has paid,' I said. 'Thus, Captain, by a bill at six months,' showing me the document. So, my dear sir, you may perceive there is a great deal of tinsel about this cotton-lord."

"Well, Duncombe, I'm not sorry to hear this—pass the bottle—for, to tell you the truth, I began to fear this man would overpower us all with his money bags, and buy up every strip of land he could purchase."

"He has bought more than he can pay for already, Colonel; and, I am told, has not yet the title-deeds of Hardington in his possession, having paid only two-thirds of the money, and the lawyers hold the mortgage."

"Then the son is not of course quite out of the fire yet, that is, independent of his father's speculations?"

"Oh, no; quite the reverse—nothing of his own—not at all a safe investment."

"By the way, Duncombe, talking of investments, I must buy something for Edith to ride; her pony is old and broken-winded, and I want one a trifle higher on the leg for her now, she has grown so tall; about fifteen hands, not over, just to keep her habit clear of the dust; quiet and gentle, with a good mouth, for she is not much of a horsewoman—rather timid, Duncombe, you understand?"

"Exactly, my dear sir, and I know the very thing to suit her; a beautiful bay, with four black legs, Arab built, handsome as a picture, and has carried Farmer Tomkins's daughter the last six months; gentle as a lamb, and steady as a pack-horse, rising six years old, and warranted all right."

"Well, well, but the price, Duncombe?"

"They are asking thirty-five guineas; and although cheap as dirt at the figure, for a park-hack, I make no doubt I could get him for thirty pounds. But I will ride him over to-morrow morning, and you can judge for yourself; put the side-saddle on his back, and let Miss Maxwell try him."

The following day, about eleven o'clock, the Captain made his appearance at Morton Grange, mounted on the aforesaid nag, whose paces he exhibited to great effect before the Colonel and the ladies, who expressed their admiration of his appearance and movements. He was then taken to the stables for an exchange of saddles, and being well dressed over, was again brought round to the hall door, with the Colonel's cob, and the servant's horse for Captain Duncombe, who, from long experience with his sisters, vaulted Edith upon the back of the nag with the ease and precision known only to experienced hands in such matters, at the same time adjusting her habit with the air and importance of a riding-master. In this little movement the Captain displayed a good deal of taste as well as coquetry. The little foot was inserted in the stirrup with a gentle squeeze of his hand, which seemed to linger about it rather longer than necessary; then a little bit of the habit must be added, to keep the skirt in its proper place, which gave occasion for another pressure of the hand, and an up-turned, inquiring look at the fair equestrian, which caused a slightly heightened colour; but there was a serious expression upon her face, which told the Captain that his attentions to her foot might have been dispensed with. She did not wait to hear a very pretty compliment as to her seat and figure, just issuing from his lips as she moved forward to the side of her father, where she remained during their ride; and upon their return home, she sprang from her saddle before the Captain could render his offers of assistance.

"Well, Duncombe," the Colonel said, "I think he will do; and both Edith and myself feel much obliged by your kindness in bringing the horse over for our inspection. We must, however, I fear, give you a little further trouble, in concluding the bargain for us."

"Not the least trouble, my dear sir; I will ride the horse back to Farmer Tomkins, make the best deal I can, and return with him here again as soon as possible."

"And I hope dine with us this evening," the Colonel added.

Farmer Tomkins was standing at his barn door, hands in

pockets, watching the threshers, apparently not in the best of humours, when the Captain rode up to his homestead.

"You ha'e gied that young hoss a pretty good spanking this morning," he said, turning round to Duncombe, "and knows his paces by this time, I reckon."

"Come, Tomkins, you needn't be grumpy because the beans don't yield so well as you expected; the extra price will make up for the loss in the measure."

"I warn't thinking about the bains, Captain; but Jack baint at home to dress the hoss down after the whisking he ha'e had, all covered wi' dirt and lather."

"He is sadly out of condition, farmer, for I gave him only a bit of a canter across your twenty-acre field, and at the end he came out as white as a sheet; but there, that don't signify, if we can agree as to the figure."

"I told you afore you had un out that I wouldn't ha'e un galloped about the country, because he were not in condition, and you've been on his back this four hours."

"I never buy without a fair trial, Farmer Tomkins, and that you know, so if we are to do business, name your price, for I've got other fish to fry this afternoon, which won't admit of much haggling about your nag."

"I wants forty guineas for that young hoss, Captain, and he is worth every shilling of the money."

"I can buy as smart a hack as that, farmer, any day of the week, for twenty-five pounds, and quite thorough-bred into the bargain; besides, you asked only thirty-five at Barton fair, and could get no offer above thirty. I've got three tens in my pocket, and you may have that, or the horse back, as you like."

"Won't do, sir. I'll have t'other five, or you put un in the stable." And Farmer Tomkins buttoned up his breeches' pockets with the air of a man who had made up his mind, and turned again to look at the threshers.

Duncombe saw he was determined now, so he said, "Well, Tomkins, you are a hard man at a deal, but if you'll throw in a bag of beans I'll take the horse."

"Well, Captain, as we ha'e had dealings afore, I won't stick at a bag o' bains;" and thus, the matter being adjusted, the money was paid, and the Captain returned with his purchase to Morton Grange, soliloquising thus, as he rode leisurely along—"A bad morning's work for me; no plunder out of this deal, but it may turn out well in the end. I told the Colonel I could get him for thirty, and that must stand, so I am four pounds out of pocket; and yet, as there is every prospect of my getting on with the young lady, it is not quite a fool's bargain. She's a ticklish filly to handle, however—starts and springs aside from the touch of my hand, like a three-year old; but I think I've got the cavesson on now, and by giving her her head for a while, she will come up to the halter quiet enough, after a little more coaxing; and when I've once got the ring on, she won't toss her head again, I'll engage. Mettlesome young things, when well broken in, generally prove the most steady and manageable."

Thus reasoned Captain Duncombe, about whose delicacy of sentiment we need make no remark; but such was the man, and such his ideas about women. I do not draw from my own imagination, but endeavour to represent realities; and whether handsome or plain, interesting or the reverse, amiable or repulsive, they are true to the life. I don't attempt to paint snub noses as aquiline; sallow faces pink and white, or crooked figures straight; and the Captain, although possessing great taste in dress, and well practised in the conventionalities of polished society, borrowed many of his ideas from the stable.

That evening Edith was in high spirits, being greatly pleased with her new horse; and that pleasure was greatly enhanced by her father's promise of giving her pony a run for life; for she was not the girl to neglect old friends for the sake of new. She also felt much obliged to Duncombe, and expressed her thanks in such graceful and grateful terms as to confirm his previous impressions of her preference for himself above all other men in that locality; and he indulged a silent laugh at the pretensions of his friend Alphonso.

The Colonel, upon the strength of the new purchase, which afforded him great satisfaction, ordered an extra bottle of claret after dinner, for the Captain and himself to discuss, and then proposed joining the ladies in the drawing-room; where, sitting in his snug arm-chair near the fire, he became very soon so deeply engrossed with the contents of a new agricultural magazine as to pay little attention to any one or anything else. Mrs. Maxwell had also taken in hand a piece of work as his *vis-à-vis*, whilst the Captain and Edith were engaged at the piano, the latter playing and singing alternately, as requested by her mother and companion.

Even in the presence of papas and mammas a quiet little flirtation may be carried on with great effect, by two young persons, before this instrument, when there is no third one to interrupt their harmony. During the intervals between song and air, the lady is apparently searching for a new piece of music through her manifold scraps and books, which somehow or other are always mixed together in the most careless and provoking manner; and pending this search, her left hand still lingers upon the keys, to drown any sweet notes of her companion's voice which may be uttered above a whisper.

The Captain, anxious to know Edith's opinion of his *protégé*, asked, "What do you think of young Shuttleworth?"

"I really never think about him," she said, carelessly.

"That is very ungrateful towards one who thinks so often and deeply about you, and says so many sweet things in your praise."

"By sweet you mean silly things, I suppose, since I have scarcely ever heard him make a sensible remark."

"It is not considered a proof of folly to speak in rapturous terms of those who are entitled to our highest admiration."

"When admiration passes the limits of moderation it becomes ridiculous."

"Then you are not of an enthusiastic nature, and do not approve of such feelings in others?"

"People are often led astray by such feelings, which are frequently the result of a too fanciful imagination."

"Then, however much I may admire, I am not permitted to express the extent to which my admiration is carried by the contemplation of the most lovely form I have ever beheld?"

"Barefaced compliments are not very agreeable, even to the most weak comprehension——"

"Even when truly expressed, and as truly felt?" the Captain added.

"No," she said; "truisms sometimes are not palatable, and in this case vanity itself might feel outraged by too open flattery."

"Well, then, I must show by sighs and looks, and outward signs, the deep admiration I have long felt for——"

"Edith, my dear," exclaimed Mrs. Maxwell, "your tea will be quite cold—pray come and take it."

Edith rose quickly from her seat, and the Captain was prevented from finishing his sentence; nor did she afford him an opportunity of renewing any further private conversation with her that evening. With the intuitive perception natural to her sex, Edith guessed the climax to which the Captain was advancing, and she felt relieved by her mother's interruption, which prevented the necessity of her refusing him; for although not in the least disposed to encourage his addresses as a lover, she had no desire to offend him, or lose him as an acquaintance. Moreover, he had always appeared much too light-hearted and gay to fall in love with any one; much less did she expect he had ever entertained any serious thoughts about herself; until that evening, his manner and conversation had never impressed her with the idea that he possessed any depth of feeling, and even were he to propose, she had resolved to laugh it off, as proceeding from a mere fanciful imagination of his brain, rather than from any strong affection of the heart. She had, however, decided in her mind to treat him for the future with more reserve, and avoid giving him another opportunity for renewing the subject.

CHAPTER XII.

I MUST now ask the courteous reader of these pages to travel with me in imagination to the ancient university of Oxford, where, in an old-fashioned, oblong room, dull and gloomy, at one end of which is a range of fixed seats or benches, rising from the floor gradually almost to the ceiling, we shall find Edmund Knightley, seated at a long table in the centre, covered with books and writing materials. There are some half-dozen other young men, occupied with pens and paper, at the same table—and one standing, book in hand, to whom a gentleman in a long gown, with a square cap on his head, is addressing some remarks.

"A little slower, if you please, Mr. Fitzpatrick—that will do, sir; now will you render it into English?" which the young man essayed to do, with a very strong Irish brogue, and at a very rapid rate.

"Really, Mr. Fitzpatrick," exclaimed the examiner, "I cannot follow you, neither do I understand the Irish language."

"Sure, it is jist me own mither tongue, sir, and the manner in which I have been accustomed at school to rinder it."

"Well, sir, you are indeed rending Horace into figments and fractions; we require a literal translation of the Latin into the English language. You compress whole sentences together."

"Thin, it's jist nonsense I'll make of it the other way,"

replied Pat, beginning to construe every word singly and literally, as thus :—

"'*Quid*, what, *agis*, do you do, *dulcissime*, most sweet or dear, *rerum*, of things?' By the powers, now, is that the way to address a friend in the street on shaking hands with him? and isn't me version the natural and correct one?—How di do, my jewel?'"

Roars of laughter from the gallery, which completely upset the gravity even of the examiners.

Pat proceeds—"'*Suaviter*, sweetly :' that's not so bad; '*ut*, as, *nunc*, now, *est*, it is, *inquam*, I say'—and mane it too: that's cutting the language into smithereens; '*et*, and, *cupio*, I desire, *omnia*, all things, *quæ*, which, *vis*, you wish.' Well, isn't it asier to say at once, making him a leg, 'Your most obedient, sir?'"

Pat continues to render word for word without comment, until he comes to "'*Demitto*, I let down, *auriculas*, my ears—I had a dacent pair, until ould Father Flanagan laid hold of 'em, and lugged me by them through the Greek Grammar, and over the *pons asinorum*; '*ut*, as, *asellus*, a young donkey, *iniquæ mentis*, of an uneven mind.' Sure that's an iligint way of telling a donkey he isn't quite a gentleman."

"That will do, sir," said the examiner, unable to suppress a smile; "you may sit down, Mr. Fitzpatrick."

Edmund Knightley was then upon his legs for nearly an hour, during which time his courteous demeanour towards the examiners, and the appropriate and eloquent language in which he rendered the Latin and Greek authors into English, as well as his quiet though pertinent replics to the many questions put to him, elicited the warm approval of his questioners; and at the conclusion of his examination, which had now lasted two days, *vivâ voce*, and on paper, he was intensely gratified on being told—

"We are much obliged, Mr. Knightley, and will not trouble you with any further questions."

A low murmur of applause was heard amongst the visitors, on which, turning his head, Edmund beheld some of his college friends, seated on the lowest benches, whose joy-lit faces bespoke the satisfaction they felt at his success.

Half an hour afterwards, on the school-room doors being thrown open, he was surrounded by them, with congratulations on the splendid examination he had passed.

When this is over the masters hold a consultation with

closed doors, as to the merits of the students who have appeared before them, and to those who have given satisfaction a little printed strip of paper is awarded, as a passport to taking their degree, which is most anxiously waited for by the friends of those who have exhibited any signs of failure; certain it is that this ordeal of a public examination is, to the nervous and timid, a most severe trial, and I have known instances of young men so thoroughly enervated by long and continuous reading, and low diet, as absolutely to faint away in the school-room.

Albeit not naturally nervous, Fitzpatrick experienced certain uneasy sensations as to his fate that day; for although of good abilities, and well read in the classics, as to logic, he just knew that a horse-chesnut could be converted into a chesnut-horse; and it was on his account that the examiners were rather longer in their deliberations than usual that evening, one being for plucking and another for passing him.

"Well," exclaimed the latter, "Mr. Knightley has passed a splendid examination, for which he is entitled to rank in a double first-class, and Mr. Fitzpatrick, being of the same college, I vote we give him his *testamur;* he is certainly clever, although I suspect an idle dog. This manuscript of his is the most curious piece of caligraphy, with the most extraordinary hieroglyphics I have ever seen, and the language so unintelligible that I must send it to my friend, the Orientalist, in the Bodleian Library, to decipher."

A hearty laugh being indulged in at Fitzpatrick's expense, the little slip of paper was signed, and his friend O'Connor, who had been in waiting outside the door, seizing it from the hand of the official, whose duty it was to distribute these much-coveted documents, ran home to his college, on reaching which, his Irish yell of triumph rang through the quadrangle, echoed back by Fitzpatrick down three pairs of stairs—door to the left. We need scarcely say that the two Irishmen, with sundry others of their party, made such a night of it afterwards that Mr. Fitzpatrick was obliged to draw very largely on his stock of blarney the next morning, when summoned before the dons, to prevent instant dismissal from the University.

Edmund Knightley, on the termination of the examination for that term, returned home in the highest spirits as a double first-class man, the Earl being not less delighted than his father at his honourable conclusion of college life; but the warm reception he experienced from Lady Agnes gratified him more than all other congratulations from relatives and friends. He had toiled and laboured hard to obtain her approbation; for her sake he had burnt the midnight oil; love for her had proved the incentive to renewed exertions of mind—her favour his coveted reward.

"Dear Edmund!" she exclaimed, on their first meeting, "how pale you look! but I am overjoyed at your success."

"Your approving smile, dear Agnes," he replied, "is more than a sufficient reward for laborious days and sleepless nights; air and exercise will soon restore me to health again."

"Indeed, I hope so," she said; "I shall feel proud of a double first-class man for my especial knight-errant in our rides and drives; and it must be admitted, Edmund, that we have had rather a dull time these last two months without you."

"Then you miss my agreeable society, sometimes, Agnes?"

"Indeed, we all do at Woodborough, even down to the little herd-boy, who was always asking 'when Master Edmund might be coming home?'"

"Well, Agnes, such kind thoughts are most gratifying; but I fear now you will be tired of my continual presence, as I shall not again return to Oxford, except for a few days, to take my degree."

"If you do not leave us until we are tired of you," Agnes said, with a cheering smile, "your visit will be a very long one; and you know papa is never quite happy unless you are here."

"And you, Agnes, do you wish me to remain?"

"How can you ask that question, you silly boy?—man I must now call you, I suppose, Edmund—are you not to me as an only brother? So now, as it is a fine afternoon, you must drive me over to Morton Grange—Edith will be so glad to see you, with all your blushing honours thick upon your brow. You know you have always been a great favourite of hers, and she ever takes your part, even against me, when we have any little differences of opinion."

Edith's reception of Edmund appeared less joyous than that of Agnes; perhaps she did not feel well—did not care much about him; perhaps it was on account of her mother's presence—yet so it was, that a certain restraint in her manner towards him was very perceptible. But Edmund's heart was too much occupied with selfish happiness to think of any one but Agnes—he had neither eyes nor ears for any one else then.

Soon after Edmund's return to Woodborough Park, where,

after a week spent with his own family, he had now become domiciled as usual, the Earl issued cards of invitation to all the surrounding families for a ball and supper on a large scale, to inaugurate his daughter's introduction to the world, who was now to preside at the head of his table; but from this list the Shuttleworths had been excluded, greatly to their dissatisfaction, although the clergyman of their parish, Mr. Sherrard, had received an invitation. This grand *fête* formed the general topic of conversation for a fortnight previous to its taking place, and Alphonso expressed to his friend the Captain a great desire to be one of the party.

"I am sorry to say, Jack, that I cannot assist you in this matter; your governor gave great offence to the Earl by writing that off-hand letter about St. Austin's. Had he consulted me, I should have told him the place could not be sold; but that is his weak point—believing everything may be had for money. The nobility and gentry of this country are particularly stiff-necked, and won't stand that sort of thing."

"Well, Duncombe, but the governor thought he was paying him a compliment by offering to purchase it at his own price. Would not you be pleased with a man making a good offer for one of your horses?"

"That's a different thing altogether, Jack; I am not a peer, but a poor Captain of Dragoons, and people know I don't refuse to sell a horse at a good price. Moreover, horses and dogs are marketable commodities, often changing hands. You might bid the Marquis even a large price for a hunter without giving him offence, and your governor might try to buy a wife for you by offering a fine settlement to her father, and this would be taken as a compliment—for when young ladies come out in the world it is tantamount to trotting a horse out at Tattersall's. Half of the girls are educated and brought out to be married—prepared for disposal or sale to the highest bidder—and papas and mammas are flattered by compliments paid to their children; but talk of purchasing their patrimonial estates, and, by Jove, sir, you will raise a hornet's nest about your ears in a moment! Your governor had shown more wisdom in asking the hand of Lady Agnes Gerard for you, than offering to buy St. Austin's."

"Well, what sort of a girl is she, Duncombe? prettier than Miss Maxwell?"

"Handsomer, Jack, I think, with finer features, more of a Grecian cast; in short, I consider her a splendid specimen of female beauty—to my mind, quite faultless in form and feature, with eyes like diamonds."

"By gad! Duncombe, I should like to have a look at her; she might do, if the other failed."

"Oh, exactly," replied the Captain, with a sneer; "Lady Agnes Shuttleworth would be just the ticket to please your mamma; but you must wait, my boy, until the annual hunt ball, after Christmas, when I will try and introduce you to her."

"Thank you, Duncombe; but is there no chance of seeing her before that time?"

"Very little; unless you find out when she may be calling at Morton Grange, and pop in unexpectedly; or you may loiter about the road near Woodborough, or hide yourself in the pleasure grounds behind the lawn, to get a glimpse of her face; only beware of spring guns and man-traps, and two huge keepers who are always prowling about the premises. There is also a brother Oxonian now staying at Woodborough, a double first-class, and a double-fist man, not unlikely to handle any fellow roughly, whom he may think poaching after his game."

"Who's he, Duncombe?"

"Young Edmund Knightley, a finer man than Reginald, but, like him, of a saucy, spicy temper, when put upon his mettle. And now, Master Jack, having given you these few hints, I must say good-bye for the present."

CHAPTER XIII.

THE eventful evening of the ball arrived, for such it was destined to prove to more than two or three of the chief personages in this tale. It would be needless to say that, directed by the good taste of Mrs. Egerton, all the arrangements were most complete, and the supper table laid out in a style not inferior to that of the first London confectioner; while of viands, in the shape of poultry, game, &c., there was a very abundant supply from the Earl's own yards and preserves.

Edith Maxwell had being staying at Woodborough during the last week, sharing with Lady Agnes the delightful anticipations of pleasure to be derived from their first ball; and as the clock struck the hour of nine, the two friends, radiant in their youthful charms, entered arm in arm the grand saloon, now tastefully decorated as a ball room, of which, as yet, the only occupants were the Earl and Mrs. Egerton. Edmund was soon added to the group, looking well, but more thoughtful than usual, and there was a faint, unfelt smile on his face as he addressed some complimentary words to Lady Agnes, which came not from the heart.

With all her apparent cordiality and affection, Edmund had his misgivings that Lady Agnes did not love him so deeply as he had long and fondly hoped; and this ball, although inevitable, he had been looking forward to with great anxiety and even aversion, as the dreaded ordeal to be encountered, decisive of his future fate. She was now coming forth in all her dazzling beauty, to be admired by eyes perhaps more fascinating than his; to be addressed in language more soft and winning, and assailed by all those little flattering attentions which men of the world could pay with much greater effect than himself.

Amongst the two hundred guests invited that evening, who could say his most bitter rival was not to be found? Who could say that she might not prefer one of that throng, even a stranger, to himself? Such thoughts rendered Edmund gloomy and abstracted; he tried to dispel them from his mind, but like unpleasant visitors, they would remain. The company were now, however, beginning to arrive, with the majority of whom being acquainted, his attention became otherwise engaged.

The ball was opened by Agnes and Edmund dancing together in the same quadrille with Reginald and Edith; and about half-past ten o'clock, the Marquis and Marchioness of Dunkerton, with Sir Digby Colville, made their *entrée*, being the last of the party expected that evening. The Marchioness was not less distinguished for her commanding figure than her graceful and dignified deportment; and not having yet reached her thirtieth year, was then in the full prime of woman's loveliness, possessing fine, handsome features, expressive of those kind and gentle feelings which circulated through her heart, and without a particle of pride or affectation.

After dancing with Sir Digby, the Marchioness accepted Edmund for her second partner, and the Baronet having been introduced to Lady Agnes, they took their station as *vis-à-vis* in the next quadrille.

"You look pale and woe-begone, Edmund," the Marchioness remarked, for he was her especial favourite of all the young men with whom she was acquainted. "Your studies have been too severe; but I am rejoiced your ambition has been rewarded by all the honours you could desire."

"Call it not ambition," he said; "I wished to please my father, and my too kind godfather; for their gratification I have toiled, and most thankful am I to have succeeded."

"Was there no other approving smile you wished to win also?" she asked, casting a meaning glance towards Lady Agnes.

Edmund's changing colour confessed the secret he was unwilling to acknowledge; but not answering her question, the Marchioness said—

"You mistrust me, Edmund."

"Indeed, I do not; I would trust you with my heart's deepest secret, and you only; but this is not the place to talk of such matters. I shall see you soon again. But now tell me what you think of your first partner this evening?"

"He is Dunkerton's friend," she said, in a low tone; adding, in one still lower, "not mine."

"I understand you; are you engaged for the next dance?"

"No," she replied; "I am not very fond of dancing, and shall sit down, or take your arm into the next room, which is less crowded."

The Marchioness and Edmund had been sitting together some short time, engaged in conversation more earnest than that generally current in a ball-room, when their attention became arrested by some remarks made by two gentlemen standing near them, to whom Edmund was unknown.

"Well, Roberts, as you are a phrenologist and physiognomist, tell me your candid opinion of the two fair *débutanti* of this evening?"

"I do not like answering idle questions, Chetwynd; they are, however, both very beautiful—the fairest flowers from that once noble tree planted in the garden of Eden my eyes have ever rested upon."

"Their characters, their dispositions, Roberts, I would know; their faces are patent to all, radiant in loveliness. I am now like Cœlebs in search of a wife; which would you recommend to a true friend? Lady Agnes appears to my sight divinely beautiful, and the other strikingly handsome."

"Reverse your terms, Chetwynd, and they will then be correctly applied. The first possesses every personal attraction to beguile the senses of man, but heart and mind are wanting to hold him her willing slave. The soul of love, benevolence, and every pure and gentle feeling beams in the soft eyes and heaven-born smile of Edith Maxwell; it would be worth years of labour to obtain her heart and hand—a treasure *gemmis venalis nec auro.*"

"What does that Latin phrase mean, Edmund?" asked the Marchioness, when the two gentlemen moved further on.

"'A treasure not to be bought with jewels or gold.'"

"His opinion is mine also," continued the Marchioness; "a more lovely, amiable girl than Edith Maxwell does not, I believe, exist."

"Do you think her then superior to Agnes?" inquired Edmund, in surprise.

"Were I a man, Edith would be my choice," she replied; "and now we will return to the ball-room, or my Lord may feel jealous of my sitting so long with you."

The words of the Marchioness, "Edith would be my choice," rankled in Edmund's mind, as rebellious to his long-cherished love of Agnes; but they held a place in his memory for many years afterwards. He was vexed and angry with them that evening, so much so that he did not even ask Edith to dance. Edith felt hurt also that Edmund had failed to show her this little mark of attention, although she had no lack of partners for every dance, save one, the valse. Edmund's heart at last smote him when he saw her sitting down, and approaching her he said, "Will you take a few turns to this enlivening air?"

"Thank you," she replied, "for the compliment, but you know I never waltz."

"Agnes does, why should not you?"

"I do not like the dance, and am sure it would make me giddy."

"Are you engaged then for the next quadrille?"

"Yes," she replied, "to Sir Digby Colville."

"Ha!" he muttered, "that man seems the ladies' great favourite to-night," and with a bow he moved on.

"Edmund appears sadly out of temper," Mrs. Maxwell remarked; "do you know the cause, Edith?"

"No, mamma, unless he is vexed with Agnes dancing twice with Sir Digby Colville."

"Ah, very likely, my dear; she really does seem very much engrossed with the handsome, gay baronet; but I have been told, my dear Edith, by one who ought to know, that he is quite a man of the world; therefore you must not believe all the fine complimentary speeches he may address to you."

Forewarned is to be forearmed, and her mother's remarks were not forgotten by Edith, when dancing afterwards with Sir Digby, whose conversation, replete with soft nothings, failed to make the same impression it had produced on Lady Agnes. The gallant baronet soon discovered his mistake, in believing Edith to be a young silly girl, ready with simpers and blushes to appropriate his pretty little compliments. He therefore altered his mode of attack, for he had a point to gain; he wished to know more of Lady Agnes, and after descanting on her beauty and great attractions, he said, in a careless tone, "Your friend is engaged already, I hear, to Mr. Knightley."

"I cannot tell," Edith replied.

"I conclude you could tell," he added, "were such really the case, for young ladies seldom keep such interesting matters secret from their dearest friends."

"Sir Digby Colville could scarcely expect I should reveal a friend's secret to a stranger, if I possessed it."

The baronet felt considerably annoyed by this rejoinder, and saw very clearly that his desired information could not be obtained through Edith Maxwell, who possessed more discretion than he had given her credit for; however, as she was one of the prettiest girls in the room, and in the baronet's opinion the belle of the party, he politely petitioned for another dance after supper, which was as politely declined; but as the dining-room doors were now thrown open, he had the pleasure of sitting between her and Mrs. Maxwell at the supper-table, the Marquis with Lady Agnes being opposite to them.

A full hour having been devoted to refreshment, dancing was resumed with greater spirit than before, particularly on the part of the gentlemen, who had made rather free with the Earl's champagne, of which the supply was most abundant. Edmund had taken more than he usually did, because Lady Agnes refused him a second dance; she pleaded engagements half a dozen deep at least, and Edmund, annoyed by what he thought excuses only, expressed himself rather warmly on her dancing so often with Sir Digby Colville. Agnes retorted by saying she thought she had a right to please herself in her selection of partners, and she should waltz with him again after supper; he was a delightful waltzer, so graceful, so quiet, so unlike country-taught dancers.

Edmund could not trust himself to reply, he felt too indignant; and to stifle his glowing resentment, he drank more wine, which added fuel to the fire now raging within his breast. Again to his glaring vision the form of his beloved was presented, whirled round and round by his detested rival, her head almost reclining on his shoulder.

The sight maddened him almost to desperation; he turned aside from the sickening spectacle, and his blood-shot eye fell upon the face of Edith Maxwell sitting with her mother. There was a soft, sad expression on her generally smile-illumined features, which seemed to say, "I feel for your distress, and would relieve you if I could."

Edmund could not resist that look; it reminded him of all her gentle interest in his welfare, of the part she had often taken in his defence. He was by her side in a moment, softened and subdued.

"You are engaged, I suppose, Edith," he said, "half-a-dozen deep, like Agnes, and cannot now dance with me?"

"I am," she replied, "for the two next quadrilles, but in the third I will with pleasure be your partner."

"Thank you; this room is very warm, will you take a turn with me in the next until this valse is finished, if you, my dear madam," addressing Mrs. Maxwell, "have no objection."

"Certainly not, Edmund; but she must return in time."

They passed on in silence through the throng into the second room.

"It is not cool even here," Edmund said; "let us go into the hall, it will be more refreshing there."

"What has so excited you this evening?" Edith asked, in a gentle, anxious tone.

"I have been worried and provoked, Edith, by Agnes acting in defiance of my advice. I warned her against that Irish baronet, and she has already danced with him three times."

"Agnes would never suffer dictation," she replied; "how can you expect her to bear it now?"

"Advice is not dictation, Edith; I merely told her what I had heard of him."

"Which, I suppose, she did not choose to believe," added Edith, "and therefore resolved to judge of him herself."

"Would you have danced with a stranger so often on the first night of your introduction? and did he not ask you for a second?"

"Yes," replied Edith, "he did, but I declined; for, although agreeable, Sir Digby's very pretty speeches abound in too much flattery to suit my taste."

"Did he ask you about Agnes?"

"It is really so much more than cool here," she said, without answering this question, "that I would rather return to the ball-room."

"No, Edith, not there; come with me into the library, for I am really so thirsty to-night, I must have a bottle of soda-water."

"Then you must be quick, Edmund, or Mr. Addleby will miss his quadrille, and mamma be angry with me for disappointing him."

"Let the mad fool wait," exclaimed Edmund, impatiently; "you would not marry that fellow, Edith, would you?"

"Oh, no!" she replied, laughing; "what could put that into your head?"

"I heard him speak in such rapturous strains of your beauty after supper, three glasses of wine always making him crazy, that I verily believe he will propose to you this very night; but for Heaven's sake, Edith, don't let father or mother persuade you to accept him; there is madness in his family, and my belief is he will end his days in a lunatic asylum."

Edith shuddered, saying, "Poor man! I pity him."

"Pity him to a certain extent if you like, Edith, although pity is a dangerous feeling for a girl to indulge in towards man. Let no considerations on earth, let no persuasions, induce you to link your fate with his. The horror of such an alliance, you, dear Edith, cannot now understand; but the lot of her who becomes his wife will be fearful indeed."

"Rest assured, Edmund, Mr. Addleby would never be my choice."

"I am rejoiced to hear you say so, for I take a deep interest, of course, in your future happiness. Now tell me what this plausible Irishman said of Agnes?"

"Only what you might naturally suppose, that she was divinely beautiful, the most charming, delightful young lady he had met in his walk through the world."

"Did he ask no questions about her?"

"Yes, he asked if she were not already engaged to Mr. Knightley?"

"Ha! so I thought; and what answer did you return, Edith?"

"That I could not tell him; and on his pressing the question, added that if the case were so, he could not expect I should reveal a friend's secret to a stranger."

"You spoke discreetly and properly, Edith; and I now perceive, as I before suspected, this man's purpose."

"Well, Edmund, I really must return to the ball-room, or mamma will be very angry, and you will have a lecture also for detaining me so long."

"Not exactly contrary to your inclination, I hope," he said, rather more cheerfully, as they left the library; "but you will not, of course, repeat the conversation that has passed between us to Agnes."

"Certainly not. I would not make mischief between you for the world; and now take my advice, as you so often give me yours, do not even mention the name of Sir Digby Colville to her again, for she has no doubt acted towards you to-night from a feeling of (perhaps a little pardonable) resentment for your presuming to question her conduct. We are both now released from lectures and lessons," she said, with a playful smile; "we are now become women of the world."

"That *you* will never be, Edith, I would answer for," he replied; "but there stands Addleby, I declare, before Mrs. Maxwell, and the sets are already forming; don't forget my caution and my quadrille. And now, my dear Mrs. Maxwell," he said, on releasing Edith's arm, "I will do penance for my sin in detaining her so long, by sitting with you until she returns, if that cracked Addleby does not run away with her."

"You appear cracked yourself this evening, Edmund," Mrs. Maxwell said.

"Not unlikely," he replied, good-humouredly; "too much learning has, perhaps, made me mad, as Festus said to Paul; however, there is no hereditary failing of this kind in my family; but poor Addleby is quite crazy sometimes; his father died in a mad-house."

"Are you serious, Edmund?—quite sure of this?"

"Quite, my dear madam; my father saw him there; but if not crazy, he is certainly tipsy to-night; look at his dancing—Edith seems quite perplexed what to do. I must go to her assistance if necessary."

Edmund was in a moment by Edith's side, her partner being at that moment performing a *pas seul* with such extraordinary skips and hops, and so intent upon his performance, as to excite the merriment of all beholders save poor Edith and Major Townsend, who was standing close to her.

"By gad! Knightley," the Major exclaimed, loud enough to be heard by those around, "that fellow's as mad as a hatter!"

"He is not in a fit state to dance with any young lady," remarked the Rev. Mr. Sherrard; "half the room is attracted by his crazy feats."

At this moment Addleby, with a spring somewhat resembling that of a wild Indian, crossed over to his partner, and seizing her hands, swung her round with such violence that she fell against Mr. Sherrard, who being a little, spare man, was knocked down by the force of the concussion, while Edith was saved from a similar fall by Edmund's arm.

"Take her away, sir," said the Major, "or I will myself." But Edmund had already decided on this step by placing her arm within his, when Addleby following, demanded furiously "what right he had to take his partner?"

"I will answer that question, sir," said the Rev. Mr. Sherrard, greatly excited by his fall. "I advised Mr. Knightley to do so. You have knocked me down, sir, by your violence, and that young lady must have fallen also but for his timely assistance. You are not in a fit state, sir, to be in ladies' society."

"And who are you that dare insult me thus?" Addleby said, savagely, now turning his glaring eyes on the diminutive pastor.

"My name is the Rev. J. Sherrard, of Hardington, as you know perfectly well."

"Yes, I know you for a canting parson, but your cloth protects you from being dealt with as you deserve."

"My cloth, sir!—my cloth shall *not* protect me," retorted the little vicar, beside himself with excitement; and tearing his coat off, he threw it on the floor.

"Take up your coat, sir," the Major said. "I have a word for your private ear, Addleby; come with me into the supper-room for a moment."

Addleby followed the Major as if mechanically, and when there, said impatiently, "Now, Townsend, what have you to say?"

"That you have made a confounded fool of yourself to-night by taking too much wine; and that when you are sufficiently sobered, by drinking the mixture I am preparing for you, your first business is to make the most ample apology to Miss Maxwell for your rough usage. By gad, sir, I never saw any poor girl so frightened in my life; you treated her shamefully; every one was remarking it."

"I am really distressed to hear you say so, Townsend, but I was not aware of it until you told me. I will go directly, and make every apology."

"No, not yet. Remain here half an hour at least, and drink this"—pouring out a few drops from a small bottle he drew from his pocket, into a wine-glass of water—"which will soon sober you."

Edith's pale face and trembling frame revealed to her mother that something unpleasant had occurred between her and Mr. Addleby, which was quickly explained by Edmund, greatly to Mrs. Maxwell's horror, and confirmed immediately afterwards by others who had witnessed the scene. But great was her surprise when Mr. Addleby, shortly afterwards—quite sobered by the Major's prescription—stood again before her and Edith, offering the most humble apologies for what he chose to term his awkwardness, and soliciting another dance.

"My daughter is engaged, sir," Mrs. Maxwell said, in a tone which none could misunderstand; "and were she not, I should not again permit her to become subject to a repetition of such behaviour."

"I wish to convince you, Mrs. Maxwell, it was purely accidental—by losing my balance; you could not suppose it intentional."

"You have had my answer to your application, Mr. Addleby, from which I shall not depart;" and she turned her head away to address Edmund, who was sitting between herself and Edith, on which Addleby retired without another word.

This little occurrence—for this scene did actually occur nearly as related—had diverted Edmund's thoughts from dwelling too much on the conduct of Lady Agnes, whom he saw engaged in every dance, waltz as well as quadrille. He had now also resolved to show her, by an assumption of gaiety towards Edith, his indifference to her flirting with the Baronet; but Edith was not deceived by his pretended lightness of spirits. His wandering eye and uneasy look towards Lady Agnes proved to her what his thoughts really were.

The ball was now brought to a close with the usual dance on such occasions, in which Edith again became the partner of Edmund; and thus terminated the festivities of the evening.

CHAPTER XIV

THE next morning, at a late hour, the family party at Woodborough were assembled round the breakfast table, with looks expressive of anything but pleasure from their last night's *fête.* The Earl seemed gloomy and dissatisfied, Mrs. Errington very serious, Edmund pale and dejected, Edith thoughtful, and Lady Agnes was decidedly in a very bad humour; for her father had spoken rather sharply to her on her flirting (as he called it) with Sir Digby Colville, saying, "that although he had been staying with the Marquis once or twice previously, he was comparatively a stranger to them all."

Lady Agnes pouted her pretty lip, scarcely deigning to recognise Edmund's morning salutation; and after drinking a cup of tea, without eating anything, she rose from the table and retired to her own room, under the plea of a bad headache. She was followed soon after by Edith, who, on asking if she felt better, received a laugh in reply.

"I have no very bad headache, Edith," she said; "but I expected another lecture from papa, and I shall not venture down stairs again till luncheon time. It seems very hard that, at my first ball, I should not be allowed to please myself by selecting agreeable instead of disagreeable partners; and as to dancing one quadrille, and waltzing twice with Sir Digby Colville, what impropriety can there be in that? Other girls were waltzing with the same partners much oftener than I did with him, and I dare say if he had asked you, Edith, you would not have refused."

"I did refuse, Agnes, to dance with Sir Digby Colville a second time."

"But why did you refuse him, Edith?" she inquired in surprise; "he was decidedly the most handsome, *distingué* looking person in the room, and most agreeable in manners and conversation."

"I do not appreciate the gentleman or his conversation sufficiently, I suppose; but I am not fond of high-flown compliments, which mamma says are the general language of men of the world like Sir Digby Colville, and mean nothing."

"Did he pay you any compliments, then?" asked Lady Agnes, rather anxiously.

"More than I liked to hear, and therefore I thought he had better repeat them to more attentive ears than mine."

"But I saw you dancing twice with Edmund," Lady Agnes said, rather spitefully; "you found *his* conversation very agreeable, no doubt?"

"Not particularly, my dear Agnes, but I could not refuse an old friend like Edmund—that is quite a different thing altogether; with him or his brother I should not hesitate dancing twice, or oftener, but certainly not with any other gentleman."

"Well, Edith, which of the two brothers do you intend to accept, as they seemed equally attentive to you last night, although Edmund appeared the most favoured?"

"I have never thought of accepting either, my dear Agnes; neither do I believe either of them regards me in any other light than that of a friend."

"I should prefer Reginald," Lady Agnes continued; "he is handsomer, and more lively and chatty than his brother, who, between ourselves, dear Edith, bores one sadly sometimes with his advice and lectures. He would just suit a girl of your sober, domestic ideas, my dear; but I must have something more gay for my future partner in life."

"I fear, dear Agnes, you will find little prospect of happiness with a gay man of the world; but we are both too young and happy to think of marrying yet; so now let us take a stroll through the pleasure grounds, or my head will ache seriously, for the music has been ringing in my ears all the morning."

"We shall meet Edmund, I fear, and he looked at breakfast just in the humour for another lecture, although I expressed my sentiments on that subject very freely last night, and I hope, for the future, he will confine his advice to one young lady instead of two; in short, if he ventures on reproof or remonstrances to me again, we shall have some serious quarrel, which I should very much regret, as he is such a favourite with papa."

"You need not fear meeting Edmund or a lecture," Edith replied, "as he has gone on horseback over to St. Austin's."

"To lecture the two Miss Duncombes, I suppose," added Lady Agnes, "for their violent flirtations last night; now, *they* are flirts, if you please, Edith, although I ought not, perhaps, to say so to you, who are such a favourite with their brother. I rather think, my dear," she continued, with a laugh, "the Captain stands first on your list of admirers, even before the Messrs. Knightley."

"He is a very pleasant companion, Agnes, but certainly not the person I should fall in love with."

"Well, I admire your caution, Edith, for papa says he is little short of a gentleman horse-dealer."

"And I was told last night," replied Edith, "that Sir Digby Colville is of the same profession—living by his wits and luck at cards."

"Edmund's information, I conclude, or some of the Knightley family's."

"You are quite mistaken, Agnes; it was given me by a gentleman I had never before seen, until he was introduced to me last night, and who said he was well acquainted with Sir Digby."

"Some ill-natured person, jealous of his superiority."

"I should think not, Agnes, as my informant appeared very good-tempered, and, I think, quite as good-looking as Sir Digby."

"Then you asked him these questions, I suppose?"

"Indeed, you do me great injustice; Sir Digby Colville is nothing to me, and how can you think I should ask a perfect stranger questions about him? I have no such indelicate curiosity, but being our *vis-à-vis* in a quadrille, my partner volunteered the information by saying, 'That is Sir Digby Colville, a man I meet frequently in London during the season, who, by horse-dealing, card-playing, and betting at races, contrives to spend two or three months in town, and lives the remainder of the year upon his friends. He is as well-known at Almack's as the Dowager Duchess of C——, and her three unmarried daughters, with as little prospect of changing his state of single blessedness as those young ladies; but perhaps he may fare better in the country with girls in their teens.'"

"Well, Edith, such remarks are very ill-natured, even if true; and I conclude your partner, having taken a fancy to you himself, feared you might feel a preference for Sir Digby."

"But, Agnes, as *I* have not taken a fancy for either of these gentlemen, I hope neither will take a fancy for me; so now put on your bonnet whilst I go for mine."

We need not relate further conversation between the two friends during their walk, on the conclusion of which Edith had arrived at another termination, that Agnes was not really in love with Edmund Knightley, if he was with her. She also perceived that the Irish Baronet had made a very favourable impression upon her friend. Of the Earl's wishes or intentions, with regard to Agnes and Edmund, Edith was profoundly ignorant, so closely and carefully had these been concealed within his own breast; but, from his partiality for Edmund, she surmised that the Earl would be well pleased by Edmund's union with his daughter; and, in conformity with these ideas, she had resolved to do all in her power to heal the breach between them.

Edmund had ridden over to St. Austin's for the sake of a good gallop, by which to dispel, if possible, the gloomy thoughts that had taken possession of his mind. His visit was not intended for the ladies, but to inspect some alterations in the buildings of the home farm, which, on taking possession of the property, he purposed keeping in his own hands. He was not in the humour that morning for making calls upon any one, much less upon two flirting girls, such as the Miss Duncombes. He did not like them, their mother, or their brother—the last least of all; to whom his dislike had been increased by his particular attention to Edith Maxwell the previous night—but what was, or could it be to him, with his heart devoted to another? She was a kind, affectionate, and most amiable girl. "Yes," he soliloquised, "perhaps more amiable than Agnes, although not so beautiful—yet others think differently; and the words of the Marchioness, what were they? 'Edith would be my choice.' She is not mine, but a dear, good girl, nearly as dear to me as my own sister, and I must prevent her, if possible, forming a bad marriage. By the way, I may as well call and lunch at Morton Grange; Mrs. Maxwell will be glad to hear her daughter is not the worse for her first ball—and I shall give her a quiet hint about the Captain—not to encourage his visits to Morton Grange; he is a plausible, smooth-tongued fellow with women, like that confounded Irish Baronet—both dissipated men of the world—reckless and extravagant—to whom the idea of domestic happiness is unknown."

Having despatched his business at St. Austin's, in a very off-hand and impatient manner, so unlike his usual custom, Edmund began to retrace his steps towards home, jogging leisurely along, his horse keeping pace with his now more sober reflections. He was calmly reviewing the past night's events; the impatience of Agnes, and her resentment at his well-intended advice; and, before reaching the Grange, he had resolved for the future on an entire change of conduct towards her; "for, like myself," he exclaimed, "she may be led, but not driven."

Mrs. Maxwell was at home; the Colonel was out riding, so

that Edmund had a cosy chat with her before the luncheon hour arrived; in the course of which he touched upon Edith's partners of the previous night, making comments upon and noticing Captain Duncombe's particular attentions.

"I believe he is a favourite with both yourself and the Colonel," Edmund said.

"We like him very well, Edmund; he is agreeable, sensible, and well informed."

"Then perhaps you think him desirable as a son-in-law?"

"Why, really, Edmund, I have never thought of him in that light, but you have some reason, I suppose, for speaking to me on this subject; you do not think Edith is attached to him?"

"Indeed, I hope not," Edmund said, "although he is a person likely to take with a young, artless girl like her; but I conclude you will require some more essential requisites in your future son-in-law than a handsome face and agreeable manners. The latter can easily be assumed, and I doubt their being natural either to the Captain or that Irish Baronet. Now, what we know of the former is that he is a half-pay Captain, with about three hundred a year—quite the outside of his income, without further expectations except from an aunt. Aunts are very convenient persons; and with horse-dealing, book-making at races, and a bit of luck at cards occasionally, he makes a great show with his half dozen hunters—all for sale. Now, my dear Mrs. Maxwell, is this the sort of man, let alone his habits of life, which would be destruction to a wife's happiness, you and the Colonel would select for your sweet-tempered, beautiful Edith's husband?"

"No, Edmund, certainly not; but we have been told that Captain Duncombe possessed his clear fifteen hundred a year, independent of his mother, although we never thought of him in any other light than as an agreeable acquaintance."

"It is not the case, my dear madam; whoever gave you this information, it came most likely from himself, for he is neither more nor less than a fortune-hunter, possessing not a shilling more than I have told you, if so much; and *my* information may be *relied upon*, as derived from the fountain-head. Mrs. Duncombe's lease has, I am happy to say, very nearly run out, and I shall not let St. Austin's again to any one. I may add, that as the Captain finds his trade of horse-dealing succeed very well in this county, he may be calculating on his board and lodging *gratis* for the future at Morton Grange instead of St. Austin's."

"That, I am quite sure, he will not realise, Edmund; neither do I think Edith is in the least attached to him, although perhaps we have been rather imprudent in receiving him here so often."

"Then," he replied, "be careful not to renew the imprudence, for the evil may be avoided by a little more caution in future. You will not, of course, repeat my communication to her, or make the slightest allusion to it; for young ladies are rather averse to dictation, and forbidden fruit is, I fear, as attractive still as to their first parent."

"Oh, no, Edmund. I am much obliged by your communication, but will not mention a word you have spoken to Edith."

The Colonel entering the room soon after, and luncheon being announced, put an end to further conversation on this subject; but after Edmund's departure Mrs. Maxwell mentioned to her husband what she had heard respecting the Captain.

"Pshaw! my dear; I never dreamt of Duncombe as a son-in-law—the thing is absurd; and as to Edith, she is too young to think of marrying; besides which, I am in no hurry to part with her yet, and am quite sure she would accept no one without first consulting you."

"I begin to think," Mrs. Maxwell said, "that Edmund is attached to Edith, notwithstanding the Earl's wish—as we are told—that he should marry Lady Agnes; St. Austin's is a beautiful place, and within an easy distance."

"What has put this fancy into your head, my dear?" asked the Colonel; "you women are always match-making."

"I noticed them particularly last night, Colonel, when Edmund was exceedingly attentive to her, and here he is again this morning talking in such a manner about the Captain, and fearing that we should encourage his attentions, that I feel almost sure he is in love with her himself."

"Well, my dear, I cannot possibly have any objection to Edmund, who is a great favourite with me as well as yourself; but pray don't meddle in the matter, or you will counteract your own wishes, and Edith can remain another week at Woodborough if she likes."

From this day Edmund had resolved on an entire change of conduct towards Lady Agnes, in the hope of regaining her confidence; and he never again alluded to Sir Digby Colville, or questioned her right to act as she thought proper. At dinner that evening he appeared in his usual good spirits and most entertaining mood, for Edmund could be very amusing, and few could resist the influence of his witching smile, which was noticed even by strangers, as imparting a peculiar brilliancy to his handsome features; even Lady Agnes, when stealing a glance at his expressive face, reproached herself for having given him pain by her sharp speech on the previous night.

"You appear in high spirits this evening, Edmund," Mrs. Errington remarked; "I suppose the young ladies at St. Austin's made themselves very agreeable, as your visit was rather a long one."

"I have paid no visit to-day except to Colonel and Mrs. Maxwell," he replied, "with whom I took luncheon on my return, thinking they would like to know how Edith was after her dissipation of last night. I merely made a call on the carpenters and workmen at St. Austin's; but the high-stepping Miss Duncombes are a trifle too fast for one of my quiet jog-trot ideas."

"Well, Edmund," the Earl added, "you must admit they are very accomplished dancers. I think I never saw two more graceful performers in that way. I wish they would give a lesson or two to Addleby."

"I hope and trust one of them may, dear uncle, for he appeared to patronise Miss Charlotte very extensively, and she is just the person to keep a wild, refractory husband in order, quite as good, I should think, as a strait waistcoat to him, when he gets into one of his crazy fits. The scene between him, his pastor, and Major Townsend, I am told, was something quite *unique*—the latter exclaiming, 'Don't be alarmed, ladies; they won't bite, although both are as mad as hatters.'"

"I was distressed to see a clergyman so forgetful of his profession," remarked Mrs. Errington.

"Sherrard is a most excitable man after dinner or supper," Edmund replied, "when his spirits lead him sometimes into trifling excesses. He is, however, generally most even-tempered, with a truly Christian disposition, and in the pulpit an excellent preacher; but Addleby cannot boast of *his* amiability, being fierce and ungovernable on certain occasions, and so much so that he is only fit to be a bachelor."

CHAPTER XV

THE following afternoon, immediately after luncheon, the Marquis of Dunkerton, with Sir Digby Colville, called at Woodborough, selecting that time as the most likely to find the ladies, or rather the Lady Agnes, at home, for whom their visit was more especially intended. A little disappointment, however, awaited the Baronet on his discovering the whole party in the drawing-room, just arranging for a drive.

The Earl came forward to receive the Marquis with a friendly shake of the hand, and the Baronet with a stately bow indicative of his wish for no nearer acquaintance. The moment he entered the room, Edmund directed a furtive glance towards Lady Agnes, over whose features the heightened colour suddenly spread, which was almost as suddenly succeeded by an unusual paleness.

His eye then rested for a moment on Edith's fair face, which remained perfectly composed, without the slightest change. After paying his compliments to the ladies, the Marquis greeted Edmund in the most friendly manner, engaging him and the Earl in conversation, whilst his friend, Sir Digby, was paying his devoirs to Lady Agnes, speaking of her ball in the highest praise, everything being so well arranged, and then turning, in an easy style, some pretty little compliments to herself, which were received very graciously, with an occasional increase of vermilion when his dark piercing eyes rested upon hers.

The Baronet, from his deep study of female physiognomy, drew certain conclusions from the looks and manner of Lady Agnes, that he had made a favourable first impression; and being satisfied on that point, he now diverged into other topics with her and Edith, fearing the Earl might notice any particular attention to his daughter. But the Marquis, observing his impatient glances towards the Baronet and Lady Agnes, rose, saying "he feared they had already detained the ladies too long from their drive;" and on their leaving Edmund felt relieved of a weight which seemed to press him to the ground. He could not join Edith and Agnes whilst his rival remained, but sat talking with Mrs. Errington, and by his unconnected language, in addressing one person whilst thinking of another, she formed a tolerably correct idea of what was passing in his mind.

On the pony carriage being brought round to the hall door, Edmund did not proffer his services as charioteer, thinking the young ladies might prefer being alone, as Mrs. Errington had declined going with them; for, having resolved to maintain an independent course of action towards Lady Agnes, he kept to his determination. There are undoubtedly certain occasions when young ladies prefer their own society to ours, when they can discuss sundry little matters interesting only to themselves, and this happened to be the case now. Lady Agnes longed to talk about the Baronet, and had no sooner left the pleasure-grounds than she entered on this delightful subject by saying abruptly—

"Now, is he not handsome, Edith?"

"Well," replied her friend, not choosing to comprehend her meaning, "I think the Marquis is very handsome indeed."

"The Baronet, I mean, Edith; don't you think him the most charming, delightful person you have ever met? And I am sure he is far better looking than the Marquis."

"Why, dear Agnes, I cannot quite agree with you, for I think the Marquis the most agreeable person of the two, quite as handsome, and more sensible in his conversation. Sir Digby talks of nothing but balls, and parties, and London fashionables, the opera, the theatres, and such things, which I suppose he thinks we take so deep an interest in as to wish to hear of nothing else."

"Well, Edith, I shall enjoy exceedingly a season in London, and hope to induce papa to take me there in May next, and I dare say you would not dislike seeing a little of town life also."

"I should have no objection to spend a month or six weeks there, which would be quite sufficient, if not more than sufficient, to satisfy my taste for gaiety; but a London life would not suit me."

"You do not know until you have tried it, Edith."

"Yes, dear Agnes, I know myself well enough to feel I could take no pleasure in continual dissipation, for I have scarcely yet recovered from the effects of my first ball."

"Suppose you were to marry a man of fashion, one who liked to live in London half the year?"

"Such a person would never suit me."

"Perhaps a duke or marquis might, my dear?"

"If I ever should marry, dear Agnes, it will be one whom I can both love and respect for his virtues and good disposition. Titles and wealth have no attractions for me in such a serious affair as this, and last of all in my opinion is he whom you call a man of fashion."

"Well, dear, our ideas are very different on these points. I wish to see more of the world, to mix more in society, and spend five or six months in London every season, then travel about for amusement and recreation during four more, and perhaps vegetate the other two in the country. But I have had quite enough of Woodborough Park all the year round."

"And yet, my dear Agnes, that time may and most likely will come, should you live long enough to gratify all your wishes to their full extent, that you will look back on the days spent at dear Woodborough as the happiest you have ever known."

"Ah! Edith, you are a pretty little moralist, and I conclude will at last settle down as a contented clergyman's wife, railing against the follies and vices of the world; but, whatever may be your lot, my own dearest Edith, you will ever be the same to me. And now let us change the subject to one more cheerful."

On their return home, the Marquis and Sir Digby were also occupied in canvassing the relative charms of the young ladies.

"Well, Digby," asked the former, "what think you of our country belles in their morning costume? Did you see anything superior to them in town last season?"

"No, I think not. They are very beautiful girls, and will create quite a sensation when produced at Almack's. Lady Agnes is in my opinion the finer woman of the two, and Miss Maxwell the most lovely."

"Precisely my idea also, Digby; the one commands, the other engages your attention. The last would be my choice were plurality of wives in fashion here as with the Turks and Jews."

"I am not a friend to Hymen, as you know, Dunkerton."

"Unless Hymen proved a great friend to you. Your liberty is not worth more to you than a hundred thousand pounds, and that you may get, with a handsome wife, by marrying Lady Agnes."

"Well," replied the Baronet, in a careless tone, "I may think about it, for she seems rather favourably inclined towards me, if the money is really forthcoming; but just fancy my predicament with a fine fashionable wife and no increase of means to support her. She has been accustomed to every luxury, and the interest of a hundred thousand pounds would barely keep a girl of her rank in that style of living. I believe it is far more prudent to remain as I am, for there are a great many hitches in those marriage settlements, and the Earl looks like a man who would tie one up pretty tightly."

"Then you know how to manage him. Get a tight hold first on his daughter's heart, which I think you can do very easily, and then you will have the Earl in hand. But you must proceed quietly and regularly—no runaway match or any thing of that kind; and I think you have blarney enough, my dear fellow, to get over him at last. The *suaviter in modo* you understand very well. The Marchioness shall send an invitation to the party to dine here next week, when you will have an opportunity of reporting progress. Win her if you can, for all the Earl's funded and landed property (save the entailed portion) will be hers, and the run of Woodborough House is worth at least two thousand per annum, where you will of course take up your winter quarters, and keep your half-dozen hunters for nothing."

"Your suggestions, Dunkerton, are worth consideration, but I am not cut out for a family man."

"Put your brats, if you have any, out to keep at Woodborough too, as we send our whelps to walk at farm-houses. Grandpapas are always fond of children. So these difficulties being arranged, I must look out my pack for to-morrow's hunting."

Edmund Knightley had now resumed his place in the hunting field, where he was an especial favourite, and with none more so than with his father's huntsman, who thought great things of Master Edmund, from his entering thoroughly into the sport and the business part, as Will called it, of the profession.

"Mr. Reginald is very well in his way," he remarked to old Squire White, on Edmund's first appearance. "He likes the riding part, and can do it very cleverly; but I'm a-thinking, squire, Master Edmund is the man for hounds, and the farmers likes him better; he's more come-at-able—ain't above shaking hands with old Mr. Thickthorn, who has bred us a litter of cubs in Thornydown bushes the last forty years. 'Ah!' said he to me this morning, 'we shall do now again, Will. Master Edmund's come home, and they do say he's a-done a power of bookwork at Oxford college.'

"'Carried all afore him, Mr. Thickthorn,' says I, 'and comed in the winner of the first prize!'

"'Well, Will, he has had enough of Latin and Greek to last him all his days, and now I hope he will settle down regularly to the pigskin.'"

"He is more like the old squire. Mr. Reginald is too hasty, and too proud for a master of fox-hounds; but here comes the Marquis, with the Irish Baronet, who, they say, has done a trick or two across Leicestershire as well as over the card-table."

"Shouldn't wonder, squire; he looks a wide-awake man, but I hope to give him the slip to-day. I'm most afraid of that young Shuttleworth, who rode in slap among the Marquis's pack when they were at check the other day."

"I think Mr. Reginald will look after him, Will, for he hates him like poison."

After an interchange of civilities between the two masters, and an inspection of the hounds by the Marquis, who complimented Will Lane on their splendid condition, the order was given for Thornydown Brake, so called from its thick blackthorn bushes, and from which a fine old fox almost immediately broke away on the far side, over a splendid grass vale, with eighteen couples of hounds within a hundred yards of his brush, although screened from view by a thick double hedge-row, just outside the covert, which was the most awkward in the whole country to get away from, on account of the stiff fences by which it was surrounded, some water meadows, and a deep brook, lying on the lower side, over which foxes generally took their line.

There was a large field of horsemen out on this occasion, and a strong muster from the Marquis's hunt, for there is a fashion in fox-hunting with the majority of sportsmen so called, as well as in other things—such as the little absurd bonnets, and wide, ridiculous, crinolined dresses of ladies—and the Marquis having expressed his intention, two days previously, of meeting Mr. Knightley's hounds at Thornydown Gate, nearly all his supporters residing on that side the country deemed it imperative almost upon them to be there also, the hope of a bow or nod of recognition from my Lord Marquis being the chief inducement with many to patronise his pack. It seemed a great thing for men of little minds and great bodies residing in the fashionable watering-place of Waterton, to strut up and down their High Street, in pink, on the afternoons of hunting days, and boast of having been out with the Marquis; they had always capital sport with his hounds, whether the fox ran one mile or ten, or was chopped in covert. It was always the fashion to say so, although the meet was all they went out to see, and to take off their hats to the Marquis.

On the hounds being away from Thornydown Brake, a rush was made by this heavy brigade for a bridge just in the contrary direction to that taken by the fox, whilst the *riders* of both hunts, stirred up by a little jealous feeling for first places, set to work with the difficulty before them in good earnest. Alphonso, on Mameluke, felt constrained to follow Duncombe, who, having an eye for an easy place, got through the first thick blackthorn hedge, and over the drop leap into the water meadows below, without any casualty; but our hero, by pulling with all his might at Mameluke's mouth just on his taking the leap, gave himself the benefit of a cold bath in the dyke, which the Captain observing, hallooed out, "Give him his head, Jack, and come along;" and well for him it was he followed his leader's advice, since, from being just behind a first flight man, the water and dirt thrown back into his face prevented his seeing a yard of the ground he was traversing, until Mameluke, taking the brook in his stride, landed him safely on the opposite bank.

Mameluke now strove hard to catch the hounds, two fields ahead of him; and the fences being of more moderate dimensions, Alphonso kept his seat tolerably well for about a mile, gradually creeping up to those in advance; the leading phalanx consisting of the two Messrs. Knightley, Sir Digby Colville, Duncombe, and two or three others, with Will Lane, and Charley the first whip. Our hero, hating Reginald, was fired by ambition and jealousy to take the lead out of his hands, and Mameluke, having the speed of his rival's horse, passed him as they were approaching a high blackthorn hedge, for an opening in which Will Lane was making, when Alphonso, crossing from his own line to the same place, knocked the huntsman, with his horse, over upon their backs into the next field. The collision was a fearful one for poor Will, who had two ribs broken by the fall, and feeling himself seriously hurt, he told Charley to take his horn to Master Edmund, and ask him to go on with the hounds.

Reginald came up immediately after, having seen the accident, and how caused; and after ordering the second whip to attend Will Lane and see him home, he rode furiously away, determined to wreak his vengeance on the young cotton cub, which he was soon enabled to do by the fox being headed back from a small brake on rising ground. Then bearing down again into the vale, Reginald found himself unexpectedly in the same field with Alphonso, upon whom he now waited, and seeing him again intent on the same trick of crossing his line, he watched the opportunity, and rode his horse at an acute angle right against him, which sent him spinning out of the saddle, head foremost, into the ditch, and Mameluke falling upon his prostrate master, he was nearly stifled by mud and water, as well as seriously bruised by the horse's exertions to get out.

"Ah! serve him right," exclaimed a young sporting farmer as he passed him, now partly recovered, and leaning against his horse, "for knocking over poor Will."

At the same time a fox-hunting surgeon, thinking he had a case in hand, dismounted to tender his services.

Edmund had also a rival to contend with in this run; no other than the Irish Baronet, who, for the honour of his country, seemed determined to keep the lead. From the fox turning down wind, the pace had slackened sufficiently to enable Sir Digby to ride close upon the hounds, when, in the middle of a large grass field, they were brought to a check by a herd of cattle following the fox; the leading couples feathering away to the right towards Sir Digby, who, seeing Edmund turning his horse to the left, with a few old hounds still working on the line, tried to hold the others on still further, most irrelevantly taking upon himself the office of huntsman.

Edmund immediately rode up to him, saying, "I will thank you, sir, to let the hounds alone; we can do very well without your assistance."

"The huntsman is not up, sir," retorted the Baronet, "and this is the line of the fox."

"I am up, if the huntsman is not," replied Edmund, "and will not permit you to interfere."

"And who are you, sir?" asked the Baronet, his Irish blood boiling up at Edmund's tone of voice.

"You may easily find out," was the rejoinder; and at that moment Charley came up, telling him that Mr. Lane, having met with a bad fall, had sent his horn to him, and begged him to go on with the hounds.

"Then turn them to me, Charley," was the quick reply, and, with a short blast or two of the horn, the pack followed Edmund, who holding them a little forward over the stained ground, where the fox had turned now with a side wind, they set to work running as hard as at first, the moment they reached the other side of the fence, whilst Sir Digby, fully persuaded that he was in the right direction, had continued moving his horse leisurely on, talking to Duncombe about what he called young Knightley's impertinence.

"By gad, sir," the Captain suddenly exclaimed, "he has given us the slip; there go the hounds running like wildfire up that hedge-row yonder. We are done; how quietly he and Charley have managed it!—not a scream or note of the horn this windy day."

"Done on purpose, I'll be sworn," replied the Baronet; "but we will soon catch them again; they can't go the pace like the Marquis's pack."

"Can't they, Colville? You will be satisfied now on that point; so come along."

Riding to catch hounds running with a good scent, and a start of two fields ahead, is almost a forlorn hope to the most zealous fox-hunter, for he well knows the difficulty, almost impossibility, of seeing them again except by an accidental check. Sir Digby rode fast and furiously to recover his lost honour of being leading man that day, but it was to little purpose; no check of any consequence occurred to let him in again; and on meeting the Marquis they both gave up the attempt, and were riding home by a short cut through the park, when they met Edmund returning with his fox's head.

"Why, Knightley," exclaimed the Marquis in astonishment, "where are you coming from? what have you done?"

"Killed our fox, Dunkerton, in the middle of your lower park—ran into him in the open."

"The deuce you have! Well, that's not a bad day's work for the first time of handling the horn; so come and have some luncheon, and feed the hounds in my kennel if you like. You are too far from home to draw again; and as for your field, they are scattered all over the country."

"I am much obliged by your kind offer, Dunkerton," Edmund replied; "but as Will has met with a serious accident, I am anxious to see how he is."

"Well, in that case I will not detain you; but mind, we expect you to dine with us to-morrow, with the Earl."

"With much pleasure I will avail myself of your invitation;" and Edmund passed on.

"That young gentleman seems inclined to be impertinent," remarked the Baronet.

"It is not his general character to be impertinent to any one, Digby, but quite the reverse; how was he so to you?"

"By speaking very sharply to me to-day, when, the hounds being at fault, I was trying to recover the line."

"The impertinence was on your side, then. I will not permit any man to speak even to my hounds, and you ought to know you were out of order in taking such a liberty when one of the family was in the same field with you, and close to the hounds."

"I wanted to keep the lead, Dunkerton, that's the truth; but I will not submit to be spoken to in the tone he addressed me, and I shall call him to account for it."

"You will do nothing of the kind, Digby, whilst under my roof. A pretty story it would be for people to circulate through the country: here is the Marquis, who blows people up sky high for overriding his hounds, encouraging his particular friend to call out young Knightley for merely telling him he could do without his assistance."

"Then I must wait for another opportunity, after I have left Huntingshire; we shall, I dare say, meet again somewhere."

"If you ever meet Edmund Knightley, Colville, in a hostile manner, you will meet with your match; he is a good shot with gun or pistol, possessing a steadier hand and stronger nerves than you have. But, independent of these considerations, if you have any serious intention towards Lady Agnes, you would incur her father's unfailing resentment by quarrelling with his godson. The Earl would never forget or forgive you for such an act; and as to marrying his daughter afterwards, the idea is quite absurd."

It is almost unnecessary to add that Sir Digby, being open to conviction, received the advice of his host and friend with the greatest complacency, and no further allusion was made to the subject.

On Edmund's return to the kennels, his first act was to feed the hounds, which had cheerfully followed their young huntsman, and his next to repair instantly to Will Lane's house, with whom he found his father, endeavouring to console his suffering servant.

"Well, Master Edmund," asked Will, the moment he entered his bed-room, seemingly oblivious of his own pain, "what did you do with him?"

"Finished him off handsomely in the Marquis's park, Will. But how are you now? how do you feel?"

"I feels, Master Edmund, as if I could jump out of bed for

joy that the Marquisites haven't got the laugh agin us this time; and then taking him home so nicely, and winding of *him* up just there and then in the Markis's park."

After answering other questions about the run, Mr. Knightley interfered by saying, "Talking will do you no good now, Will, so we must leave you for the present, and I suppose Charley must hunt the hounds until you are able to hold the horn again."

"Well, sir, I am a-thinking, if Master Edmund don't mind the trouble, the hounds will do better with him than Charley, who is wildish at times, sir, as you knows, and they won't follow him pleasantly, as he is always rating and knocking 'em about. Now, sir, the hounds is very fond of Master Edmund, and, as soon as they hear his voice in the kennel, I can't keep e'm quiet, and I am a-thinking, sir, besides this, that Mr. Edmund knows our business pretty well, and, as a huntsman, he'll beat the Markis hollow."

"Well, Will," Mr. Knightley replied, "if Edmund has no objection, you shall have your desire."

"I have not the slightest, my dear father; but perhaps Reginald would like to hunt the hounds; so we will consult him first, or he may take offence."

"As you please, Edmund, although I am quite satisfied your brother is too impatient to make a huntsman, and, moreover, he cannot bear kennel work. We will pay him the compliment if you like; but I see Will does not fancy his handling his favourites, so I must give my vote in your favour. Does that satisfy you, Will?"

"Oh, yes, master. Mr. Reginald ain't so fond of hunting as he is of riding, and I expect he and Charley would play old gooseberry with the pack."

"That is just my opinion also, Will; so now rest contented and get well as fast as you can, by keeping quiet in bed. I shall see you again to-morrow morning," Edmund said, as he left the huntsman's bedside, after giving him a friendly shake of the hand.

On returning to the house, where they found Reginald at luncheon, his father, to avoid increasing the jealousy already existing between his two sons, asked him if he would like to hunt the hounds during Will Lane's illness.

"No, thank you, Governor," was the reply; "that is not exactly in my line, and I hate kennel business. Why can't Charley do it?"

"Will thinks him too wild, and the hounds don't like him."

"Then you know, Governor, I am as wild as Charley, and the hounds hate me more than they do him, for giving them whip-cord whenever they come in my way. Why not let Edmund hunt them? He is always pattering about the kennel, and being a double first-class man, I have no doubt he will show equally good talents in the science of fox-hunting."

"Very well," replied Mr. Knightley, not noticing the sneer of his eldest son, "you shall try your hand with the horn, Edmund; so, that point being settled, I will take off my boots."

CHAPTER XVI.

It will be gathered from the closing scene of my last chapter that a jealous, envious feeling existed in the heart of Reginald towards his younger brother. Edmund was his superior in disposition and abilities, and, from inheriting his uncle's property, was in a more independent position than himself. He was moreover his father's favourite son, although Reginald had not the slightest cause for murmurings or complaint, since both had been equally indulged, and the elder brother ruled at Wychwood quite as much or more than Edmund did at Woodborough. Reginald was consulted by his father on nearly all occasions, and the keepers and shooting over their landed estates were entirely under his control, although in the hunting field Mr. Knightley still held the chief power.

It was with a feeling, therefore, of ill-suppressed satisfaction that Reginald so readily assented to the proposition of Edmund succeeding Will Lane in the management of the hounds; knowing the difficulties of his new task, and anticipating his certain failure. In Edmund's present frame of mind, alternating between hope and despair, the idea of more exciting occupation was a relief—a means of escape from dwelling too intently on one harassing subject—his increasing misgivings as to the nature of Lady Agnes's affection for him.

Since the night of the ball her behaviour had been distant and constrained; and his to her more deferential in consequence. Little differences like these had, however, frequently before existed between them for a time, but, after the lapse of a few days, they had become friends again. Agnes had pouted, and fretted, and looked very cross; but all the while it was evident she felt uncomfortable; and if not openly so, was secretly most desirous of terms of peace. She was altogether different now—with a composure of manner and courtesy towards him which Edmund could not well understand. Suspense had become agony, yet in their present position he dared not reveal the nature of his regard for her. He could, however, endure this coldness no longer; and finding her alone in the drawing-room on his return from hunting, which she rose to leave as he entered, the exclamation almost involuntarily escaped his lips—"Dear Agnes, have I so deeply offended you that you cannot now even bear my presence?"

The tone in which these words were uttered, and his pale looks, went direct to the heart of Lady Agnes. She turned immediately, and holding out her hand, said, "Indeed, Edmund, you have not deeply offended me."

"Then why do you avoid meeting me alone, Agnes?"

"Because," she replied, with a forced smile and deep blush, "I feared you might favour me with another little lecture."

"That time has passed away," he continued, in a serious tone; "you are no longer a girl, and if I have sometimes ventured on offering you advice, it has been dictated by the most pure unselfish regard for your happiness; and the Searcher of all hearts knows the sincerity of mine towards you. The world is now opening before you, with all its allurements and fascinations. Flattery and falsehood are its peculiar characteristics; and when sated with adulation, the insincerity of which you will soon discover, you may perhaps call to mind the homely though truthful admonitions of the companion of your childhood and friend of your youth. From me, Agnes, you will never hear advice or remonstrance more. My father wishes me to return home; and as my presence here has of late become so irksome to you, my resolution has been taken, to leave Woodborough to-morrow."

This announcement, so totally unexpected, dispelled every tint of colour from the cheeks of Lady Agnes, who, sinking into a chair, said imploringly—"Oh, Edmund, do not leave us, I entreat you not to go—my father will say it is my doing, and it will make me very unhappy. I confess I have been greatly to blame in treating you so coldly; but forgive me, such conduct shall never be repeated towards you again."

"The Earl shall not know the true cause of my leaving Woodborough," Edmund replied, "for which I have now a very good excuse. On that point, therefore, Agnes, you need feel no anxiety."

"Whatever you say, Edmund, my father will suspect the true cause of your departure, for he has already shown his displeasure towards me. Once more, then, I entreat you not to leave us now. Dear Edmund, must I plead in vain?"

"No, my dear Agnes," he said, taking her hand; "that you know you can never do. Is it not my greatest happiness to comply with your wishes when I can? But now I am rather in a difficulty how to act, and I will frankly tell you my position—that, observing your continued avoidance of my presence, I accepted my father's offer to-day of hunting the hounds during poor Will Lane's illness."

"Why, what has happened to him, Edmund?"

"He was very seriously injured to-day, whilst out hunting, by that young cotton-spinner riding against him and knocking him and his horse down together. Two of his ribs were broken, and he is otherwise sadly bruised; and, poor fellow! seeing it was his wish I should hunt the hounds, as he does not like Charley, the first whipper-in, I promised him to do so, thinking it would set his mind at rest."

"Well, dear Edmund, that is one of your kind actions—always thinking of others: but, indeed, I am grieved to hear of poor Lane's accident—he is such a favourite with all of us. Yet why cannot Reginald assist his father, instead of you?"

"He declined doing so; and therefore, with the view of pleasing all parties, I will divide my time between Woodborough and Wychwood, sleeping there the night after hunting. By this arrangement all cause of suspicion will be removed from your father's mind. I can do no more now, dear Agnes; will this satisfy you?"

"Yes, Edmund; and I am so much obliged by your compliance with my wishes, that I will get up early every hunting morning to make breakfast for you, instead of Mrs. Errington."

Edmund had taken her hand, and was about making an impassioned reply, when the Earl entering the room, he suddenly relinquished it, yet not before the Earl's eye had seen the act; and the heightened colour in the faces of both assured him of their perfect reconciliation, if not of something more. A cheerful smile passed over the features of the fond father on perceiving his daughter's happy though embarrassed look, and his softened address, in his usual mild, affectionate manner, convinced her of his forgiveness for her late distant and petulant behaviour towards his godson.

"Have you seen Edith lately, my dear father?" she asked, raising her still beaming eyes to his.

"Yes, my child, you will find her and Mrs. Errington in the library."

"Well Edmund," observed the Earl, "if I may judge by appearances—soiled boots, and a happy though scratched face—you have had a satisfactory day's sport."

"Save for a serious accident to Will Lane, my dear uncle, it would have been very satisfactory indeed."

He then related the occurrences, concluding with his father's desire for him to hunt the hounds, until his huntsman could resume his place.

"I shall, therefore," he added, "be obliged to spend three evenings out of the seven at Wychwood; as the days are now so short, it would be out of my power to return to Woodborough after hunting, in time for your dinner-hour."

"Then it has been a bad day for me, as well as poor Will; but I can, of course, raise no objection to your proposal. Your father has the first claim upon your services, and I must be content; so now change your dress, and we will talk over these matters after dinner."

That evening was the first really happy one the family at Woodborough had spent together since the night of the ball. All were in good humour and light of heart—Lady Agnes remarkably so, who felt convinced, by her father's cheerfulness, that he had been satisfied with Edmund's explanation.

"Well, Edmund," he remarked, "I hope you will win honours in the field, as you have done in the schools of learning, although your competitor, the Marquis, does not appear to be a first-class man in his self-imposed undertaking of huntsman. Whatever may be your success, however, I hope you will not forget your good temper, which you must expect to be ruffled sometimes; and I sincerely trust young Shuttleworth will not serve you as he has poor Will Lane."

"From what Charley told me," replied Edmund, "I think that young gentleman has fared little better than our huntsman, to revenge whose fall, Reginald appears to have given him a *quid pro quo*, or tit-for-tat, by knocking him and his horse into the ditch together, where, to use Charley's expression, his favourite steed, Mameluke—late Duncombe's—gave him 'a precious good pounding.' But don't be alarmed, Edith," he said, laughing, "your rubicund admirer is not very seriously hurt, although it appears the aforesaid Mameluke seemed intent on making a roly-poly pudding of him, instead of a shuttlecock. No bones were broken, but Charley said he looked 'uncommon squeamish' when first pulled out of the ditch. Our hunting doctor rode up directly to offer his assistance, and, on my meeting him afterwards in the village, said the young gentleman was more frightened than hurt. Well, Edith, are you not rejoiced at his fortunate escape?"

"I am sorry to hear of accidents befalling any one," she replied, very gravely; "but beyond a fellow-feeling for sufferers generally, I have no further sympathy with Mr. Shuttleworth, although truly grieved for your huntsman."

Nothing worthy of note occurred at the Marquis of Dunkerton's dinner-party the following evening, which consisted chiefly of guests staying in the house, with the only addition of the Earl of Woodborough and Mr. Knightley's families; for the Marquis was not on visiting terms with many of his neighbours, although once a year it was his custom to give a grand ball and supper to all the supporters of his hunt, to whom, in addition, a biennial present of venison was made in August and about Christmas; and by these and other means—being also Lord-Lieutenant of the county—his influence was maintained, without the onerous necessity of paying and receiving visits from the neighbouring gentlemen's families, the Knightleys, from their relationship to the Marchioness, being the exception to this general rule.

On the ladies retiring, the Marquis began joking with Reginald on his tilt with Shuttleworth junior the previous day.

"He required a practical lesson, Dunkerton, of that sort, to prevent his doing further mischief."

"He feels very sore upon the subject, I am told, Reginald; and I should not be surprised at his calling you out."

"I am not particularly nervous as to what such a cub may say or do, and I rather think, for the future, he will know how to keep his proper distance. Are men's lives to be jeopardised by such an upstart fellow as this? I suppose we are to provide fresh huntsmen weekly for his amusement to ride down. But I think, between your lordship's lectures and my practical essays, he has been taught a lesson which he will not soon forget."

"Duncombe says he declares he will never go out with your hounds again."

"I am rejoiced to hear it, Dunkerton, and I suppose, therefore, when sufficiently tamed, he will become a valuable member of your hunt."

"Not just yet, I think. But what are you to do now Will Lane is placed *hors de combat*—Charley, I suppose, takes the horn?"

"Oh, no! we are to have an amateur huntsman, in the person of my brother Edmund, who has been voted by the authorities as the most eligible to fill that important situation, and no doubt we shall have some new light thrown in upon the 'noble science' by our double first-class man."

"He has commenced well, however," replied the Marquis; "and in my opinion a better man could not have been selected, except yourself, Reginald; but I think you are like me, a little too hasty to hunt hounds."

"That post, I think, befits those best who are educated for the profession, although we do find occasionally some gentlemen huntsmen, like your lordship, Tom Smith, and Osbaldeston, who excel in everything they undertake, even down to a game at skittles; but as I am not fit for a gentleman huntsman, I am a-thinking, as Will says, I might succeed as a gentleman horse-dealer, which appears to be the fashion in this neighbourhood, provided your lordship will give me a share of your patronage." This was uttered in a sneering tone, and with a glance across the table at Sir Digby Colville, which the Marquis well understood, but turning it aside in joke, he replied—

"Just the thing for you, Reginald, you are a sharp hand; a trifle too sharp sometimes; but now pass the bottle, and when that is finished we will join the ladies."

Sir Digby Colville bit his lip at Reginald's remark about gentlemen horse-dealers, feeling it was intended for himself; but a look from the Marquis suppressed his rising choler, although he felt inclined to fight with both the brothers. On joining the ladies, Reginald also stood fearlessly in his path, by pertinaciously affixing himself to the side of Lady Agnes during the remainder of the evening, for no one could render himself more agreeable to ladies. He possessed also a good voice and ear for music, which Sir Digby did not; and to tell the truth, Lady Agnes preferred the attentions of Reginald that evening to those of the Irish baronet. He had always been a favourite with her, and she was just the person to suit him as a wife, being light-hearted, high-spirited, and without sentimentality. Reginald disliked sentiment in man or woman; it was, in his opinion, either pedantry or hypocrisy. He did not subscribe to the doctrine of a highly-talented and poetical novelist, "that love in woman is a sentiment." We must make allowance for a little stretch of poetical fancy; and although differing entirely with Reginald Knightley's ideas, we cannot quite admit that the love of woman is merely a sentiment, although with those of pure and chaste ideas, it undoubtedly is so; yet I fear this feeling must be taken rather as the exception than the common rule.

With regard to Lady Agnes, Reginald saw clearly before him certain insurmountable obstacles. One was the Earl's great partiality for his brother. He would have also his own father as well as hers opposed to him. Taking these things into consideration, Reginald saw no prospect, at present, of his obtaining the hand of Lady Agnes; but no one could prevent him flirting with her, and paying her the greatest attentions. It gratified him to do so, and to observe that they were so well received; and when Edmund was present he experienced great satisfaction by showing before others the preference she evinced for his society. Although unable to obtain her himself, he was resolved to frustrate the intentions of others, and the Irish Baronet, from his attentions to her on the night of the ball, had now increased his animosity.

Mr. Chetwynd, a relative of the Marchioness, of whom we before made mention as greatly taken with Edith Maxwell at the ball, was then staying in the house, rather as her guest than her lord's, since with the Marquis he had little community of taste or ideas. Mr. Chetwynd was neither a fox-hunter, card-player, racing-man, nor gambler; but having spent several years in North America, and passed much of his time amongst the Indians, accompanying them to their hunting grounds, he was a superior marksman with rifle or gun. He had now reached his fortieth year, being still a bachelor, although the possessor of large property, and a fine old place a few miles distant from Dunkerton House.

At an early age, immediately after finishing his university education, he had formed a strong attachment for a young lady of great personal attractions, to whom he was engaged to be married, when she was seized with a severe pulmonary attack, which terminated in her death, on the day fixed for their marriage. Overwhelmed with grief for the loss of one on whom his fondest love had been fixed, Chetwynd became a wanderer in foreign lands for several years, until he had travelled over the greatest part of the habitable globe; but having now reached the age considered the turning point of human life, he deemed it a duty he owed to the country of his birth to spend the remainder of his days there; and accordingly the family mansion, hitherto occupied by the old housekeeper and butler, man and wife, was prepared for his reception about a month previous to the ball, to which, from the Earl's acquaintance with himself and his father before he left England, he had been invited.

In bodily frame Chetwynd was well adapted to the laborious and hazardous life he had led, being tall and well-proportioned, with fine intellectual features, which, on certain occasions, exhibited great resolution and sternness of character; but this was scarcely perceptible in ladies' society, to whom he possessed the power of rendering himself most agreeable, irrespective of personal recommendations; for his black curly hair still retained the unmixed hue and luxuriance of youth, and his face, although bronzed by warmer climes, presented the full development and perfection of matured manly beauty.

Since the ball, Chetwynd had dwelt unceasingly upon the loveliness of Edith Maxwell, his admiration being increased by the high opinion expressed by the Marchioness of her much greater loveliness of disposition, and his attentions were almost exclusively devoted to her during this evening; she also became deeply interested in the recital of his various adventures.

CHAPTER XVII.

The day following, Chetwynd rode over to Woodborough Park, and being invited by the Earl to take luncheon with them, remained there several hours. The afternoon turning out stormy, he joined Lady Agnes and Edith in the library, where they were amusing themselves with their pencils and paint-brushes, the former copying a landscape with Tyrolese scenery.

"With your permission, Lady Agnes," Chetwynd said, "I think I could impart a little more life and spirit to your sketch, by the insertion of a Tyrolese huntsman in that blank space beneath the over-hanging rock."

"Oh, pray do!" she said, offering him the pencil, "for I think with you, it would be a great improvement to the scene."

Chetwynd sat down to his task, which he executed in a few

minutes, much to the surprise and admiration of his two fair lookers-on.

"How beautifully it is done!" exclaimed Lady Agnes; "you are a most superior artist, Mr. Chetwynd; do you paint in oil colours as well?"

"Yes," was his reply; "and if Lady Agnes would honour me with a sitting, I think I might produce something worthy her notice, although, of course, not equal to the original."

"You are very kind in offering to take so much trouble, and I think papa would be pleased with my picture."

"Then with his consent, Lady Agnes, I shall have the greatest pleasure in exerting my humble talents to make it deserving his and your approbation. I am not yet a fox-hunter, although I have joined in the pursuit of buffaloes in the wild prairies of the far West, and in lion and tiger-hunting, both in India and Africa; but now, having returned to my native country, I conclude it will be deemed imperative upon me to follow the chase of the fox. As, however, my stables cannot yet boast of horses fitted for that purpose, I must in the meantime amuse myself in other ways, and painting from nature being one of my chief pleasures, I can thus beguile the heavy hours of a bachelor, at this most gloomy season of the year."

"You have, then, I dare say, a fine collection of original paintings at Dropmore Hall?" Lady Agnes said.

"A large collection of trash, I fear," he replied, "executed by my own hand from sketches taken in my travels of Red Indian warriors, Caffirs, Hottentots, Arabs, Turks, and Infidels, of nearly every nation under the sun, with their weapons of war and chase. I have also buffalo hides, tigers' and lions' skins, with those of various other animals and birds—in short, my old house looks more like a menagerie than the residence of a country gentleman."

"How charming!" exclaimed Lady Agnes, in delight; "I should like so much to see these curiosities!"

"It will afford me the highest gratification to become showman to Lady Agnes and her fair friend, if they will honour me with a call," was the polite reply.

"Oh! that we will, most certainly," Lady Agnes said; "and you must come over when you can, to take my likeness for papa."

"What are you saying of me, my dear?" asked the Earl, who had just entered the room.

"Oh! papa, Mr. Chetwynd has kindly offered to take my

likeness, anu you have often said. you wished to have it done."

"Yes, my child, it is very true; but I cannot think of giving Mr. Chetwynd that trouble."

"You fear, my lord, I should make a caricature instead, I suppose?"

"No, no, Chetwynd, although I remember your taste for that sort of thing when a boy, and my catching you taking a sketch of myself by no means flattering."

"Ah, yes, my dear lord, I believe I was considered rather a pickle in my youth; but I will promise you now a faithful portrait of your daughter, after three or four sittings, if you will allow me that honour."

"Well, well, Chetwynd, we will think about it," said the Earl; "I will drive over and pay you a visit, when the weather permits."

"I shall feel proud to receive you, my lord, and show you all the lions and tigers about the place, an account of which I have been giving the ladies."

"Oh! papa," interposed Lady Agnes, "I long so to see Mr. Chetwynd's curiosities and paintings; pray let us go there to-morrow!"

"I think the ladies will be amused by an inspection of my old curiosity shop."

"Well, if the day is fine, you may expect us about eleven o'clock."

Soon after, Chetwynd having gained his point, returned home in high spirits. He cared little about taking a portrait of Lady Agnes, save as a preliminary step to a nearer acquaintance with Edith Maxwell; and in persuading her to sit for her picture, he hoped for an opportunity of ingratiating himself into the favour of her fair friend.

On entering the old spacious hall of Dropmore the following day, Lady Agnes started back with a cry of surprise and terror on finding two large buffaloes confronting her, with glaring eyes and shaggy manes, looking like life, standing on either side of the grand staircase, after a nearer approach and closer examination of which her courteous host directed her attention to other rare specimens of stuffed animals and birds, occupying the entire space on one side of the hall, the other three side walls being ornamented with almost every kind of weapon of defence—spears, buffalo shields, assiegans, bows and arrows, tomahawks, clubs, old fashioned rifles, and numerous other instruments used by the various nations amongst whom he had sojourned, arranged with great taste, above and around, with beautifully painted portraits of their warriors or chief men. The floor of the hall was also nearly covered with tiger, leopard, and lion skins; as mats at the entrance to each room lay the hides of black and white bears; and above the doors were fixed the antlers and horns of the deer kind, from the huge elk and moose down to the smallest antelope.

The ladies were occupied with the Earl for more than an hour inspecting the contents of the hall alone, which presented the appearance of a museum on a small scale; but on entering the drawing room, their eyes were almost dazzled by the splendour of its furniture and fittings, which were more costly than any they had yet beheld. Chairs of the most elaborate and varied workmanship—tables of every description, inlaid with gold and silver—ottomans and settees, covered with the richest and most costly damask, as well as the most beautiful embroidery from Turkey. Vases adorned with precious stones. Screens composed of feathers from birds of the most brilliant plumage—and an abundance of articles of vertu scattered about here and there, with large jars of rare and curious Chinese manufacture, standing in the four corners of the room, from which the most delightful perfumes were wafted; and yet, with all its luxurious appendages, the apartment presented the appearance of comfort and repose, from the taste with which everything was arranged. Whilst the party were occupied in examining some interesting specimens of Indian mechanism, a black servant entered the room, who with noiseless step approached his master, addressing him in an unknown language, to which a short reply being given in the same tongue, he disappeared. Chetwynd then said: "Now, with your permission, Lady Agnes, we will visit the dining-room, where I hope to prevail on you to take some refreshment." On the door being thrown open, a most elegant luncheon was presented to their view, consisting of various made dishes, pastry, dried fruits, &c., the table being decorated with massive silver wine coolers, containing champagne, hock, and other light wines. To each person was also allotted a drinking cup, of highly polished buffalo horn, inserted in a stem of chased silver.

"Why, Chetwynd!" exclaimed the Earl, "instead of luncheon you have provided a dinner suited to an Eastern prince!"

"Nothing very particular, my lord; but I thought the

ladies would prefer something piquant after their cold drive; and my Indian servant is a good hand with curries and light dishes to suit the ladies' tastes."

After the repast was finished, Lady Agnes and Edith expressed their wish to return to the drawing-room, having scarcely examined half the curious things that attracted their attention. Having taken a further survey of them, their host threw open the folding doors leading into the saloon, which requires a more lengthened description, as being the finest room in the mansion—I might say the county—and of noble dimensions, extending fifty-five feet in length, and forty in width, with height corresponding to its size. The ceiling being arched, was divided into compartments, each composed of paintings from some scene in classical or mythological history—not poor, every-day paintings, but magnificent specimens of art executed by first-class Italian painters, who had been engaged five years in the completion of their undertaking. The frame, if I may so call it, round each, was of elaborate carved workmanship, painted white and gold. On three sides of the room against the walls stood pilasters, most exquisitely carved in every kind of fruit and flower, which were also white and gold, and, the spaces between them filled up with paintings of the same description as the ceiling. On the fourth side were three large windows, which at night were shut from view by superb mirrors, so contrived as to slide into the wall during the day. Each window was draped by curtains of gold-coloured satin damask, from the looms of Lyons, and the effect, when the room was brilliantly lighted up, and reflecting back all its beauties, was something truly magnificent.

The chairs and settees, of the style of Louis XIV., were of white and gold, covered with the same rich material as the curtains; while interspersed about the room were tables of rare marbles, supported on pedestals of white and gold, to match the rest of the furniture. The floor of this unique apartment was composed of inlaid woods, highly polished; but, except when used as a ball-room, covered with one of those luxurious carpets in which the foot sinks as into moss. At the end of this room, opposite the folding doors leading into the drawing-room, were large double ones of plate-glass, through which you entered into the conservatory, like everything else at Dropmore, of great magnitude, and laid out with exquisite taste. There was one broad walk through it, dividing parterres of the choicest flowers, with seats of all kinds; while on each side of the walks, at intervals and in arches over them, supported by light iron trellis work, hung the most beautiful and rare creepers; and suspended from these arches were Chinese lanterns, which when, lit up, sent a soft and subdued light through this lovely spot, like an Arabian-night scene.

Great was the admiration expressed by all, mingled with regrets at not being able to devote more time to all these varied and beautiful things.

After passing through the library, they were conducted into Mr. Chetwynd's studio, around which sketches and half-finished paintings were suspended, and facing his easy chair a blank piece of canvas already prepared, which, attracting the attention of Lady Agnes, she asked for what it was intended.

"If you will do me the honour of taking a seat in this chair," placing one for her in a favourable light, "the canvas itself shall give you an answer," he replied, with a smile; and thus taken by surprise, the Earl found himself in a few minutes looking intently and eagerly on the canvas, which was receiving the first outlines of his daughter's features. Chetwynd sat carelessly with his palette in hand, telling stories and relating adventures the while, so that an hour had passed for Lady Agnes's first sitting, before the Earl became at all aware of the lapse of time.

"I will not detain you any longer now," Mr. Chetwynd said, addressing Lady Agnes, and laying aside his brush; "the light is not so good as I could wish."

"Which reminds me," said the Earl, "that it is high time we took our leave."

"I hope then, my lord, you will allow the young ladies to resume their inspection of the other parts of my Noah's ark on the next fine day; and I think they will be more pleased with the contents of the conservatory, which they have not had time to examine to-day, than anything they have yet seen."

"Well, Chetwynd, I believe it would be of little use my putting a veto on your proposition, or an end to their curiosity, until they have seen all. If not otherwise engaged, I hope you will dine with us to-morrow?"

The invitation being accepted, and the carriage at the door, the Earl took leave of his entertaining host, Lady Agnes expressing rapturous delight with the curiosities of the place, which had excited her highest admiration.

CHAPTER XVIII.

THAT evening the two girls sat rather later than usual in Lady Agnes's dressing-room, discussing the wonders and beauties of Dropmore, as well as the courteous conduct of its owner.

"Really, Edith," remarked Lady Agnes, "Mr. Chetwynd is exceedingly good-looking and entertaining, beyond any person I know; and his house fit for the reception of a princess. Would not you like, dear Edith, to be the mistress of such a place?"

"No, Agnes, indeed I should not; those fierce-looking creatures would haunt me every night in my dreams, and you will laugh at me for saying I felt quite relieved when the carriage was announced to take us home."

"My dear Edith, what childish ideas!—one would suppose you were still in the nursery. I am quite in love with the house and all its luxurious comforts, and nearly so with the owner of it; for although not so young as Sir Digby, he is quite as handsome, equally agreeable, and far more clever and entertaining."

"Well, Agnes, in all these points, I agree with you: he is his superior; but there is a wild, stern expression sometimes in his dark eyes which makes one quail beneath their gaze, and induces one to think he is not good-tempered."

"Only one of your fancies, dear Edith; for I read that expression differently, as exhibiting firmness of character and resolution. I like a man of spirit and courage; but I really believe, Edith, you think no one equal to Edmund."

"We have both cause to think highly of him, dear Agnes; and now I must wish you good night."

The Earl, who had been taken by surprise in allowing his daughter to sit for her portrait to Mr. Chetwynd, was deliberating at first how he might extricate himself from the difficulty in which he found himself so unexpectedly placed, without rudeness to Chetwynd, of whom he entertained a very high opinion, although he could not bear the idea of his daughter's forming an attachment for him; but on due reflection, he thought it best of two evils to choose the least. Chetwynd was a man of well-known good fortune, and his appearance betokened regular and steady habits of life. His agent, who was also the Earl's man of business, spoke of him, whilst absent, as not spending more than half of his income, which exceeded ten thousand a-year; and this was evidence of his being a prudent as well as a wealthy man, which the Irish Baronet was not. His being a neighbour also was another recommendation; so that the Earl, from dread of his daughter forming an attachment for Sir Digby Colville, deemed it more prudent to comply with her wishes, and consented to her taking some more sittings in Chetwynd's studio, with Edith and Mrs. Errington, or himself, as her companions.

Edmund entertained no doubt as to Chetwynd's real intentions, from the conversation he overheard at the ball, and his particular attentions to Edith afterwards at the Marquis's dinner party. He had heard him express his decided resolution never to marry any woman for rank or money, having more than a sufficiency of the latter; and from his long sojourn in America he had imbibed rather too independent ideas as to the aristocracy of his own country, although closely allied to that class. Edmund, therefore, met Chetwynd with cordiality the next evening when he dined at Woodborough, and, from his observation of his conduct towards the two young ladies, felt confirmed in his previous opinion that Edith was the object of his choice, and that he was making Lady Agnes the stepping-stone to his further advancement in her friend's favour.

The next day, therefore, Edmund volunteered to accompany the ladies to Dropmore, to inspect the conservatory and other curiosities; and if persuaded before, he became now thoroughly satisfied, by Chetwynd's peculiar manner towards Edith, that he had no cause for jealousy. Lady Agnes also remarked it; and on seeing him occupied in pointing out to her the beauties of some rare exotics, she could not forbear saying to Edmund in a pettish tone—

"Mr. Chetwynd seems to forget he has any other visitor than Edith. I have seen and heard enough of the contents of the conservatory, so let us walk out into the pleasure-grounds."

Edith being reluctantly detained in looking at a rare plant, and listening to its various properties, with her back to Lady Agnes and Edmund, who were, as she supposed, still occupied near her with other rarities, was not aware of their having left the conservatory until, turning her head, she exclaimed—

"What has become of Lady Agnes?"

"She is not far off," replied Chetwynd; "stay a few minutes longer, Miss Maxwell, that I may show you a favourite flower of mine?" This was asked in a low and peculiar tone of voice.

"I must join my party," Edith replied, without noticing his question. "Agnes is not very fond of flowers, and will not be pleased, perhaps, at my remaining here so long."

"Perhaps she is more agreeably engaged," Chetwynd said, with a meaning smile; "and would rather dispense with the presence of a third person."

"I think we had better follow her," Edith continued, very gravely, advancing directly towards the lower door, through which her friend had disappeared.

Chetwynd, noticing her serious looks, saw at a glance this was neither the time nor place, nor Edith Maxwell the girl to listen to soft speeches from a person with whom she had become so recently acquainted, so he merely said, in a more deferential tone, "Miss Maxwell's wishes are commands to me, which I shall ever feel the greatest pleasure in obeying;" and opening the door, he immediately conducted her to Lady Agnes, who appeared out of temper with something or somebody—not this time with Edmund, whom she requested to order the carriage, much to the surprise of Mr. Chetwynd, who expected she would remain for a second sitting.

During their drive home she scarcely made a remark to Edith, and continued in a very uncommunicable mood during the remainder of the evening, until Edith went into her room to wish her good night, when she said—

"It seems, Agnes, that I have offended you to-day, but how, I am at a loss to understand."

"Oh, no, dear. I have not felt very well, and am sadly out of spirits;" but assuming a livelier tone, she said, with a forced laugh, "Well, I suppose, Edith, Mr. Chetwynd made a declaration of love to you in the conservatory, where you were so long alone this morning; nothing less, I conclude, from the serious looks of both when you joined us?"

"Mr. Chetwynd could not, with common propriety, upon our short acquaintance, have ventured on such a subject; and if he had, you have already heard my opinion of him."

"Oh," replied Lady Agnes, "girls' opinions change every day; Dropmore, with twelve thousand a-year, might reconcile the most particular young lady to a much more disagreeable person than Mr. Chetwynd."

"Twenty thousand a-year would not induce me to accept him or any other gentleman, unless really and truly attached to him—and you know my impressions are not in favour of the owner of Dropmore—so now, Agnes, good night."

"Well, dear Edith, I hope you are not too angry to refuse me a kiss?"

"I am not angry with you, dear Agnes, only annoyed by your expressing such an unfair opinion of my feelings, which you well know are quite different from those you have just now accused me of."

On Edith retiring to her own room, and reflecting on the occurrences of the day, she felt persuaded that the ill-humour of Lady Agnes proceeded entirely from Mr. Chetwynd's attentions to herself the short time they were in the conservatory together; and to avoid a repetition of any further unpleasantness of the kind, Edith resolved to return home the next or following day, and accordingly wrote a short note to her mother, requesting her to send the carriage, or call for her, as soon as it was convenient.

When Mrs. Maxwell called for her daughter, no one suspected, save Agnes, the cause of her leaving Woodborough; and when pressed to stay a few days longer, Edith excused herself by saying she had already exceeded the time of her intended visit by more than a week; and as her mother had a dinner party the next day, she wished her to be at home, which was really the case; and it must be confessed that just at that time Lady Agnes was not very reluctant to part with her friend, of whom she began to feel rather jealous, from the admiration she had excited at and since the ball. Being a spoilt child, and of an impatient and selfish disposition, with an abundant share of vanity, she could not bear, without secret envy, the praises and attentions paid even to her dearest friend.

Some ten days had now elapsed since Edith's departure, when Chetwynd, having daily expected another visit from the young ladies, called again at Woodborough, where, much to his chagrin, he found Lady Agnes alone, and more formally inclined towards him than heretofore; but not appearing to notice her altered manner, Chetwynd expressed his hope that she would favour him with another sitting, that he might complete the picture to present to her father; and, after a few excuses about engagements, bad weather, &c., an assent was given, and a day fixed; and Chetwynd, having regained by a few compliments her ladyship's favour, soon after took his leave.

The secret spring of Chetwynd's behaviour was his desire of remaining on the best terms with Lady Agnes, with whom he had learnt Edith was frequently staying, that thus he might have further opportunities of meeting her, and gaining a clearer insight into her true character and disposition. For this purpose he thought greater facilities would be afforded him at Woodborough Park than in her father's house; for although on visiting terms with Colonel Maxwell, he was not so great a favourite with him as with the Earl.

After a few more sittings for her portrait, during which Chetwynd had reinstated himself in favour with Lady Agnes, the picture was completed, and pronounced by all who saw it to be a faithful likeness, as well as a highly-finished painting, quite equal to any of the best modern artists; and Chetwynd, having become on intimate terms with Edmund, paid frequent visits to Woodborough, in the hope of again meeting Edith there; but finding she was not expected, he called on the Colonel, by whom he was invited to dine at Morton Grange, and thus his path lay open for more intimate acquaintance with the family. Lady Agnes, meanwhile, from his frequent visits and polite attentions, had brought herself to believe that the owner of Dropmore had fallen a victim to her superior charms, although not seriously in love with him herself; for hers was the love of conquest, not that of the heart.

CHAPTER XIX.

We must now take a retrospective view of Edmund Knightley's brief career as a gentleman huntsman. On his first appearance in public he found, like others entering on higher situations of responsibility, envyings and jealousies conspiring to render his assumption of office as disagreeable as possible. His brother Reginald, with Charley the first whip (who thought himself the most proper person to succeed Will Lane), were ranged against him on opposition horses, in the hope of marring his sport, and making him retire in disgust and discredit from the post he had presumed to fill. Edmund, however, was not the character to be deterred by difficulties and opposition from executing with energy his *almost* self-imposed task; though, on his first appearance at the place of meeting with his father's hounds, Charley's sulky looks gave him warning of what he was to expect.

The covert to be drawn that morning abounded in foxes. The day proved boisterous, and Edmund saw he had to contend with conflicting elements within and without. A large field had congregated to witness the first throw off of the new huntsman, amongst whom old Squire White looked most conspicuous. The Captain also was there, having come out with rather malicious intentions towards Edmund.

The hounds had not been in covert ten minutes before a leash of foxes were on foot, upon which they rang the changes for some twenty minutes more, when, the pack dividing, Charley began playing the part of huntsman to one division, whilst Edmund was occupied with the other. Jack, the second whip, was in close attendance upon his young master, who, guessing Charley's trick, sent him to desire he would stop the other hounds, and send them to his horn.

Charley gave Jack for answer that he might stop them himself if he liked, for he couldn't get at them in the high wood; but this was only an excuse for himself to get outside the covert, and wait his chance of the fox breaking. This he did shortly after, and away went Charley directly with the greatest part of the field, hallooing and screaming to get the other hounds away also, to join the five couples with him, which it was his business to have stopped, and to have supported the huntsman with the body of the pack. Jack, seeing how matters stood, returned quickly to Edmund, reporting what had occurred.

"Then stick to me, Jack," was his reply, "and come along, for our fox is the right one, and will break the lower side now those coffee-housing fellows have left it."

In a few minutes more Edmund's prediction was realised, and a view-holloa from his father told him the fox had broken, and that the hounds were away over the best of their vale country. Edmund and Jack were quickly in their wake, with old Squire White and some half-dozen farmers, who alone remained out of the large body of horsemen, the majority having gone in the contrary direction with Charley, Reginald, and five couples of hounds.

On passing his father, Edmund briefly told him Charley's trick, adding, "Never mind, my dear dad, we have the best of the pack, and the fun to ourselves; so pluck up your spirit, and ride hard for the brush."

"Go along, Edmund," roared out old Squire White; "I mean riding to-day, with none of those fire-eaters to knock one over."

In this order, then, they settled down to the work before

them, Edmund leading with Jack and young Farmer Springfield in close attendance; immediately behind them, Mr. Knightley senior, old Squire White, and four other farmers of middle age, staunch supporters of the hunt, and men difficult to be shaken off, even when the pace was first-rate.

Woodland foxes generally prove the stoutest runners, and this old sly-boots, having given the hounds the slip by some two or three fields, held on his course in a straight line for the Morton Grange woodlands, some seven miles distant, passing through the pleasure-grounds of Woodborough Park, where Edmund was cheered on by the Earl and the ladies on the lawn. Fortunately for our young huntsman the fox ran the drive all the way through the Morton Grange woods, some two miles in extent, and again faced the open, turning away to the right, into the Marquis's country, for a well-known large gorse covert, which he seemed little inclined to leave. Here the hounds had been steadily working their game for nearly half an hour, a brace of fresh foxes having been disturbed before Mr. Knightley, with two farmers, came up, the pace having been too severe for old Squire White and his mare, when Edmund begged his father to enact the part of first whip on the other side of the gorse, young Springfield taking up another position to view him away. Jack was called to his assistance to get the hounds together the moment the fox broke.

"Mind," cried Edmund to his father, "*our* fox is a large, very light-coloured one, with a long white tip to his brush."

"Don't you think, you young donkey," replied the old squire, laughing, "I know a hunted fox from a fresh one?"

"It's more than I do, daddy dear, sometimes; so don't make a mistake."

Mr. Knightley had been at his post some five minutes when he saw their game stealing stealthily through some patches of gorse outside the covert; and when clear of these he crept through the next fence, as if undecided whether to go or tarry. His movements were watched by the master, who sat perfectly motionless on his horse, behind a thorn tree, until the fox had crossed the next field, casting one longing, lingering look behind before he jumped the outside fence, as if doubtful of the policy he was pursuing in deserting the stronghold which had so often afforded him shelter. The parting scream uttered by the master on viewing him clear away seemed to bring conviction to his mind (if he had any) that, a return being now very hazardous, he must depend on his speed and craft to reach some other place of refuge, of which he knew many.

Edmund and Jack experienced some difficulty in stopping the hounds from another scent to which they had now changed; but the farmers riding up to their assistance, their object was effected in a few minutes more, when, hearing their master's well known view-holloa, they dashed away directly, their heads well up, and soon settled down again on the line of their first fox. By this welcome check to their speed, horses, hounds, and fox had recovered their wind, and another dashing effort was made by the latter over five more miles of country for Dropmore woods, wherein was a strong head of earths.

"He saves his brush at Dropmore, Edmund," exclaimed the old master; "the earths are open."

"I'm not quite sure of that, my dear dad; the Marquis was there yesterday, and I'll bet a trifle those lazy earth-stoppers have not opened them yet."

Such was found to be the case; and after a ring round the covert, where the hounds got up to the fox, he was obliged again to fly, and turning away to the left, set his head for St. Austin's.

"Now, Jack," cried Edmund, "get forward as fast as you can for the main earths in Park Coppice—you may reach them before him; and you, Springfield, must help me as whipper-in, if wanted."

"Ay, sir, most willingly; this is a glorious run, and I'll bet Mr. Reginald and Charley are sorry for what they've done by this time; now we go again, sir, he can't reach Park Coppice at this pace."

"Well, I hope not, Springfield. I should like to finish handsomely."

Two more miles had now been passed at a rapid pace, when a small patch of gorse intervened.

"If he lingers a moment here," exclaimed Edmund to his only companion, Springfield, "we shall have him."

Just as the hounds were approaching the near end of the gorse, Springfield cried out, "Yonder he goes, sir, by Jingo!"

"Quick, then, Tom," was Edmund's reply; "put them on to me;" and cap in hand, their young huntsman hurried his ready followers round the gorse with a scream which seemed to set them crazy.

"Forward, my lads!" he cried, as the hounds caught sight of their game crossing the next large grass field.

Up went their heads, and the race for life and death recommenced more furiously than ever. For another mile, however, the gallant old fox held his place, the fences breaking the hounds' view; but when emerging on an open common, they again caught sight of him, and with a scream from Edmund cheering them on, they spread over the heath, every hound straining for the lead, until they ran in and rolled him over, within a hundred yards of the wood hedge.

The whoohoop of Tom Springfield echoed far and wide through the dells of St. Austin's, and was borne back on the breeze to Dropmore, where old Squire White had just pulled up, sadly in want of a glass of sherry, which Chetwynd was giving him at the hall door, when Springfield's piercing whoohoop caught his ear.

"They have him, by Jove, sir!" he cried, throwing down the glass, and setting spurs to his old favourite; "I must be off."

Edmund, having thrown the fox to his eager and hungry subjects, remained on the spot until joined by his father and Jack, with two other farmers, when their small party, delighted with their day's sport, set out on their homeward track, on which they met old Squire White and his jaded mare, who could barely make out a trot.

"Glorious run, by Jove, sir!" exclaimed the old sportsman, "the finest I ever saw in my life; twenty miles, if it was a yard! and done in an hour and forty minutes, including stoppages," as he pulled out his huge hunting watch, about the size of a small turnip. "Give me your hand, Teddy," riding up to Edmund, "I congratulate you with all my heart—nothing could be better done—first-class huntsman, Knightley, by Jupiter! as well as a first-class scholar; beats the Marquis hollow!"

"It is pretty well, for a young beginner," replied Mr. Knightley.

"Save for you, my dear dad," added Edmund, "he would have beaten us; so the merit of catching him belongs to you."

"I just gave you a lift from the gorse, my boy; but your handling the hounds throughout could not be surpassed by Will himself—if done so well."

"Here Jack," cried old Squire White, diving into his deep waistcoat pocket, "here's a guinea for you, my lad; you're worth a dozen Charleys, and stick to your young huntsman as you ought to do. And as for you, Tom Springfield, you young dare-devil, I thought you'd have broken your neck over the Woodborough Park palings. Well, by Jove! Knightley, I vote we draft that wild harey-starey fellow Charley, and get Tom to play first fiddle, as an amateur head whip. The d—— a fox would ever escape him and Teddy, with Jack to bring up the rear guard; and as for his holloa, sir, I heard him at Dropmore four miles off."

"I am right glad to lend a hand at any time, squire," replied the young farmer, "and wouldn't have had this fox beat us for fifty pounds of my own money, after the trick served us by t'other party."

They had been jogging leisurely homewards some five or six miles, when Tom Springfield's quick eye caught sight of a solitary red coat galloping across country towards the road they were pursuing.

"Ha! ha!" cried Tom, "there's the Captain coming along over the fields yonder, and I'll warrant, by the pace he's going, Charley didn't give 'em much to do."

"Confound him!" said old White, "that's a fellow I detest—a dandified, jockey-like, horse-dealing chap—always riding in upon the hounds, when there's a bad scent, to sell his cattle; and that Irish baronet is just such another."

"He's mounted on a raw four-year old to-day," remarked Tom Springfield, "which he bought of my neighbour, Tomkins, a month agone, for sixty pounds, and I warrant he sticks him into the young cotton lord for a hundred and twenty."

The object of animadversion—the Captain—now made for a gate close to the road, which he was endeavouring to open, when the hounds were just passing.

"Holloa!" he exclaimed on seeing Edmund, "why, where have you been running to, Knightley? I didn't expect to meet you in this quarter. What have you done?"

"Tolerably well," was Edmund's short reply, as he passed on, and the Captain's horse swerving from the gate at sight of the hounds, he had no time to ask further questions.

Soon after, however, they met Welford on the same road, who gave them an account of Charley's proceedings thus:—"We had a quick burst for a couple of miles, when the hounds threw up their heads on a piece of fallows. Charley made a brilliant cast forward, without hitting off the scent; went to a holloa half a mile ahead; got upon a hare; ran her for a couple of fields; jumped up in view, Reginald and Charley rating and screaming; stopped the hounds; then a consultation what to do; Reginald was for drawing another covert; Charley said it was no use, with five couples of young hounds, and he must go back to the pack. Trotted on for several miles here and there to recover you, and at last gave up in disgust. Then said it was no use, and went home. That is the pith of the story."

"Just as I expected," muttered old Squire White, "a flash in the pan; and that's not all—unsettling the young hounds, which were just got steady—yet what do your steeple-chase fellows care whether they are after hare or fox, provided they get their gallop?"

"Well, then, sir," asked Welford, "what have you done?"

"Something to tell about, sir, for the next month; twenty miles, sir, in an hour and forty minutes, and there's his head hanging behind Jack's saddle. Found at Spirthill, and killed him at St. Austin's. Put that in your hookah, Mr. Welford, and smoke it."

"Slow, of course, Mr. White, or you would not have been there."

"I was not there, sir," retorted the old sportsman; "twenty stone couldn't see such a thing—neither would you, light as you may be—none but a thorough good rider to hounds could have witnessed the finish of this magnificent run," with which he resumed his road.

On reaching the kennels Charley came out very obsequiously (having had due time for reflection), to take Edmund's horse, and touching his cap, said, "he hoped he had had a good run."

"Yes," was the short reply, "although you did your best to spoil it."

"I beg pardon, sir, but I could not stop the hounds for a couple of miles, when I got back as fast as I could to join the pack."

"You need not tell any more lies about it," Edmund said, very gravely. "I have heard the truth, and the mischief you have done by lifting the young hounds on to hare."

"It wasn't my fault, Mr. Edmund; for Mr. Reginald would make me go on."

"You knew perfectly well," replied Edmund, "if you pretend to know your business as whipper-in, that it was your duty to maintain to the huntsman, and obey his orders instantly. I sent Jack to desire you to stop the hounds, and instead of doing so, you halloed them out of the covert, thinking to have a run by yourself. Now, Master Charley, I have only thus more to say, that the very next time you attempt to handle the hounds, or disobey my orders in the most trivial matter, that time shall be the last you and I ever hunt together with my father's hounds—*you* shall leave them, or *I* will."

"I am very sorry, Mr. Edmund, to have given you offenee, but it shall never again happen."

Charley saw clearly he had made a very great mistake in supposing Edmund would entirely overlook his offenee, and he knew that, once resolved, he would keep his resolution. He knew also that his old master, having selected him to hunt the hounds, his own discharge would certainly follow any further deviation from duty; but he could not refrain afterwards venting his ill-humour on Jack, by accusing him of telling Mr. Edmund he would not stop the hounds if he could.

"I told him what you said," retorted Jack, "and no more; in course you know'd best what to do."

"I don't want you to teach me my business, Mr. Jack."

"And I don't want you to tell me mine, Mr. Charley," was the rejoinder; "I ain't whipper-in to you yet, and don't think you be likely to get the horn by sarving young master such tricks as you did to-day—a pretty job I shall have again with them young hounds after being halloed on to hare, when they'd just got steady to a fox scent."

Further bandying of words between the two whips was cut short by the master entering the stable, who told Charley he wished to see him when the horses were made comfortable and littered down for the evening. But we need not repeat the lecture given him by his old master, to whom every servant in the establishment was very deeply attaehed, from his kind disposition, and almost paternal interest in their welfare.

Reginald, having an invitation to dine at Morton Grange that evening, avoided a meeting with his father, in the dread of a little lecture also; and being annoyed at the failure of his scheme, and greatly out of humour, he spoilt the sport of Chetwynd—as he had attempted to do that of his brother in the morning—whom he perceived intent on paying attentions to Edith Maxwell, by appropriating her to himself at the dinner-table, and afterwards by sitting with her during the remainder of the evening.

The next morning being the Marquis of Dunkerton's hunting day, Edmund's run was the general topic of conversation at the place of meeting, and many questions were asked of

Tom Springfield, the only man in the field who had seen it from find to finish.

"Well, then, it was a clipper, I suppose, Tom," remarked the Captain, "and the pace good, eh?"

"Just as fast as hounds could go, Captain, and barring a couple of pulls up, at the gorse and Dropmore, I should not have been there to tell the tale. It was just the very best run I ever rode in my life, and the way in which Mr. Edmund finished him off at last shows what I always said of him, that if he did take to hunting hounds, he'd make the best huntsman of the day. He's very quiet with them, gives 'em time when they ought to have it—knows the run of a fox as well as old Will; but when the time comes for a spurt, he's just the quickest man I ever see. He won't have meddling or hark hallòing, however, Captain, and he is right; so you may depend upon it, if Charley comes that dodge again he tried yesterday, you won't see him head whip another day."

"Oh! then we are to be kept in drill order now, Tom, eh?"

"Mr. Edmund, Captain, although very good-tempered, with as kind a heart as need be, won't stand any nonsense from anybody, as you knows; and there are some of his field that means to stick to him."

"You are one, I conclude, Springfield?"

"Just so, sir, as I did yesterday, and means to do again to-morrow."

"Very well—you won't keep me in order though, Springfield."

"With Mr. Edmund's orders, sir; as Charley don't seem very willing to attend to them—I shall prevent mischief being done, if I can help it."

"By which you will get into trouble yourself, Tom."

"I've two strongish arms to help me out of it, Captain, and don't mind a bit of a turn up, to suit anybody, who's inclined to be uncivil; but Master Edmund shan't be put upon."

The opinion of Tom Springfield, who was well known in both hunts as a bruiser, in more respects than across country, produced the effect he desired, for he knew the cabal entered into by certain ill-disposed persons to spoil Edmund's sport; and the Captain rode off to report the information he had received to the Marquis, who, contrary to his expectation, declared his intention of hunting with Edmund the next day.

CHAPTER XX.

THE news of Edmund's superior run having spread far and wide, his next fixture in the higher part of their country attracted a full attendance of sportsmen from both hunts; it being a common impression that one good day is almost sure to be succeeded by another: why or wherefore, no one acquainted with the mysteries of the "noble science" can tell; since, to afford good runs, there must of necessity be good, stout, well-seasoned foxes; and when one of this sort has been dispatched, masters of hounds don't expect to find his brother in the next gorse brake.

It does not always follow as a matter of course that good hounds make good foxes; for as with the human, so it is with the vulpine race, a great diversity of opinion prevails as to the best mode of self-preservation. The generality of foxes are on the look-out for earths or drains to hide their precious carcases from view as quickly as possible. Others, bred in woodlands, retain their shelter by dodging and foiling the hounds; and a few—the *élite* of the fraternity—stretch boldly across the open, in the hope of beating their pursuers by speed and stout running.

Then we have the regulator of all sport—scent—to damp or encourage our exertions, as the case may be, with the weather; and the odds against catching a good fox, on a bad scenting day, are about fifty to one in favour of the wily animal.

Will Lane's favourite opinion about scent was that it was in the *hair;* and according to his orthography and phraseology, this doctrine is not far from being right, since the scent of the animal exudes through the porous tissues of the skin, more than from the breath. The ground over which the animal travels has a great deal to do with the scent, as well as the atmosphere, and the pace also at which he is going; for as long as hounds can press their game, the scent will hold good; but when turning down wind, or loitering by the way, the case is reversed.

We will now return to Edmund Knightley. On his appearance at the place of meeting, within half a mile of a fine piece of gorse, lying on the side of a hill, which was the first draw that morning, a cheerful smile rested on his manly face, as he sat in his saddle, surrounded by eighteen couples of the lady pack, averaging in height rather above twenty-three inches.

Charley is at some little distance, looking very serious, and Jack the picture of good-humour. The turn-out is as complete as need be, the horses as well as hounds in first-rate condition, and looking well-bred and fit to go. The men neatly dressed, and looking as if they had paid especial care to their toilet that morning. The Marquis scans the group with a master's eye, but there is nothing he can detect out of place; neither can the fastidious Sir Digby Colville.

"Well, Edmund," exclaimed the Marquis, riding up to shake hands with him, "I congratulate you on the success of your essay as huntsman, and hope you intend treating me to a gallop with another fox of the same sort."

"That, Dunkerton, would be no easy matter; but we will do our best to afford you sport."

After the quarter of an hour allowed for late comers, and the usual interchange of civilities, Edmund moved off for the gorse covert, into which the hounds immediately dashed, at a word or two from their young master, Charley riding away for the farther end. There was no unnecessary noise or cracking of whips, and for a few minutes stillness reigned around—men looked serious. The Irish Baronet remarked to the Marquis, "He is a cool, quiet hand for a novice; there's no life in him; your man Dick would crack a fox out of that gorse before Mr. Knightley finds him. He is only fit to hunt harriers."

"Softly, Colville," the Marquis replied; "we are come out to take a lesson, you know, and I rather think it has already commenced. Our young huntsman has been accustomed to fox-hounds ever since the day that he could toddle into the kennel, when Will Lane used to take the child in his arms to see them; and he is not the sort of character to let anything pass without due observation. Now, what think you of that screech? The ladies are at him, and their huntsman too," as Edmund was seen jumping and springing his horse over the gorse.

The Marquis had taken up his position, at one end of the covert, where he was joined by several others, when Tom Springfield, riding down to him and taking off his hat, said, "Master Edmund's respects, my Lord, and he will be obliged if you will leave this corner open for the fox to break."

"Are you then head whip to-day, Tom?"

"No, my Lord, I am only a *yeoman pricker*."

"Well said, Tom Springfield! your old mare can verify that assertion, for you prick her along with the spurs most confoundedly."

"I think, my Lord," Tom replied with a laugh, "she will want a new pair to-day."

"Well, your fox shall have free scope at this point, Tom," as the Marquis moved away; "but I suppose you want to catch another in my country?"

"We don't care where he goes, my Lord, if we can catch him at last."

Tom Springfield now posted himself alone behind the high gorse just at the angle of the covert, where he could see everything below him without being himself seen, where he sat in his saddle, motionless as a statue; and whilst thus sitting we may give a slight sketch of him. He was a fine, handsome young man, standing six feet two inches without his shoes, of exceedingly powerful frame-work, with great activity of limb. He was in his thirtieth year, and the son of a tenant of Mr. Knightley's, who rented a large farm of five hundred acres, principally pasture land, the management of which devolved chiefly on Tom, who possessed more than a common knowledge of his business, being thus early in life considered one of the best judges of cattle and stock in the whole country, as well as a clever agriculturist in other respects; so that Springfield's farm was cited as a model for others to imitate.

His father being in his seventieth year, and reputed rich, Tom was regarded—to use a homely phrase—"a young man well to do in the world," and a great match amongst farmers' wives and daughters, although, to use his own words, he had too many irons in the fire already to want another. Besides which his mamma was not the best of tempers, and he knew a young wife would have a sorry time of it with her; for his father being an easy, good-tempered man, Mrs. Springfield ruled the household.

Tom had remained stationary at his post some five or six minutes, when he saw the fox poke his nose out of the gorse to reconnoitre the ground, and seeing all clear, spring out quickly and away for the fence. When safe on the other side, a view halloa greeted his ear, which gave wings to his flight, and brought the ladies out in a body, with their huntsman and Jack in close attendance.

"Now for a spurt, Mr. Edmund," said Tom, "'tis a young one this time, and he's got his mouth open already;" and before the rest of the field could molest them, the greater part being on the other side with Charley, the trio were a field ahead, with the hounds running, as Tom expressed it, "like blazes;" the

Captain, Sir Digby, with Reginald and Charley—the first straining every effort to catch them—and in this order they went for five and thirty minutes, without a check, the ladies running from scent to view, and pulling down their fox in the open.

"That's just the ticket, sir," cried Tom, who was third up at the finish; "the Captain won't call us slow coaches after this, I think, nor the Irish Baronet boast of his Leicestershire clippers. But here comes Mr. Reginald first, he has got the foot of 'em all to-day, and Charley close in his wake; I'll just give 'em a shriek, sir, to wake up the Marquis, or he may think of going home because he couldn't catch us."

Tom's whoohoop roused up more than the Marquis to renewed exertions; for many were so far behind as to have given up all hopes of catching the hounds again, when Tom's yell set them going, to be there or thereabouts, and see a second fox found, if not the first eaten. Reginald, pleased at having distanced the Captain and Sir Digby, could not forbear, in the excitement of the moment, from expressing his delight at the burst, by saying, "Well done, Edmund! you and Tom managed that very cleverly; I give you both credit for the performance."

"I'm glad you're pleased, sir," Tom replied; "but where's the Captain?"

"He will be here presently, I suppose, Tom, but he got grassed by going too fast at a double, and that Irish Baronet had a noser at the same place."

By this time the gentlemen inquired after made their appearance, racing over the last field neck and neck; but both pulled up directly they caught sight of the hounds, which, having eaten the fox, were now, some standing, some lying around their huntsman.

"Found an open drain, I conclude," the Captain said to Tom, when he came up.

"A good many," replied Tom, laughing; "he's gone down the red lane."

"What! killed and eaten already, Springfield?"

"Just so, sir, and we have been waiting the last ten minutes, to see how our field were coming in. Have you seen the Marquis lately, Captain?"

"He is on the road, as I heard a tremendous 'getting up stairs' between his lordship and somebody else at a bullfincher about three fields behind."

"*Damsons* is very plentiful this year," remarked Tom, "but there is generally a pretty good crop in some places."

The Marquis having now arrived, not in the best humour, let loose at Springfield for spoiling his start.

"All fair, my lord," Tom replied; "you would have spoilt ours, and we ain't so overburdened with foxes as to chop 'em in covert."

"You are an impudent dog, Tom Springfield; I shall speak to Mr. Knightley to keep you in better order."

"Much obliged, my lord," returned Tom, touching his hat, "we will try to please you with our next, and there he goes, by jingo!" as a fresh one, disturbed from a thick hedge-row, crossed the corner of the field in view of the hounds, which set to work running at the top of their speed. "Now, my lord," cried Tom, "we have all a fair start this time;" which was not the case exactly with regard to wind, the horses of the first division having had the advantage of ten minutes' breathing time, which enabled them to keep the lead, Sir Digby, the Captain, and a few others, straining in vain to beat them; both Edmund and his brother Reginald being mounted on thorough-bred horses, as well as Charley, the first whip. The yeoman pricker spurred on his old mare, and at the end of five miles, accomplished in sixteen minutes, the ladies, which no horse could catch, pulled down their second fox, before he could reach a large covert in the Marquis's country.

"A glorious finish, by Jove, Edmund!" cried Reginald. "We have given those horse-dealing fellows a thorough good dusting to-day, so don't draw again to oblige anybody."

"Well, Captain," asked Tom Springfield, as that individual rode up, "was that fast enough for you?"

"Quite, Tom; I think hounds could not go faster."

"Just my opinion, Captain; you see they can run as well as hunt; but I'd rather have an hour and forty minutes with some difficulties in the way, to test the hounds and huntsmen, than such things as these we have had to-day, galloping and spurring from find to finish."

The ceremonies attending the whoohoop were delayed for some little time, to enable the Marquis and others of the second-class riders to come up, on whose arrival the second fox was given to the hounds.

"Well, Edmund," the Marquis observed, "you have given us two splendid scurries this morning, and must confess your lady-pack can go the pace; perhaps you may show us now how they hunt, as it is only one o'clock."

"We don't intend drawing again, Dunkerton, two foxes in one day being the outside number we can afford to kill; independent of which, our next fixture is made already for Frampton Wood, the nearest covert we could draw, on this side of our country."

"I think you are quite right, Edmund," was his reply. "I, for one, have had quite enough to breathe our horses."

"My lord," the Captain observed, "I don't call this a day's sport."

"Then, pray, may I ask," Reginald said, "what Captain Duncombe *does* consider a day's sport?"

"Drawing, of course, till two or three o'clock in the afternoon," was his reply.

"*We* measure sport by its *merits*, not by the *hour*," Reginald remarked, with a sneer, "and regret we cannot subscribe to Captain Duncombe's opinion. Come, Edmund, the governor says we cannot spoil our next fixture, to please anybody. Good morning, Dunkerton, we will give you a slow thing from Frampton, if you will honour us again on Friday."

CHAPTER XXI.

ABEL WHITE gave his annual dinner-party like other great personages in high places, for Abel was the premier of fox-hunters in those parts, being the oldest man who regularly attended the fox-hounds. As some little return for the many good dinners he enjoyed at other people's houses, Abel invited them all to dine with him once a year, *en masse*, the week before Christmas; not that this was the only occasion when the spirit of hospitality acted upon him, for little bachelor dinner-parties formed the *rule*, not the exception, at Westwood Manor; the old squire seldom sitting down to a solitary meal at six o'clock, and when failing to find a friend in the hunting field willing to partake of his good cheer—for Abel lived upon the fat of the land—he would toddle down to the gate, which stood close to the parish road, about four o'clock in the afternoon of non-hunting days, with the hope of meeting some acquaintance, or even a decent traveller riding or driving by, to whom he courteously offered the rites of hospitality, with a shake-down for his horse.

His annual dinner had now, however, become a regular thing—an established custom for more than thirty years, and every gentleman of the hunt made a point of attending it. It was, as Abel called it, a meet for the dog pack, no ladies being invited; for being still a bachelor, the softer sex could not be included, and, as it was, the old dining-room barely sufficed to contain his male guests upon this occasion. Westwood was an old-fashioned looking place, suitable only to old-fashioned people; standing upon low ground, and abutting upon two roads, one parochial, the other dignified by the name of turnpike, although, save for a little more wheel room, the former presented a more even surface than the latter, thanks to its proximity to Abel White's residence; who, by dint of coaxing and scolding, had persuaded the farmers of his parish to mend their highways much more readily than their pastor could their private ways; although, it must be admitted, by the more potent argument of John Barleycorn, a powerful auxiliary, generally called in by the squire to determine little controversies of this kind with his neighbours. Notwithstanding its proximity to the aforesaid highways and byways, the front approach to the old mansion was barred by strong double doors, at either end of the carriage drive, a high wall occupying the space between, and extending quite round the lawn; the back entrance was guarded by a large white ferocious bull-dog, the terror of beggars and children, the very sight of Billy, as they peeped into the court-yard, being sufficient to deter the most brazen-faced from setting foot over the threshold of the dark green door, which generally stood invitingly half open. Billy occupied a little snug stone hut, just in the corner under the window of the housekeeper's room; his tether of chain extending to within a few feet of the back door, and his barking and furious efforts to attach himself to the persons of strange intruders into his private domain, were sufficient to appal the stoutest heart; his frantic efforts to break his chain—looking from constant friction upon the gravel as smooth and white as old Peter's silver forks and spoons—were fearful to behold; for at every rush Billy performed a sort of *pirouette* in the air, coming down with his hind legs foremost, scratching and throwing up the dirt and gravel in a violent manner; and whilst people stood confronting this infuriated animal, dreading every fresh effort to disengage himself from his chain might prove the last, Ralph, the raven, would, unperceived, steal gently behind them, sending his sharp, powerful beak into the calves of their legs—for Ralph and Billy were great friends, and the bird seemed to enter into the dog's feelings, by aiding and abetting, as far as in him lay, to drive strangers from the yard.

Ralph was a grave-looking, methodistical bird, like other personages of the household. There was something dignified in his deportment, even whilst sending his beak into people's legs. He performed this operation methodically, and with judge-like gravity, delivering his charge, and then stepping back with a knowing and consequential air, to see how it was received; at the same time there was a provoking leer in his upturned eye, plainly asking, "How do you like it?" Ralph would bite, in his way, nearly as sharp as Billy; and it was highly amusing to see with what agility little boys, when calling for their jugs of skim milk, would skip about the yard, to avoid his treacherous attacks from behind.

Every one and everything at Westwood looked old-fashioned. The head servants, butler and gardener, numbered as many years as their master, and it was nothing surprising that they looked staid and demure with their silvery locks; but Richard the footman, and Jim the groom, neither of whom had attained the age of thirty, looked equally stiff and antiquated in their old style of dress, cut out after the antique and time-honoured fashion, from which the old squire would permit no deviation; and ensconced in which, the boy of all work under Richard, commonly called Dolliger, but whose Christian name was Adonijah, presented as long a visage, when assisting at the dinner table, as his instructor Peter the great, who was of somewhat the same corporeal dimensions as his master. Mrs. Wise, the housekeeper, when seated in her high-backed arm-chair, and dressed in her laced cap and frill, resembled the bird of wisdom of the white species, with his sharp beak and large grey eyes; a strange contrast to Peggy the cook, a big, burly, bustling woman—fair, fat, and forty—who presided over the culinary department with the air and dignity of a dowager duchess. Her kitchen was the picture of comfort and cleanliness, everything being arranged in punctilious order. The two shelves of pewter plates ranged over the dresser had, from long use and constant cleaning, assumed almost the appearance of silver; and so bright were the metal covers of all sizes—from that capacious enough to conceal a haunch of venison, down to protecting a hot mutton chop in its transit from the kitchen—that they hung suspended against the wall like so many old-fashioned mirrors.

The only other legalised occupier of the kitchen besides Peggy and Dolly, the scullion and dairy-maid—a blooming round-faced wench, with dark eyes and luxuriant black tresses—was a large white cat, sitting as composedly upon a stool near the fire as if the house and all it contained belonged to her, and not pussy to the house. Peggy permitted no one else to intrude upon her privacy, except during business hours, that is, dishing-up time; all the male portion of the household, save Peter, being obliged to content themselves in the servants' hall; although Richard the footman and Jim the groom would venture in occasionally to get a chat with Dolly on the sly when Peggy was out of the way.

"I won't have them men littering about the kitchen," she would say, when the mark of their shoes upon her smooth, white, stone floor caught her eye; "they be always a hankering arter you, Miss Dolly, and I won't ha' it. Them sloe black eyes of your'n will bring ye into trouble, if thee'lt 'courage the men to be peering into 'em; thee beest too young by a score o' years to think o' marrying yet, and I tell 'ee no good 'll come on it."

It was the morning now of Abel's grand annual festival, and Peggy and Dolly had been at work two hours by candlelight in getting things forward for the feast. There was a deal to be done that day, and scarcely time for their own breakfast and dinner. There were the plum puddings, new college puddings, and other puddings to be got ready, for Abel dealt largely in the substantials of every kind. Mrs. Wise, too, was busy with her jellies, blancmanges, trifle and mince pies, and other confectionery appertaining to her department. Richard was burnishing up his forks and spoons, and Dolliger, the boy, upon his legs the live-long day running hither and thither.

Six o'clock at last arrived, and at the head of his table, faced by the master of the foxhounds, old Squire White took his seat, flanked on either side by a dozen of his friends and neighbours, among whom were the two younger Knightleys, Colonel Maxwell, Chetwynd, Welford, Addleby, Major Townsend, and other members of the hunt. Grace was said by the little vicar; the covers of two large soup-tureens, of solid silver, heirlooms in the family, were simultaneously removed by Peter and Richard, sending forth a thick fragrant steam of mock-turtle, and rich gravy soups. When the contents of these had been dispensed to all around, two huge dishes of turbot and cod-fish were ushered in, with the same precise movement, occupying the place upon the table where the tureens had lately stood, and with these now commenced Peter's busy time, in handing round milk-punch and sherry.

"I am sorry to say, Knightley," the jolly old squire remarked, "that case of champagne, which I ought perhaps to have tasted long ago, has not yet been loosed out of dock, but milk punch is not, I believe, a very bad substitute at this time of year."

"Capital, White, nothing can be better, and as to champagne, I don't think it's worth your paying the duty upon it, as long as you have a cargo in hand of such soft milky stuff as this; and I must trouble Peter for a second glass."

"Ay, ay, Knightley, glad to see you like it; no poison in that cup, home manufactured; a bottle of it wouldn't hurt any man's feelings the next morning."

"By gad, sir!" exclaimed the Major, "if my mother had nourished me with such lacteal fluid as this, I shouldn't have been weaned by this time."

The hum of cheerful voices now commenced all round the table, and a huge sirloin of beef smoked upon the board, with its *vis-à-vis* of a turkey, weighing before dressed twenty-five pounds; the rest of the fare equally solid.

"We live in a plain old-fashioned manner, Mr. Welford," the host said, "and I fear our substantials may not comport with the tastes of those who are accustomed to French kick-shaws. My housekeeper and cook belong to the old school, with the knowledge of only plain roast and boiled."

"Which I think they exercise to perfection, Mr. White, for we seldom find French *artistes* who can send up joints or poultry in such perfect style as yours are done."

"Ay, ay, sir; Peggy has the art at least of doing things to a turn, well done, not overdone into rags and tatters, and she's her hands pretty full of work to-day, for there's another lot of hungry hounds to be let in upon the troughs, after the dainty ones have picked out the tit-bits. There's Charley and Jack, with the keepers and earth-stoppers, at the long table in the servants' hall, to begin their work when we have done, and another such dinner as this prepared for them. We keep it up pretty late, Mr. Welford, on the '*nanniversary*,' as Will calls it; but there's a morning moon, sir, to light folks home who feel a little staggery."

The more substantial viands had been removed for game and wild fowl, plum puddings, new college ditto, large, trembling moulds of jelly, blancmange, &c., with mince pies, &c., for side dishes; the centre of the table being occupied by a large silver epergne, bearing a deep glass dish of trifle. The old squire did not press his guests to take wine, leaving every man to follow the bent of his own inclination; but when cheese was placed upon the table, for he would have everything done in old style, half of an old Cheshire at top, and a large mellow cream, one from his own dairy, at the bottom, every man knew it was expected he should swallow the contents of the tall spiral glass handed to him by Peter, with the ears of barley prettily stamped upon its brim; and few would decline, who had become previously acquainted with its flavour, to taste the light amber-coloured liquid offered with old Peter's insinuating and persuasive smile. Up to this time, however, all had enjoyed their freedom of action; but when the dessert had been placed on the table, an uneasy glance was directed by Welford towards a silver fox's head, which Peter had set up beside his master's plate, well knowing the rule of the house as regarded this little ornamental drinking cup.

"Ah! Mr. Welford," the squire said, catching his eye; "I believe you do not quite like my little friend here on my right hand, a little too bacchanalian, I fear; but we excused you the last time on the plea of ill-health, and the same indulgence shall be granted now, although a bit of that anchovy toast will give it a relish. You have your choice, however, water or wine."

"Thank you," Welford said, "of the two, if needs be, I prefer a draught of water."

Our host had now risen, and, after a hem and haw, said, "As good wine needs no bush, gentlemen, there is no necessity for my enlarging upon the merits of fox-hunting in the presence of fox-hunters. I shall therefore drink the toast with the usual honours, and I hope, as long as life and health are given me, to have the pleasure of seeing you all here, at my little annual gathering of friends and brother sportsmen. I drink success to fox-hunting, my friends, and may its shadow never grow less!"

The cup was raised to his lips with a steady hand, the contents drained to the last drop, and the cup then handed to his next neighbour, Peter standing obsequiously at his elbow, with a fresh half-pint bottle of old port wine, which was used only upon this occasion.

"Ay, ay, Colonel," remarked the host, "you have known the flavour of that vintage before this night. It is not corked, I hope?" as he took a draught first, and then set it down to rest awhile on the table, still supported by his right hand.

"Oh, no, White, good as ever—so good, that I enjoy the aroma: it is as sweet as a bouquet of flowers."

"Never make two bites at a cherry, Maxwell; the old cup which stands there on the sideboard holds a full bottle, but to suit the present generation, who haven't half the hearts or heads of their fathers, I have lowered the measure to just half-a-pint; and if a man can't put that out of sight pretty quickly, he hasn't much business in the hunting field, according to my ideas."

"I conclude, sir," the Captain observed, addressing his host, "that the old gentleman who is looking down so complacently upon us from the canvas opposite to me, has often handled that cup upon the sideboard, but from the dents in the picture he seems to have met with rough usage."

"Yes, Captain Duncombe, that is my disgraceful work, for many's the bottle of wine that has been shied at his head by his scrapegrace of a grandson, when I was a youngster like yourself, with an empty head upon my shoulders, for entailing this house and property, and cutting me out from doing with it as I then wished. Yes, sir, this unworthy hand has dealt him many a hard blow, but I have dealt myself harder since—*here*, sir," laying his large bony fist upon his heart. "Our young warm blood leads us all astray; we want to have things our own way, like young impetuous hounds, impatient of restraint; but there's many a day I've seen, when, but for old Solomon putting them right upon the line again, and curbing their hot fancies with a bad scent, we should have gone home without our fox's head. And you, Captain, are a deal too hasty sometimes, making more rents than you can mend. It won't do, sir, pull up, and give them time, if you would have the name of a good sportsman."

"I hope to profit by your advice for the future, sir," the Captain replied.

"Glad to hear so wise a resolve, and hope you won't forget it, when we next meet at Skurry Gorse."

The next toast proposed that evening by the old squire—

"The Master of the Foxhounds"—was received with rapturous applause, and no sooner had the plaudits died away than their echo was borne back from the servants' hall with a loud ringing cheer which pierced through every ear.

"Ay, ay, gentlemen," cried the old squire, rubbing his hands with great glee, "Charles has found his fox at last, and the other dog pack are running right merrily now!"

CHAPTER XXII.

OUR friend Alphonso did not recover from the pommelling he received in his fall with Mameluke for more than a week, and feeling very sore, in more respects than one, expressed his disgust of hunting altogether, telling the Captain he should sell his horses and retire from the field.

"Oh! of course," replied Duncombe, "and realise the predictions of your enemies, that you are a chicken-hearted fellow, and afraid of a fall. What are your few bruises in comparison with Will Lane's broken ribs?—for which he has to thank you, since you rode right across him, and knocked him over."

"Reginald Knightley served me the same trick, then—so we are quits on that score."

"No, you are not, Master Jack, but a long way from it; Knightley saw you were intending to cross him also, and by waiting his time, caught you cleverly on the hop. That's how it happened, and he served you quite right—tit for tat, my boy, that's all. So now I will trouble you to inclose a ten-pound note to Will Lane, regretting the accident, and hoping he is in a fair way of recovery. You should have done this the next day, but it is not too late now. This will bring you into favour with Mr. Knightley, who is generosity itself, and he will know how to appreciate good feeling in others."

"Well, Duncombe, I will do as you suggest directly, but I won't go out hunting again with their hounds."

"Because you are afraid of being horsewhipped by Reginald, I conclude,—as every one else will also conjecture."

"I don't care a d——n for Reginald, or all the Knightleys put together," replied Jack, waxing bumptious.

"If you will repeat that boast in the presence of any one of the Knightley family, Jack, I will believe you mean what you say; but on one point I am quite satisfied, that not one of them cares a rap for you, unless you get in their way; so don't imagine it to be any concern of theirs whether you hunt with their hounds or not. Your fellow Oxonian has, however, created quite a sensation in the sporting world, and it has become the fashion to hunt with him, in preference to the Marquis; in short, the Marquis himself patronises him nearly every week, so take wit in your anger, and come out with him again."

"If I must hunt," replied Alphonso, "I shall meet the Marquis; but how about the hunt ball? my mother wants to go also, and the governor."

"Very well, I will get tickets for them and you: it will be a grand affair—half the country there. By the way, Jack, which of the young ladies do you mean to patronise?"

"Why, upon reflection, I think Miss Maxwell will suit me best. Lady Agnes, by all accounts, is too much of a high-flyer to marry a commoner, and from what I saw of her at Morton Grange, I don't like her half as well as Edith. We got on uncommonly well together the last time I dined with them, and I begin to think she is in love with me already."

"The deuce you do! and what makes you think so?"

"Why, you see, Duncombe, she colours up when we first meet, and seems very shy of me sometimes when I am talking to her; and I have heard mother say that is a sure sign of a girl liking a man."

"Well, then, when is the governor to pop the question for you?"

"I think I can manage that little matter better by myself; and mother says she should like to meet her first at the ball, and see how she behaves there, as very pretty girls often turn out very great flirts."

"Of course, there is nothing like looking a horse well over, and seeing his paces, before purchasing; and I dare say your mamma is a better judge of young ladies than her son is of horseflesh. So now, good morning, and tell your governor I will dine with him to-morrow evening."

On leaving Hardington, Duncombe rode straight away for Morton Grange, unburdening his mind by muttering certain anathemas against his friend Alphonso. "That fellow's impudence does astonish one! Edith Maxwell, indeed, in love with such an unlicked cub as that! By Jove! it's enough to make a cat laugh! and yet money may do it. I must look alive—there's no time to be lost now!"

The Captain's present intention was to sound Edith on this matter, but, to his surprise, he found her occupied in receiving a lesson in sketching from Mr. Chetwynd, whom he knew only by sight. On his entering the drawing-room, however, Edith rose to meet him, with her usual sweet smile, though in Mrs. Maxwell's manner a little more formality was perceptible; and as Edith appeared disinclined to leave her occupation, the Captain was perforce constrained to address his observations on the weather, &c., to Mrs. Maxwell, and he sat on, in the hope of seeing the drawing lesson finished, and Mr. Chetwynd's horse at the hall door.

It was now about twelve o'clock; he had called thus early to find the young lady at home, intending also to take luncheon there, which he had been generally asked to do. He was not asked now, yet still held on until it was announced; but Chetwynd remained and took luncheon also, and after it was over, the carriage came round to take Mrs. Maxwell and Edith over to Dropmore. The Captain, not being invited to join the party, felt exceedingly disgusted, twisted his moustache, tapped his leg with his riding-whip, and began humming an opera air; when suddenly recollecting himself, he apologised to Mrs. Maxwell for absence of mind, it having just then occurred to him that he had forgotten an engagement, and abruptly wished her and Edith good morning, giving Chetwynd a look of defiance as he passed.

The Captain's reflections on his road home were not of the most pleasant nature. Here was another rich man evidently standing in his path, far more dangerous than Alphonso; but still believing Edith preferred his society to any other person's, he set his brain to work out his new rival's discomfiture.

The following evening, when dining with Mr. Shuttleworth, he again alluded to Rushmeed farm, by saying that another party had made an offer for it, and unless Mr. Shuttleworth came to terms, without delay, with Farmer Perrin, it would be disposed of. This communication produced the desired effect upon the money maker, whose agent concluded the bargain the very next day by paying a deposit on the purchase; but the land was not to change owners until the following Lady-day. The particulars of this transaction were known only to the Captain, who now waited his opportunity to turn this information to some account, feeling assured a rupture must ensue thereon between the Colonel and Mr. Shuttleworth, which would secure him from any further advances on the part of his esteemed friend Alphonso.

His mind being set at rest on this point, his next effort was directed against Mr. Chetwynd, about whom he made diligent inquiries. Lady Agnes had been made acquainted by Edmund with Chetwynd's visit to Morton Grange, which opened her eyes to his real intentions, causing her considerable annoyance; and Edith's disinclination to renew her visit to Woodborough, added confirmation to her previous impressions, that her friend, although denying it, had secretly given encouragement to Mr. Chetwynd's advances, from their first *tête-à-tête* at Dropmore—and things continued in this unsatisfactory state until the night of the hunt ball.

Now a county or hunt ball is an event of great importance to young ladies and single gentlemen, where they expect to see a great many people who live out of visiting distance, as well as those in whom they take a deep interest. They also feel at liberty in a ball-room to do a little bit of flirtation which could not be safely done under the surveillance of mammas and papas at home, or at a dinner-party, or even after dinner; which are the only opportunities they have of meeting in the country—save and except an occasional pic-nic or archery meeting;—for unless quite unexceptionable as to their means of providing for a wife, mammas take good care not to allow young gentlemen to be left alone with their daughters during morning calls.

The Captain had made two unsuccessful attempts at a private conference with Edith, but on both occasions Mrs. Maxwell pertinaciously adhered to her seat the whole time of his visit; so that he perceived the ball was his only chance. Sir Digby Colville also looked forward to the ball, as of considerable importance to himself; and Lady Agnes, piqued at Chetwynd's non-appreciation of her charms, longed for the ball, when she might show him how she was admired by others. Alphonso also longed for the ball, to dance with Edith, and get her into some quiet corner, where he might feast on her beauty, as Johnny Horner did on his Christmas pie. Mrs. Shuttleworth was eager for the ball, to display her diamonds to the haughty dames of the country who had not called upon her. Well, and Edith too—she rather longed for the ball—not to flirt or dance with any gentleman in particular, but because she was fond of music and dancing.

A county ball is the arena on which all the young ladies for miles round are openly presented to view. Scores and hundreds would pine in single blessedness, and their beauty fade away in lonely places—seen only by a few country neighbours—whose parents cannot afford taking them to London or watering places—save for the county ball. What chance was there of the Misses Duncombe getting off hand except at the county ball? They were too well known in their narrow circle of neighbours to be caught up there—but at the ball they would meet strangers from other parts of the country, who might be fascinated by their charms. In short, a county ball may be not unaptly likened to a horse fair, where all the nags are furbished up and decked out to the best advantage—and we know that many a horse too well known to be sold at home, goes off at the fair.

On the night of *our* hunt ball, the Captain, arrayed in his splendid uniform, was waiting at an early hour in the lobby, to engage Edith Maxwell for the first or second dance, knowing that on entering the room she would be directly assailed by many solicitations of this kind, from her numerous admirers—for Edith's beauty had been the theme of conversation amongst the young men of the country since her first introduction.

On the Captain making his bow, and asking her for the honour of the first dance, he was informed that favour had been already granted to Mr. Chetwynd—but the promise of the second consoled him for his first disappointment—with which he made off, not to seek another partner, but to hover near, and watch her manner and looks when dancing with his rival. Now, Chetwynd had never entered a dancing academy in his life, and dancing over the prairies in the far west is a far different thing to measuring one's steps on the floor of a ball-room. Chetwynd proved, therefore, rather an awkward partner, which the lynx-eyed Captain was not slow to perceive; and Edith's sly laugh at one or two *gaucheries* he committed induced him to think she was not yet in love with Mr. Chetwynd—so that, on obtaining her arm, he remarked, "Your first partner does not show to much advantage in a ball-room—or perhaps he was intent on exhibiting the steps of the Cherokee Indians in their war dance, from whom he has borrowed some rather strange ideas also."

"To what ideas do you allude?" Edith asked.

"About religion," the Captain replied. "Perhaps you are not aware that he is a Deist, who laughs at church-going people. The clergyman of his parish was lamenting to me, the other day, that Mr. Chetwynd had never entered the church since his return to Dropmore, and when venturing to remonstrate with him on this neglect of duty, and the evil influences it would produce on his poorer parishoners, he was met by a violent outbreak of temper."

"I am quite astonished to hear such an account of Mr. Chetwynd," Edith said, gravely; "for he appears very amiable."

"In ladies' society," added Duncombe, "although I should think, unless blinded by prejudices, or some other softer feeling, any lady might gather from his look that he is not good-tempered; but no doubt Miss Maxwell has the power of converting the heathen to Christianity, and rendering him as harmless as one of his stuffed tigers."

"I really do not comprehend your meaning, Captain Duncombe. Mr. Chetwynd is a recent acquaintance, and you cannot suppose I should presume to speak to him on such a subject as his religion."

Duncombe continued—"He gives you lessons in drawing; why should you not, in return, give him a lesson on theology?"

"He has given me only one lesson, which you saw," Edith replied; "and that was neither solicited nor desired by me."

"Ah! indeed!—well, the world is given to tell tales!—since it is reported Mr. Chetwynd had laid himself, with his buffaloes, lions, and tigers, at your feet, all of which you had been most graciously pleased to accept, as well as a most costly Indian shawl."

"I did accept, with Lady Agnes, an Indian shawl, as a loan, on the cold day we first called at Dropmore, but not as a present, since it was left by me at Woodborough to be returned; and as to the report you have mentioned, there is not a word of truth in it."

"For your sake I am rejoiced to hear it," the Captain replied, "for even to a man there is something dreadful in the idea of marrying a heathen."

Having thus expressed his opinion, he turned to other topics of conversation, until the close of the quadrille, when he said, with his most insinuating smile, "I suppose I must not ask for a second dance this evening!"

"Perhaps you had better not," she replied, with a laugh; "it will save me the unpleasantness of a refusal, as I scarcely know for how many I am engaged."

"Well, then, will you think of poor me, if the list is not quite filled up; for I do not care about dancing with any other girl in the room except yourself?"

"I suppose," said Edith, "I must reward you for that gallant speech, if possible; but at present I can make no promise."

We must now turn our attention to Lady Agnes, who had renewed her flirtation with Sir Digby, to the extent of attracting very general observation, and greatly to Edmund's annoyance, who did not expect a repetition of the scene at their first ball. The Earl was not present on this occasion, and Mrs. Knightley having consented to act as her chaperon, Lady Agnes felt more at liberty to follow the bias of her own inclinations; as for Chetwynd, she refused point-blank to dance with him at all, without even the usual excuse of being engaged. Edmund and Edith were also both out of favour, and with the purpose of vexing them, knowing their objection to Sir Digby, the spoilt beauty flirted with him the more, the consequence of which was, that the Irish Baronet, with the impetuosity of his countrymen, proceeded almost to the length of a proposal.

Our friend Alphonso had primed himself at supper with a sufficient quantity of wine to proceed to like extremities with Edith, to whom he paid all the compliments his heavy head could devise; but in attempting to say something more sentimental than common, Edith could no longer restrain a laugh at his failure, which so discomposed our hero, that his heart failed him at the critical moment. *Vox faucibus hæsit*—Anglicè—he could not get it out.

"Well, Alphonso," asked his mamma, after the quadrille, "have you done what you said you would?"

"No, mother," he replied, in a low tone, "I made a hash of it by saying something very silly, which made her laugh, and I could not then go on."

"Well, Alphonso, I dare say the young lady guessed what you intended, and laughed at your want of courage to speak out."

"There, mother, it can't be helped now; I must wait for Dunkerton's *fête*, or some other opportunity."

"She will be snapped up before that time by some of these gay sparks, buzzing about her like bees round a jar of honey, and so, my dear boy, you'd better let papa speak to the Colonel, as you seem so afraid of speaking to the young lady. There's nobody like her in the whole room; and as for that Lady Hagnes, she's a hoity-toity, flirting, flaunting miss, and not to be mentioned on the same day of the week with Miss Hedith."

But notwithstanding Mrs. Shuttleworth's hopes and expectations with regard to her son, the Captain considered *himself* the most favoured of all Miss Maxwell's partners at the close of the hunt ball; and, truth to speak, he was not far wrong in his reckoning at that time.

CHAPTER XXIII.

Edmund's state of mind, after the renewed flirtation of Lady Agnes with Sir Digby Colville, may be more easily imagined than described; and to a man of his particular ideas about women, her conduct was most objectionable, unless she intended giving serious encouragement to his addresses. The veil had been removed from his eyes since her first introduction to the world, and as her true character became more clearly developed, the spell cast over him by her youthful charms was beginning to lose its effect. The contrast between her manners and those of Edith Maxwell had never struck him so forcibly as at the hunt ball, and to judge by the numerous suitors for her hand in every dance, and the observations which reached his ear, Edith's modest, unassuming loveliness attracted many more admirers than the dazzling beauty of Lady Agnes; and as to disposition, he knew too well the marked difference between them.

"Notwithstanding," Edmund would exclaim in the words of Byron, "*Agnes*, with all thy faults I love thee still." But the question must be now resolved, whether she loved him, on which point doubts had lately arisen in his mind, rendering this state of suspense no longer endurable. At first, Edmund thought of speaking to the Earl before making a declaration of his passion to his daughter. This was the most honourable course for him to pursue, although well aware of her father's preference for himself; but there were other considerations which induced him to act otherwise. He could not avail himself of the Earl's influence over his daughter, and if rejected, he might be spared the unpleasant discovery of his refusal by his child. Edmund, therefore, sought an opportunity of meeting Lady Agnes alone in the garden one afternoon, about a week after the hunt ball, when, with all the impassioned eloquence of a first love, he poured forth the long-subdued feelings of his heart.

Lady Agnes listened to his address at first with surprise;

and then, with a laugh which sent the blood rushing to his forehead, said, "You silly boy! how can you talk such nonsense to me, who have always regarded you as a brother? Pray let me hear no more on this subject."

Not the words, so much as the careless, ironical tone, and manner with which they were spoken, sealed at once the lips, and extinguished every hope in the hitherto sanguine mind of Edmund Knightley; when Lady Agnes, taking advantage of his silence, added, "Come, Edmund, let us remain the friends we were before, for I never have and never can think of you in any other light."

Edmund still continued silently walking by her side, until they reached the hall door, but no other word proceeded from his lips; his heart was overwhelmed with conflicting emotions, and too full to give utterance to his feelings; and having opened the door for her, with a deep-drawn sigh, that spoke more forcibly than words the anguish of his heart, he turned again down the steps, walking hastily to the stables, mounted his horse, and rode rapidly away.

To those who, like him, have experienced the bitter disappointment of a first unrequited attachment, his state of mind will be easily understood; but few, perhaps, in a similar situation have had to support the additional burden of insult to which he had been obliged to submit from one whom he had ever regarded with the tenderest affection since early boyhood. This was the blow which, like that dealt by Brutus, paralysed his efforts at resistance; at such a moment anger or resentment found no place in his heart. He saw at once that further pleading would be useless. His eyes were opened to his true position: Agnes had never loved him—not even with the affection of a sister or friend. She made no attempt to soothe the bitterness of his disappointment, but rather appeared to exult in the pain she had inflicted. Although haughty and pettish, he had believed her possessed of a woman's heart, and that she would pity and alleviate his distress, if she could not remove it. It was true, upon reflection, she had altered her tone, and asked to be regarded still as his friend; but was not even such a proposal hollow and insulting? Had she ever regarded him in that light, she must have sympathised with him at such a moment. But he knew the cause of this after-thought—the dread of her father's displeasure. It proceeded from no feeling of compassion or consideration for himself. The idol he had blindly worshipped, idolised as a warm-hearted, generous, though wayward girl, was now broken in pieces, displayed to his astonished vision in all its deformity. He had bowed himself down, like a besotted heathen, before a finely-chiselled, beautifully-painted image, which he now discovered to be a mere block of stone. But older and wiser men than Edmund Knightley have had their mental vision blinded and their senses bewildered by woman's beauty. On reaching home, Edmund's pale and haggard looks were noticed by his sister Emmeline, who, meeting him in the hall, exclaimed, "My dear Edmund, what has happened? you look so ill and agitated."

"I am not ill, dear Emmy," he replied, in as careless a tone as he could assume, "but I have been a good deal worried to-day;" and he began ascending the staircase to avoid further questions.

His sister said no more, but in a few minutes her gentle knock was heard at her brother's door, which, after a little parley and attempted resistance, was at length opened for her admission. On entering the room his things lay scattered about in various directions, one look at which by his sister revealed her brother's intentions; and the tears still standing in his eyes, though he turned away his head to avoid her seeing them, betrayed to her what had occurred.

Taking his hand in one of hers, with the other laid gently on his shoulder, she said, in the most soft and soothing accent, "My own dear Edmund, do you love your sister?"

There was no resisting that appeal; for a second only he gazed on her beautiful features and melting eyes, fixed lovingly on his face, and then, bursting into tears, caught her to his heart.

"Dear, dear Edmund," she whispered, as her tears mingled with his, "I know what has so distressed you. Come, my dearest brother, let us sit down on the sofa. You must not leave home."

"Indeed I must, dearest Emmy, for the present. I cannot remain here now."

We need not relate the whole conversation between the brother and sister; it may suffice to state that Emmeline drew by degrees a full revelation from Edmund of the scene between Lady Agnes and himself, and the cold, insulting manner in which she had rejected his suit; when she said indignantly, "And for this heartless girl, my own beloved brother, you would leave your dear, affectionate father and mother, and poor sister Emmeline?"

"No, dearest Emmy, not now; your gentle pleading has not been in vain. I see my folly in having madly loved one who has never returned my affection, and now treats it with ridicule and contempt."

"There is one, dear Edmund, far more lovely, more amiable, and more affectionate, from whom, had your choice happily so fallen, you might justly have expected all the blessings and happiness which this world can confer."

"I know to whom you allude, dear Emmy, for the contrast between these two girls has also often struck me, although then under the influence of blind and misguided passion; but do not now, my own dear sister, talk to me of other love."

"And yet, dear Edmund, I have long foreseen that your misplaced affections would meet with this return; and believe me, my dear brother, although you may not admit it now, the time will come when you will look back upon this, which you now consider a grievous affliction, as a providential escape from a wretched union, by which your whole future life would be embittered. Lady Agnes is not the person to suit your ideas or disposition. She is selfish, self-willed, and haughty, frivolous and bad-tempered. What prospect of happiness could you reasonably entertain with such a wife? Indeed, my dear Edmund," she added, in a more cheerful tone, "you have had a most fortunate escape; and now, Teddy, dear," she said, playfully, "rouse yourself from this deceptive dream, in which you have too long indulged, and prove yourself a man, instead of the 'silly boy' she called you, to fret and cry about the loss of a worthless toy. Lady Agnes dare not reveal what has passed between you to-day, and pray do not you, by your looks or conduct, give others reason to suspect what has occurred. You have sufficient excuse, were any needed, to spend more of your time at home than at Woodborough, since poor Will Lane is still incapable of resuming his place in the hunting-field; and your rejection by his daughter—for she had of course a right to accept or refuse your proposal—will, I hope, cause no difference in your behaviour to the dear old Earl, who loves you as his own son; you must, if possible, spare him the sorrow of knowing that, which I feel assured would grieve him to the heart. Neither must you absent yourself entirely from Woodborough, or he will guess the cause; and as Lady Agnes has treated you so lightly and cavalierly, your proper pride, dear Edmund, ought to suggest to you a similar line of conduct."

The wholesome counsel of his beloved and affectionate sister produced the effect she desired upon her brother, who, upon reflection, after the first burst of outraged feelings and disappointed hopes, was obliged to acknowledge that he had never received the slightest encouragement from Lady Agnes to persevere in his suit. The love had been all on his side, and the conviction began gradually to steal over his mind that he had been guilty of great folly in proposing, with the certainty almost of being rejected.

We must now take a glance at Woodborough on the evening of Edmund's abrupt departure. He had been expected to dine there, but when the dinner hour arrived, the Earl, who had seen him walking with his daughter in the pleasure grounds, began to question her as to the cause of his absence.

"What has become of Edmund?" he inquired, when the family had assembled in the drawing-room.

Mrs. Errington did not know.

"Agnes," said the Earl rather pointedly, "did Edmund tell you he should not dine here this evening, as you were walking together, not more than two hours since?"

"No, papa; he said nothing about dining here."

"But you know, Agnes, he had promised to remain, and Edmund never breaks his engagements. Something very unusual must have occurred to make him do so now; do you know the cause, Agnes?" and his eyes were turned full upon her face.

Agnes made no reply: but, blushing scarlet, fixed her eyes upon the carpet.

At this moment a significant look from Mrs. Errington satisfied the Earl that her conjectures corresponded with his own; and the confusion of Lady Agnes, coupled with Edmund's abrupt departure from Woodborough, without a word of explanation to either of them, could be accounted for only in one way—his rejection by Lady Agnes.

No further remark escaped the Earl during the dinner-hour; but that sad, gloomy silence was more distressing to his daughter than the most severe reproof. She read in his melancholy looks and averted eye the pain she had inflicted on her too fond, indulgent father, by the refusal of his beloved godson, and the heartless manner which had accompanied that refusal smote her now as unworthy of herself, and insulting to him, whom, if not to love, she had every reason to respect. She might have spared his feelings that bitter, taunting laugh, which had struck like a dagger to his heart, and rendered him speechless in her presence. She saw the iron aimed by her hand had entered his soul; it had been a moment to her of proud revenge, to humble him in the dust for presuming to speak of her flirtation with Sir Digby Colville. She had had her revenge; to her it was sweet for the moment, but for the moment only. The next brought as quick repentance for her unfeeling conduct towards the friend and companion of her youth.

As they walked side by side towards the house, she longed to say something in palliation of her bitter irony, but pride sealed her lips. She walked slowly in the hope—yes, in the hope—that Edmund would say something more; his silence was irksome to her now; but nought save the sound of that deep-drawn sigh reached her ear. In after years, when the day-dreams of youth had passed away, when the beauty, of which she was now so proud, had faded, the remembrance of that scene and sigh haunted her like a dark vision of the night; to the last day even of her existence it was not forgotten.

The sad, reproachful look with which Edmund regarded her, on parting at the hall door, went home to her heart; and on reaching her room, she burst into tears, exclaiming, "Oh, Edmund! how have I in a moment of pique rewarded you for all your kind, generous feelings, and the deep interest you have ever taken in my happiness! I might have bid you still love me as a brother, and we might have still remained friends, but now that hope is lost to me for ever!"

It was now that Lady Agnes felt also the estrangement of that other friend, the warm-hearted, gentle Edith, whose feelings she had also outraged. She at once wrote to her, asking forgiveness for her pettishness, and for her ill-natured and undeserved remarks; adding, that being ill and out of spirits, she hoped Edith would forget what had passed, and resume her visit to Woodborough, if only for a day or two.

This letter was answered immediately by Edith in person, who, incapable of harbouring resentment even for an hour, flew to the assistance of her friend, who, by the expressions used in her letter, she believed to be seriously unwell; and we need scarcely say, that at this particular moment the visit of Edith Maxwell was hailed with delight by the Earl and Mrs. Errington, with whom this gentle, affectionate girl was an especial favourite, as well as with the whole household. Every servant in the establishment loved Miss Edith, to whom pride and haughtiness of demeanour were unknown, and who, anxious to spare them any extra trouble on her account, rewarded their attentions by gracious words, and a sweet smile, which went to the hearts of all.

The presence of Edith imparted something of her cheerfulness and good humour even to Lady Agnes, who, however, carefully withheld any allusion to what had transpired between herself and Edmund. A week had now passed since this event, when the reluctance of Edmund to return to Woodborough, even for an hour, was overcome by his sister's remonstrances on his apparent neglect, and rudeness to his ever kind godfather.

"No other consideration on earth," replied Edmund, "should induce me to set foot in that hall again whilst she is there; but what can I say to my dear, kind godfather? Not for the world would I acquaint him with the heartlessness of his daughter; but my rejection by her cannot be concealed when we meet. I see, however, dear Emmy, that the evil hour cannot be longer deferred. Pride must be humbled, and I will endeavour to meet her with something like indifference. It is a hard task, dear Emmy, you will admit; but as to dining at Woodborough, that, my dear sister, is quite beyond my power of endurance yet."

"The Earl will not, I hope, ask you to do that, dear Edmund; and if he should, you can easily decline, as your father is far from well, and requires your attendance here."

With a sinking, sick sensation at heart, Edmund summoned resolution to ride over the next morning to Woodborough, hoping to meet the Earl in his usual after-breakfast walk to the farm; but as he turned the angle of the road, most unexpectedly Edith Maxwell met his view. His first impulse, in his then agitated state of mind, was to turn his horse, and fly even her presence; for he feared Lady Agnes had acquainted her with his rejection. A moment's reflection, however, on the cowardice and incivility of such an act—for Edith must have seen and recognised him—altered his purpose. There was another consideration, also, which induced him to proceed. Did Edith even know of his rejection, he felt sure of her secrecy and deep sympathy also, in his distressing position. As Edmund dismounted to take her hand, his own trembled with a convulsive grasp in hers, his quivering lips and heightened colour betraying unusual emotion; but by a furtive glance at her face, he saw that hers also was suffused with a deep blush, and her agitation little less than his own.

"Where so early and alone?" he at last asked, in an assumed cheerful, though faltering tone of voice.

"I was going to see the shepherd's wife," she replied.

"Will my company be an intrusion, Edith?"

"Oh, no! I only wished to know how one of her children is who has been ill with fever."

"And are you not afraid of catching the infection, Edith?"

"We ought not to think of a little risk to ourselves, when others are in distress, and need our assistance," she replied.

"Yes, Edith, your life is too precious to all who know and love you, to be risked for a shepherd's child. I am glad to have met you here, and cannot permit you to enter the cottage; the inquiries you wish shall be made by me, and I will take care that everything required shall be sent to the shepherd's family."

As they walked forward, Edmund's silence as to Lady Agnes confirmed Edith's supicions that some rupture had occurred between them, but of what nature she was ignorant, although, from his embarrassment at their first meeting, the true cause of his absence occurred to her; and after leaving the shepherd's house, they proceeded towards Woodborough Park, on reaching which, they parted at the stables, Edmund going by the back entrance to the Earl's private room.

We need not describe the affecting interview between the poor old Earl and his beloved godson, from whom a reluctant confession was at last elicited as to the cause of his late absence; but so far from alluding to his daughter's ill-timed levity, Edmund said all in his power to palliate her conduct.

"It was a sad mistake on my part, dear uncle," he urged, "to talk of a different love to her, who has, perhaps, always regarded me as a brother; and to confess the truth, having these misgivings myself, I would not, as I ought to have done, consult you previously on the subject, before speaking to her."

"I fully understand your motives, my dear Edmund, in withholding this confession of your affection for my child, well knowing the pain her refusal of your suit would inflict upon myself; for this union of our children has been long dwelt upon by your father and me, who have witnessed your increasing attachment with the greatest pleasure, and we lived in the hope of seeing the accomplishment of our wishes. Even now, I do not yet despair of their being realised, for since your departure Agnes has been very dejected and thoughtful, more so than I have ever seen her before, and I really believe she already repents her too hasty decision."

"I dare not so hope, my dear lord," Edmund replied, sorrowfully.

"Then, to oblige me, Edmund, will you endeavour to forget what has passed, and continue your visits here as usual, if I am not asking you to do violence to your own feelings?"

"I fear, dear uncle, Lady Agnes may have bestowed her affections on another, and will never alter her opinion of me."

"I know to whom you allude, Edmund—that spendthrift Irish baronet; but I would rather almost see her in her grave than married to such a fortune-hunting man of the world, whose true character is well known to me. No, Edmund," the Earl continued vehemently; "my consent to her union with such a reprobate shall never be given."

"Oh! make not, my dear lord, any rash vow; his character may have been misrepresented to you, as well as to me."

"I fear not, Edmund; yet I still hope the evil may be averted if you will return. Edith is now here, and I hope her influence will also be of service to Agnes, for I know her dislike to Sir Digby Colville; but your continued absence would afford him greater hopes of success, since it will be certainly attributed to the true cause."

"It shall be then as you desire, my dear uncle," Edmund at last said; "and the day after to-morrow I will promise to dine with you."

CHAPTER XXIV.

THE third morning after the occurrences related in the last chapter, as Colonel and Mrs. Maxwell were sitting at their breakfast table, the servant entered the room, with a letter from Mr. Shuttleworth, the purport of which was a proposal of marriage between our friend Alphonso and Edith, couched in these terms:—

MY DEAR SIR,

I am commissioned by my eldest son and heir, who is too bashful and nervous to address you himself on such a momentous subject, to ask the favour of your consent to his becoming a suitor for the hand of your daughter; and as he flatters himself that reciprocal sentiments already exist between them, I shall feel obliged by your naming an early day for the adjustment of the preliminaries regarding settlements, &c., which I purpose making on such a liberal scale, that of course there can be no further impediment to the happiness of the young people.

I am, dear Sir,

Yours faithfully,

T. SHUTTLEWORTH.

"Cool!" remarked the Colonel to his wife, handing her the document; "deuced cool indeed! too cool by half!" he continued, his choler beginning to rise. "I call it impudent, my dear. What does the fellow mean by addressing me in this strain? as if my daughter, the daughter of a Maxwell, were to be bought, like a bale of cotton in market, by the highest bidder! I say it is downright insolence—give me the letter, my dear, or throw it into the fire."

"Stay, my dear Colonel, you are very excited this morning, and forget that Mr. Shuttleworth has not been accustomed to the forms and etiquette of genteel society. He is a well-meaning man in his way, and of course intended no insult to us, and no doubt means to act very liberally in his settlement on a daughter-in-law, although his son is not the person I could approve, unless Edith is really attached to him."

"Do you then believe your daughter attached to this young fellow, madam?" asked the Colonel, as he rose from the table and began poking the fire very vehemently.

"No, Colonel; I believe she is not attached to any one."

"But my opinion of Edith is," resumed the Colonel, "that she has sufficient of her father's spirit neither to marry for money, nor beneath her position; and as she will inherit all my property, as well as yours, she has a right to aspire to a higher connection than that of a cotton-spinner. But I will ride over directly to Woodborough, and know Edith's true sentiments—so give me the letter."

"Please, sir," said the footman, just then entering the room, "Mr. Shuttleworth's servant wishes to know if he is to wait for an answer to his master's letter?"

"No, sir," replied the Colonel in a sharp tone; "he is not to wait."

"Please, sir," continued the official, "Mr. Grappler, the steward, is waiting in the housekeeper's room to see you."

"I can't see him now—tell him to call to-morrow."

"Please, sir, Mr. Grappler says, he wishes to consult you on very particular business, and hopes you will see him, if only for a moment."

"Show him into my study, then, directly, and tell John to bring my cob to the door in half an hour."

"Well, Grappler," asked the Colonel on entering his sanctum, "what do you want to bother me about this morning? Quick, man! out with it, as I am in a hurry."

"I calls it, Colonel, just as ungentlemanly a proceeding as

I ever hear of—a nasty under-handed job, as a real gentleman would scorn to have a hand in—that's my opinion, Colonel."

"Hang your opinion, sir; what is the job you complain of?"

"Neither more nor less, Colonel, than that this Mr. Shuttleworth has set his agent to work with old Farmer Perrin, and has bought Rushmead Farm over our heads, by giving two thousand pounds more than we offered. I picked it all out, bit by bit, of his son last night, at the Fox and Goose, when he was about three parts drunk, by giving him another glass of brandy-and-water, pretty stiff, Colonel; I mixed it stiff to get all out of him."

"I wish *you* were stiff and buried too, you old fool!" exclaimed the enraged Colonel, "for allowing yourself to be hoodwinked in this manner. I told you, sir, to buy this farm without fail, and offer another thousand, rather than let it fall into other hands."

"I'm not to blame, Colonel, begging your pardon. Mr. Perrin as good as sold me the property at the price you offered; it was made a bargain of over a glass of brandy-and-water."

"Hang your brandy-and-water, sir!" again vehemently interposed the Colonel; "you are drinking brandy-and-water instead of minding your own business, sir."

"Begging your pardon, Colonel, I only takes a drop now and then, to facilitate business—just to suck people's brains a little."

"And muddle your own, you confounded old fool!" exclaimed the Colonel, now boiling over with rage. "Get along with your very particular business; I shall see Perrin myself."

Within half an hour, the Colonel was cantering along the road leading to Rushmead Farm, instead of that leading to Woodborough Park, where, finding old Farmer Perrin at work in his fields, he began to upbraid him for his breach of faith.

"Why, you see, Colonel," Mr. Perrin said, "I meant no offence; but Mr. Grappler is a hard-dealing man, and I couldn't get him beyond the five thousand; then Mr. Mapping comes along one morning, and offers two thousand more if I'd settle the job at once, as he were a-going from home next week, and shouldn't be back for a month; so he pulls out a roll of bank notes, 'mounting to two hundred pounds, and I signs an agreement to the bargain, and gives him an acknowledgment for the money paid down."

"I wish to know, Mr. Perrin, if you told this fellow I had made you an offer for the farm?"

"Why, 'is, Colonel, I told 'im all about it, and said I must speak to you first, before I could close the bargain. 'That's nothing to me,' says Mr. Mappin; 'you may take the money or not, but I sha'n't offer it again;' and he got up to go away, when I thinks to myself, two thousand pounds more would set up John and Thomas in business; so you see, Colonel, I couldn't afford to lose so much money, and I thought you and Mr. Grappler wouldn't come up to the same pint, and that's the long and short of the business."

"And I call it, Mr. Perrin, a very dishonourable piece of business altogether," added the Colonel, as he turned away, and rode towards home, muttering to himself—"A confounded cotton-spinning rascal! And this is the fellow I have patronised and invited to my house. Knightley warned me not to do so, but, like a fool, I would not listen to his advice."

We may suppose the irritable Colonel in no very placable humour on reaching home, when, sitting down in his den, the following laconic epistle was immediately penned to his friend the cotton-spinner:—

Colonel Maxwell presents his compliments to Mr. Shuttleworth, and begs to decline any alliance with his family.

Morton Grange.

Having finished this consolatory epistle, a violent pull at the bell brought Thomas to the door, to whom he said, "Tell John to ride over directly with that letter to Hardington."

"Is he to wait for an answer, sir?"

"No, sir, not a minute."

Exit Thomas, and the Colonel, seizing his hat, sallied forth to cool his excited brain by a walk over his farm.

Captain Duncombe having dined and slept the previous night at Hardington, and being an early and wide-awake bird, rising betimes in the morning to see that his horse was properly attended to, saw the letter given to the under-groom, with instructions to go to Morton Grange, and wait for an answer. "Ha! ha!" thinks the Captain, "the governor and Jack have kept it pretty snug, but I suspect 'that's the agreeable news,' the old woman said I should be startled with to-day. She seemed quite cock-a-hoop about something last night; but I have been beforehand with you, old lady, and now the mine is sprung which will blow you all to the d—l! The Colonel knows all about Rushmead Farm by this time," and shoving both his hands into his pockets, he walked forth into the park, humming the old tune of "A frog he would a-wooing go."

When the bell rang for breakfast, Duncombe took his place at the table in the most cheerful mood, and it added considerably to his high spirits to notice the fidgety state of Papa and Mamma Shuttleworth, as well as the nervous anxiety of his *protégé* Jack, who, to use the Captain's phraseology, "was quite off his feed"—*i. e.*, unable to eat his breakfast.

"Why, Jack," exclaimed the Captain, when they were left alone, "you seem uncommonly down in the mouth this morning; what's the matter, old fellow? Have you got the megrims or the fret?"

"I don't feel very peckish, Duncombe, that's all."

"But that is not all, Jack," replied the Captain, "begging your pardon; you have been doing a little bit of business on the sly, and thought I should not find it out; but did you ever catch a weasel asleep, my boy?"

"No, Duncombe, I don't know much about weasels."

"Or ferrets either," added the Captain; "but as I am a ferret, and can smell a rat a long way off, I'll tell you what's the matter with you, Master Jack; you are in a deuced funk about the reception of that little billet-doux sent off to Morton Grange this morning; and instead of keeping me in the dark about it, you would have acted more wisely by consulting your friend on the matter, since two heads are generally considered better than one; and I shall find out all I wish to know, as to this very secret missive of yours, before to-morrow night."

"Well, Duncombe, you need not take offence, for I have not written any letter at all."

"But it was written on your behalf, although penned by your governor."

Alphonso, struck home by this remark, made no reply, neither did any further allusion to the subject escape the Captain, who resolved to maintain his ground at Hardington until the next morning, hoping by that time, or before, an answer would arrive from the Colonel.

After breakfast the Captain strolled down to the stables, again attended by Alphonso, who now wished his prying friend at the Land's End, which Duncombe perceiving, he added to Alphonso's annoyance by sitting on the corn-bin, and leisurely smoking his cigar.

"I say, Duncombe," Alphonso suggested, "we had better go to my den, where you can enjoy a pipe, instead of that cigar.

"This suits me exactly, old fellow," was the reply as he continued puffing away, kicking the side of the bin with his heels, as an accompaniment to some occasional snatches of an opera air; "smoke my weed and see my horse dressed at the same time just suits me to a T, this wet morning—killing two birds with a stone."

Alphonso was in a fix, fearing to leave his friend alone, in expectation of his cross-questioning the groom, whose return he was so anxiously awaiting.

The Captain had maintained his position about half an hour, seemingly disposed to hold it for half the day, when his quick ear detecting the tramp of a horse in the yard, he sprang with a violent kick from his heels against the box, which made the horses jump nearly over their stalls, and rushed to the door; so did Alphonso, in double-quick time, shaking all over with agitation.

"Where's the ticket for the governor, Bill?" the Captain asked.

"Haven't got any, Captain; Thomas the footman said there warn't no answer to master's letter."

"Deuced queer!" muttered the Captain; "but I say, Bill, was the family at home?"

"Only the Colonel and Mrs. Maxwell, sir; Miss Hedith was a staying over at Woodborough."

Alphonso's face brightened up at these words, and Duncombe's countenance fell.

"Hang it!" he thought; "the Colonel takes time to consider: I may be sold at last."

"Well, Duncombe," Alphonso said, in a more cheerful tone, when relieved from present apprehensions; "they say no news is good news, and I take it the Colonel means to consult the young lady before he sends a reply."

"Then that settles your hash, my boy; for although the Colonel might say 'yes' on account of the money, I'll back the young lady to say 'no' on her own account."

"Why do you think so, Duncombe?"

"Just because there's a chap a deal better-looking than Alphonso Shuttleworth, with as good a house as his, and more money than your governor will fork out, of good old family also, and highly connected, who has been paying particular attentions to Miss Maxwell for the last month."

"Oh, you mean Chetwynd, I suppose; but my governor can outbid him."

"Oh, of course, Master Jack, if the young lady thinks more of the money than the man."

It was now the Captain's turn to be fidgety, and to kill time he proposed a game of billiards, at which, being out of temper, he was beaten by his pupil. The luncheon hour had arrived, and as they were all seated at table, the butler entered, salver in hand : "A letter from Colonel Maxwell, sir."

The Captain kept his eye intently fixed on the face of Mr. Shuttleworth as he hastily broke the seal, the varying colour and fierce expression of which, on perusing the contents, afforded him incontestable evidence of the failure of his proposal. Without saying a word, Mr. Shuttleworth consigned the letter to his pocket, his looks preventing either his wife or son making any inquiry as to its purport.

Duncombe, now thoroughly satisfied as to the result, resumed his usual spirits, helping himself to another glass of wine, and working away at a turkey's leg as if he had not dined for a week. "Ha, ha!" thought he with secret glee, "the cotton market is dull this morning; old Moneybags has got a settler," as his respected host rose from table, quickly followed by the old woman, who had not tasted a morsel of anything since the arrival of the letter.

"Well, Jack," the Captain said, when his papa and mamma had left the room, "you may as well follow suit, and hear the news; I don't mind being left alone, so stand upon no ceremony with me, old fellow, as I mean to finish off with that cranberry tart before I've done, and then, as I see my room is more agreeable than my company, I shall toddle off home."

"Oh, don't leave yet, Duncombe; I will be back in a few minutes, and I want to see you before you go."

Leaving the Captain with his tart, we will peep into Mr. Shuttleworth's sanctum, where papa is storming about the room, and mamma exclaiming, "Well, I never see'd anything half as imperent as that old snappish Colonel's letter; I never would have believed it of him; who would have thought it?—so agreeable and purlite as he has always made himself when we have dined there. Oh, dear! oh, dear! my poor boy; to be snubbed like that!"

"Well, mother," said Alphonso, entering the room, interrupting her exclamations, "what's it all about? Let's see the letter."

"Oh, my dear boy, such a nasty, spiteful answer from that crabbish old Colonel!"

"But what is it, mother? I want to see it," as she still held it back.

"It's all over, my dear, with Miss Hedith, and so you will see."

"Bill said Miss Maxwell was at Woodborough, mother, so she could have had no hand in it, and I'll serve the Colonel out for this, by running away with Edith to Gretna Green."

"Well, my dear, it is some comfort to know that sweet, pretty angel wasn't concerned in it; and if I were in your place, Alphonso, I would do as you say."

"But what's to be done with the Captain, mother?" for his father had left them together; "he says he shall go home directly after lunch, and if I don't tell him all about it, he will blow me all over the hunting field to-morrow."

"Then you must get him to dine here to-night, and I'll ask him to keep it quiet."

On returning to the dining-room, Alphonso found the Captain standing with his back to the fire, warming himself, and tapping his leg with his riding-whip.

"Now then, Jack, I'm off; any commands for Morton Grange, where I shall call *en route*?"

"No, Duncombe, don't go yet; mother wants you to dine here to-night."

"Can't afford to lose more time now, Jack, as I wish to learn the news."

"What news, Duncombe?"

"Oh," he replied, in a careless tone, "whether Miss Maxwell is to become Mrs. Alphonso Shuttleworth; I can pick out all about the matter from Mrs. Maxwell this afternoon, and shall have it ready for Dunkerton's lawn meet to-morrow."

"You won't serve a fellow such a scurvy trick as that, Duncombe, by telling family secrets?"

"You have confided nothing to me, not a scrap, Master Jack, but, *tout au contraire*, kept me quite in the dark, instead of consulting me as a friend. I have no secret of yours in my keeping, or it had been held sacred, and I shall speak therefore of what I hear from others precisely as I think fit."

"It was father's doing, Duncombe, who would not allow me to speak to you as I wished, and he and mother thought to surprise you this evening with the agreeable news of my being accepted."

"Very prettily intended, no doubt, Jack; but just look me well over once more, and say if you see anything in the physiognomy of Tom Duncombe to warrant your opinion of his being such a confounded flat as to swallow all that trash about the agreeable surprise; so now I shall wish you good morning."

"Stay, Duncombe, a few minutes longer, and you shall see the letters;" and off went Alphonso, now in a precious fright, to obtain them from his mamma, telling her it was his only chance of keeping him quiet.

As usual, the Captain was still tapping his leg with his riding-whip when Alphonso, returning, placed the letters in his hand without further remark.

"'Pon my life," he said, when he had read the proposal, "that governor of yours has a rum notion of doing business in the matrimonial line. By gad, sir! I never read such an off-hand, flippant piece of literature in the shape of a proposal; it is downright insulting. Why, your governor must have been thinking of making a cotton bargain, when he penned that epistle to the Colonel about his only child; and, of course, here follows the answer, short and rough, like a jackass's gallop. Well, I should like to know what other answer you could expect from a gentleman of old family and high connections, like Colonel Maxwell, upon receiving such an offensive proposition, telling him, in plain terms, that his daughter was to be bought for money? But there it is: that governor of yours, although a good sort of man in his way, knows no more of the etiquette and usages of polished society than a hippopotamus."

"Well, but, Duncombe, what's to be done?"

"Nothing that I can see now," was the reply; "you have shut me out from your counsels until it is too late. Your governor, by his letter, has set the Colonel's back up, and there's an end of the affair, at least for the present."

"But, Duncombe, stay and dine, there's a good fellow, and we will talk it over after dinner."

"Well," replied the Captain, "as it seems setting in for a wet afternoon, I may as well change my mind, and go home to-morrow after hunting."

After drinking a larger quantity of wine than usual that evening at dinner, the Captain, with his chum, retired to his private room, to finish off with mulled claret and a grill, whilst discussing which Alphonso amused his companion by declaring his intention of proposing a runaway match to Edith, when they met at Dunkerton's ball; adding, "I know she likes me better than Chetwynd, so I'll have a go at Gretna Green."

"You'll have a go at another place, you conceited fool," thought the Captain, "before you can persuade Edith Maxwell to take that trip with a snob like yourself;" but he merely said, "Oh, of course, if the young lady is willing, there is nobody to prevent you, except the Colonel."

"Ah!" exclaimed Alphonso, highly elated with his new project, "I don't care a rap for him, and now we may as well go to roost."

CHAPTER XXV

WE have little worthy of note to record before the Marquis of Dunkerton's grand annual *fête*, to which, as before stated, every gentleman's family possessing landed property within the limits of his lordship's hunting country was invited, except that Edmund was observed to ride much harder than usual, and from Will Lane's bad state of health, consequent upon his fall, he still continued to hunt the hounds with uniform success. In short, with a mind ill at ease like his, the excitement of the chase brought relief to his troubled spirit; he sought it with feverish avidity, as men seek dissipation, or drink wine, to drown for the time distress or cares; and Edmund's love seemed transferred from Lady Agnes to his spotted favourites.

Their first meeting had been very embarrassing on both sides, for Lady Agnes felt now how unkindly she had treated him; but that passed, his usually deferential manner of late was resumed, and Edith Maxwell being again a guest at Woodborough, prevented the unpleasantness of their being left alone. None of his friends, not even Edith Maxwell, knew or suspected Edmund's rejection by Lady Agnes, and thus matters stood until the evening of the Marquis's *fête*, to which, although sick at heart, and little inclined for gaiety, his reluctant consent had been given to accompany the Earl, Lady Agnes, and Edith.

The Colonel, rendered savage by Mr. Shuttleworth's underhand conduct, as regarded Rushmead Farm, made no secret of the transaction, or his insolence in asking for the hand of his daughter; and Edith, offended at Alphonso's presumption in daring to associate her feelings with his, as well as his father's trickery, felt little hesitation in complying with the Colonel's mandate to give the whole family the cut direct. Our friend

Alphonso, although not very tall in stature, was sufficiently portly to be rather a conspicuous personage even in a crowd, and being himself aware of this fact, it appeared somewhat strange to him that Edith—for he had the assurance still to call her by her Christian name amongst his friends—should not be able to recognise his features, even when standing before her and making his bow. Alphonso knew she was short-sighted, and, as she turned her head at the moment, supposed she did not see him ; but believing, from a very romantic novel he had been lately perusing, that young ladies were invariably addicted to act in opposition to their parents' wishes with regard to marriage, and being also under the delusion that Edith's sweet smile, with which she always received her friends and acquaintances, had been fraught with a more especial meaning towards himself, he could not dispel the monomaniacal hallucination of her being certainly in love with him ; and while pondering over these things, a well-known voice whispered in his ear: "Have you settled the trip to the north?"

"Hang it, Duncombe," he said, turning sharply round; "don't talk of these things here; you will be overheard."

"No one will guess to what I allude," was the reply ; "but I wish to know if the young lady is agreeable?"

"Confound it, Duncombe, I haven't asked her yet; don't bother a fellow so."

There are some men too conceited, and others too obtuse, to see a joke cut at their expense. Alphonso was one of the former, so wrapped up in self-sufficiency and money-made importance as to think no one could be guilty of laughing at him ; and he was fully bent on making a proposal to Edith Maxwell of a trip to Gretna Green before he left Dunkerton House.

Some short time after, observing her walking with his friend the Captain, on the conclusion of a quadrille, he seized that opportunity of now fairly presenting himself to her view, by obstructing her further progress, and saying, "that he hoped to have the honour of dancing with her."

"I must decline that honour," she replied, with a haughty inclination of her head, as she passed on, leaving Alphonso perfectly astounded at this reception from one he had been contemplating as the willing partner of his northern flight. The look and manner of Edith Maxwell could not be mistaken, for although it was foreign to her disposition to take offence lightly, she felt justly indignant at the familiar terms in which her name had been coupled with his in that off-hand proposal penned by his father.

"You are not aware, perhaps," the Captain remarked to his fair partner, "of the loss you have sustained by declining to dance with Mr. Shuttleworth."

"What loss do you mean?" she inquired.

"The loss of a most pleasurable excursion, in a travelling chariot with four horses, as far north as Gretna Green, which that young gentleman had intended proposing to you this evening."

"You are joking, for Mr. Shuttleworth could scarcely be so very impertinent as to think of such a thing."

"I am quite serious, Miss Maxwell; for, notwithstanding the Colonel's rebuff, Mr. Alphonso persists in his belief of having inspired you with a flame as fervent as his own."

"Really," she said, "this is too ridiculous to be true, unless, poor man, he is of very weak intellect."

"Oh! not in the least; the son and father think themselves as strong in the head as they are in the pocket, and that all things, not excepting young ladies, are to be had for money."

"Then I hope they are now undeceived," as Edmund came up to offer his arm.

"Has it ever struck you, Edith," Edmund asked, "how ridiculous people appear to a looker-on, when hopping about, and jumping up and down, like a set of puppets moved by strings?"

"No," she said; "I have been generally too much engaged in the performance to notice the absurdity of the exhibition."

"And too fond of dancing," Edmund added, "to give up the amusement, if ever so absurd."

"I believe I like dancing more for the music than anything else."

"Except the company of a gay captain of dragoons."

"Or, I must substitute, an agreeable partner," she said.

"Then," he replied, "the Captain, I suppose, is included in your category of agreeable, gay, and handsome, and the most particularly interesting of all your partners."

"He may be all the former, without the latter," she replied, with a slight blush.

"Edith," he continued, "would you prefer joining in the dance to walking with me through the saloon, as I have had a fatiguing day, and do not feel up to dancing much to-night?"

"Then I think you had better sit down and rest yourself, which I shall be glad to do also, instead of performing puppet."

Having found two vacant chairs in the smaller saloon, which was nearly empty, Edmund addressed his fair companion in a low tone, from which all levity was banished.

"Edith," he said, with a sigh, "I have incurred the displeasure of one whom I have long regarded with the deepest feelings of affection and interest, by offering her advice when I knew it was needed. I will not run the risk of losing your friendship also, by perhaps ill-timed, unpalatable remarks. It is my failing—a natural one, of which I cannot divest myself—to love those I do love intensely, and to endeavour to avert from their heads, with greater eagerness than is consistent with the usages of social life, the evil I believe impending over them. This failing has cost me the favour of Agnes. Yours I cannot afford to forfeit in like manner, for I have regarded you as one of the very few friends I possess, and whose esteem and confidence I value most highly."

"I shall always consider your offering me advice, when you think I require it," she replied, "as the greatest proof of your friendship."

"Once before, Edith," he continued, "allusion has been made by me to the same subject, and now, since here, remarks have reached my ears, which compel me to warn you against receiving those attentions from Captain Duncombe which have attracted the notice of others. Oh! let me not see you also, like Agnes, blindly courting a fate wretched as hers; for the character of Captain Duncombe is precisely similar to that of Sir Digby Colville—the reverse of all that is noble or virtuous in man."

"Indeed you are mistaken," she replied, "in thinking Captain Duncombe ever has been or ever can be anything more to me than an acquaintance."

"I hope and trust, for your sake, Edith, that the case is so; but the world, judging by appearances only, thinks otherwise. You patronise him too much in public for merely a common acquaintance."

"You shall see, then, for the future, that I am not indifferent to your well-intended advice;" and the words had scarcely passed her lips, when the Captain made his approach, and, with a bow, said, "he believed Miss Maxwell had kindly promised him the honour of another dance?"

"You must have mistaken my meaning," she replied; "for what I said was that I could *not promise* you another."

"Am I then so unfortunate as to find you engaged for the whole evening?"

"I can only repeat my first answer," Edith said, rather formally, "that I must decline making any further engagement with you;" upon which the discomfited Captain withdrew.

"Are you engaged, then, for the next dance?" Edmund asked.

"No," she replied, "not for that, although I believe I am for nearly every other; but you see I have not forgotten the advice you gave me at my first ball."

"Will you dance with me then, Edith, the next quadrille, since I have kept you sitting here quite long enough, listening to my dull remarks?"

"With pleasure, if you do not feel too tired."

They were about rising to leave the saloon, when Sir Digby Colville entered with Lady Agnes leaning on his arm, and, from her downcast looks and blushing face, it was evident that some very interesting conversation was passing between them. Sir Digby appeared also unusually grave, addressing her in a very low tone of voice; and they were both so engrossed with themselves as to have approached within a short distance of Edmund and Edith before either was aware of their proximity, when Lady Agnes, on lifting her eyes and beholding them, started back in affright, and turned instantly round, but not before Edmund had observed her extreme agitation and confusion.

"Alas!" exclaimed he, as they retreated precipitately, "I fear my worst anticipations are realised—that Agnes has accepted that unprincipled man."

"I fear so too," was Edith's reply.

"But could not you, Edith, dissuade her from such folly?"

"No," she replied, sadly; "my influence has been unavailing, for, knowing the Earl's and your opinion of Sir Digby Colville, I have said all I could to induce her to refuse his attentions, and we had a serious disagreement on this subject, when she desired I should never mention his name to her again."

"Oh! what a fate will hers be," Edmund said, "if married to a spendthrift, gambler, and libertine! How infatuated women and with these heartless, plausible hypocrites, these men of the world, who talk of love and sentiment, unknown and unfelt by them, as pity by a tiger! And you too, Edith, with your sound sense and deep feelings of religion, appear to be taken also with a character equally worldly as that needy Irishman.'

"Indeed, indeed you are mistaken, Edmund; for nothing would induce me to accept Captain Duncombe: such a thought never entered into my mind."

"Oh, keep to that resolution, dear Edith," he said, earnestly; "and may God grant you a happier lot in marriage than that of your deluded friend. But oh! what a sad blow will this prove to my dear, kind godfather! Come, Edith," he said, abruptly rising, "I must not detain you here—my heart is too heavy now for dancing; yet come with me, I will soon find you a more cheerful partner."

"Oh, no, thank you; my thoughts, like yours, are gloomy also, at the prospect of this grievous disappointment to the poor Earl."

Edmund resumed his seat, for he felt how soothing to his wounded feelings was the gentle sympathy of this sweet girl, who showed by those melting eyes, and lowly modulated voice, how much she pitied his distress; but even to Edith, dearly as he loved her, like his own sister, he would not reveal the secret of his heart, and, fearing she might guess the truth, he turned the conversation into a more pleasant channel.

Whilst thus conversing together, Mrs. Maxwell entered the room in search of her daughter, exclaiming, "My dear Edith, I wondered what had become of you, not having seen you for the last half hour, and there is Mr. Chetwynd hunting everywhere for you, as you are engaged to him for this quadrille."

"I really beg his pardon, mamma, but I did not think we had been absent so long from the ball-room."

"It is all my fault, dear Mrs. Maxwell," Edmund said; "I alone am deserving your reproaches; but having had a hard day's hunting, I have felt in a very lazy humour to-night, and persuaded Edith to indulge me here, instead of dancing with her, where, I suppose," he added, with a laugh, "from your account of the lapse of time, I may have forgotten all about it, by indulging in a nap."

"Come, come, Edmund," said Mrs. Maxwell, cheerfully, "that is not very likely; you would scarcely treat Edith so unceremoniously; but now let us return to the dancers, for I do not wish her to appear rude to Mr. Chetwynd."

"You are not very angry with me, dear Mrs. Maxwell?" Edmund said, in a pleading tone.

"Not very, Edmund, if you will promise to be a good boy, and not commit the same fault again."

"Until the next time," he added, "that I am so tired as to wish to be lulled to sleep by Edith's sweet, musical voice."

"So you think, Edmund, by singing Edith's praises, to avoid my displeasure."

"Well, but dear Mrs. Maxwell, has she not a soft, sweet, silvery voice, like your own?"

"I will hear no flattery from you, Edmund; anything but that I can forgive; but, come, we really must return to the ball-room, for the Colonel is very irate, having been searching for Edith in vain; and here he comes, looking in a very irritable mood."

"Where have you been, Edith?" he asked, in a sharp tone. "I have been pacing through nearly every room on the ground-floor in search of you."

"Only here, dear papa," Edith answered.

"It is not proper for young ladies to be sitting with gentlemen in a room by themselves; it causes remarks to be made, which are not pleasant to a father's ears."

"We were not alone, dear papa; this room is open to the company."

"My dear Colonel," interposed Edmund, "pray spare poor Edith reproaches of which she is wholly undeserving; it was my fault, if fault it is, in detaining her contrary, I believe, to her own inclination, because I felt too tired by my day's exertions, or too lazy, if you will, to dance. Punish me as you please—I care not how severely—but pray spare the innocent."

A look from Mrs. Maxwell turned her lord's wrath in a moment.

"Well, well, Edmund," he replied, "we won't say any more about it; but having heard remarks to-night, and some very severe, too, on the flirtation of Lady Agnes, I did not like the idea of similar ones being made on Edith."

"Of that, my dear sir, you need not entertain the most remote apprehension; and I hope you will believe me as jealous of Edith's fair name as yourself."

"Yes, yes, Edmund, I do believe you; but I am rather out of temper to-night, by meeting that confounded cotton fellow here, whom I, of course, cut dead at once."

"I have felt my hand itch to horsewhip him, and his son too, ever since you told me of their conduct."

"Very bad; very dishonourable indeed, Edmund; but you must not quarrel with either on my account."

Fortunately for Edith a valse intervened, which saved her from appearing oblivious of her engagement to Mr. Chetwynd, upon whose approach Edmund sauntered through the crowd, and took up a position from which he could see the dancers; and his eyes were directed towards Edith and her partner with a closer scrutiny than he had ever regarded her with before. Whilst loving, and believing himself beloved by Lady Agnes, Edmund had not felt so deep an interest in her as to watch her movements and behaviour when dancing or conversing with other men. How was it that he found himself thus engaged now? It would be absurd to suppose him in love with Edith also; but, if asked by his dearest friend the true nature of his feelings towards her at that moment, a definition of them would have been impossible to himself.

When rejected by Lady Agnes, he felt desolate, dejected, and alone; his sister being the only friend to whom he dare confess the true feelings of his heart. Her sympathy had soothed him into something like resignation; he loved her more than ever for that sweet counsel she had given; for those soothing words she had spoken to calm his troubled breast. Again had that breast been pierced by another dart, when beholding Lady Agnes bestowing her affections on one whose name and character he detested. It was, then, while smarting from this fresh wound, that Edith Maxwell's sympathy, expressed more by looks than words, fell like the gentle dew upon parched ground, lulling his agonised feelings to rest. To her he had made no confession; of her he had asked no sympathy; he had never trusted her as a friend, yet had she shown a deeper interest in his happiness—for to her, it was clear, the cause of his depression was surmised, if not known—than he could have expected from any but his own sister. A feeling of deep gratitude sprung up forthwith in his heart towards this dear, gentle girl, and from that hour he resolved to watch over her with a brother's love, and a brother's jealous care. A new feeling towards her had now arisen; a new channel opened, into which his troubled thoughts might be diverted; there was one other being whom he could, and felt he must now love, as one sent to comfort him from a brighter sphere.

Whilst these thoughts occupied him, Major Townshend, whose nose, like that of Paul Pry, was ever poking and peering into odd corners and little by-nooks, whispered in his ear, "All settled, I see, Knightley; give you joy; you have made the best bargain of the two, by gad!"

"I don't understand you, Townshend; what do you mean?"

"Well, just come with me into the supper-room, and I will explain. Now," said the Major, helping himself to a glass of wine, "you know I am not a dancing man, so to pass the time, I just took a survey of the apartments, and on passing into the Marchioness's boudoir, by gad, sir! there I saw that long-legged Irish baronet kissing the hand of Lady Agnes up in the far corner."

"Nonsense, Townshend! your eyes must have deceived you."

"But my ears did not, Knightley; for, by gad, sir! I heard the smack; and if you had seen them when I coughed, by gad, sir! they sprang up as if a powder-flask had burst at their feet. Well, then, on peering into another room, I saw Edmund Knightley sitting with Edith Maxwell; and from his looks and manner, I jumped to the conclusion, that he had been doing pretty nearly, if not quite, the same thing; so I think, my boy, you have got the best of the two, although I did hear you were cut out for the peer's daughter."

"You are greatly deceived, Townshend, in supposing me making love to Miss Maxwell. I have never dreamt of proposing for her."

"Then, by gad, Knightley, begging your pardon, you are a bigger fool than I gave you credit for. Why, hang it, sir! a young fellow like you *must* be in love with some girl, and if not with Edith Maxwell or Lady Agnes, who is now bespoke, by gad, sir! I should like to know with whom you are in love?"

"Well, Townshend, suppose I don't choose to enlighten you on this very interesting subject?"

"Then I shall just draw my own conclusion—and, by gad, sir! I'll bet you a cool hundred that you marry or are engaged to Edith Maxwell before the opening day of next hunting season."

"You know I am not a betting man, and never risked more than a shilling upon any event in my life; but I give you my word—that as regards myself your conjectures are wholly unfounded; and, for the young lady's sake, I trust you will not express these chimerical opinions to other men."

"No, Knightley, I promise you I will not; although entertaining myself a very strong impression that there is love on one side, if not on both. And now, as Mrs. Major is impatient to return to her brats, I must say good night."

CHAPTER XXVI.

The Major was gone. Edmund Knightley stood alone in that long, lofty room. A new light had burst suddenly in upon his mind, from Major Townshend's words. He became abstracted and thoughtful, and, advancing to the fire-place, sat down in an easy chair, where, removed from view by a large screen, he could meditate for a while undisturbed.

"It may be," he thought, "as the Major says—it may be possible that Edith does regard me with warmer feelings than those of friendship—what then? I have no such love to offer in return; I can never love again. There is a void, a vacancy in my heart, which none other can fill; it is cold—too cold now to be warmed again by woman's smile. No, Edith, I trust you do not thus regard one who can make you no return. May you never feel what I have felt these last few weeks! May your first young hopes of joy and love never be withered in the bud like mine! May you never know that utter desolation of hope—that listless despondency of mind, which follows unrequited affection! But where could Edith love, and not be loved in return? and yet——"

The current of his thoughts was here interrupted by the approach of footsteps, to within a few feet of his position, and the well-known voice of Chetwynd struck his ear, who, after presenting an ice to his companion, said in a low tone, though every word seemed conveyed through the screen as a sounding board to his now excited attention—

"Dear Miss Maxwell, we are now alone, perhaps for a few brief moments only—but these are to me precious ones, long and eagerly sought, when I might lay open the feelings of my heart, whose every pulse since our first introduction has beaten for you alone."

"Mr. Chetwynd," interrupted Edith, in a gentle though firm voice, "I cannot listen to such language from you—pray spare me saying more."

"Oh, Edith! Edith! let me not appeal to that gentle heart in vain. Oh! could you know the deep abiding love, the respectful admiration, with which I have so long regarded you, you could not—would not, I feel, consign me to hopeless misery! Let me still live in hope that you may yet be propitious to my suit. I may have been too hasty in this early declaration of my sentiments—you may look upon me as nearly a stranger from our short acquaintance—but, oh! do not reject my suit until you know me better—until time shall prove the steadfast, unwavering love I feel for you."

"Pray cease, Mr. Chetwynd," Edith said, having made fruitless efforts to check his impassioned address; "spare me the pain of hearing more;" and the expression of her features showed how painful her feelings were.

"I see you feel for me," he continued; "your gentle nature revolts at the misery your words inflict. Oh, dearest Edith! give way to those gentle feelings of your heart; on my knees, I implore—entreat you—do not pronounce my doom;" and seizing her hand, he threw himself on one knee before her.

"Rise, Mr. Chetwynd," she said; "I cannot allow you to indulge the thought that time will effect any alteration in my sentiments towards you; pray release my hand."

"Edith," he continued, rising, and letting her hand fall, "is it then, as I fear, that you love another?"

Edmund listened eagerly—intensely—painfully for her reply. For a second or two, which seemed an hour of suspense to his excited mind, none was returned. "Hah!" he thought, "she does then love another!" when her voice after this slight pause was again heard, but now in an offended tone.

"Mr. Chetwynd will excuse me for saying he has no right to question my motives for declining his addresses, and I must beg instantly to return to the ball-room;" with which she turned away from the table towards the door, followed by Mr. Chetwynd, who said, "I beg your pardon, Miss Maxwell, if I have by any word of mine given you offence; but pray allow me to hope you will still regard me as a friend?"

To this there was no reply.

As they quitted the room, Edmund breathed more freely. His situation had been most painful—most distressing to an honourable mind. He had listened to a confession intended for Edith's ear only. But anxiety to know the secret of her heart had kept him silent—motionless—almost breathless in his chair. At first he thought of rising and poking the fire to warn Chetwynd of his presence, or of feigning sleep and snoring, but ardent curiosity prevailed.

"Will my fate be his also?" he asked himself. "Can Edith resist such earnestness of manner—such a deep, fervent appeal as his? No," he thought; "her gentle heart will melt on beholding his lowly position—his deep devotion. She will pity his feelings, and spare him even at the sacrifice of her own."

Such were the thoughts which passed rapidly and tumultuously through Edmund's mind as he listened to Chetwynd. He was astonished at her firm refusal of his suit, and her indignant manner when questioned as to her love for another. Who could that other be? Was it Duncombe or Reginald upon whom her first young affections had been bestowed?

Edmund was now turning from the room, and as he passed the place where Edith had been standing at the table, a little *vinaigrette*, in the shape of a heart, caught his eye, which, in her confusion having been left there, was instantly transferred to his pocket; and on reaching the ball-room he found the Earl, with Lady Agnes, Edith, and Mrs. Errington, waiting only for him to return home.

After a late breakfast the next morning, Lady Agnes excusing herself from appearing by being over-fatigued, Edmund said, "Edith, will you take a walk with me this fine day? It will restore the colour to your cheeks."

"Most willingly," she replied.

"Then I will be ready to escort you in half an hour, as I have two letters to write, and you will find me in the library."

At the time appointed, Edith made her appearance with a pretty new bonnet on, which became her exceedingly; and Edmund, lifting his eyes to her face, seemed for the first time struck with her surpassing loveliness.

"Will you put these letters for me in the letter-box in the hall," he asked, "while I fetch my hat?"

In a few minutes after they were walking in the pleasure-grounds, when Edmund said, "So, Edith, you lost your heart last night at the ball?"

"No, indeed I did not," she replied, with a deep blush, as she thought of Chetwynd's proposal.

"Excuse me, Edith, for contradicting you, but although not perhaps aware of the loss, you did certainly leave your heart behind you, and it was my good fortune to find it—see, here it is," producing the *vinaigrette*.

"Oh, yes," she said; "I remember now—I did leave it there, but where I could not tell."

"I found it lying on the supper-table," which caused the colour again to rush even to her forehead; "but I shall prize this little heart of yours dearly, if you will allow me to keep it."

"It is yours, Edmund, if you think such a trifle worth your acceptance."

"It is no trifling gift to me, dear Edith, and I shall ever value it most highly for your sake. Will you be here the day after to-morrow?" he asked, as they walked on, "for I must return to Wychwood this afternoon, and to-morrow being my hunting day, I shall remain there also that night."

"I fear mamma will be anxious for me to return home, although Agnes has begged me to remain with her a little longer."

"To help her to bear the storm which I fear is gathering," said Edmund, mournfully; "for I was told last night she had accepted that confounded baronet."

"Indeed, Edmund! I hope not, for the Earl has taken a great dislike to him; but Agnes has made no allusion to the subject, having scarcely mentioned his name."

"If what Townshend told me he saw last night be true," Edmund said, "we shall soon hear more about this unfortunate affair; and for the Earl's sake, dear Edith, let me beg you to remain at Woodborough a few days longer; but neither to him, Agnes, nor Mrs Errington, must you give intimation of what I have now told you."

"That you need not fear," she replied, "and I will endeavour to persuade mamma when she calls to extend my visit."

The next afternoon, when her mother called, Edith petitioned to remain a few days longer at Woodborough, upon which Mrs. Maxwell said—"Well, my love, as I fear there will be some dreadful work between the poor Earl and Lady Agnes, when he hears what I heard the other night, that she has accepted Sir Digby Colville, you can remain here another week, where your presence may be of some use to your kind old friend."

That same afternoon, whilst Edmund was out hunting, and Mrs. Maxwell had scarcely passed through the lodge gates of Woodborough Park, Sir Digby Colville called, and asking if the Earl was at home, was shown into the library, where, after a few preliminary remarks on the common topics of the day, he began breaking the object of his visit in the most courteous and deferential language—extolling the beauty and charms of Lady Agnes to the skies, and avowing the very deep impression she had made upon his heart.

When in the midst of this most enraptured harangue, the Earl's impatience could no longer be restrained, who said—

"I must decline, sir, listening to anything more on this subject, for I cannot possibly countenance your addresses to my daughter."

"May I beg, my lord, to be informed on what grounds, since I am quite willing that all necessary inquiries respecting my connections, fortune, and position should be made by your lordship, which I feel assured will prove quite satisfactory."

"I have neither the wish nor the intention of making any such inquiries, Sir Digby Colville, because they are wholly uninteresting to me."

"My lord, I am already assured that Lady Agnes reciprocates my sentiments; and I trust, therefore, your lordship will not thus summarily dismiss my suit."

"If, sir," continued the Earl, rising, "you have already attempted to win my daughter's affections without consulting her father, that fact, sir, alone is sufficient for me to decline at once the honour you purposed conferring on my family, by your contemplated union with my only child; and I must refuse hearing another word on this most painful subject."

Sir Digby Colville, perceiving by the Earl's excited manner that further pleading at that time would only increase his irritation, prudently withdrew, after expressing his deep sorrow for the premature disclosure he had made of his affection for Lady Agnes, which he hoped the Earl would pardon, on account of the overwhelming feelings with which her beauty had inspired him. Not another word, however, could be elicited from the indignant father, who sternly bowed him out of the room.

When his agitation had somewhat subsided, the Earl, returning to the drawing-room, found it tenanted only by Mrs. Errington, Lady Agnes having fled precipitately upon seeing Sir Digby riding up to the hall door.

"I fear, my dear lord," Mrs. Errington said, observing his perturbed looks, "you have had an unpleasant visitor."

"Yes, indeed I have, and dread, from what he admitted, that my infatuated child has already accepted this Irish speculator without consulting me."

"I suspect, my dear lord, something has occurred, from the altered demeanour of Lady Agnes since the *fête* at Dunkerton House, coupled with the remarks which reached me of her great flirtation with Sir Digby Colville that evening."

"Then, my dear Mrs. Errington, may I beg you to inform my daughter that I wish to speak with her immediately in my morning room."

On this message being delivered, Lady Agnes became excessively agitated, in anticipation of a severe lecture, if not more, from her father, whose just displeasure she felt conscious of having deserved.

"Oh! dear Mrs. Errington," she exclaimed, "I fear I have done wrong in accepting Sir Digby Colville; but indeed, indeed, I have become so deeply attached to him that life would be insupportable to me without him."

"You have been frequently warned by me, dear Agnes, not to encourage the attentions of this gentleman, of whom your father has heard very unfavourable accounts, so much so that I have told you that his objection to him will never be overcome. As your best friend, therefore, I advise you to give up all thoughts of ever marrying this Sir Digby Colville."

"Oh! that I cannot—will not do," she exclaimed, passionately; "I would rather die than give him up!"

"Well, my dear, I can say no more than I have already on this most distressing subject. The Earl is waiting to see you in his own room, and my last words are, be careful not to offend your father further, who has already spoilt you by too much indulgence, for on this point he seems very determined."

"So am I," *thought* the petulant beauty, as she descended the staircase.

Upon entering her father's room, she cast a timid glance at his face, and was struck by the sad and solemn expression of his features, as he desired her to take a chair.

"I have sent for you," he said, "to speak on a very serious matter—most serious it is to you, as concerning your future happiness, both in this world and that which is to come. I have warned you several times against accepting the attentions of Sir Digby Colville, but, notwithstanding, I have been grieved—most deeply grieved—to find that so far from my advice and warning being heeded, you have positively accepted that man for your guide and protector through life, and would leave your too indulgent and fond father to mourn alone the misery which, by such a rash step, you would entail upon me in my declining years."

"Oh! no, no, my dearest father—I would not leave you for all the world. Sir Digby has promised that I shall remain with you, at least half the year, if not longer, if I wish; that in this respect, as in all others, my wishes shall be his guide."

"Oh! no doubt," replied the Earl, with a bitter sneer; "this arrangement would be most agreeable to a man of his broken fortunes."

"Oh, no, papa—you are greatly mistaken and deceivedas to his fortune; he has a very fine place in Ireland."

"Which, of course," added the Earl, contemptuously, "every Irish gentleman has, mortgaged up to the lawn on which it stands; but as to income or money to support a wife, he has not sufficient to maintain himself, without horse-dealing and gambling! I have heard all concerning him—he has been for four or five years what is called a man about town—in other words, one who has been attending all fashionable assemblies there, in the hope of marrying a woman of fortune, to retrieve his lost estates and support his extravagance; but having failed to find any woman there silly enough to become his wife, he has now come down here in search of an heiress, and you, Lady Agnes, are the victim he has selected—the deceived, wretched dupe of this man's false pretensions and deep machinations. You are young, artless, and unsuspecting, and like a foolish girl, taken with the handsome person and plausible manners of this cunning man of the world. *I* am not so deceived, and to save you, my child, from misery, degradation, and want, I have positively refused Sir Digby Colville's proposal for your hand."

"Oh, papa," she said, imploringly, "you are, indeed, misinformed as to his true character; he is most amiable, most kind-hearted, and surely it is sufficient that he is Lord Dunkerton's most intimate friend. Can you suppose the Marchioness would permit such a person as he has been represented to you, to remain a guest in her house for more than three months?"

"The Marchioness has no voice in the matter," the Earl replied; "and his being Lord Dunkerton's most intimate friend is no recommendation to me. Once more, Lady Agnes, I repeat that this Irish baronet shall never, with my consent, become your husband; and I insist upon your never holding any further communication with him."

The Earl rose indignantly from his chair, and approached the fire-place, but when he again turned his head Lady Agnes was gone. Rushing to her own room, she locked the door, and gave way to an uncontrolled burst of passionate tears, inveighing bitterly against her father's cruelty to herself, and unjust reflections upon her lover.

CHAPTER XXVII.

UPON Edith's gaining admittance—not without considerable trouble—to her room half an hour after, she found Lady Agnes still indulging her grief, and refusing to be comforted.

"Oh, Edith!" she exclaimed, "you have never known what it is to love—and love with all the intensity of a first affection, or you would not mock my misery by advising me to give up all thoughts of marrying Sir Digby Colville."

"I give you, dear Agnes, the advice I should myself follow, not to marry, in direct disobedience to my father's wishes, any one, however estimable—however deserving of my affection. Of Sir Digby Colville's character and disposition you know nothing; all that you can know of him is what I know also, that he is handsome, agreeable, and of highly-polished manners; but upon such a very slender, superficial foundation as this, no girl with common reflection could expect any reasonable hopes of happiness for life. I have always given you my candid opinion of him since his first introduction to us; and I am sorry to say, dear Agnes, that opinion has been more confirmed every time we have since met."

"Oh! you are so prudish and particular, Edith, in your ideas of men, that you will never find one to realise such Utopian expectations—unless it be Edmund, whom I should think just the person to suit you; so amiable, so strict, so full of sentimentality and morality, that he is fit to become, as he is called, the Abbot of St. Austin's."

"If I ever do marry, Agnes, it will be one whom I can respect as well as love for his virtues, not fear for his vices; but as we shall never agree upon these points, it is useless my saying more; yet pray do not increase the Earl's displeasure by refusing to appear at dinner."

"You must excuse me, Edith; but after papa's cruel conduct and severe reflections upon Sir Digby Colville, I shall remain in my room—you can say, what is the truth, that I have a severe headache, and no wish for anything more than a cup of tea."

"Well, my dear Agnes, I have no doubt this must be the case, and I will come up and sit with you as soon as we leave the dining-room."

It is needless relating more of the pettishness and insubordination exhibited by Lady Agnes that evening and the following morning. Rejecting all counsel from Mrs. Errington and Edith, she continued to indulge her ill-humour and steadfast determination not to marry any other person than Sir Digby.

The next day, when Edmund arrived at Woodborough, he was informed by the Earl of all that had occurred and his fixed resolution never to accept Sir Digby Colville as his son-in-law, adding, that he felt not only surprised but exceedingly indignant at Lord Dunkerton's entertaining such a person in his house for so long a time, and abetting him in his attempt to deprive him of his only child.

"I must confess, my dear uncle, an absence of all surprise at the conduct of Lord Dunkerton, whose character will bear, perhaps, as little investigation as that of his friend, for you know the very trite old saying—'Birds of a feather flock together.' Dunkerton is not overburdened with morality, although for appearance' sake professing to observe certain conventional rules of society; but what can you expect from a confirmed racing and betting man, as well as gambler? He has already lowered himself, in the opinion of all honourable men, by inviting black-legs to his house, and treating such persons as his familiar friends, so that they even talk as lightly of him as one of their own class—and the poor Marchioness mourns and laments in silence her husband's depravity, without daring to utter a word of remonstrance—for Dunkerton has a fearful temper; in short, since his connection with these black-legs and blackguards he has lost all respect, even for himself."

"I was not aware of these things, Edmund," the Earl replied, "or should not have been present at his ball."

"It would be hard, uncle, to punish poor Emily for the sins of her husband; and on her account many visit there who would not otherwise be seen at Dunkerton House."

"Then, my dear Edmund, it is the more incumbent on me strenuously to resist, as I have already, any further overtures from this Irish baronet, and save my child from a more wretched fate than that of the Marchioness."

"There can be little doubt, I fear, dear uncle, as to the ultimate result, should Agnes persist in marrying this man; but the question is, how can it be avoided? for if treated with too much severity, I fear, from her haughty disposition, she will break out into open rebellion; and she may possibly by you, and by you only, be led—although I am quite sure she will never be driven to act contrary to her own inclinations. I would, of course, my dear uncle, do anything in my power to dissuade her from this false step; but you know my influence is entirely gone, and she now regards me with suspicion, if not aversion."

"Ah, Edmund! it is a sad, sad return I have experienced from this wayward, undutiful girl; but Mrs. Errington has often warned me that she would be spoilt by my too great and culpable indulgence—she has never been refused or checked in anything."

"You, my dear uncle," added Edmund, "have allowed her to have her own way so long, I fear she will have it still."

"Have you no interest with your friend," Edmund asked, when he and Edith were alone in the afternoon, "to dissuade her from the contemplation of such a wretched connection?"

"No," Edith replied, "I fear none—neither has Mrs. Errington, to whom she expressed her determination, if obliged to wait by her father so long, to marry Sir Digby when she became of age—but that nothing should induce her to give him up. This Mrs. Errington dare not tell the Earl; neither must you, Edmund, for it would only increase his unhappiness."

"You do not think then, Edith, she will run away with this fortune-hunter?"

"I really cannot say, Edmund, although she is so infatuated as to do almost anything he might suggest, if treated here with too great severity."

"Would you act thus, in disobedience to your father's wishes, Edith, were you attached to a person he did not approve?"

"No," she replied; "how can you suppose I would?"

"Well, no, I did not suppose you would; but should the Colonel press you to marry any one you did not love?"

"I do not think papa would be so unkind."

"Well, but suppose he were to do so—for he is very peremptory sometimes?"

"As I would not act in opposition to his wishes, neither would I marry any person in opposition to my own."

"Well, Edith, I think this stipulation is most fair and reasonable, and I trust for your own sake you will maintain this very prudent and proper resolution—for marriage is indeed a most serious obligation, and seldom viewed by young girls in its really solemn light. Parents, also, think too much of worldly things to consider sufficiently their children's true interest, in seeing them *well* married, instead of being richly married."

Lady Agnes, continuing to indulge her ill-humour, did not choose to appear at the dinner table that evening, which passed heavily away, unenlivened even by a note of music. The week had now expired, when Edith was to leave Woodborough, which she could now do without reluctance, all her efforts to induce Lady Agnes to alter her behaviour towards her father having proved unavailing—in fact, her patience had become exhausted by the persevering pettishness of this self-willed girl, with whom she now felt little community of feeling. As a last attempt, however, to divert her mind from dwelling so entirely upon this subject, she endeavoured to persuade her to spend a few days at Morton Grange, and this invitation being also declined very positively, Edith returned home.

During her absence, Mr. Chetwynd had called upon the Colonel, renewing his proposal formally to her father, whose consent was readily obtained to favour his suit; for Chetwynd, having discovered his reluctance to part with money during his lifetime, had entered fully into the business part of the matter, offering to make a very handsome settlement upon Edith, without requiring anything in return.

"You see, Chetwynd," the Colonel remarked on his first broaching the subject, "I have not the slightest objection to yourself, but just the reverse—yet Edith is my only child, and I shall indeed feel, as will Mrs. Maxwell also, quite lonely without her—in short, I do not wish her to marry for a year at least. Moreover, my income is chiefly derived from land, except a few loose thousands in the funds, which it would be ruinous work to sell out at present prices; and as a friend and neighbour I may tell you, that I intended investing all my spare cash in the purchase of a few fields here and there interspersed with my property, to render it more complete, so that at my death Edith will reap the benefit—since all I possess will of course go to her and her husband, if she selects one I approve."

"You have quite mistaken me, my dear sir," Chetwynd replied, "if you suppose my proposal for your daughter's hand influenced in the slightest degree by mercenary motives—for not one shilling of the money would I deprive you of that you proposed investing in the improvement of your estates. I have enough, and more than enough already; so that I propose settling on your daughter five hundred a year as pin-money, to be at her own disposal, and two thousand a year in the event of my decease. The rental of my other estates, exceeding ten thousand a year, would provide for any children of the marriage.

"Very handsome indeed, Chetwynd—nothing can be more liberal; but as to pin-money, I shall, of course, make Edith a sufficient allowance to render her in that respect totally independent of her husband."

"Then, may I hope, my dear sir, Mrs. Maxwell and yourself will use your influence to further my hopes of happiness with your most lovely and amiable daughter, to obtain whose hand I would cheerfully resign all I have in the world—in fact, my dear sir, she has inspired me with a passion so fervent and devoted that I feel I cannot exist without her."

"Well, well, Chetwynd, this sounds very romantic; but knowing you to be of a sanguine temperament, I dare say you feel what you express—although men at your time of life don't often die for love."

"I have never, Colonel, really known what love was, until bewitched, as I most certainly am now—fascinated—enraptured by the irresistible charms of Miss Maxwell."

"Well, well, Chetwynd, but we really do not wish to part with her yet, as she is very young, and has seen nothing of the world; I cannot go further than by saying, we thoroughly approve and shall be happy to sanction your addresses, although we do not wish her to enter into any positive engagement just at present."

"I thank you, dear sir, for your good wishes, most heartily and gratefully; but I should have told you that I did venture, at Dunkerton's ball, to express my sentiments to Miss Maxwell rather warmly, by which she appeared so taken by surprise, that I requested she would consider and reserve her final answer until we met again."

"Very well, Chetwynd; after what you have now told me, I should advise you to defer re-opening the subject for some time, and continue your visits as before, in your previous character of a friend."

"Yes, my dear Colonel, perhaps it will be best for me to adopt your suggestions; afterwards, when supported by yourself and Mrs. Maxwell, I have every reason to hope for success."

CHAPTER XXVIII.

Many hours had not elapsed before Alphonso's bad luck in his wooing was communicated to the Marquis, by his esteemed friend Duncombe, in a manner so confidential, that it had, within a brief space of time, become public property; that is, everybody knew everything about it, and a great deal more than had actually occurred; the story, snow-ball fashion, having gained considerably in its rolling progress, so that our poor hero had been represented as kicked out of Morton Grange by the peppery old Colonel, for daring to aspire to his daughter's hand. There is a very trite, though true old aphorism, "Save me from my friends;" and it must be confessed that Alphonso's particular chum, enraged by his presuming to act for himself, set the ball a-going with a very malicious kick.

The Captain, whose inventive faculties were generally on the stretch to assist others as well as himself, volunteered a little private suggestion to the Marquis on this event.

"What think you, Dunkerton," he asked, "of this soft young gentleman for your cousin Lady Gertrude? He will be just in the humour now to catch at a pretty bird like her."

"Well, Duncombe, it is not a bad idea; but her little ladyship is as proud as a peacock, and will never put up with the old lady bear as a mamma-in-law."

"Oh! confound the old woman," exclaimed the Captain; "she can be muzzled or strangled, or something of the kind; of course she would never think of living with her; but the cub is not so much amiss, and may be licked into something bearable; and the Governor, as he is called, will pass muster well enough."

"That cotton fellow is a shrewd, sharp-witted man of business, Duncombe, and if he lets me into a secret as to these railway shares I will patronise him; but the Marchioness won't stand that *has*pirating old woman."

"For which I cannot blame her, my lord; but you can invite the papa and son to a dog party, and that sort of thing, without that piece of vulgarity being included."

In somewhat less than ten days after this conversation had taken place, Lady Gertrude Lennard made her appearance at Dunkerton House, and the day after her arrival the Captain and his victim were asked to dine there, after hunting with the Marquis.

Lady Gertrude, as to stature, might be about two inches above the standard of a pocket Venus; of fair and almost transparent complexion, and light auburn hair. She was now in her twenty-sixth year, having seen several London seasons; and being the eldest of a family of three sons and four other daughters, her mother, the Countess of B——, began to entertain certain misgivings as to her adopting any other name, and thereby making way for her younger sisters, two of whom had already made their *début* in fashionable life; and it must be confessed, Lady Gertrude herself began to feel rather solicitous about changing her state, and possessing a home she could call her own, provided it contained the neeessary comforts and luxuries to which she had been accustomed.

To say that at first sight the appearance of our hero comported in the least degree with her preconceived ideas of what a husband out to be, would be absurd. She had moved too much amongst polished men of the highest orders, not to be struck immediately with the contrast; but having youth and tolerably good looks in his favour, she thought he might be made, with a good deal of drilling, presentable after a time to her aristocratic acquaintance. He seemed soft and plastic enough to be moulded into something passable, so that, if she could make up her mind to marry him, she had every reason to think he would become a very obliging and obedient husband.

Alphonso, on the other hand, felt not only flattered, but exceedingly pleased, with her animated and agreeable conversation during the dinner hour, when he sat next to her; the little heightened colour which occasionally visited her cheeks, with a very bewitching smile, rendering her most interesting in his eyes, and he never felt so much at home with any young lady before. Lady Gertrude chatted away as if she had known him for two years, instead of two hours; in short, to use his own expression, "she did all the talking for him." He never could get on with Edith Maxwell; she was not a talkative young lady; and although her smile seemed to invite, her reserve repelled him. Alphonso began to think he had committed a great mistake by fancying himself in love with her. She was not, he thought now, at all the person to have suited him.

How fortunate it is, for some people, they can be so easily satisfied, that the grapes which they cannot reach must be very sour! Although Alphonso might be supposed still smarting from the effects of Cupid's darts, yet in reality there existed no such feeling as pure love within his heart; he had never experienced what true love was, and the Captain very naïvely remarked, "that he hadn't got it in him." There was not the most infinitesimal part of it to be detected by the most accurate analysis, in the whole composition of his frame, physical, spiritual, or mental. The material of which our hero was composed resembled a bale of cotton, not gun cotton, for there was not a particle of explosive matter belonging to him. His passions even moved slowly and sluggishly, like a deep sulky stream, with a heavy muddy bottom.

The character of Alphonso is not an over-coloured picture; it is true life. I have known more than one original Alphonso, who never have loved, and never could love anybody but themselves, from boyhood to manhood, and from manhood to old age; disinterested affection has been a stranger to their hearts. They have married, some more than once, and would have married half a dozen wives if they could, yet have they never experienced what true love is. Alphonso was nettled—a term very expressive of his mental feelings, as compared with that bodily irritation experienced from the sting of that weed or plant, the bite of which most men have had cause to remember—by the treatment he had received from the Colonel, and by his daughter's haughtiness at the ball, the cause of which yet remained *in ambiguo*.

He and his father had been received and *fêted* at Dunkerton House, and here he was now, sitting beside Lady Gertrude Lennard, who, if not so handsome as Edith Maxwell, yet appeared nearly as fascinating, more agreeable, quite as good-tempered, and, what was of immense consequence in his sight, a lady in her own right. "Ah," he thought, "if I could persuade her to become Lady Gertrude Shuttleworth, that would be a go indeed. To be cousin to the Marquis of Dunkerton! my lucky stars!" reasoned Alphonso, "what a go that would be; going right a-head of the fussy old Colonel, and all the country squires in Huntingshire!"

The close of the hunting season had now arrived. It was the last lawn meet with the Marquis of Dunkerton's fox-hounds. A grand breakfast has been prepared, to which all are welcome, yet of which few partake. At eleven o'clock the lawn in front of the house presents a most animated spectacle. There are at least five hundred horsemen there assembled in every variety of costume. The pink coats of the Knightley hunt contrasted favourably with the more sombre, yet more coveted dark green livery of the Marquis. Beyond this concourse of equestrians is a half circle or outer ring formed by carriages of all descriptions, drawn up as on a race-course, containing the female portion of the neighbouring gentlemen's families ; the wives and daughters of the principal tradesmen from the fashionable town of Waterton, who patronise the Marquis's hunt, are also there, to see and be seen. Every man and boy, living within a radius of ten miles, who can muster horse or pony, adds his quota to the cavalcade.

On the outside of this group, between the ring formed by carriages and horsemen, a space is left for the hounds and their attendants to parade up and down for the gratification of the ladies, until the Marquis makes his appearance on the lawn. On the gravel drive in front of the house, with a few others containing particular friends, stands the carriage of the Marchioness, now, as the clock strikes twelve, occupied by herself and Lady Gertrude Lennard; at one side our friend Alphonso is stationed, on his favourite hunter Mameluke, attempting to say some pretty things to the fair Gertrude, who, being mischievously disposed that morning, and observing Mameluke's dread of her parasol, gave it an occasional twirl, thereby occasioning Mameluke to make sundry sudden retrograde movements, greatly to the discomfiture of Alphonso (who was twice all but unhorsed), and the extreme delight of her little ladyship, who enjoyed the fun so much that she was obliged to lower her parasol, to prevent her admirer observing her exceeding merriment at his expense. Having, however, tormented him in this manner for some twenty minutes, the offensive flag was dropped for a time, to admit of his nearer approach.

"Your horse seems very nervous, Mr. Shuttleworth," she remarked, with the most provoking *nonchalance.*

"It is your parasol which frightens him, Lady Gertrude, and I wish to goodness you would put it down for a few minutes."

"Well, I can oblige you thus much, until the sun again breaks forth. I have been introduced to Miss Maxwell this morning, and so far from agreeing with what you said about her yesterday, I think her the most interesting, lovely girl I have ever seen—quite beautiful, Mr. Shuttleworth."

"Ah ! some people think her so," he replied, "but I don't."

"Have you always entertained that opinion ?" Lady Gertrude asked, with a very inquisitive, meaning look, which caused Alphonso, in his confusion, to give Mameluke a dig in the ribs. Not relishing this treatment, he dashed forward, bringing his master's knee between the hind wheel and pannel of the barouche, whereby he was forthwith dislodged from the saddle, and thrown upon his back, just opposite Lady Gertrude, who could not suppress a rather loud laugh at his grotesque position, which was further increased by an exclamation from an adjoining carriage, "Oh! me gracious! if there ain't our Halphonso kicked off by that nasty Marmeluke!"

Our hero never picked himself up so nimbly before, and, to use the Captain's term, "he cut away like a thief who had prigged a pocket handkerchief," for he felt that Edith Maxwell's eyes, as well as Lady Gertrude's, were bent upon him.

As Alphonso precipitately retreated, Reginald Knightley rode up, and addressing Lady Gertrude, said, "How can you patronise such a cub?"

"Dunkerton patronises him, why should not I, Mr. Knightley?"

"If from the same motive," Reginald replied sarcastically, "some excuse may be made for you."

"I don't understand your meaning," she said, rather haughtily.

"If you do not, then there is no necessity for giving you any further explanation; but is that the sort of person you would like to be seen dancing with at Almack's?"

"Perhaps not, Reginald; yet he is passable in the country."

"*Im*passable anywhere, Gertrude, without striking one as a clod."

"Well," she replied, "he is reported as passing rich, which will pass him anywhere, even at Almack's."

"There are some animals which are dear at any price, and that fellow is one of them. He may be had on easy terms, no doubt, by any pretty woman like yourself, who will take the trouble to catch him; but what a fish to hook!"

"A gold fish, at least, you must admit, Reginald," she said, laughing.

"But were I a woman, which, thank goodness, I am not—don't misunderstand me as reflecting upon the sex, but their unlucky position as compared with ours—I would much rather have a silver one, that is, a poorer man and a gentleman; but what have we coming this way?" he exclaimed, on turning his head; "by all that's ludicrous! *Père* Shuttleworth, as I live! (bowing to the Marchioness) in your ladyship's livery! Well!" he continued, "I have heard of a hog in armour, although why one of the porcine race should ever have been encased in a coat of mail I never could understand; but, pray look, Emily," addressing the Marchioness, "do look at this extraordinary figure."

"I had rather not, Reginald, or he may see me; pray move your horse to screen me from his sight," which Reginald did as desired, just as Papa Shuttleworth, on passing, had raised his hat; and as at the same time he gave his horse a prick with his spur, that animal lashed out with his right leg, giving the cotton-spinner such a crack on his boot that, losing his equilibrium, he rolled out of his saddle, and lay sprawling on the ground.

"Oh, Reginald!" exclaimed the Marchioness, in affright, "what have you done? I fear the poor man is sadly hurt."

"Merely followed your Ladyship's instructions," Reginald said, in the most unconcerned manner; "but my horse is apt to lift his legs rather high sometimes, especially when he does not like his company."

"Ah, Reginald, you are more wickedly inclined, I fear, than your horse."

"The most innocent, harmless young man in the whole county, begging your ladyship's pardon."

To account for Mr. Shuttleworth's appearance at the lawn meet, we must state that, although decidedly disinclined to equestrian exercise, he had been induced, by Captain Duncombe's representations, to honour the Marquis by his attendance upon this gala day, having been offered the button, the badge of honour, as the proprietor of some large fox coverts in his lordship's hunt.

"Riding, my dear sir," the Captain replied, in answer to his excuses, "is out of the question on this occasion; you can sit on horseback, I suppose, like scores of others you will meet there; you will show yourself on the lawn, half the county will see you in the Marquis's livery, as a member of his hunt, you can appear at the public breakfast, sip your glass of liqueur, re-mount your horse, take a look at the hounds, make your bow to the Marchioness in her barouche, and when we trot off to find our fox, you can trot home again."

The little disaster incidental to his polite bow to the Marchioness suggested to Shuttleworth senior the necessity of adopting the latter part of the Captain's advice without a moment's delay; for the crack upon his leg, coupled with his roll out of the pig-skin, had not only caused most uncomfortable sensations about his whole corporeal, but little dazzling lights were also playing before his eyes, inducing the belief that he was surrounded by myriads of shooting stars, rather than the horses, and hounds, and gay equipages attending the Marquis's grand meet.

Escaping from the throng, Mr. Shuttleworth rode for an open gate leading into a grass field, through which he had passed in the morning, and feeling unable to retain his seat much longer, reeled out of it and lay upon the ground, where he remained for some ten minutes unconscious of all around him.

"Ah, he'll do now," were the first words which reached his ear, as he opened his yet dull and heavy eyes, staring vacantly around him.

"Better have a drop more, sir," continued the voice of one of the under-keepers; "you be all right again now," putting the mouth of a small bottle to his lips.

Revived by the spirit and water, Mr. Shuttleworth attempted to rise from his sitting posture, in which he had been supported by the knee of the keeper.

"Better bide still a bit longer, sir; you bain't yerself yet."

"Why, where am I? what has happened?"

"Just a mossel of a faint, that's all, sir. Bill there's a-holding of your 'oss, and the hounds be sure to come our way, when they've done with that ladies' fox in the gorse."

"Show me the road home, my friend," exclaimed Père Shuttleworth, roused to energetic action by the dread of being again involved amongst hounds and horsemen. "Oh, dear!—oh! my leg pains me so, I cannot walk."

"Get on your 'oss, then, sir," suggested the keeper.

"No, no, my friend, I could not sit him now; can't you get me a conveyance to Hardington?"

"All the gentlefolk's carriages be gone whome, sir, but there's the butcher's cart a-coming from the park."

"Ah! well, that must do—anything but riding;" and after rewarding the under-keeper, and giving directions to Bill to bring his horse home, thus ingloriously returned the proud moneyed man from the first and last of his lawn meets.

CHAPTER XXIX.

We must now return to Woodborough Park, where we left Lady Agnes indulging bitter feelings against her father for his refusal to accept Sir Digby Colville. During the first few days after this her grievous disappointment, she gave way to her uncontrolled bad humour, resolutely refusing to leave her room, under the pretext of severe indisposition, and notwithstanding Mrs. Errington's gentle expostulations and unceasing endeavours to induce her petulant pupil to view her father's decision in its proper and true light, as solely solicitous about her own future happiness, she continued obdurately sullen and silent, not condescending at last to make her fondly attached governess and friend any reply.

In the second week, however, a gradual change in her manner was perceptible. She became more cheerful, expressed to Mrs. Errington contrition for her past conduct, and made her appearance at the breakfast and dinner table as usual. Another week passed, and the Earl, hearing from Edmund that Sir Digby Colville had left Dunkerton House, began to think, from his daughter's apparent return of affection towards himself, that she had now seen the folly of her choice.

Not so reasoned Mrs. Errington, who suspected some latent cause for this smooth surface, which to her seemed as a lull before some gathering storm, though she felt reluctant to communicate her suspicions to the Earl, since there was no foundation for them. On the night of the last lawn meet at Dunkerton, Lady Agnes retired to her own room rather earlier than usual, complaining of a bad headache, which from its frequent occurrence excited no further attention, and Edmund not being expected to return that evening, the Earl and Mrs. Errington soon after sought their own apartments.

That night a presentiment of coming evil took such possession of Mrs. Errington's mind, that she could not sleep; although weary, she felt nervous and restless, with that throbbing pulsation of the head, when laid upon the pillow, which forbids repose. As she lay thus agitated without any apparent cause—for nothing had transpired that day to occasion her any fresh uneasiness or alarm—she fancied she heard a step near the bedroom door of Lady Agnes. She listened in breathless suspense. The sound again reached her ear; she sprang instantly from her bed, and hastily putting on her dressing-gown, approached the door of her own room. Here she again stopped to listen—all was silent through that long corridor—so silent that she could hear the beating of her own heart. Still she was not satisfied, she felt convinced her ear had not deceived her. The cold was bitter, piercing to her limbs, which shivered as she stood, yet dared not move.

The house clock struck the hour of twelve; it was midnight, the time when strange sounds are heard, strange sights are seen by the superstitious. Mrs. Errington was not one of these; yet as the last stroke told out its dying tale of departing night, with its long-drawn sigh through the old oak hall below, a feeling of dread—for what she could not account—crept over her trembling frame. She dreaded to remain longer there, yet feared to return to her bed. The embers in the grate still sent forth a red lurid light, and drawing her easy chair close to the fender, she sat down to warm her chilled feet; her sense of hearing stretched painfully to its utmost limits, to catch the least passing sound. Silence still reigned around, broken only at intervals by the low moaning of the wind.

Again one stroke from the old clock rang through the house; but ere its last echo had died away, another sound smote upon her ear. She sprang quickly, though noiselessly to the door, and on opening it she confronted a slight, trembling form gliding hastily along the corridor. It was that of Lady Agnes, equipped in travelling costume, who, thus suddenly surprised, stood motionless and confounded before her.

Mrs. Errington, fearing to disturb the Earl, laid her hand upon her pupil's arm, whispering only, "Come with me." On returning to her room, Lady Agnes threw herself upon the sofa, and covering her face with her hands, burst into tears.

"Oh! Agnes," exclaimed Mrs. Errington, sitting down beside her, and taking her trembling hand in hers, "is it thus, my poor deluded child, you would steal from your father's house, like a thief in the night?"

A fresh outbreak of grief followed this pathetic address, and throwing herself into Mrs. Errington's arms, she wept bitterly. Mrs. Errington did not attempt at first to check her falling tears, but straining her to her heart, and pressing her lips upon her burning cheek, gave way herself to her pent-up feelings, and mingled her tears with those of Agnes. For some moments neither spoke; the heart of each, during that trying scene, being too full for the utterance of words. At length Mrs. Errington whispered, "Agnes, will you leave me now?"

No response followed this touching appeal, but again her tears flowed fast, and she pressed the hand of her kind instructress to her lips.

"Agnes," she continued, "listen to my words—do not bring misery and disgrace upon your poor father by such an unhallowed act as this. If resolved to marry this man, which I see you are, let that ceremony be performed in the light of day, and with proper witnesses to attest its legality, as befits the only daughter of a noble house. Promise me not to make another attempt to attain the object of your wishes in this clandestine manner, and in return for that promise, should you continue in the same mind, I will endeavour to obtain the Earl's consent, and no allusion to what has now occurred shall ever escape my lips. Will you give me this sacred promise, Agnes?"

"Yes, dearest Mrs. Errington, I will," Lady Agnes faltered out.

"I thank you, my dearest child, for that promise, which will save you from those bitter reflections invariably attending such unblessed unions as these. You are young and inexperienced in the ways of the world, and in the opinions of worldly men. Sir Digby Colville would be the first to despise you for this too ready compliance with his wishes—and treat you afterwards with cold indifference or contempt; for man's disposition is to despise even the woman he loves, if, in consenting to become his wife, she forgets the respect due to her sex. And now, my dear child, I will leave you to your rest, and to thank the Almighty, I hope, for this providential interruption to your intended wretched flight."

Whatever the faults of Lady Agnes—and she had, like ourselves, many—falsehood was not one. She would speak the truth; and her promise often given to Mrs. Errington on previous occasions, even when a child, had never been broken.

Mrs. Errington, upon calm reflection, felt she had prescribed for herself a most difficult, and perhaps thankless task; yet, under these extraordinary circumstances, she believed it to be the wisest course she could have adopted, from a thorough knowledge of her pupil's determined disposition; for if placed under restraint and surveillance, she would assuredly rebel against them, and renew her attempts to escape. She had heard also sufficient of Sir Digby Colville to doubt his faith and honour in a clandestine marriage with this infatuated girl, if celebrated after the Scotch fashion; and even if properly and legally performed, all her own money would inevitably pass into her husband's hands. Strong in the conviction, therefore, that she had pursued the most prudent course, her next step was to induce the Earl to acquiesce in her views, with whose scruples and deeply rooted antipathy to the man of his daughter's choice, she had to undergo a severe contest.

The Earl at first was quite astounded by Mrs. Errington's proposition; but as she gradually and most feelingly proceeded to unfold her opinion of the case, his attention became more engaged, and he began to see the hopeless position in which he was placed.

"You cannot coerce, my dear Lord," she said, "your too long spoilt, though deeply-loved child; she has always been allowed, and will still have, her own way; and it is to avoid her certain misery and disgrace, by being thrown entirely into the power of this man, that, after long consideration, I give you that advice, however painful to my own heart, which I should be compelled to adopt were Lady Agnes my own daughter. And you know, my dear Lord, I could scarcely love her more, were it even so. You can then have secured to her, for life at least, the money to which she is entitled, and save it from her husband, by whom, in the other event, it might be squandered, and she left penniless, or solely dependent on his will."

"You have, I fear, my dear friend," the Earl replied, "given me the best counsel, although it is hard, very hard, for a father thus to yield to his child; but I feel now, when, alas! too late, the consequences of my mistaken indulgence. Still I must have time for consideration, and weigh well all you have said."

"And I, my dear Lord, shall still use all my power to avert the evil, though I fear we cannot now avoid it."

After two days' deliberation, and long consultation with Edmund, the Earl was induced to give a reluctant consent to the marriage taking place at the expiration of three months, stipulating that the settlements should be drawn up by his own solicitor, that the marriage should be strictly private, and solemnised in the parish church of Woodborough, although he should not be present at it.

The result of this decision being communicated to Lady Agnes, her promise was obtained, by Mrs. Errington, to comply with these conditions, and in the event of Sir Digby Colville not agreeing to them, the match should be broken off. Both the Earl and Edmund believed that no gentleman would submit to these humiliating terms; but they were yet more disgusted with Sir Digby's character, upon learning a few days afterwards, from Mrs. Errington, that under pretence of the excessive love he felt for Lady Agnes, her hand would be a sufficient recompense for the indignity offered him by her father.

The true state of the case was: the Irish Baronet, having ascertained that she had fifty thousand pounds at her own disposal, and so much more on attaining the age of twenty-one, resolved at any hazard to clutch this prey which had so unexpectedly fallen in his way, when all his speculations on a successful venture in a matrimonial bargain had through many previous years been doomed to disappointment.

A week had not elapsed since Sir Digby Colville's acquiescence in these conditions, as communicated by letter to Lady Agnes, when the Earl was astonished by his appearance at Woodborough, but at the same time so indignant, that, refusing an interview, he requested Mrs. Errington to inform him that any communication he had to make must be addressed to his solicitor, as he should decline any conference with Sir Digby himself.

The Irish Baronet seemed exceedingly mortified by this repulse, having indulged the hope of being now received at Woodborough as the Earl's son-in-law elect; but he now found the old peer composed of much sterner stuff than his friend Dunkerton (to whose house he had again returned) had led him to suppose. The fact was, that the Earl still hoped by these rebuffs to debar Sir Digby from proceeding further in his suit; but he little knew, until it became gradually developed, the true character of the man he had to deal with, who, to gain his point, would submit to almost any indignity. The Earl, however, resolutely maintained his determination not to admit Sir Digby to any private interviews, and his communication with his daughter was therefore carried on by letter.

We need make no further comments upon this most unpleasant and unsatisfactory state of things at Woodborough. It may suffice to state that the settlements were drawn up by the Earl's solicitor, in the most stringent manner possible, although by the will under which Lady Agnes became possessed of a hundred thousand pounds, bequeathed by her grandfather, she had the free disposal of this property at her decease, if dying without issue.

Two months had now elapsed; the conditions in the settlement had been assented to by Sir Digby Colville; and as it appeared to Edmund nothing now could intervene to avert the fate of Lady Agnes, his resolution was taken to leave home, in the hope that time and travel might in some measure alleviate his bitter feelings of disappointment and sorrow, which he had struggled in vain to subdue. There was distraction in the thought of witnessing the union of her he had once loved so entirely, with another, and that other a man he despised and detested more and more for his servile and worldly character. The certain consequences to Lady Agnes also preyed upon his mind, so that he told his sister he could remain no longer in that part of the country, unless she wished to see him in a madhouse.

"Go, then, my dear Edmund, I will not oppose your intentions now—you have endured many weeks of trial and sorrow to oblige me. I would not harrow up your past feelings by asking you to remain another week. Our old friends the Egertons are at Florence, why not join them? You can make a tour to beguile your thoughts, and return to us, I trust, before the next hunting season, with amended spirits and a lighter heart."

No sooner had Edmund obtained his sister's approval of his plan than he became impatient of its execution. He felt a feverish longing now to leave those scenes with which his first budding hopes of love and happiness had been so intimately blended, and by escaping from which he hoped to escape also partly, if not wholly, from the harrowing thoughts those scenes continually presented to his harassed mind.

The Earl could offer no opposition to his wishes.

"It is better you should leave us now," he said, "my poor, dear boy, since you cannot do any good by remaining longer, neither could I expect you to be present at a ceremony which even my eyes will never behold. Go, my dear Edmund, for the present—change will perhaps soften, if not obliterate, the remembrance of the past. You are young, and another love may warm your heart. Mine is now cold and crushed for ever."

"Oh, say not so, my dear, kind uncle—things may turn out better than we expect. Sir Digby Colville may prove a good husband, and, when married, may change his former course of life—let us at least hope for the best."

"Hope, which comes to all, comes not to me, my dear Edmund," the Earl replied, sorrowfully; "I am desolate and alone."

"Oh! not alone, dear uncle, I will soon return and never leave you more."

"Then go, dear Edmund—go at once; do not delay your

departure now another day—you will the sooner return to me again; but write, write by every post; your letters will be a consolation, something to cheer me day by day, till with God's permission we meet again. And now, my dear boy, not to prolong my misery at this parting, may the Almighty bless and protect you!" and folding him in his arms, the old peer, unable to suppress his emotion, burst into tears; but quickly recovering himself, he brushed them away, and, after one more silent and fervent embrace, left the room.

Edmund could not in his present state of feelings trust himself to a last interview with Lady Agnes, to whom he requested Mrs. Errington to convey his kind regards and best wishes and hopes for her future happiness. He had now only one more farewell visit to pay; he must bid adieu to Edith Maxwell, and, as he rode on to Morton Grange, a new train of thoughts occupied his mind. "Would she be Edith Maxwell still when he revisited her present home again?" He thought of the many happy days he had spent with this sweet, lovely girl, and an envious, jealous feeling crept over his heart when he contemplated her as the wife of another man. "Ah!" he murmured, "a barrier will then be placed between us, which none may pass. She will be the property of another; his will and wishes a law to her, upon which friendship must not trespass. Alas! how soon have the once happy day-dreams of my youth passed away; how changed now are all my prospects of happiness! The two dear companions of my happiest hours will have been in a few short months lost to me for ever; and I left, like my poor old friend, to mourn alone the absence of those so long and fondly loved."

Edmund's reverie was suddenly broken by the appearance of that object about whom his thoughts had been so painfully engaged. Edith was walking alone in the glen, by which the carriage drive led to the house, when, tying his horse to the palings which separated them, he was quickly by her side.

"Edith," he said, after their first salutation had passed, "I am come to bid you farewell. I leave home to-morrow for a long journey, and who can tell when I may return?"

"Oh, Edmund!" she faltered, in surprise and agitation not to be controlled; "why do you thus suddenly leave us—why are you going?"

"Well, dear Edith, as I have never seen any save my native land, I think, now the hunting is over, of spending a few months on the Continent; after which," he added, with a sickly smile, "I hope to return a polished man of the world, since in these times travellers appear to be the especial favourites with ladies, by whom we poor stay-at-home fox-hunters are completely thrown into the shade."

Although surmising to whom he alluded, Edith made no response, her mind being too much occupied with other painful thoughts.

"Ere that time comes," continued Edmund, "you, like your friend, may be changed in name as well as heart towards the companion of your youth."

"Oh, no, no, Edmund!" she said, as her tearful eyes were raised for a moment to his, "my affection for you will never change."

They walked on in silence, the hearts of both being too full for words, when, as they reached the little gate opening to the lawn in front of the house, where large evergreens hid them still from view, Edmund said abruptly, "Here, here let us part, dear Edith—I could not bid you farewell in the presence of others—my heart is too full."

Poor Edith, unable to check her emotion, offering her hand, burst into tears, when Edmund, on the impulse of the moment, caught her to his heart, whispering, "Dear, dear Edith, forgive me this embrace, I did not think you loved me thus. Now God bless you, my dear, sweet girl; I will soon return."

Edith sprang from his arms, and turning into another path, was quickly lost to his view; and Edmund, after wishing the Colonel and Mrs. Maxwell a hasty good-bye, mounted his horse and rode rapidly away.

Edith, on reaching her own room, gave way once more to an uncontrolled flood of tears. The veil had been suddenly removed from her mental eye—her heart's true feelings were disclosed—she knew and felt now for the first time that she loved Edmund Knightley with an affection widely different from that with which she had before believed she regarded him.

CHAPTER XXX.

"Have I then no tears for thee, my father?
Can I forget thy cares, from helpless years,
Thy tenderness for me? an eye still beam'd
With love—a brow that never knew a frown—
Not a harsh word thy tongue. Shall I for these
Repay thy stooping, venerable age
With shame, disquiet, anguish, and dishonour?"

It is the last morning of May. A dull heavy mist hangs suspended 'twixt earth and heaven, like a dark curtain o'erspreading this lower hemisphere, which the rays of the sun attempt in vain to penetrate. There is not a breath of air to shake from the hawthorn tree its loaded dewdrops, but an oppression in the atmosphere portending thunder, and all nature seems mourning in this heavy gloom the departing hours of blithesome spring.

"Hush'd are the birds, and closed the drooping flow'rs."

It is the bridal morn of Lady Agnes. Beneath the large portico of Woodborough House two carriages are in waiting, one belonging to the Earl, the other to Colonel and Mrs. Maxwell, who, with Edith as bridesmaid, are to accompany the bride to the parish church. As the clock strikes eleven Lady Agnes appears in the hall, supported by her friend and instructress, Mrs. Errington. She is weeping bitterly, and scarcely able to support her trembling frame. The last agitating parting with her kind, indulgent, but now almost broken-hearted father has caused those tears to flow, that obdurate heart to palpitate with those awakened feelings, too long suppressed. The voice of conscience will be heard at last—the claim of nature can no longer be denied. It comes too late for retraction—the die is cast, but the first tears of repentance have been shed—the beginning of that sorrow for wilful disobedience which will never cease.

The poor old Earl has shut himself up in his private room, to mourn in silent and secret sorrow the impending fate of his wayward, though still dearly loved child, which he has in vain, by entreaties and expostulations, attempted to avert. Even the servants move noiselessly and stealthily about the house, as if the funeral, instead of the bridal, of their young mistress were about to take place. The face of Edmund's favourite footman, Thomas, is sad and pale; and the old butler, who stands bareheaded, with his silvery hair, at the hall door, cannot suppress his strong emotion, for down his wrinkled cheek the expressed drops of sorrow are slowly trickling, and his choking voice refuses to utter the words hovering on his lips—he cannot falter out the common farewell, "God bless you!"

As Lady Agnes passes the threshold of her once loved and happy home—a home to her no longer now—the old Newfoundland dog, Hero, raises his shaggy frame from the door-mat, and, slowly wagging his tail, fixes his large mournful eyes upon the face of his young mistress with an appealing look which strikes her to the heart. Stooping low to conceal her tears, she imprinted a hasty kiss upon his honest head, and then rushing down the steps, threw herself into the carriage, giving way to a fresh outbreak of grief.

Colonel Maxwell stood alone, the only unmoved spectator of this trying scene, his stern, rigid features unrelaxed by the tears and sorrows of those around him; when, having assisted his wife, Mrs. Errington, and Edith into the Earl's large carriage, he calmly entered his own, with that grave composure which scenes of strife and bloodshed, cries of pain and anguish, in many a hard-fought field, had stamped upon his brow, which appeared impervious to all human suffering.

As they approached the porch of the old ivy-clad church, the Marquis of Dunkerton and Sir Digby Colville, with Lady Gertrude Lennard, attired as a bridesmaid, were waiting to receive the party; and as they traversed the long, damp, dreary aisle leading to the altar, echo returned from the deserted pews the sound of their own passing footsteps only; for, save the officiating clergyman and clerk, not another human being was visible in that house of God—not even the happy faces of thoughtless curious children, to cheer with their smiles the bridal of Lady Agnes—so deep was the sympathy of the whole village for the kind-hearted, charitable old Earl in the bereavement of his only child by this ill-fated marriage.

The ceremony began—the clear, full, though tremulous tones of the venerable vicar rang through that vaulted roof, startling by their distinctness the ears of all assembled; but when, with more than usual impressive solemnity, he pronounced the charge, "I require and charge you both, as ye will answer at the dreadful day of judgment, when the secrets of all hearts shall be disclosed"—the face of Sir Digby Colville paled, his lips quivering with ill-suppressed emotion, and the head of Lady Agnes fell buried in her hands, with a shuddering, overpowering sensation, on the cushioned rail beside her. The Marquis even trembled, as he stood surveying the unhallowed work of his own devising—and with a cold shiver beheld his prostrate victim, bound with cords woven by his own hand, before the altar of an offended God.

On the question being asked, "Who giveth this woman to be married to this man ?" the stiff, formal Colonel came forward to perform the ungracious part allotted to him, and then falling back, with folded arms and compressed lips, gazed steadfastly upon the kneeling forms before him.

All is over now ; Lady Agnes is assisted in rising by a man she has just sworn, in the presence of her Maker, to love, honour, and obey ! How strong, how passing strange in its very strength, is the power of that passion we call love ! which tears the timid maiden from her home, leaving parents, brothers, sisters, friends, all behind—all, all forsaken, for the love of one, almost a stranger, whom she has invested with perfections conjured up by fancy's dream, and for whom she has rudely reft asunder all other ties—for whom she has bartered the long-tried, constant loves of all else beside !

Lady Agnes had made her cast on this one die, despite the warnings of relations and friends ; she had now obtained the object of her morbid fancy ; she was now the wife of a man whom she knew not, save by name, and whose name she must now bear, whose fortunes she must follow, through all the strange vicissitudes of life, for weal or woe !

After one more parting embrace from Mrs. Errington and Edith, Lady Agnes Colville was handed by her now smiling husband into a travelling chariot with four posters, in waiting at the churchyard gate, and whirled rapidly away. The Colonel and Mrs. Maxwell returned directly to Morton Grange, whilst Edith and Mrs. Errington were borne back in the Earl's carriage to Woodborough Park ; not amidst a merry peal of bells, for not the chime of a bell was heard that day to greet the bridal of the Earl's daughter.

On reaching home, both immediately ascended to their rooms, to change their gay attire for one more sombre and befitting this mournful occasion, to which, by tacit consent, no further allusion was made. The hour of luncheon arrived, but the Earl still remaining shut up in his own room, Mrs. Errington said, "Perhaps, my dear Edith, you may induce our afflicted friend to take a glass of wine and a biscuit, for he has not tasted anything the whole of this day."

The hint was sufficient, and the next minute Edith's light tap was heard at his door.

"Who is there?" the Earl asked, without opening it.

"Edith Maxwell."

"What, you still here, my dear?" the Earl inquired; "I thought you had returned home with your mother."

"No, my dear lord; I wished to remain with you a few days, if my presence will not be irksome to you."

"That, my dear child, you know it never is," as he opened the door to admit her; "why have you brought me this, my dear?" he asked, taking from her hand the glass of wine and biscuit, and placing them on the table.

"Not to remain there," she said, with her sweet smile; "you will not be so ungallant as to refuse the glass of wine which I have taken so much trouble to bring you, without spilling a drop. You must drink it now," she said, cheerfully, taking it again from the table, and offering it.

"Well, my child, to oblige you, I will do as you desire, although I do not require anything."

"Yes, my dear lord, indeed you do; you have not taken anything the whole morning; neither have I had any breakfast, will you, therefore, give me a little luncheon? for Mrs. Errington has gone to her room, and I cannot eat alone."

"Well, my dear, then I will go with you," and they entered the dining-room together, where both sat down and made a slight repast.

The wind had now risen, rolling the thick mist away, like a folded curtain, to the tops of the hills, and the meridian sun burst forth in its full splendour, enlivening all nature with its cheering rays. Even the heavy heart of the afflicted peer could not wholly resist its gladdening influence, and at Edith's earnest solicitation, he was induced to take a short stroll with her through the pleasure grounds. The soft tones of his companion's sweet voice fell like gentle melody upon his ear, and he felt grateful for the presence of this dear girl, to comfort him in his bereavement, who, whilst walking by his side, beguiled him of his melancholy thoughts.

The next morning, the Earl, in deference to his young guest, appeared as usual at the breakfast table, when he was cheered by a long letter from his favourite Edmund, who wrote from Paris, in better spirits than might have been expected, concluding thus: "I hope dear Edith may be with you when you receive this letter, to cheer you in your solitude. She is a sweet, affectionate girl, and pray assure her of my most tender regard."

"Here, my dear," the Earl said, handing her the letter, "there is a message to you from Edmund."

The heightened colour with which Edith perused its contents did not escape the notice of Mrs. Errington, but the Earl was too busy with others to observe the change.

It was generally at this season of the year that the Colonel and Mrs. Maxwell spent a month with an old brother officer in Yorkshire; and the third day after the marriage of Lady Agnes, Mrs. Maxwell called at Woodborough, to take her daughter with them. The old Earl's countenance fell when apprised of her mother's intentions, and he sat for a moment thoughtful and abstracted, which Mrs. Maxwell observing, said, "Dear Lord Woodborough, perhaps you would like to have Edith a little longer?"

"I would not detain her in this melancholy place, my dear madam; she has suffered sufficient penance already; and I am sure change of scene will be of great service to her, and not before it is needed."

"Well, then, we will leave Edith to determine whether she prefers going with us for our usual month in Yorkshire, or remaining at Woodborough; what say you, my love?" Mrs. Maxwell asked.

"I would much rather remain here, dearest mamma, if you do not require me with you."

"Not in the least, my dear child, and you know Hursley Hall is not very gay with our gouty old friend, the General; so, my dear lord, if you are not tired of her, Edith shall be your guest until we return."

The Earl cast a grateful look upon Edith, as he replied, "I fear your dear child will be tired of my disagreeable society long before I shall feel tired of her cheerful companionship; but if she prefers remaining here, I must exert myself to render her visit as pleasurable as I can make it."

"Then," said Mrs. Maxwell, "as I am now rather busied in preparations for our long journey, I must wish you good-bye;" and after a warm embrace between mother and daughter, Mrs. Maxwell left Woodborough, more pleased than ever with Edith, for her generous sympathy with the unhappy Earl.

That evening, after dinner, the Earl appeared to have recovered some of his usual serenity, and turning to Edith, said, "You have made a very bad choice, my dear, in kindly remaining with me; but having done so, I must afford you all the pleasure and amusement in my power. I know you like horse exercise, and Edmund's horses being here, I shall select his favourite hack, Marmion, which has often carried his sister, for your especial use, and I am sure he will be delighted to hear he is so highly favoured by your riding him. Now, therefore, my dear child, you will find me always at your service as your cavalier after breakfast, leaving you to drive Mrs. Errington in the pony carriage during the afternoon."

We need hardly say that the charitable object of this kind-hearted, affectionate girl was accomplished, in diverting, by her presence and unwearied attentions, the mind of her venerable friend from dwelling too long on his desolate condition. For three long dreary months the Earl's mind had been on the rack, distracted with doubts, fears, and hopes—expecting something might intervene to prevent his daughter's marriage taking place; but now the worst had happened, he felt relieved of that dreadful burden—even more insupportable than actual suffering—the burden of suspense.

A few days after he had commenced his rides with Edith, the Earl received another letter from Edmund, expressing his joy at finding her still with him, and speaking in the highest terms of her affectionate conduct to his dear uncle. "Tell her from me," he added, "that I fully appreciate her kind motives in remaining at Woodborough, and that she must henceforth consider Marmion her own property, as a gift from her old and true friend, Edmund, who is delighted to hear of his carrying her so well, and that on my return home I hope to bring with me something more worthy her acceptance."

Edmund's letters were always handed by the Earl to Edith, and the pleasure she derived from their perusal, generally containing some kind message to herself, proved a sufficient reward for the little attentions bestowed by her upon his godfather.

CHAPTER XXXI.

THERE is an old proverb in regard to marriage, the truth of which has always appeared to me very questionable, "Happy the wooing that's not long a-doing."

It seems, however, that our friend Alphonso entertained a different opinion to mine on this subject, by the haste with which matters had been progressing between Lady Gertrude and himself; although it must be admitted that he was strongly urged on in his wooing by his backer the Captain, who with his *protégé* had been invited to dine several times during the past month at Dunkerton House. Alphonso felt not a little elated, and conceited also, by the favour shown him by a nobleman in the position of the Marquis of Dunkerton, whose name was now continually on his lips. "The Marquis did this, or said that;" in short, almost everything he said or did in his presence, was detailed, with an assumed air of consequence, to his friends and acquaintances. He had also remained one whole night at Dunkerton House, of which he informed Major Townsend the next time he met him by saying, "The Marquis is a good sort of fellow, Townsend—I dined and slept with him the other night."

"Did you, by gad?" remarked the Major; "that is coming to close quarters; and, by gad, sir! much as I like Dunkerton, I should be deuced sorry to have him as a bed-fellow; for he is just the fellow to kick one pretty hard on the shins, as my old companion between the sheets used to do at school."

"Oh no, Townsend, I didn't mean that. I should have said, I slept at Dunkerton House."

"Well," added the Major, "that is nothing particular to boast of, for I met Tom Savage the other day, who had been staying there a week, and what do you think he said? That the Marquis wasn't bad company, although not so smart a fellow over the mahogany as the Duke of B. Dunkerton backed Tom heavily in his late fight with Bill Barker."

"He must be an impudent rascal, Townsend, to speak of the Marquis in such an impertinent manner."

"Very likely, Shuttleworth; but you have heard the old saying, 'Too much familiarity creates contempt;' and if Dunkerton invites such fellows as these to his house, he must expect to have some of their sauce. But I am told you are likely to become a relative of Dunkerton's."

"Well—no—can't say much about that at present, Townsend. Lady Gertrude is a clipper, and no mistake; but, you see, she is a high stepper too, although a deuced pretty girl."

"Well, she'll raise you a step or two, my boy, in the scale of society; and if I were a single man with plenty of the needful, like yourself, I should try my luck with her. Thoroughbred cattle are always the best—figure and form, sir! there you have it—looks like a filly to win the Oaks; and somehow or other these spicy ones make the best wives, when brought into training. There was Dashwood of ours, who married the daughter of the Duke of Tadcaster, and, by gad, sir! although a delicate little thing to look at, she roughed it with him through the whole Peninsular war—killed half a dozen Frenchmen with her own hand one night when they broke into camp, and saved her wounded husband's life."

A few days after this conversation with Major Townsend, Alphonso consulted his friend the Captain upon the subject of Lady Gertrude.

"I say, Duncombe, what do you think of that young woman up at the big house yonder?"

"You mean Lady Gertrude, I suppose?"

"Yes, that's the ticket."

"Well, I have told you more than once what I think about her."

"Will she do, then?"

"Do for what?"

"Why, for me?"

"Yes, she *will do* for you, my boy." Aside—"In more senses than one."

"Well, Duncombe, you see the governor has bought that Grimstone Hall, which he says he shall give me when I am coupled up, and I've a great mind to set up in business on my own account."

"Which means, I conclude, to get married?"

"Just so, Duncombe. The governor has become very fidgety, and mother is always kicking up a row about my coming home so late at night; and if you had heard her the other day, when my dog Billy followed me into the drawing-room, and had a set-to with the cat on her best hearth-rug, you'd have thought the house was on fire. So I think the old pair of birds will do best by themselves, and I shall look out for a nest of my own, and a wife to help keep it warm."

"Oh! of course," the Captain *said;* and *thought,* "Lady

Gertrude will warm your ears, my boy, if you bring that devil of a bull-dog into her drawing-room."

"Well, but Duncombe, I made a bad shot at Miss Maxwell—by the way, she looked very seedy at the lawn meet—quite gone off——"

"Your books, of course," the Captain added, "because the grapes are sour."

"Well, Duncombe, never mind about her now; but as they say in France, *revenons à notre mouton*—I think Lady Gertrude will suit me; but that popping the question is worse than the great go at Oxford."

"Well, you made a bad go there with the classics—and your governor made as bad a go here with his didactics to the Colonel—so now you had better have a go at the young lady yourself."

"I shall never go up to the scratch, Duncombe, unless I can get some fellow to back me."

"How? leading you up, as his second does a pugilist, to face his opponent?"

"No, Duncombe, I mean in the pen and ink line; and if you will just come up to my den, you might lend a fellow a hand."

"Oh, willingly; although I am not over grand at composition."

Pen and paper being produced, Alphonso sat down to write at the Captain's dictation.

"Well, Jack, how will you begin?"

"By Jove! that's just what has been puzzling my head the last week; I don't know how to begin; but if I could once make a start, I might then get on."

"Now, what do you think of this beginning? 'My dearest Angel——'"

"That's coming it pretty strong, eh, Duncombe? Gad! she may flare up at being called an angel."

"Not a bit of it; but she would if you called her a woman, like an old tramper I met on the turnpike road yesterday."

"What was that?"

"Why, I saw a big, powerful woman dragging an unfortunate little pedlar about by the hair of his head; and upon my inquiring the cause of this rough usage, the virago said, 'I'll sarve him out for calling me a woman.' 'Then what are you,' I asked, 'a man in petticoats?'

"'No, I ain't, Mr. Saucebox,' she replied, 'but a respectable female!' So you see, Jack, women must not be called women—but angels, divine creatures—that sort of thing."

"Well, let it stand then—so now for the second go, *in medius res*—into the pith of the letter."

"Your divine charms have inspired me with a passion that is rapidly consuming the very vitals of mv heart, which will very soon be reduced to powder."

"That's pretty stiff, Duncombe."

The Captain proceeds—"I am burning like a volcano to lay myself at the feet of my adorable enchantress, and become for ever your devoted and enraptured slave!"

"By Jove! this is hot work"—taking off his coat—"I vote we have a bottle of iced champagne."

"With all my heart, Jack—pull the bell." Duncombe continues—

"Oh, dearest Lady Gertrude! deign to bestow one kind, approving look at him who lives only in the sunshine of your smiles. Let me not appeal in vain to that soft heart, to save me from endless misery and despair."

"Well, that will do, Duncombe, won't it? What's the use of writing more?"

"Let us finish the champagne, and then we can add something a little more spicy, to top up with;—some poetry, for instance—hand us some books, and see if we can find anything suitable—ah! here's the very thing!

"'Sweet are the charms of her I love,
More fragrant than the damask rose;
Soft as the down of turtle-dove,
Gentle as air when zephyr blows,
Refreshing as descending rains
To sun-burnt climes and thirsty plains.

"'True as the needle to the pole,
Or as the dial to the sun,
Constant as gliding waters roll
Whose swelling tides obey the moon!
From ev'ry other charmer free,
My life and love are all for thee.'"

The letter being finished, and sealed, Alphonso said, "Now, Duncombe, how are we to send it?"

"By post of course, Jack, then nobody here will know anything about this go of yours for a wife; and I will ride over to breakfast with Dunkerton to-morrow morning, and speak a good word for you."

The amusement of Lady Gertrude, at Alphonso's expense, when reading his love letter, was so great that she burst out into a fit of laughter, and handing it to her cousin, Dunkerton also was no less edified with its contents, saying, he had never thought Jack a poet before; "but, by Jove!" he added, "that fellow may be made something of—he has a very lofty imagination."

"Well, Charles," she asked, "what am I to do with him?"

"Just what you please, Gertrude. I think that is clear enough; and if the governor, as he is called, will make you a thorough good settlement—say three or four thousand a year—my advice to you is to accept him, and I will see things properly done—leave the bargaining part of the affair to me."

"Well, Charles, I must consider it well before giving my final answer."

"You may as well make up your mind at once, Gertrude, for we go to town the beginning of next week, and I had better arrange the preliminaries with Mr. Shuttleworth before I leave the country."

"I cannot answer his letter until the afternoon," Lady Gertrude replied, in a very serious tone; "and now, Charles, you will excuse me going to my own room."

Upon the Captain's arrival a short time afterwards, the Marquis and himself enjoyed a hearty laugh together over Alponso's curious epistle, in the concoction of which Duncombe explained how he had taken the greatest share, amidst renewed roars of merriment.

"Well," the Marquis said, "I thought some mischievous fellow like yourself had a hand in it; but don't tell Lady Gertrude this, or she will think the whole affair a hoax, and I really think they will do very well together, if Père Shuttleworth will bleed freely."

"Stick the lancet in pretty deep, he is a plethoric fellow as to money, and will bear draining; but make sure of what you can get, for these speculators are ticklish men to deal with—here to-day and gone to-morrow."

That same evening, upon calm reflection, Lady Gertrude resolved to accept our friend Alphonso, for better or worse, and wrote him a quiet, lady-like letter, expressing her desire to relieve him from the anxiety under which he appeared to be suffering, but at the same time stating her disinclination to receive his addresses before consulting her father and mother.

Our hero was in ecstacies on the receipt of her letter, reading it at least fifty times, and immediately after breakfast drove over to Dunkerton House, to express in person his grateful feelings to Lady Gertrude, in thus far conceding to his wishes. A few days after, upon his calling again, his happiness was completed by the information that the Earl and Countess of Bragborough had consented to Lady Gertrude's marriage, provided there were sufficient means to render them comfortable in wedded life, and as befitted their daughter's rank.

Alphonso, after throwing himself at the feet of his enchantress, vowing eternal love and fidelity, and almost devouring her hand with rapturous kisses, set off directly for Hardington, to acquaint his papa and mamma with the successful issue of his suit.

"There, mother," he said, "you will now have a real lady for your daughter—and such a dear, charming little thing—you will soon be as much in love with her as I am."

"I don't know that, my dear John, for these high-bred ladies don't suit my taste, they always give themselves so many airs; Miss Hedith was my choice—but there, 'tis no use crying for spilt milk."

His papa, however, was of a very different opinion—ambition being his ruling passion; and by his son's marriage with a peer's daughter he hoped, through this connection, and with the aid of Lord Dunkerton, to obtain the long-coveted advancement into aristocratic circles. With this view, therefore, his proposals of settlement to the Marquis, on the marriage of his cousin, were exceedingly liberal—far beyond his expectations—proposing to give Grimston Hall, with eight thousand a year, to his son, and four thousand as a jointure to Lady Gertrude. The Marquis expressing his satisfaction with this handsome proposition, it was agreed that the settlements should be drawn up by his lordship's solicitor, and the marriage solemnised in town, from the Earl of Bragborough's residence.

CHAPTER XXXII.

A FORTNIGHT had now elapsed since the marriage of Lady Agnes, during which Mrs. Errington and Edith had been each favoured with a letter from her, expressive of her great happiness with Sir Digby Colville, whose devotion and attention exceeded her most sanguine hopes. They were now travelling on the Continent, intending to remain abroad some months, and Mrs. Errington's kind influence with her father was solicited to obtain his forgiveness for her late waywardness, and receive her upon her return to England.

To this request the Earl so far conceded as to say, he should be glad to see her at Woodborough, although he must decline a visit from her husband.

To Edith Maxwell the time passed as happily as her now awakened feelings would admit, in her present doubtful position. She looked forward to the receipt of letters from Edmund to the Earl with nervous anxiety, and any kind notice of herself was treasured up in her mind, with an earnestness she could no longer conceal. She would often ramble alone through paths and walks which they had trod together, in the careless, joyous days of early youth, as boy and girl. "What are his feelings now towards me?" she would ask. "Are his changed like mine—or"—she shuddered at the thought—"have I allowed myself to love in vain?" and yet Edmund's last words, and fervent embrace when parting with her by the little wicket gate at Morton Grange, tended to nourish the seeds of hope, which had now taken root, and were springing up in her heart.

To Mrs. Errington alone had her secret been revealed, by observing her varying colour and nervousness of manner when the Earl handed her Edmund's letters to peruse; although she carefully avoided any expression of her conjectures to Edith, fearing to encourage her with expectations which might never be realised; yet both herself and the Earl, when alone, could not forbear expressing their wishes that Edmund might select Edith for his wife.

Chetwynd called several times at Woodborough, and was invited once to dine there by the Earl, although receiving no encouragement from Edith, whom he could never find alone, and her behaviour in no wise tended to induce the belief of her sentiments having undergone any change in his favour, since her rejection of his proposal at the ball; but, supported by the Colonel's approbation of his suit, Chetwynd resolved to persevere.

We must now pass over two months. It is the beginning of August. Colonel Maxwell, with Edith and her mother, is seated at the breakfast table, when the servant enters with the letter bag.

"Here Edith," her father said, "is one for you—it looks like the handwriting of Lady Agnes."

She broke the seal, and continued quietly reading the contents, until the last sentence, which sent the blood rushing back to her heart, her face assuming the paleness of death, when, feeling about to faint, she rose hastily from the table and left the room.

"Edith has had some bad news this morning, I fear," Mrs. Maxwell remarked; "I must go and hear what it is." And on reaching her daughter's room, she lay fainting on the sofa, with the open letter on the carpet, where it had fallen from her hand. Mrs. Maxwell rushed to her child's assistance, and, with the help of restoratives, she was soon brought back to consciousness; but to her mother's question of what had happened, she made no reply, and covering her face with her hands, burst into tears.

Mrs. Maxwell seized the letter, hastily scanning its contents, until these words caught her attention:—"Edmund is here, and the Egertons; he is constantly with them, and report goes, engaged to be married to Lucy. I thought him *épris* with you, dear Edith, as you would just have suited each other."

The truth flashed directly upon Mrs. Maxwell's mind—the cause of her child's sudden fainting fit was revealed—she loved Edmund Knightley.

"Oh, my own dearest Edith!" she cried, throwing her arms round her neck, "do not give way thus, it is only a report, it may not be true."

"Yes, dear mamma; I feel it is too true; a foreboding of evil has been hanging over me for some time; but, oh! this dreadful feeling now! I am overpowered with shame, to think I should have loved one who has never sought my love; but, oh! in compassion to my misery, do not let my father know the secret you have discovered, of my misplaced attachment. I feel I have done very wrong, but thrown as we were together so much, I could not help feeling more than common regard for one so amiable and so good. Yet not until our last parting here, did I know myself the true state of my heart."

"Do not distract yourself, my own beloved child, with these sad reflections, for even I thought Edmund attached to you, and still it may be the case."

"Oh! no, no, my own dear mother, let me no longer indulge such fond delusive hopes. I will rouse myself from this too happy dream, and no one but yourself shall ever know that I have loved in vain."

For three days Edith struggled to suppress all outward show of the anguish which was wringing her heart; but on the third evening she was seized with cold shivering fits, succeeded at night by a burning fever. The Colonel and her mother becoming much alarmed, their medical attendant was immediately sent for, who prescribed everything his skill could suggest; but "who can minister to a mind diseased?" For several days poor Edith seemed to hover between life and death, during which her mother scarcely quitted her bedside; but at last a change came for the better; the fever gradually abated, although leaving her weak and almost helpless as a child.

Pending her illness, Chetwynd called every day, expressing the deepest grief and anxiety, and sending presents of the choicest fruits and flowers his hot-houses and gardens produced; and his excessive delight when informed of her amendment, and gradual recovery, convinced the Colonel and Mrs. Maxwell of his strong affection for their child. Emmeline Knightley had now become an inmate of Morton Grange, sharing with Mrs. Maxwell her anxious watchings over her afflicted friend; who, now that the crisis had passed, began slowly to recover her lost strength, and at the end of three weeks, although pale, weak, and almost the ghost of her former self, poor Edith again descended to her little morning room, from which she could walk out upon the flower-garden, leaning on Emmeline's arm, and cheered by her soft winning smile and heart-felt compassion into a more complacent frame of mind.

Although not before suspecting it, the cause of Edith's illness became revealed to her friend, by the agitation she exhibited one morning when reading part of a letter received from her brother, still at Florence, in which he wrote of Lucy Egerton as wonderfully improved, and now become a most delightful, entertaining companion. On her reading these words, Edith turned deadly pale, and fell back almost fainting in her chair.

"Dearest Edith," cried Emmeline, springing to her side in a moment, "you are, I fear, very ill—what can I get for you?"

"A little sal-volatile only, dearest Emmy; I feel faint, perhaps from the heat of the room."

When recovered a short time after, Edith could not resist her impulsive desire to know the worst, by asking, whilst a hectic hue suffused her face, "Is not your brother engaged to Lucy Egerton?"

"Oh, no, Edith, not that I am aware of, and I think Edmund would certainly have told me had such been the case."

Edith breathed more freely, and, for a moment, one of her former happy smiles stole over her expressive and now animated features.

"It is enough," thought Emmeline; "I know now the secret of your heart, my own dear, sweet sister—you love my brother Edmund—and that love I hope and trust to see returned."

Emmeline rose, and clasping Edith to her heart, with more

warm and tender feelings than she had ever felt towards her before, said, in a low tone, "May your hopes, and mine also, be realised, my own dearest Edith!"

The same afternoon, Emmeline Knightley was obliged to return home, but she had the satisfaction of leaving her friend much improved in health and spirits, for a ray of hope had been thrown upon Edith's heart by Emmeline's opinion that her brother was not engaged to Lucy Egerton; the thought, however, occurred to her upon reflection, "He may be attached to her; there must be some cause for his protracted stay at Florence."

The next day, Mrs. Errington again called, and remained with her the greatest part of the morning; the Earl or herself having driven over to Morton Grange every day since her illness. Mrs. Errington said the Earl had received another letter from Edmund, who appeared quite in love with Florence—(poor Edith thought of his love for Lucy Egerton)—speaking in raptures of that beautiful city, its grand palaces and picturesque villas on the side of the hills, surrounded by olive groves, with a view of the beautiful Arno winding through the town and valley; "but he says," continued Mrs. Errington, "that the heat is so oppressive there, that he is going next week with his friends, the Egertons, to the Lucca Baths."

Mrs. Errington little imagined the pang her last words had sent through the heart of her she had come to comfort and console, and after her departure, poor Edith sought her own room, there once more to weep and mourn her ill-fated love for Edmund Knightley.

"Oh!" she murmured, "it is, alas! too true; he loves another, and thus ends my happiness for life. Yes—though I blush to own it—I do love, esteem, and feel for him what I never have felt, never can feel for another; but those feelings I must never again indulge. Oh! from this hour let me strive to obliterate the memory of the past. My pride forbids me ever again to betray those emotions which it is my duty to suppress. I may think of him only as a brother or friend; but better, far better, could I think of him no more!"

From this time Edith kept a careful watch over her thoughts and feelings; and strengthened by her better judgment, strove, by constant employment of her mind in reading wholesome and religious books, to divert her ideas into a more healthy channel; and with her high sense of religion, she began to view this afflicting trial as a warning to set her affections more on things in heaven than upon those on earth. "A few years more," she thought, "and all here will be as if it had never been; our joys, our hopes, our sorrows, and our sufferings will all have come to an end. In that better, happier world beyond the skies, love will be without dissimulation, pure and holy, such as angels feel. There will be no fear, no care, no anxiety about those we love; no bond or marriage tie to hold loving hearts together."

Thus Edith reasoned and reflected, until she could look even upon Edmund's marriage with Lucy Egerton without jealousy, if not with complacency. Time passed slowly on—it ever passes slowly to the sorrowful and afflicted,—but it brought healing on its wing to the wounded heart of Edith Maxwell. There was a feeling also of degradation in the thought of having given her affections, unsolicited, unsought for, to one who had never regarded her in any other light than that of a friend. She had now recovered from her illness, the cause of which was known only to her mother; and even her knowledge of it became now a source of uneasiness. "But," she exclaimed, with sudden energy, "none other shall ever have reason to suspect the humiliating truth! Henceforth I will rouse myself to appear cheerful and happy as usual in company, and in my own room alone throw off this disguise!"

She had been told by her mother of Mr. Chetwynd's unremitting attentions and genuine sorrow during her illness, but she had been told nothing more. Not a remark further passed her mother's lips, who felt too acutely for her child to say one word as to the too evident object of his visits; and, to confess the truth, Edith's choice would have been her mother's also, for she loved and esteemed Edmund Knightley far above all the young men in the county. Edith, however, pondered on these things. She possessed a feeling and grateful heart, and after Chetwynd's deep interest in her welfare, she could not receive him with her former indifference.

Chetwynd marked the change in her conduct towards him, and hope began to revive in his breast. His visits were continued; they were left sometimes alone, but there was a restless look and nervousness in her manner, which checked the renewed expression of his love, when hovering on his lips. Chetwynd had become changed also; a softened, mellowed expression beamed in his dark hazel eyes, which had entirely lost their former fierce and piercing look. His voice had assumed a low melodious tone, and his manner a most deferential character, although coupled with the most tender anxiety; and Edith could not fail, with her warm heart, to appreciate all his little attentions, although it pained her to think she could make only one return—that of gratitude.

CHAPTER XXXIII.

It was now the last week in October. Edith had nearly recovered her strength and health, and Chetwynd was becoming tired with this—to his naturally impetuous disposition—long probation of his love. It was now that his impatient, restless look again attracted her attention. The expression of his wild, piercing eye again filled her with apprehension as to his real disposition, and the words of Captain Duncombe recurred to her memory, "Would you marry a heathen?" There was horror in this thought. Eight months had elapsed since Chetwynd had obtained the Colonel's approval of his suit, which, in compliance with his suggestions, he had forborne to urge further; but his patience having now become completely exhausted, he entreated the Colonel's kind aid and assistance, by speaking to his daughter upon the subject, or permitting him to plead his own cause.

"Well, well, Chetwynd," Colonel Maxwell said, "you are certainly entitled to our best wishes for all your attentions and devotion to my child; and I have now no hestitation in using my influence with her, since I have had so many proofs of your constant and sincere attachment."

The same evening the Colonel was proceeding to lay before Edith Mr. Chetwynd's proposal, in his usual methodical manner; when she said, "Dear papa, I have already told Mr. Chetwynd, when he spoke to me before, it was out of my power to regard him otherwise than as a friend."

"Well, well, my dear, second thoughts are sometimes best; you have not, perhaps, sufficiently reflected on the many advantages you would derive from this connection, which it is my duty, as your father, to point out *seriatim*, and to which, without interruption, I request your particular attention. In the first place then—which I consider of greater importance than wealth—Chetwynd is a thorough gentleman, of very old family, clever, generous, and possessing a very warm heart, and what young ladies regard, perhaps, more than these, exceedingly good-looking. Yes, my dear, you must admit that he is a fine, handsome man; and as to age, just in the prime and vigour of manhood, having now reached his fortieth year, a period when men's habits and opinions become confirmed, when they attain that stability of character rarely to be found in young gentlemen of twenty-five, and therefore more likely to prove a faithful and attentive husband. A man of forty who has passed through the ordeal of life, with fortune and constitution unimpaired by extravagance and gaiety, gives security for a long and healthy term of life, so that at sixty he would still be hale and hearty; and you see, my dear, the disparity of age is therefore of no moment, but rather an advantage. Moreover, my dear Edith, your marriage with Mr. Chetwynd would have a great recommendation to us in another respect, that your mother and myself would have the comfort and consolation of your living so near to us that it could scarcely be called a separation; and our properties, which now join, would become eventually consolidated in one family. Lastly, Mr. Chetwynd has made the most handsome and liberal offers of settlement, and surely after the excessive devotion and attention he has shown you, you cannot doubt the strength of his attachment."

"Although very grateful, dear papa, to Mr. Chetwynd, and flattered by the preference he has shown for me, yet there is a vehemence and impetuosity in his words and manner sometimes, even in ladies' society, which has inspired me with fear rather than any other feeling, and although fully sensible of his many good qualities, he is a person I really never could marry."

"Oh, he is a little hasty sometimes, my dear—rather excitable, I admit; but men of his sanguine temper are far preferable, to those of a slow, phlegmatic disposition."

"Pray, dear papa, do not press me further, for surely you would not wish me to marry one I could not love."

"Well, well, my child, I shall say no more at present—but let me advise you to consider well to-night all I have stated in respect to the advantages of this connection; for such an offer may never be in your power to refuse again."

"I shall never change my opinion, dear papa, in his favour, which I told him very decidedly at Lord Dunkerton's ball; and I am surprised he should have renewed his proposal to you, which it is very painful for me again to decline."

"Well, well, think it over, think it over once more, Edith, and reserve your final decision until to-morrow; we will dismiss the subject for this evening."

The absence of all irritability from the Colonel's address

to his daughter will be accounted for by Mrs. Maxwell's advice to her husband, not to press Mr. Chetwynd's proposal upon her.

"My dear Colonel," Mrs. Maxwell had remarked, "I have lately heard some strange reports about Mr. Chetwynd's religious principles, which, if true, are most objectionable, and would cause our dear child endless misery."

"Tut, tut, my dear!—old women's scandal—village gossip, to which I never attend. Chetwynd has, I dare say, as good moral and religious feelings as the generality of men. Very few of us, my dear, prove to be saints when temptations come in our way—but when married to a young wife, depend upon it he will be steady enough, and attend church regularly, like other husbands, for the sake of appearance, if from no better motive. You forget, too, he has been roaming amongst wild Indians for some years past, which has made him rather inattentive, perhaps, to these spiritual matters; but marriage will soon alter his habits and ideas in this respect—you women have always some crotchet in your heads about a man's morality and religion."

"And it is very necessary we should, for, without the influence of our example in society, men would become perfect heathens."

Seeing himself likely to be on the wrong side of the argument, the Colonel forthwith retreated from the controversy, leaving his better half sole mistress of the room.

Just after the luncheon hour the following day, Mr. Chetwynd called again at Morton Grange, when Edith, seeing him approaching the house, made her escape to her own room, whence, after hastily putting on her bonnet and shawl, she descended by the back staircase to the shrubbery behind the stables, through which there was a long meandering walk, leading to a sequestered plantation of rhododendrons and other evergreen shrubs, a small but deep piece of water occupying the centre, studded with a variety of reclaimed wild-fowl.

This secluded spot was a favourite retreat of Edith's during the heat of summer, where, within a pretty grotto, around whose entrance roses and creeping plants hung suspended in graceful festoons, she sat reading or working; the birds, having become familiar with her voice, approaching the bank, and some, more bold than others, entering the grotto to be fed by her hand with crumbs of bread or grain. It was a bright though cold October day, and the breeze from the little lake sent a chilling sensation through her frame, which caused her to draw her shawl more closely around her; but here Edith had resolved to remain until she could hear the sound of Mr. Chetwynd's horse, returning by the carriage drive, which passed close at the back of the plantation.

In the meantime, Chetwynd had been in conference with the Colonel, who had explained to him his daughter's resolution to decline his proposal, notwithstanding the arguments he had used to alter her purpose.

"I have urged all I could think of in your favour, Chetwynd, but the young lady appears very determined, and I regret very much the failure of your suit."

"A thousand thanks, my dear sir, for your kind advocacy of my cause; but with your permission, I should wish to make one last appeal to Miss Maxwell herself."

"To that I can offer no objection, although I am bound to tell you my belief, that your pleading will meet, I fear, with no better result; but Edith is gone out for a walk, and I cannot tell in what direction."

"With your leave, I will soon find her," Chetwynd said, and taking up his hat, he left the house in great agitation, and on meeting with the gardener, who had seen her, soon ascertained the path she had taken.

As Edith sat watching the movements of a pet moor-hen, picking up crumbs at the entrance of the grotto, the bird darted suddenly away with a shrill scream, and fled across the lake, when, hearing approaching footsteps, she sprang to her feet, but ere she could reach the entrance, Mr. Chetwynd stood before her.

"I trust, Miss Maxwell," he said, in the most deferential manner, "you will not consider me intrusive, but having heard that you had taken a walk in this direction, I could not resist the opportunity of once more pleading the cause ever uppermost in my thoughts, in the hope that your sentiments may have undergone some little change in my favour, since I first ventured to address you at Lord Dunkerton's ball."

"I must beg, Mr. Chetwynd, you will not renew that subject, since, as I then informed you, my feelings will never change."

"But why," he asked, "have you taken such a dislike to me?"

"I have taken no dislike to you, Mr. Chetwynd, but on the contrary, have felt most deeply your kind solicitude during my long illness, for which I shall ever be grateful, and shall always be glad, as I hitherto have been, to meet you as a friend; but my conduct, I am convinced, has never given you the least cause to suppose I ever have, or could regard you in any other light."

"I had, indeed, indulged the pleasing hope," he continued—"do not call it delusion—that you had begun to entertain more gentle feelings towards me, since my frequent visits to Morton Grange."

"This on your part must have been merely imaginary, since I do again assure you I have never intended to receive you otherwise than as a friend."

"Oh! speak not, dear Edith, in this cold, repulsive manner; but—perhaps—may I ask if you are engaged to Mr. Edmund Knightley, or any other person?"

"I must decline giving you any reply to such a question, which you have no right to ask; and I must beg you will now permit me to resume my walk alone."

"Stay, Miss Maxwell," he said, standing in her path, "I had some right to ask that question, since I have obtained your father's approval of my suit."

"Which will not induce me, sir," she replied, with her father's spirit, "to alter my determination."

"Is it thus, then," he said, "you will consign me to hopeless despair?—is it thus you would break a heart too fondly, too unalterably your own?—thus dash from my expectant lip the cup of happiness I had believed nearly filled to the brim? Oh, Edith, will you thus send me from your presence, again to become a wanderer on the face of the earth, without one word of consolation? Oh, no!—no!" he continued, with increasing vehemence, "it cannot, must not be; I could not now exist without you; without you life would become a burden I could not bear, unless—that withering thought!—your hand and heart are pledged to another; answer me that question in the affirmative, and I must be content."

"I am not engaged to another, Mr. Chetwynd," she replied, haughtily, "but never will be engaged to you."

"Then, by Heavens!" he exclaimed, giving way to his violent, ungovernable temper, "mine you shall be in life or death! Consent to become my wife, or beneath the waters of that lake both of us shall sleep in death!"

"Release me, sir!" Edith screamed, terrified by the fierce expression of his eyes; "I would rather die than become your wife!"

"Then die you shall, within these arms," he cried; "welcome death with you, rather than life without you!" And seizing her in his grasp, he dragged her to the brink of the water, the plantation resounding with her cries for help. His foot rested on the last spot of earth, from which he was about to take the fatal spring with her into the deep water below!

CHAPTER XXXIV

SUDDENLY a hand was laid upon his coat collar from behind, and he was thrown by a powerful jerk upon his back, Edith, as he fell, being released from his arms.

"Ha!" he exclaimed, springing again to his feet, "it is you, then, my hated rival, who have saved her life! but yours shall be the forfeit for this daring interruption—yours she shall never be!" And the next instant Edmund Knightley found himself wrestling in a death struggle with this now infuriated madman, who, with almost supernatural power, was forcing him to the brink of the water!

For a moment Edith stood as if paralysed—every faculty of mind and body suspended—her bonnet torn off in her struggle with Chetwynd, and her long, dark, dishevelled hair hanging in wild disorder over her neck and shoulders; she could scarcely realise the scene before her—all had passed so quickly, that it seemed like some horrid vision of the night. Could she believe her senses? Was Edmund in reality there: the preserver of her life? All this passed like lightning through her brain. She pressed her hand upon her brow as if to assure herself of being really awake; and at that moment a savage cry from Chetwynd roused her at once to life and action. She sprang forward to Edmund's assistance, who, as we have said, was being dragged to the very brink of the lake—another effort from Chetwynd had consigned them to destruction. With both hands Edith seized Edmund by his shooting-jacket pocket, with a resolution and strength of which she never could have believed herself capable—the whole energies of mind and body were concentrated in that one desperate effort. Giving way to this sudden jerk they fell back together, Edmund rolling over Chetwynd, whom he now held firmly to the earth.

It was at this moment, when Edmund had got his opponent

on the ground, although still unable to disengage his fearful hold, that Green the gardener, a young, powerful man, with his assistant, alarmed by Edith's piercing shrieks, rushed down to the spot, just as Chetwynd had seized Edmund by the throat in the hope of strangling him.

"Save Mr. Edmund!" cried Edith, frantically, "or he will be killed!" and in another moment, Chetwynd was pinioned by the gardener and his assistant, who knelt by his side, each holding an arm.

"Oh, Edith! Edith! my own dear, courageous girl!" Edmund exclaimed, quickly advancing to take her hand; but no word escaped her lips—her head sank on his shoulder—and she fell senseless in his arms. Alarmed by her death-like looks, Edmund carried her to the grotto, and laid her unresisting form upon a garden chair, where, kneeling by her side, with the assistance of the little vinaigrette she had once given him, and which he always carried about him for her sake, she was gradually recovered.

"Oh, Edith," he said, as her eyes, slowly opening, rested for a second on his, and then closed again, "thank God you are restored to me once more, never, I trust, to part again!"

Edmund's words sounded like soft strains of music to her ear, although as yet she felt powerless to rise.

"Then you were not engaged to that madman, Chetwynd?" Edmund continued.

"Oh, no! no!" she exclaimed, with sudden energy, roused by his now dreaded name; "I never did or could think of him otherwise than as a friend—and this he knew."

"Then you did not love him, Edith?" he asked.

"Oh, no! I never did."

"Did you love another, then, dearest Edith?" he asked, in a low, tender voice.

She turned her head away, blushing deeply, but made no reply.

"Oh, Edith!" he continued, "relieve me from this suspense: did you—could you love him who is now kneeling at your feet? May I take this dear little hand, and keep it as my own?"

He took her trembling hand in his, which lay passive and unresisting in his grasp, and Edith, turning her face to him, burst into tears—tears of joy and inexpressible delight, that all her fondest hopes were at that moment realised.

Edmund caught her once more in his arms, and implanting

one first hallowed kiss upon her lips, whispered, "My dear, sweet, loving girl, you are then indeed my own!"

By that moment of ecstatic bliss, Edith felt rewarded for days, weeks, and months of anxious solicitude and heart-rending despondency. Her restless nights and long sufferings were all repaid by the ineffable happiness, the tumultuous feelings she now experienced, when pressed to that heart, to whose beating, throbbing pulsation her own now responded.

"Come, dearest," Edmund whispered, "you must now return home—this is no place for you."

"I will not go without you, Edmund," she said, firmly, "and leave you here again at the mercy of that madman."

"Well, then," he said, "we must release him, and let him go." But at this moment Chetwynd had regained his feet, and gnashing his teeth with rage at his defeat, said, "We shall meet again, Edmund Knightley, where none will interrupt us." Then turning on his heel, he walked rapidly away, in a contrary direction to Morton Grange.

Colonel and Mrs. Maxwell were looking out of the drawing-room window—the former rather nervous about Chetwynd's meeting with Edith, when he exclaimed, on seeing two forms approaching the house, "Thank goodness, my dear, it is all settled—they are walking arm-in-arm together—a sure sign Chetwynd is accepted, for Edith would never take his arm before this day."

"Chetwynd!" exclaimed Mrs. Maxwell, after a steady gaze upon her daughter and companion—"Gracious Heaven! it is Edmund Knightley upon whose arm my dear child is leaning."

"Nonsense, my dear," the Colonel said, impatiently, "you are always dreaming of Edmund, who is thousands of miles away—this is only your silly fancy. It is Chetwynd you see approaching."

"Oh, Edmund! Edmund! my dear, affectionate boy!" she cried, rushing out of the room.

"Crazy," muttered the Colonel; "my wife is quite crazy—monomania, sir—decided monomania: she has taken it into her head that Edith must marry Edmund, and not all the world will persuade her to the contrary, until she is actually Chetwynd's wife. When women once get a crotchet into their heads nothing will get it out again. But, eh! what do I see? Mrs. Maxwell is absolutely hugging him round the neck—she dare not treat Chetwynd so. No, by Jove! sir, it must be Edmund Knightley!"

Whilst the Colonel was thus soliloquising, Mrs. Maxwell had indeed thrown her arms round Edmund, in her excessive joy at his return; but when released from his embrace, the first question, ever uppermost in her thoughts, was addressed to him.

"We heard you were married, Edmund, or engaged."

"I am not married yet, my dear, kind friend," Edmund replied; "but believe I may say I am engaged."

Mrs. Maxwell turned an anxious look on Edith, fearing the effect this announcement might produce; but what did she behold?—Edith's eyes cast on the ground, and her now joy-lit, smiling face suffused with blushes.

"Oh, Edmund! is it—can it be that you mean Edith?"

"Yes, my dear, kind, second mother," Edmund said; "dear Edith has promised me this precious hand, if you will confirm her choice."

"May Heaven, who has heard my prayers," Mrs. Maxwell replied, in the most fervent manner, joining their hands together, "bless and preserve you both, my own dear children; it is enough—my happiness is now complete, even to overflowing."

"Well, well, my dear," exclaimed the Colonel, now coming up; "I should think Edmund had enough of hugging and kissing by his time—but what on earth is the matter with you all? You crying—Edith blushing and smiling—Edmund looking quite wild with excitement—why, it seems to me you are all crazy together. But where is Chetwynd?"

"That, my dear Colonel, I will explain to you when we reach the house," Edmund said, now very gravely. On which Edith, with Mrs. Maxwell, made her escape to her own room, where we will leave mother and daughter to the full enjoyment of this unmixed cup of happiness.

The consternation and horror of Colonel Maxwell, when informed by Edmund of his son-in-law elect's attempt upon the life of Edith, would be difficult of depiction.

"What, sir!" he exclaimed, springing from his chair and confronting Edmund, "do you mean to tell me that Chetwynd attempted to murder my daughter—his intended wife, sir—whom he obtained my consent to marry—and for whom he has shown the most devoted, the most undeniable, and unequivocal affection? The thing is impossible, sir—I beg your pardon, quite impossible!"

"I beg *your* pardon, my dear sir," Edmund replied, very gravely; "but for God's providential mercy in sending me to her rescue, your dear Edith had now been numbered among the dead. I arrived just in time; Chetwynd had her in his arms—his last footstep was on the very brink of the lake—his last words ringing in my ears, 'Welcome death with you rather than life without you'—when I seized him, and by a violent effort hurled him back upon the ground, releasing Edith from his grasp. Maddened by my interference, he then strove by might and main to drag me into the water, and the strength of this madman was so great, that, save for dear Edith clinging to my arm, I had been his victim. Your gardener, Green, and his assistant were witnesses to this scene—ask them, sir, if you doubt my word—let me call them."

"No, no, Edmund, I do not doubt your word; but what could induce Chetwynd to act in this outrageous manner? Good heavens! sir, he must have been crazy."

"No doubt of that, my dear Colonel; for a friend of his I met at the Lucca Baths, and who had been his fellow-traveller through Egypt and Syria, when he was attacked by a brain fever, told me that ever since he had been subject to great excitement at certain periods, during which he became almost unmanageable, and his friend's expression was 'that he would end his days in a lunatic asylum.' Upon this information, and there having heard for the first time of poor Edith's engagement to him, I immediately set off on my journey home, to save her from such a dreadful union."

"Horrible, Edmund! quite horrible to think of!" the Colonel exclaimed, pacing the room in great agitation. "Good heavens! what should I have done?—consigned my dear, gentle child to the arms of a maniac! Thank God, sir—I do thank God, from the bottom of my heart"—and the tears stood in the father's eyes—"that he has saved me from being, perhaps, the destroyer of my own dear, affectionate child. God has been merciful to me—very merciful—more merciful than I deserve, my dear Edmund. I feel it here, Edmund, at my heart—I cannot express all I would say. And you, my dear boy, what reward—what return can I ever make you for your noble, fearless conduct in saving poor Edith from a watery grave?"

"There is one boon, one reward I covet, my dear Colonel, far, far above all my deserts—on which the future happiness of my life now depends—the hand of that dear, affectionate child."

"What, Edmund, what! you in love with Edith? Then why, in the name of all that is marvellous, did you not tell me this before? Could you doubt our regard for you?—Mrs. Maxwell's love—yes, Edmund, almost maternal love for her dear Edmund, as she calls you?"

"Oh, no, my dear sir, I could not doubt your kind regard for me, and Mrs. Maxwell's love, but I never knew the extent of mine for Edith—how deep and true it was—until I had left England, and was separated from her beloved society."

"Well, well, Edmund—all's well that ends well—God be praised for his twofold mercies bestowed upon me this day! But here, my dear boy, comes Edith with her mother. My heart is too full now for words—I must go to my room: tears do not become a man—give me your hand"—and placing his daughter's in Edmund's, he said, in a choking voice—"God bless you, my dear children," and hurried from the room.

Two hours afterwards, when Edmund and Edith had returned to the house from their first lover's walk together, and the Colonel had recovered his usual composure and dignity of manner, Edmund said cheerfully, "Well, my dear sir, if you will excuse my sitting down to table in a shooting-jacket, I will dine with you this evening."

"Well, well, Edmuud, rather against rules you know; but if you proposed dining in your shirt-sleeves to-day I could not refuse you; but I think my wardrobe will supply the garment you require," at which proposal both Mrs. Maxwell and Edith could not suppress a laugh.

"Then lend me John and the dog-cart, instead," Edmund said, "and I will send over for my things, and write a line to my father, telling him I do not dine at home."

"You shall have John and the dog-cart with the greatest pleasure," the Colonel replied; "so sit down and write your note whilst I tell him to get ready."

Whilst Edmund was thus employed, Mrs. Maxwell whispered Edith, who approaching him said, "Mamma desires me to tell you she will not allow you to return home to-night."

"Are these your commands also, dearest?" Edmund asked, looking up into her face with his usual winning smile.

"Dear Edmund, how can you ask me such a question, after our long separation?"

"Well, my dear girl, tell your mamma, then, I will obey her orders on one condition, that she will bear with my company to-morrow also. I will ride over in the morning and tell my father and the Earl of my present happy prospects, and dine with you again to-morrow night. Will this please you, my own dear, precious Edith?"

"Yes," she whispered, "you know it will make me so happy—so now finish your note, dear Edmund, and I will bring you the sealing-wax."

About nine o'clock that same evening, a letter was received by the Colonel from Mr. Chetwynd, expressing the deepest sorrow and horror for his frenzied behaviour to his daughter, whose pardon he most earnestly implored, and concluded by saying he intended to leave home the following day, in the vain hope that change of scene might in some degree mitigate the poignancy of his grievous disappointment. "And now, my dear sir," he added, "accept my best and grateful thanks for all your past kindness, and the many happy hours spent by me under your hospitable roof; and should I never again return to my native land, your too dearly loved daughter will receive a proof of my long-felt deep regard and esteem for her."

"Poor fellow! poor fellow!" exclaimed the Colonel, as, handing the letter to his wife, he brushed away a tear from his eye; "he has a good heart, and I must write one line to him, to assure him of our forgiveness."

CHAPTER XXXV.

It was on the following morning, when the excitement of the previous day had subsided, that Edmund and Edith were again strolling together through the pleasure grounds of Morton Grange. They were standing near the little wicket gate, and Edmund said, "This spot, my own beloved girl, witnessed our last sad parting, and now, through God's mercy, it is the scene of our happy reunion. I parted from you in the deepest sorrow; I am united to you again in heart and soul now, with a joy that passes all description. When you left me here, I had almost resolved to change my purpose and not quit England; for, on witnessing your grief, the thought first struck me that you regarded me with deeper feelings than those of mere friendship; but other thoughts succeeded to dispel from my mind this pleasing delusion; for then I believed it so, as I fancied you loved my brother more than me. Still, however, through all my travels, the recollection of our last parting has been ever present to my mind; but when my brother wrote to me in his usual sarcastic style—"The report is current here, and confirmed by his constant attendance at Morton Grange, that your dear friend Edith, for whom you expressed such Platonic affection, is engaged to be married to Chetwynd"—the letter fell from my hands, and so great was my agitation, that Egerton feared some fatal news had reached me from home. Fatal indeed it was to my peace and prospects of happiness; but I remembered that you had once refused Chetwynd: still the thought harassed me day and night, that possibly you had yielded to your father's wishes, and might become the unwilling bride of one you did not love. I wrote to my dear sister Emmeline, begging her to ascertain the truth of this report; and her reply reached me at the Lucca Baths, after having been detained some time at Florence—and oh! how cheering were her words:—

"'It is true, my own dear brother, that Mr. Chetwynd is a constant visitor at Morton Grange, and I believe has the Colonel's approval of his addresses to my sweet, affectionate friend, Edith; but after your last letter, I can no longer withhold another truth from you, which Edith betrayed to me by her excessive agitation, when speaking of your reported engagement to Lucy Egerton—that she loves you, my own dear Edmund, and you only. In writing this, I am not betraying the secret of my friend, for, with her usual reserve, she has never confided such a secret to my keeping; but I know the looks of love, and the agitation she vainly attempted to suppress convinced me beyond all doubt of the nature of her feelings towards you: come home, then, dearest Edmund, without delay, save this gentle, loving girl from misery, and give a sister to your fond and attached Emmeline.'"

"I never knew until now, dear Edmund, that your sister suspected the true cause of my illness, but I will not deny to yourself, after your candid confession to me, the agony of mind I sustained when first told of your engagement to Lucy Egerton. It was then, dear Edmund, that I felt it impossible for me to love another."

"And now, my own precious girl," Edmund said, clasping her in his arms, "our mutual confessions made, you must love me with heart and soul, as I shall you, and trust me in everything as your nearest, dearest friend; we must have no thoughts, cares, joy or sorrow, separate from each other."

"Ah!" exclaimed a soft, sweet voice, "I am sorry to interrupt this very charming scene, but I must have some kisses too, from my new dear sister," and the next moment Edith and Emmeline Knightley were locked in a warm embrace.

"There, Edmund," his sister said playfully, "now you may go—your society, although very agreeable sometimes, can be dispensed with for the next hour, during which I shall have Edith entirely to myself; so go, and pacify your papa and mamma, who have come over here in very great anger, at your presumption in daring to bespeak a wife without consulting their wishes. Go, you naughty boy, directly, and beg their pardon for this very serious offence, and tell them from me, when I have lectured Edith sufficiently for encouraging you in such undutiful conduct, I shall hand her over to receive that punishment from them she so richly deserves."

We will not relate the conversation of these two sweet girls, when linked now, in heart and feeling, by the prospect of that nearer tie which was soon to unite them in a closer friendship—as they walked arm-in-arm together, talking of past sorrows and suffering, and now partaking of mutual and unmixed joy; nor need we say with what delight the kind-hearted squire and Mrs. Knightley received their son's blushing and beautiful bride elect, who had always been Mrs. Knightley's especial favourite, although her husband had once indulged the hope of seeing him married to Lady Agnes.

"Well, papa," Emmeline said, "as you have punished this poor child so as to make her shed many bitter tears, I shall take her away from you to her own room, and I am sorry to say I must remain here this night to comfort her, for your cruel treatment."

"Then, Emmy," replied her father, "you must ask Mrs. Maxwell to send you home in her carriage, as your mother has to make some calls to-morrow."

"I am afraid, my dear sir," Mrs. Maxwell said, "that I shall be doing the same thing—and I am not quite sure," she added, laughing, "that I shall be able to spare my carriage this week, which is very provoking."

"Well, well, my dear," interposed the Colonel, "Knightley has promised to dine here on Monday—so Emmeline must remain here until that night."

"Then this point being determined as to my disposal, without my consent being asked," Emmeline said, "I shall now run away with Edith," and after throwing her arms round her father and mother's neck, the merry-hearted girl, taking Edith's hand, tripped lightly with her from the room, singing as they ascended the staircase together,—

"'Oh! dear, what can the matter be?
Oh! dear, what shall I do?
There's nobody coming to marry me,
Nobody coming to woo.'

That's my case, Edith dear, yours is the reverse; you will have lots of wooing, billing, and cooing from that sentimental brother of mine, be bored to death with him, my love, before a month has passed."

Edmund was sitting alone in the drawing-room, before dinner, occupying an arm-chair, with his back to the door, when Emmeline, entering noiselessly with Edith, and cautiously approaching him without disturbing his reverie, whispered, "A penny I tell your thoughts."

"Oh! Emmy, you silly girl," he exclaimed, jumping up, "how you startled me!"

"From a beautiful dream, no doubt," she added, "to behold a more beautiful reality. Now confess you never saw your lovely Edith looking so lovely before. I have cnacted the part of lady's maid to-night, and arranged her hair according to my fancy."

"Well, let me see," Edmund said, taking her hand to draw her nearer.

"No, Teddy, that you shall not do," guessing his purpose; "you shall not spoil my handiwork by displacing one of those ringlets."

"Then I will displace yours instead, you meddling girl," and catching her in his arms, he imprinted several kisses on both her cheeks.

"Edmund, you rude boy," she cried, "let me go directly, sir; I must now return to my room to re-adjust my tresses."

"And as it would be only one trouble, my dear," Edmund said, gently drawing Edith to his side, "you can see if Edith's require amendment also."

"If you dare to treat either of us so again, I will advise Edith to change her mind, Master Edmund, and give you up. There's that pink of *politesse*, Mr. Welford, so deferential, so respectful to ladies, that he would scarcely dare to raise the tips of his lady-love's fingers to his lips, ready to throw himself at Edith's feet upon the slightest encouragement. For the last three months he has been trying to ascertain from me whether she was positively engaged to Mr. Chetwynd or not; and I have also received two long letters from my friend, Lady Ann Eversfield, telling me that her brother can think and talk of no one else than dear Edith, since he danced with her at Dunkerton House, and not having met her, as he hoped, in town last season, he is coming down for a month's hunting with the Marquis, with the intention of improving his acquaintance with my exceedingly lovely friend Miss Maxwell. So you see, Master Edmund, she has two new silver or golden strings to her bow, and I recommend *you* to be on your good behaviour, or I shall recommend *her* to become the Marchioness of Eynsford instead of Mrs. Edmund Knightley. But here comes the Colonel, who will keep you in order, if I cannot."

Emmeline was in exuberant spirits that evening, having at last seen the accomplishment of her long-cherished hopes, and after dinner she began to attack the Colonel about giving a ball and supper upon the joyful occasion.

"Pooh! pooh! my dear," the Colonel said; "you girls are always thinking of balls and such things, but I really cannot have my house turned topsy-turvy to suit your fancies. You may have a dance upon the carpet, my dear, if you are so fond of hopping about."

"My dear Colonel, I hope you will not think me impertinent, but I am sure it would do your carpets good to take them up and give them a good beating."

"Not unlikely, my dear, but that can easily be done without giving a ball; if I must give one, however, the proper time would be on Edith's marriage."

"Oh, my gracious, Colonel, that will never do; dear Edith would not then enjoy the fun with us—nothing like the time present—we are all so happy now, just in the mood for dancing and singing; and according to the old song, 'There's a time to be merry and gay.' Besides, my dear Colonel, people did make the remark last season, that Colonel Maxwell was the only person who had not opened his house and heart like his neighbours, from the first day of hunting until its close."

"Well, well, Emmeline," the Colonel said, rather testily, "we will think about it, my dear, plenty of time yet."

The happiness of Edmund and Edith was now as complete as it was possible for that of any two human beings to be in this world. Their love for each other was founded on that only sure foundation of long and lasting affection—esteem. From being friends they had become lovers—but there was wanting that wild, passionate rhapsody of feeling, which fills the mind of youth with distempered and chaotic imaginings. Theirs was a pure, calm, unruffled affection, unaccompanied by foolish excited fancies, or rapturous expressions. Edith was not exactly an angel in Edmund's eyes, although closely approaching human perfection, but a dear, fond, affectionate girl, whom he loved more for her many excellent qualities of mind and disposition than her exceeding beauty of person.

He had loved Lady Agnes with the first impulsive passion of youth, for her beauty and charms of person only; but even at that time, when unwilling to believe in her imperfections of character, the contrast between her and Edith could not be concealed from his partial sight. Even then he would trust and consult Edith as his friend—her ideas and feelings were more attuned to his own than those of Lady Agnes. What were his thoughts now? Those of thankfulness that his first wild love had failed, and that he could now reward this sweet, confiding girl, for her long sorely-tried affection for himself, with his heart and hand. "Yes," he murmured, "my hand at least should have been hers, for her deep devotion to myself; but now I feel my heart is hers also."

CHAPTER XXXVI.

The following morning Edmund drove Edith and his sister over to Woodborough Park, where they were received with heartfelt congratulations by the Earl, who, since his daughter's marriage, had indulged the hope of seeing Edith, who held the next place in his affections, united to his beloved Edmund.

"Ah, my dear Edith," the Earl said, "I have had a sad, lonely time without seeing your sweet, cheering smile for so many weeks, and now that you are restored to health, you really must come here again for change of air. You are always well and happy at Woodborough. So now, Edmund, you must tell Mrs. Maxwell, with my kind regards, that she must spare Edith to me for a week or two at least; and your sister will, I hope, give me the pleasure of her company also, as long as she may find our society agreeable."

"I fear, my dear uncle," Emmeline said, "you will find two

wild girls, like ourselves, rather too much of a good thing; at least, I can answer for myself always getting into mischief of some kind, except at Morton Grange, where the Colonel maintains very strict discipline, and keeps me in great order."

"I am not the least afraid, Emmeline, of your wildness or mischief," the Earl replied; "you know this is Liberty Hall, where all do as they please."

"Well, dear uncle, you will, I fear, wish me at home again before I have been here two days; but as you are bold enough to invite me after what I have said, I will do myself the honour of waiting on your lordship as soon as my company can be dispensed with at Morton Grange, which I think will be on Tuesday next."

"Very well, Emmeline; then I shall take you at your word, and send the carriage for you and Edith that same afternoon."

"Which arrangement being most happily acceded to on my part, my dear lord, you will further oblige me by taking Edmund with you round your home farm, while Edith and myself have a run through the pleasure grounds to warm ourselves after our cold drive."

We will pass over the few intervening days until Edmund and Edith are once more reinstated in their old quarters at Woodborough, which had been to them the scene of their happiest unclouded days of early youth, for it had been ever to them a second home, where, without restraint, they could enjoy all the amusements and pleasures of country life unfettered and untrammelled in their innocent recreations, and the kind-hearted Earl was in every respect to them like a second and most indulgent father.

"Well, my dear Edith," Emmeline said the first day of their arrival there, "here we are once more at Liberty Hall; and to confess the truth, my love, although your mamma is one of the dearest, kindest creatures in the world, I always feel, in the presence of the Colonel, as I suppose a raw recruit would before his drill sergeant. Your papa cannot divest himself of the idea that he is still a Colonel on parade. Now, here we don't get a reprimand or austere look for being late at breakfast, or late at dinner. And now let us go down to the stables, look over Edmund's stud of hunters, and see if the ponies are—as your late admirer the Captain would say—in proper trim, and fit to go; for we will give them a breather to-morrow over to Wychwood, to see in what kind of humour the high and mighty

Reginald will receive his new sister. By the way, Edith, it is lucky for you that you selected the younger before the elder brother, since Master Reginald, although very handsome and most agreeable when on his good behaviour, is, notwithstanding, between ourselves, a quick-tempered, vicious, kicking animal—like his favourite hunter, 'Fireaway,' and will never go quiet in harness—that is, my dear, he is only fit to be a bachelor."

"I never believed, dear Emmy, he entertained any serious thoughts about me, although we have always been very good friends."

"Perhaps not, Edith; yet I would not answer for what his real feelings are, for he declared positively you never should marry Shuttleworth, if he turned Benedict himself; and I won't warrant his receiving you very complacently now, as Edmund's intended, but that is of little consequence; I never humour his pettishness, neither must you."

"Holloa!" cried Edmund, who was walking with the Earl, "where are you girls going?"

"Only down to the stables, Teddy dear, to see if the ponies are fit to appear at our lawn meet to-morrow morning, as you do not approve of your sister or wife riding and hunting."

"Wait a moment, Emmy, and I will go with you."

"Oh, no, Edmund, continue your walk with the Earl; we don't want you tied to our apron strings all the day long."

"I will punish you for this impertinence, Miss Emmeline," her brother replied. "She is very well behaved at home, my dear uncle, but here quite unmanageable, from being spoilt by too great indulgence."

"Ah, very likely," she said, "but there is a spoilt boy as well as a spoilt girl at Woodborough. So now, Master Edmund, if you want something to do, take your gun and kill us some wild ducks for dinner to-morrow—there are lots upon the lake; so good-bye until dinner time, for we are going for a long ramble after our inspection of the ponies."

"Ah, Edmund," the Earl remarked, as they turned away, "you are indeed highly favoured in possessing the affections of two such dear, cheerful girls, and notwithstanding our mutual disappointment, the Almighty has, of his great goodness, provided a helpmate worthy of you; for I am obliged to confess that Edith is far more amiable than my own child, and I am most thankful that her choice has fallen upon you, my dear boy, when I feared she had given her affections to another."

"I do, indeed, my dear uncle, feel most grateful for this

greatest of all earthly blessings, and it shall be the study of my life to prove myself deserving her deep, devoted love."

"But when do you think of being married, Edmund?"

"Not before the spring of the year. I shall then have possession of St. Austin's, and Edith says she is so completely happy now, that she would prefer it being deferred until that time."

"Well, I admire her the more, my dear Edmund, for such feelings, but you know this is your home as well as St. Austin's. Although confiding in your mutual affection, you will never be happier than at this present time; for marriage brings many cares and anxieties, from which you are now wholly free."

"Yes, my dear uncle, I am well aware that such is the case; but with dear Edith, my friend as well as wife, troubles or cares will tend to draw us nearer together. And now, to indulge that spoilt girl, Emmeline, I will take my gun, with old Hero, and try to shoot a couple of ducks before dinner."

The party at Woodborough that evening was a very happy one, and the high spirits of Emmeline had their effect upon the whole household. The old butler's face was lit up with unwonted animation, and Thomas, Edmund's favourite footman, seemed beside himself with joy at his young master's return.

"What are you about, Thomas?" Emmeline said. "I asked you for bread, and you bring me lobster sauce to eat with mutton. 'Gude faith,' as Mrs. Macpherson said, when her lout of a serving-man sent a pair of boiled fowls and white sauce into the lap of her new silk gown, 'but the mon's demented.'"

"I beg your pardon, miss," Thomas said, "but I was——"

"Just a-thinking," added Emmeline, "as Will Lane says, of something else."

"My dear Emmeline," Edmund said, "you keep running on in such an extraordinary manner this evening, that I believe you are the person demented."

"I am not at Morton Grange, now," she whispered to the Earl, "where every serving-man looks as if he had a poker down his throat, but at dear Woodborough, which would not be Woodborough to me, unless I could do and say what I like. Are you angry with me, dear uncle?" appealing to the Earl.

"No, no, my child, that you know I never can be; it always gives me the greatest pleasure that you feel so much at home here; and as you are going over to Wychwood to-morrow morning, you must ask Mrs. Knightley, with your father and Reginald, to dine here on this day week."

"I don't know about the latter," she said, "he is so snappish sometimes, that I am afraid of his biting; but suppose, dear uncle, we extend the family circle a little, by inviting a few others to make up a quadrille in the evening. We have been all very dull lately, and we ought to have a merry-making now the wanderer is returned home, and I have the happy prospect of such a charming new sister. If you will leave the invitations to me, my dear lord, I will select those I know you would approve. To begin, I would have Mr. Welford, and old Squire White, as *vis-à-vis* at the dinner-table—just the antipodes of the old and new school; Major Townsend, to tell long stories of his own manufacturing; our little friend the vicar; and a few others, not to exceed, with Colonel and Mrs. Maxwell, twenty around your festive board."

"Well, dear Emmy," the Earl said, in the kindest manner, "you shall have your wish gratified; and, in addition, you may ask a few other ladies and gentlemen in the evening."

"Oh, thank you, my dear kind uncle. We shall have such a delightful party!"

The felicitations on Edmund's return home were poured in upon him from all his fox-hunting friends, high and low, the next morning when he appeared in his new pink at his father's place, where, from the extraordinary event of the last week, many more ladies than usual graced the opening meet. Edith also engaged more than common attention and interest, from having escaped a fate so fearful; and rumours were circulated freely of her long attachment and engagement to the preserver of her life.

"Ah, Knightley!" exclaimed the Major, "so it appears I was a true prophet, notwithstanding your positive denial of the fact that a certain young lady would become your property, or engaged to be so, before this very day came round again."

"Extraordinary things do occur sometimes, Townsend, and this is one; for when you foretold this event I saw no probability of its fulfilment, being at that time entirely ignorant of the young lady's *penchant* for your humble servant."

"But, by Jove! that wild fool, Chetwynd, had nearly stopped your love-making; it was a very near thing, I am told."

"Too near to be agreeable, Townsend; so let us dismiss that subject, and as Mrs. Townsend is not here, I must tell you that my sister is commissioned to invite her and yourself to dine at Woodborough on the 7th."

"We shall come of course, Knightley, for had I a dozen invitations for that day, they should all give way to the Earl's—and, by Jove! my boy, we'll have a glorious evening—a bit of a hop afterwards, perhaps, for the young ladies."

"Just so, Townsend—so put on your dancing pumps—and now good-bye."

Of the day's sport we have nothing particular to relate, save that Will Lane, being now restored to perfect health, concluded this first regular day's fixture for the season by bringing home the heads of two foxes, which came to hand without much trouble.

CHAPTER XXXVII.

Two days after the Earl received a letter from his daughter to the effect that, her husband having engaged stables at Melton for his stud of twelve hunters, he had offered to leave her at Woodborough for a few days, in their way to that place, if her father would receive her. The proffered visit was of course accepted, and, singular enough, Lady Agnes arrived the very day of the Earl's party—Sir Digby having stopped the previous night at Dunkerton House, where, however, from not being included in his wife's invitation, he remained only two days, and then continued his journey to the emporium of fox-hunters.

The appearance and manner of Lady Agnes had undergone considerable change since her marriage. She had become very thin and thoughtful, subdued and quiet in her manner; and although trying to appear cheerful and in good spirits, the assumption of gaiety was evident to her old friends—that it was an assumption only of what she did not feel. To Mrs. Errington and Edith she spoke of her great happiness with Sir Digby, his attention and devotion to her. But neither Mrs. Errington nor Edith were deceived by these expressions of tender regard; for to their quick perceptions her restless, wandering eye betrayed an uneasy, doubtful state of mind, the very reverse of true confidence and love.

Lady Agnes, although at home once more, felt an alien in her father's house. She had incurred his displeasure by marrying a man she could not now herself esteem, although she loved and feared him—yes, the confession must be made—Sir Digby Colville had brought her once high spirit and imperious temper into subjection to his will. Five months had effected a change in her which appeared almost incredible to herself. She had realised to its fullest extent the curse pronounced upon Eve: "Thy desire shall be to thy husband, and he shall rule over thee." She had forsaken literally all to follow a stranger—unknown to her then, save by name—his true character and disposition never revealed to her until after she had sworn to honour and obey him at the altar!

Her father had received her with kindness—like the repentant prodigal—although she had expressed little contrition for her wilful and disobedient conduct; but there was a restraint in his manner towards her which was not visible in his address to Edith, who appeared now to occupy the place she once held in his heart. Edith alone was unchanged—gentle, warm-hearted, and affectionate as ever. Edmund also seemed to have forgotten her unfeeling behaviour to him by a return of his usual friendliness. There was no perturbation, no uneasiness perceptible in his look or manner towards her, even at the first moment of their meeting; for Edmund now felt fully persuaded that the loss of her love had been unspeakable gain to him; he loved one now who loved him with her whole heart and soul; and when he surveyed Lady Agnes and Edith together, amazement seized him that he ever could have preferred the one to the other. Anxiety and self-reproach had worked a sad change in the beauty of Lady Agnes, whose features had assumed a careworn, peevish expression, so that she looked ten years older than Edith.

Time passed on; there was more than usual gaiety during the winter season. The annual Hunt ball followed. Lady Agnes was there, being still a visitor at Woodborough. Sir Digby continued at Melton. He and his friend Lord W had engaged a house between them for the season, the only one to be had; small and comfortable, her liege lord wrote her, but not sufficiently commodious for more than a couple of bachelors. She could, therefore, remain at Woodborough. The Earl must be so glad to have her with him again! Lady Agnes bit her lip at this cool suggestion of her *devoted* husband; but she knew remonstrance would be useless. Sir Digby had a quiet, cool way of doing things—he was provokingly cool sometimes—but Lady Agnes knew there was no appeal from his decision, and she felt his sarcasm about remaining at Woodborough, where he had expected to have taken up his winter quarters, instead of being at Melton. He had calculated, through her intercession and influence, on being reconciled to her father.

Sir Digby was quite a man of the world; he was ever attentive and polite to his wife, but this very politeness annoyed her. He never exhibited want of temper in her presence. When she pouted, fretted, and shed tears because she could not, as formerly, have her own way, Sir Digby would stand before the mirror surveying his handsome person and twisting his whiskers, remarking, in the most *sang froid* manner, "Really, Lady Agnes, these perpetual outbreaks are very indecorous, and red eyes excessively unbecoming to young ladies. I have an engagement this afternoon, and hope, when I return to dine, you will have recovered your complacency of temper and good looks."

Lady Agnes had loved, and did still love her husband—what newly-married woman does not?—but she dared not show, even when first married, how much she loved him. He had never loved her; there was no warmth of heart or cordiality of manner about him; it was foreign to his nature. He was cold, deferential—sometimes painfully so—courteous and respectful—in short, a fashionable husband. She could not upbraid him with unkindness; she could not accuse him of speaking or treating her harshly; he was always the same—polite, apathetic, imperturbable, and she felt powerless as an infant to contend with him; so he always carried his point.

What were her feelings now, when again treading those boards? what her reflections when passing through that room where, twelve months since, she had listened with rapture to the avowal of his love? She was then in all the pride and power of youthful beauty—admired, courted, and flattered—arrogant and haughty. What was she now? a humbled and neglected wife. The same familiar faces were around her, but not with the same expression as then. They looked coldly upon her now. No soft, flattering speeches proceeded from the lips of her former admirers. Not even Captain Duncombe had one little compliment to pay. She seemed isolated; set apart from kith, and kindred, and friends—as one marked out for pity or compassion only. Remarks reached her ear also, turning her bitterness of spirit into gall. She overheard the eldest Miss Duncombe say, "Poor thing! how miserable she looks! so changed, so thin, so woe-begone, one would take her for a woman of forty!"

No name was mentioned, but Lady Agnes felt the allusion. She wished she had never attended that ball; all appeared happy but herself. Edith looked more lovely than ever; all spoke in raptures of her beauty, all seemed to bask in the sunshine of her sweet smiles, and although now engaged, she received the same homage as before.

Edmund also looked more handsome and cheerful than she had ever seen him. Would he treat Edith with indifference and neglect when his wife? Ah! no, she knew the heart of Edmund Knightley too well. Vain, worse than vain, were all such reflections now; but she might have been there then, the happy, contented, and beloved wife of him whose love she had treated with scorn! It was a relief to her over-burdened mind when the ball was over, and she returned home to mourn and weep alone.

Two more months have passed away. The ides of March have come, but not with them has come Sir Digby Colville. He is finishing the season at Melton; "he will be at Dunkerton House the middle of April, on his way to town. Lady Agnes can join him there. He hopes she has been enjoying herself at Woodborough, as he has at Melton—the place had been unusually gay——"

The marriage of Edmund and Edith was fixed to take place at the little village church of Morton Grange, on the 15th of April; and Mrs. Duncombe's lease of St. Austin's having expired, preparations were making for the reception of the young couple. The Captain had taken a cottage in the neighbourhood; his mother, with her family, having gone to the gay town of Waterton, which proved a very agreeable change to the young ladies, from a dull country life.

The 15th of April arrived; it was a bright, cheerful morning—bright and cheerful as the thoughts and feelings of Edmund and Edith, surrounded by the smiling, happy faces of their friends and relations, by whom the church was thronged. The young and happy pair pledged their troth to each other with sincerity and truth. Lady Agnes was present at the ceremony, so different to that in which she had been the principal party some few months before. All was joy and animation now. The whole neighbourhood seemed congregated here; not a pew stood vacant in that old church; even the gallery creaked under the weight of closely packed spectators, anxious to witness the union of their favourite Edmund with one who had become no less known for her beauty than her kind and charitable disposition to the poor, and her affable, unaffected manner to all.

As Edmund and Edith left the church, now man and wife, although wanting not that link to bind them in the closest unity of love, the bells sent forth their merry peal, which was quickly taken up and re-echoed from every church tower for ten miles round. In every parish where the old Squire and his son were known, the farmers had resolved, as Tom Springfield said, "to set the bells a-going, and have a merry-making on Master Edmund's wedding-day." A grand breakfast had been prepared by the Colonel at Morton Grange, of which a large party of friends, relations, and neighbours partook; but Edith and Edmund had immediately set out on their bridal tour, intending to return home again by the 1st of June.

About a week after this event, Lady Agnes joined her husband at Dunkerton House, whence, after remaining a few days, they proceeded to London for the season, and she became inaugurated into the mysteries of fashionable life, which, when the novelty had passed away, brought little additional happiness to her excited mind. Sir Digby was, as I have before said, a very fashionable husband; his wife was introduced to his fashionable acquaintances; she had her carriage and servants at her own disposal; Sir Digby had his cab and tiger. She had perfect control over the disposition of her time; she could accept invitations without consulting him; he of course did the same. Sir Digby seldom dined at home, except when he gave a dinner party, which proved of rare occurrence. He voted *tête-à-têtes* with his wife a bore. They met more frequently in public than in private, for he was generally out all night somewhere, not returning home till a late hour in the morning, and being most anxious not to disturb Lady Agnes' rest, he had his separate room.

To drown care and thoughts—those bitter, self-accusing thoughts—thoughts of that wilful perverseness of mind which, despite the warnings and advice of every true friend, she had resolutely maintained, had made her the arbitress of her now wretched fate—Lady Agnes entered into gaiety and dissipation; for to sit alone at home, moping and mourning, became insupportable. And yet many of those invitations were accepted by her, in the hope of meeting her husband there. Her wish was gratified; she had met him several times, at balls and other parties, but she never desired to meet him so again. He was the same polite, agreeable, entertaining partner to others he had once proved to her. She saw other young ladies listening in raptures, almost as she had done, to his soft, silvery, honeyed speeches, and looking with admiring eyes upon his handsome, *distingué* person, but not a kind look or word could he spare for his unhappy wife. A low, formal bow was all the recognition she received from him in public; it was not fashionable for husband and wife to be seen conversing together there. Lady Agnes had put forth her hand, gathered and tasted the forbidden fruit, and her eyes were opened. She had obtained a fine, handsome husband, but that was all; she had married a man without heart or feeling.

It was the last week in May that Edmund and Edith arrived in London, after their short wedding tour, when the former said, "Now, my dear girl, I should like to show you a little of town life."

"Which," she added playfully, "I have no wish to see, dear Edmund, or it may perhaps spoil my love for the country."

"Well, Edith, as I think there is no risk of that, we may as well spend a few days here and see some of my friends, to whom you have not been introduced. All the world is in London now, and I should like to know also how poor Agnes gets on with her fashionable husband. *You* can call and see her, although I cannot."

Accordingly, the next day, Edith, anxious to see her friend, probably the only time for many months, called upon her at the unfashionable hour of twelve, wishing to find her at home. She was at once admitted, and there sat Lady Agnes at her breakfast-table quite alone.

"Oh, Edith!" she exclaimed, "I am delighted to see you again, but I am sadly lazy this morning, having been at a very late party last night. I need not ask how you are, love! you look the picture of health and happiness. Are you very happy, dear Edith? happier than you ever were?"

"Could you expect a bride, dear Agnes, to answer such a question otherwise than in the affirmative? But I don't know that I am happier than I have ever been before, for nothing could exceed the happiness of the last few months of our engagement; but we are both as happy as Edmund and myself ever expected to be; we are old friends, although a newly-married couple, and have long known each other's disposition and character."

"Then, dear Edith, I conclude you are very happy; and

now that you are in town, you must give me the pleasure of dining here this evening."

"That, I fear, I cannot do, as Edmund does not know Sir Digby."

"There is no chance of his meeting my husband," Lady Agnes replied, with a deep sigh, "for he seldom dines at home; and to-night I know he has an engagement, so that I shall be quite alone."

"Yet as Edmund might object, dear Agnes, you must come and dine with us instead, at our hotel, when we shall have the whole evening to ourselves."

Three weeks in town proved sufficient to give Edith a distaste for fashionable life, during which she had seen nearly everything worth seeing. She had been presented at Court by the Marchioness of Dunkerton—had been introduced at Almack's—attended the opera and theatres, and been at half a dozen aristocratic balls and parties; in fact, her exceeding loveliness had attracted such general admiration, that invitations poured in upon her so thickly, she was obliged to decline more than half. The beautiful Mrs. Knightley had become, without her so intending or wishing, the fashion; and no party was thought quite complete without her. Edmund felt every day more proud of his wife, and more devotedly attached to her. She would go nowhere without him. Flattery and adulation possessed no charm for her; her husband's approving smile being the only one she coveted.

The Marchioness felt more than gratified by the homage paid to her new cousin. "Well, Edmund," she remarked one evening at the Duchess of R——'s ball, where Edith was dancing with her son, "what think you now of *my choice?* Are you not the most fortunate man in the world? Can you doubt now the evidence of your senses, which were once so blinded that you could not perceive the superior attractions of that dear, sweet girl, whose beauty is her least recommendation?"

"Ah, Emily! my eyes were indeed withholden then to her many perfections; but believe me, I do feel now most thankful, most grateful, that my wilful, boyish fancy was not gratified."

"You are the most envied man in town, Master Edmund, notwithstanding your former obstinacy; and had Edith been Miss Maxwell still, she would, to my knowledge, have been offered a choice of coronets. Old and young are equally in love with her; the old for her quiet, unaffected manners and sensible conversation, and the young for her great personal charms. In short, she has created quite a sensation; and the old Duke of Willerby, whose taste in female beauty is considered undeniable, has pronounced her to be the most lovely and accomplished woman he has ever beheld. You may suppose, therefore, how proud I am of *my choice*, and to be able to call her cousin."

"Edith and myself have to thank you now, dear Emily, for all your kind attentions to us whilst in town; but as you see my dear, precious girl has exchanged the rose for the lily in her complexion, we purpose returning home the day after to-morrow, at Edith's particular request, who prefers the healthful recreations of country life to the gay, although unsatisfactory amusements of London."

"I approve her choice, Edmund, although I shall truly regret her absence; and, to speak the truth," she said, laughing, "I think your position as her husband here is rather too much envied to be quite safe; so take your beautiful bride to the country, where you may enjoy every happiness without inducing others to break the tenth commandment by a longer display of your coveted treasure in such an unhallowed place as this."

A fortnight after this conversation, Edmund and Edith, after having spent ten days with Colonel and Mrs. Maxwell, were again at Woodborough Park, St. Austin's not being quite fit for their reception, and we need scarcely say with what delight their return was hailed by the Earl and Mrs. Errington.

CHAPTER XXXVIII.

We must now pass over a period of five years, during which Sir Digby Colville had been engaged in multifarious transactions upon the turf—racing and betting having been his favourite amusements as heretofore; and with the additional income derived from his wife's property, he had become the owner of several racehorses. The turf, however, proved not to be Sir Digby's *forte;* he was a bad hand at book-making, and somehow or other his horses seldom won any stake worth having. He had been twice so nearly ruined by backing two favourites to large amounts, that Lady Agnes was obliged to apply to her father to save him from being openly declared a defaulter. Upon the first occasion the Earl agreed to advance his daughter the sum required to save her husband from disgrace, on the condition that he discontinued keeping racehorses, and these terms were apparently complied with, although the horses had in reality been merely transferred to a friend, in whose name they continued to run.

The true state of the case having been at last made known to the Earl, he refused positively to aid him any further, and in consequence, Sir Digby, having again become greatly embarrassed, and unable to raise another shilling upon his own property—his wife's money being properly secured from his interference with it in any shape whatever during her life-time—was at last under the necessity of making a precipitate retreat from England, and had been living for the last year and a half at a retired château in the south of France. It was here that Sir Digby, becoming impatient of his seclusion from the world, exhibited his true character by fretfulness, and frequent violent outbursts of temper towards his still attached, though no longer deluded wife. The veil had been removed long before from the eyes of Lady Agnes. Their first season in London had shown her the worldly, selfish disposition of her husband, and his utter disregard of her comfort or domestic happiness, in which he took not the slightest interest. Lady Agnes could make excuses for him when in London—he had there so many friends, so many engagements; here, however, no such excuses could be made, and yet she saw nothing of Sir Digby from the hour of breakfast until that of dinner. Her husband still kept his two hunters, and she had also her carriage to take her solitary drive when so disposed.

With the old château, Sir Digby rented a large forest, on the borders of which the house stood, and here he found occupation and amusement, during the season, in shooting and hunting the wild boar; and in the summer he was frequently from home for weeks together, upon various excuses. They had spent the first winter together in Paris; but living there was so expensive that he could not afford to take her there again.

Lady Agnes had now become so dispirited, and submissive to the will of her lord, that she was as a child—helpless, powerless—in his hands. In her own room she would sit for hours, weeping and lamenting the wayward, wilful passion of her youth, in linking her fate with such a man as her husband; and yet, when a kind word was spoken by him, a seemingly interested inquiry about her health, or a regret that their limited income would not permit him to obtain for her other

Q 2

amusements and recreations, the tears—the forbidden tears—which, by a strong effort, she had been taught to suppress in his presence—would stand in her eyes, and she felt she loved him still. She continued her correspondence with Mrs. Errington, but even her letters tended only to increase her unhappy, desponding state of mind. Mrs. Errington wrote of the faithful, devoted love of Edmund and Edith, whose happiness appeared ever on the increase. Oh! what a contrast this to her sad, mournful, melancholy lot—loving hopelessly—despairing of any return!

Lady Agnes could barely summon courage, sometimes, to reply to these letters. What had she to communicate? She dared not even mention her husband's name, who had, from his late conduct, become still more offensive to the Earl. She had nothing to write about; she saw no one, knew nothing of the gay world, from which she had now, by a false step, been debarred. How she longed, when a girl, to see and mix in that world! How she had fretted then against her now dear old lamented Woodborough, like a linnet against the bars of its cage! How she panted to be free from all paternal restraint, and join in that giddy, thoughtless throng of the gay and dissipated! What would she give now to be once more at home, owning no other power than that of her kind, too indulgent father! what to be once more free within those walls—once more free to wander through the haunts of her happy youth with Edmund and Edith, the loved companions in those cheerful walks! And her words would often recur to her mind, "The time may come when you will look back on the days spent at dear Woodborough as the happiest of your life!" The prophecy had already been fulfilled. And another painful, heart-rending thought arose, "Shall I ever re-visit dear Woodborough again?"

It was now, when shut out from the world, that the lessons of religious instruction instilled into her youthful mind began to revive. When the prospect of all earthly happiness seems cut off, it is then—perhaps, then only—that we begin to turn our thoughts on heaven. It is then that the soft whisperings of our guardian angel are heard for the first time in our thoughtless, careless lives. It is in solitude and retirement that we look "from nature up to nature's God." It is when walking in the garden, far removed from the busy hum of mankind, that we contemplate the real beauties of creation. There we can dwell upon the wonderful construction of even the meanest flower—

there consider the lilies as they grow, exhibiting in their early beauty and too early decay a true emblem of human life.

It was in the pleasure garden of the old French château that Lady Agnes now sat upon a rustic chair, day by day during the spring and summer months, occupied in studying the Book of books, from whose hitherto neglected pages she could now derive her only comfort and consolation. It was here, when falling asleep from weariness and exhaustion of mind, that she beheld, like Jacob, a vision of angels ascending to and descending from heaven; here she beheld one of those blessed, happy spirits standing before her, with outstretched hand towards the sky, saying, "There the wicked cease from troubling—there the weary are at rest." She awoke—was it a dream or a reality?—and the words of Jacob occurred to her mind, "Surely the Lord is in this place, and I knew it not." That spot became hallowed ground to her ever after. There she sat, meditated, and pondered until her thoughts wandered to that happy land, with which Jacob's ladder was connected, and upon which she now almost longed to climb to the regions of immortality.

Alas! how true, how alarmingly true it is, that until visited with affliction, weighed down to the earth by sorrow and calamities, we seldom think seriously of God! When young we are occupied with thoughts of pleasure and amusement only—when older, with the business and cares of life; and it is only when we tire and weary of earthly things that our thoughts are directed towards another home. How few consider and confess, like the patriarchs of olden time, that we are pilgrims and sojourners here in a strange land—travellers in a foreign country, beset with dangers and difficulties on every side! How few of us take for our guide that star which once shone in the East to direct the wise men on their way to Bethlehem, and by the light of which our footsteps can alone be upheld through this dark valley, over-shadowed by death—until the glorious light of the heavenly kingdom shall burst upon our sight!

We must now cross the Channel, and attend to affairs at home. How different had been the result of that union founded upon esteem of character, and cemented by the bond of friendship! Edmund's love, when he married, was in its infancy. The discovery of Edith's affection for himself would have induced him, with his generous and romantic ideas, to offer her his hand, even had he no heart to give, so highly did he esteem her character, and so reluctant would he have been to consign to despair the budding hopes of this young, artless, sweet-tempered girl. But Edmund had begun to experience other feelings for her when first informed of her supposed engagement to Chetwynd. He could not bear the idea of seeing her the wife of another man. It fretted, galled, and worried him day and night. This was jealousy—it could not then be called love.

Edmund had been deeply attached to Edith, as a brother to a sister—she was very dear to him, and he was selfish enough, sometimes, to hope she would not marry at all. He wished her to remain Edith Maxwell, that he might still possess her friendship—pure and undivided; for if married, he knew that friendship would be broken by other ties. But when assured by his sister that Edith's first love had been his, his heart bounded with delight at the prospect of making her happy for life. We have seen the result. Edmund's love had been progressive—it continued to increase to that extent that he could not now bear her out of his sight. They had been married five years—they were lovers still—all-in-all to each other. They were blessed with two lovely children—a boy and girl; but much as Edith loved her children, she loved her husband more.

The little Edmund, now four years old, had become the great pet of the aged Earl, for Edmund and Edith passed a large portion of the year at Woodborough, which was sanctified to them by early associations. Here still they would ramble together through those hallowed walks, and sit beneath the shade of that old venerated cedar, where they had first confessed their mutual love. Those had been blissful days, but only a foretaste of what they now enjoyed—that calm, serene, confiding affection which had banished all fear, jealousy and suspicion from their minds.

Edith had improved much since her marriage; from being a beautiful, lovely girl, she had now become a still more lovely woman, and although rather more dignified in manner, gentle, artless, and affectionate as ever. Women are often greatly altered after marriage. I wish I could say improved, morally as well as physically—but the case is not so.

The veil of modesty is frequently thrown aside—the pure thoughts and chaste ideas of the girl exchanged for the licence and liberty of the married woman. This is more especially the case with those who have been educated in large schools, or sent to French academies, where more attention is paid to ornamental than religious instruction—where they acquire utilitarian and worldly, in place of that true wisdom which cometh from above; for unless influenced and guided by religious principles, little faith can be placed in the integrity of man or woman. To the world they may appear honest and virtuous, but at heart what are they? *To the pure all things are pure*—and those girls who have been early taught at home that their first duty is owing to God, will, in future life, whether single or married, still continue to walk before him in innocency and holiness of mind. Solomon says, "Who can find a virtuous woman? for her price is above rubies."

We must now see how the Shuttleworth family had been progressing during the last five years. Shuttleworth senior's visions of ambition had been realised to a certain extent. He was a county magistrate, deputy-lieutenant, and member of Parliament. His speculations in railways had hitherto been successful. The Marquis has also profited largely by following his suggestions; neither had the Captain been forgotten.

Mr. Shuttleworth now launched out into other schemes. He had become a man of consequence in the House of Commons, and his opinion on other railway projects was listened to with the greatest attention; he was even consulted by the Government upon matters of this kind. He had risen in his own estimation far above the County Party, who had treated him once with hauteur and disdain. He had his town house—gave grand entertainments, many of the aristocracy patronising him; in short, he had become a very great man indeed, and was represented as worth millions of money—everything he touched in the way of speculation being converted into gold. But his extraordinary good luck was beginning to make him careless. It gratified his vanity and ambition to see his name in print. He was solicited to become a director and manager in other schemes, to the success of which the magic name of Shuttleworth acted as a guarantee. He had embarked very lately in a banking concern in the city, which had previously to his joining it been thought in a tottering condition. It became renovated by his money, power, and influence, and was now doing an immense business. Still he continued purchasing land, anywhere and everywhere he could lay his hand upon it, within ten miles of Hardington, his ultimate object being to obtain a peerage, and become one of the largest landed proprietors in the county.

Our friend Alphonso had also made rapid progress towards the perpetuation of the family name, Lady Gertrude having become the unhappy mother of three little boys and two girls, all bearing a strong resemblance to Grandmamma Shuttleworth in obesity and rotundity of person; in short—and they were very short for their age—they were as plump and round as little apple dumplings. Lady Gertrude did not like children, even her own—she never was fond of noisy little brats, whose proper place was in the nursery—they interfered with her amusements; but grandmamma doted upon them.

At first, Lady Gertrude positively refused to live under the same roof, even for a few days, with Mrs. Shuttleworth—whom she designated amongst her friends as an odious, vulgar woman; but when Alphonso s papa became a great man, and a member of Parliament, with his splendid mansion, &c., in B—— Square, Lady Gertrude condescended to accept apartments there for the London season; and Mr. Shuttleworth, proud of his daughter-in-law, kept her in good humour by magnificent presents of jewellery, and money whenever she required any little assistance; and to confess the truth, Lady Gertrude was, as the Captain remarked, "a very expensive article to keep up, and far beyond Jack's means without an extra allowance from the governor."

From these largesses and liberality, Lady Gertrude really began to like her papa-in-law, for she could do much more with him than his own son. She had only to ask to have, and he had also supplied her with funds to assist her two younger brothers with their promotion in the army. Lady Gertrude felt more at home in B—— Square than in her own father's house; and Mrs. Shuttleworth being excessively fond of her grandchildren, never interfered with their mother in any of her arrangements, in visiting and receiving company, the greater part of her time being occupied in the nursery.

Our friend Jack meanwhile kept his cab and park hack, belonged to a fashionable club in St. James's Street, and, to use the Captain's expression, "cut a great swell among the nobs." During the season, Duncombe took up his residence in London, from whence he attended all the principal race-courses, having now become a well-known character on the turf, and doing a good business in the betting line, his chum, Jack, in attempting to follow his example, doing the reverse. The Captain, having taken a very convenient lodging in the immediate vicinity of B—— Square, found his knife and fork always laid out for him when the Shuttleworths dined at home; and he had also become a favoured attaché to Lady Gertrude, attending her to the opera, and other public places of amusement, whilst Jack was amusing himself in localities not less celebrated as the resort of snobs and men of very lax morality; for Jack preferred being considered a great man in a coal cellar rather than a little man in a drawing-room.

Alphonso did not fancy being tolerated in the aristocratic circle to which he had obtained access through his wife. He felt amongst them as a fish does out of its proper element; in short, Lady Gertrude, finding she could do nothing with him, left him to follow his own devices and pursuits, regarding him pretty much in the same light as her footman—a necessary appendage to her establishment; or in a higher grade, as her house steward—since her ladyship left the direction of household matters entirely to her husband—Jack having to enact the part of purveyor of all things necessary for the establishment.

The Marquis of Dunkerton, after three years' probation with the horn, having made the discovery that he possessed neither the ability, temper, nor patience to become a first-class huntsman, had prudently resigned this unpleasant and invidious office in favour of his whipper-in and kennel huntsman, Dick, greatly to the comfort of his supporters in the field, who had, during his noviciate, been treated to an over abundance of *damson pie.*

No other changes had occurred in that neighbourhood worth mentioning, since we left the portals of Woodborough House five years ago.

CHAPTER XXXIX.

It is in the month of April we return to Woodborough again. We are once more the guest of the hospitable Earl. It is the breakfast hour. Edmund and Edith are reading their letters. One in an unknown hand has just been opened by Mrs. Errington, who has scarcely glanced over the first few lines, when, a faint scream escaping her lips, she falls back senseless in her chair. Edmund and Edith are by her side in a moment, rendering every assistance, when Mrs. Errington, slowly recovering, said in a low tone—"Dear Edith, come with me to my room."

They ascend the staircase in silence, but when safe within her own apartment, Mrs. Errington, bursting into tears, exclaims, "Oh, Edith! my poor child is no more!"

The truth flashed directly across Edith's mind that she

alluded to Lady Agnes, whose last letter, received more than a month ago, was written when suffering from illness and great depression of spirits. We need scarcely add that Edith's kind heart was filled with the deepest sorrow for the untimely fate of her early friend, and her tears mingled with those of Mrs. Errington. Both wept long and bitterly until their overcharged hearts had become somewhat relieved from the deadening shock by which they had at first been overpowered.

"Oh, Edith!" Mrs. Errington said, "how can we break this sad, sad news to the poor Earl? I dread the effect it may produce upon him."

"I will speak to Edmund, dearest Mrs. Errington, when I am a little more composed myself, and he will break it by degrees gently to our dear old friend. Oh, what a dreadful blow it will be to him, his once dearly loved, only child!" and poor Edith again burst into tears.

"Edith, dear Edith," Mrs. Errington said, "you must try to suppress your grief now; see Edmund at once, my dear; give him the letter when you are out in the garden together—it will be better there."

Edmund did not express such great surprise as Edith imagined when made acquainted with the cause of her deep sorrow; for, as he handed the letter to Mrs. Errington, the foreign post mark caught his eye, and from her sudden fainting he surmised the fatal truth. Still, with his beloved wife, he could not for some time suppress his grief.

"It is my duty now," he said, "my own dearest Edith, to apprise my poor old friend of this mournful event; and we must of course remain at Woodborough until he is a little recovered from the shock of this bereavement, although I believe, like myself, he suspects what has occurred."

We will not attempt to depict the sorrow of the bereaved father when apprised of the death of his only child. Deep heartfelt grief such as his cannot be portrayed; but in this hour of sore trial and distress, Edmund was his greatest comfort, and *he* also felt most acutely for the once dearly beloved companion of his youth. The Earl had, however, other little comforters around him, in Edmund's children, especially the boy, whom he loved with quite parental fondness; and the child, in return, never felt more happy than when sitting on his knee, delighting the old man with his joyous smile and innocent prattle.

The Earl, after his interview with Edmund, had retired to his own room, there to weep and pray in retirement, when little

Edmund entering, and seeing tears rolling down his cheeks, as he sat in his old arm-chair, crept quietly to his side, and raising his little cherub face to his, said, in a soft, touching tone, "Is dear grandpapa very ill?"

"My boy, my darling boy!" the old man exclaimed, taking him in his arms. "Yes, dear child, I am very ill to-day—but you remind me I have another tie to this wretched world."

"Dear grandpa won't die," the child continued, "and leave dear mamma and papa, and little Edmund all alone?" and he burst into tears, clinging round the old Earl's neck.

"Oh, no! my darling child, I trust not yet. I may pray, for their dear sakes and yours, to be spared a few years longer."

The letter adverted to, containing the intelligence of Lady Agnes's death, was written by Sir Digby Colville, lamenting, in the most sorrowful strain, the irreparable loss he had sustained by the premature decease of his young and affectionate wife, which had occurred after a few days' illness, and, at her last request, he was now on his return to England with her remains, to be deposited in the family vault at Woodborough.

We will pass over the intervening time, spent by the Earl and his household in deep sorrow, until the arrival of Sir Digby with the melancholy *cortége*, who was received by Edmund with as much courtesy as he could bring himself to observe towards one for whom he had ever entertained the greatest contempt, and whom the wretched fate of Lady Agnes had made him now regard with still greater aversion than before; for Edmund, knowing how unkindly she had been treated, and how neglected by this heartless man of the world, attributed her death to his unfeeling conduct.

The funeral was conducted in a strictly private manner; and prejudiced as Edmund had been against Sir Digby, he was not prepared for such deep humiliation and contrition as he exhibited upon this mournful occasion; his pale face, trembling lips, and excessive agitation betokening the deepest emotion.

"That man," thought Edmund, "has a heart; although deadened by worldly ideas and long indulged dissipation, he may become an altered being—perhaps this is the only deep affliction with which he has been visited—the prodigal may be reclaimed;" and by Edmund's invitation, he remained that evening at Woodborough, winning, by his subdued manners and apparent deep grief, the good opinion of both Mrs. Errington and Edith.

The Earl, however, could not be induced to see him, even

for a moment, and the next morning Sir Digby took his departure for London, having expressed his intention of travelling on the Continent, in the hope of alleviating the deep anguish of mind by which he was oppressed; so leaving Woodborough for a while, we will now follow him through his subsequent career in life, with a few supplementary remarks.

Before quitting England for the Continent, Lady Agnes had been persuaded by her husband to make a will, by which he was to succeed to her whole property in the funds, of which, as before stated, she had the power of disposal, after her decease; and it was now his first business in town to prove her will in Doctors' Commons, as a preparatory step towards obtaining a transfer of her money into his own name. Through a well paid, clever solicitor an arrangement was made with his creditors (before they were aware of the amount of funds to which he had now become entitled) on a very satisfactory scale, so that in a short time Sir Digby might once more be seen in public without fear of arrest.

Pending these transactions, the worthy baronet again disappeared from London, as secretly as he had arrived there; in fact, none of his anxious friends of the Jewish persuasion knew of his having been there at all—his solicitor representing him as still living abroad. For many months nothing was heard of the once fashionable Irish Baronet, until in the following May he once more appeared on the London stage of life, like a butterfly emerging from its dormant state into new life and gaiety, more than twelve months having elapsed since the decease of his wife.

It was, however, remarked by all his former friends and acquaintances that Sir Digby had become an altered man. He was grave and thoughtful, and painfully sensitive to any observation made about his late wife. He eschewed gambling, betting, and playing—even to a game at cards, and in place of being the *seeker*, he was now *sought* as a desirable *parti*.

"Well, Dunkerton," the Captain remarked one evening, "your friend Colville has come out in a new phase, or rather like Proteus, in a different shape; but I see through the disguise: he is trying to get hold of another heiress, Miss Aubrey, whose mother is a Catholic, and I should not be in the least surprised to hear that Colville had changed his faith, if he ever possessed such a thing as religious faith, as I overheard him telling Mrs. Aubrey last night that his family had formerly professed that creed."

"Well, Duncombe, I have sometimes thought of turning Roman myself. It is a much more comfortable form of religion than the Protestant, and absolution is a very easy mode of getting rid of a heavy debt of sin, such as mine."

"True, Dunkerton, as to the mode—but then follows that little objectionable monosyllable *if*—yes, if a man is fool enough to believe all those priests would cram down his throat—and if he is such a fool, perhaps he is as much to be envied as pitied. Colville, however, would just as soon turn Jew or Catholic—all modes of faith being equally indifferent to him; but the women seem to think he is half a saint already. 'Poor man!' the Countess of D——— exclaimed the other night, 'how Sir Digby mourns the loss of his pretty young wife. He looks the picture of melancholy!'"

"Well, Duncombe, you must confess he is greatly changed both in appearance and conduct, and I really believe the death of Lady Agnes has made a serious impression on him."

"And I suppose," added the Captain, "that having once tasted the bliss of married life, he is bent now upon a second trial of it—or rather, that having feathered his nest well by the first venture, he is now about to try his luck again with a second shuffle."

The surmises of the Captain proved not very wide of the mark, since Sir Digby had already made a very favourable impression on Miss Aubrey, who, as to character, disposition, and personal charms, was the very reverse of the unfortunate Lady Agnes; Miss Aubrey being rather short in stature, her features, although regular and handsome, pale as alabaster, and her natural disposition unimpassioned and phlegmatic—exhibiting no outward sign or semblance of those feelings by which she was actuated; she admired Sir Digby Colville rather from an excess of vanity, because he appeared to possess the same characteristics as herself, and the worthy Baronet, upon a very short acquaintance, having discovered her *penchant* for the grave and demure, adapted his conversation and conduct to her requirements.

Miss Aubrey, however, was not, like Lady Agnes, in love with his handsome person and agreeable manners at first sight—she was not the person to be wooed and won in a hurry. Sir Digby had a long, tedious game to play—he was obliged to proceed cautiously and systematically. The mother's good opinion must also be gained as well as that of her daughter, for a deep attachment existed between them; Mrs. Aubrey being a widow, and excessively fond of this her only child. Sir Digby talked religion with her, and sentimentality with her daughter, to such an extent, and with such apparent earnestness, that both believed him sincere.

Mrs. Aubrey and her daughter both attended the Roman Catholic chapel. Sir Digby, having thrown out several hints about his family being of that persuasion, and also that, having lived a good deal abroad, he had often attended their places of worship, was politely offered a seat in their pew when he felt disposed to occupy it, which he had done now for several Sundays; and Mrs. Aubrey, like a zealous Catholic, ever anxious to obtain proselytes, requested their priest and father confessor, whom he had met several times at her house, to call upon Sir Digby, and use his influence in converting him to Mother Church, by adopting the religion of his forefathers.

Now Mr. O'Donnell was, like Sir Digby, an Irishman, and one of good family also. He was about Sir Digby's own age, quite as gentlemanly in manners, very agreeable, much more learned and clever, and, to speak the truth, quite as gay at heart as the Baronet. We will not enter upon the arguments used by Catholics, nor the texts quoted from the New Testament in support of their creed; it may suffice to state that O'Donnell, taking these for his sermons, preached thereon at various times, with such effect, apparently, that at length Sir Digby confessed himself a convert to his arguments, and expressed his intention of returning to the faith of his ancestors. Yet in truth the arguments of the priest exercised a very faint influence over his mind, in comparison with those of Miss Aubrey, who, like a moth hovering round a candle, had at last burnt her wings. And how often do we find girls, and even women of sound sense and discretion, entrapped in this net of their own weaving! They treat open flattery and adulatory compliments with disdain, but there is another kind of flattery to which they become victims —deferential regard to their own opinions—or conversion through their influence, from a state of bondage to sin, to that of slavery to themselves. From becoming a convert to her religious opinions, Sir Digby in turn, converted Miss Aubrey, gradually and almost imperceptibly, into an admission of reciprocating his sentiments; in short, she was not aware of the dangerous weapon she had been using, until it had pierced her own heart; for upon due examination she found her convert reigning there, and secure of his position. Miss Aubrey consented to become his wife, on the condition that her lover first became a member of the Roman Catholic Church, to which an assent being given, he was received by Mrs. Aubrey with joy as her accepted son-in-law. Matters had progressed thus far most satisfactorily, and the other necessary preliminaries having been adjusted, the day was fixed for the marriage ceremony, and their engagement being no longer a secret, a short time after the following announcement went the round of the London and country papers, under the usual heading of "Marriage in High Life":—

On Saturday last, Sir Digby Colville, Bart., led to the hymeneal altar the beautiful and accomplished Miss Aubrey, only daughter of Mrs. Aubrey, of G—— Square, and Pennington Park, Lancashire. The ceremony was performed at the Roman Catholic chapel in Warwick Street; the worthy Baronet having very recently become a convert to the religious tenets of his most charming and wealthy bride.

CHAPTER XL.

About a month after the announcement of Sir Digby Colville's second marriage, which created no trifling sensation both at Woodborough and St. Austin's, Edmund and Edith were sitting together at their breakfast-table, when the letter-bag was brought in, upon opening which, Edmund's eyes became riveted upon one so intensely for a few moments, that Edith could not forbear noticing his looks of surprise and agitation.

"That handwriting!" exclaimed Edmund; "surely it cannot be!—yet look, my dear Edith! You know it better than myself."

"Good heavens, Edmund! it is indeed that of poor Agnes; I cannot be mistaken."

"Break the seal then, my love—I cannot; it must have been written previously to her death. How strange I have not received it before!"

Edith did as directed, with trembling fingers; for the handwriting of those we have loved, and who have been removed by the hand of death from us, causes a painful pang through the heart. On looking hurriedly over the first few lines, she exclaimed, "Oh, Edmund, my own dear Edmund, Agnes still lives! Thank God for this wonderful mercy! Her letter is dated the very day of that wretch's false marriage with another."

"Gracious Heaven!" cried Edmund, springing to his feet in boundless amazement. "Is it possible? What a monster of iniquity that smooth-tongued villain must be! But read, Edith; read and tell me what she says," as he stood leaning over his wife's chair.

"Her handwriting is very tremulous; I can scarcely decipher it."

Edith read as follows :—

My Dear Edmund,—Should this letter reach your hands, which I fear it never may, I implore you, as the friend and companion of my happier days, lose not a moment in coming to my rescue from this dreadful place —for, alas! I am a prisoner here. My husband left me six months ago, nor have I heard from him once, and ever since his departure I feel I have been under the espionage of his two French servants, who are on the watch day and night to prevent my escape, or holding communication with any one. I have not received a letter from home or dear Edith for more than twelve months, and I know not, therefore, whether my kind father is still living, or what has become of dear Mrs. Errington. Sir Digby told me I need not expect to hear from home again, after my last application for money. Oh, Edmund! I am sadly altered; you will scarcely know me again—but I am indeed, thanks to God, changed in heart and feeling also. Oh, come as soon as you receive this letter and save me—for I fear the worst—I may be removed to some other place.

Your broken-hearted

Agnes.

"Oh, Edmund!" exclaimed Edith, "what can we do to save poor Agnes, if indeed still alive?"

"Do, my beloved? I must leave home this very day, and travel with all speed, to prevent some fearful tragedy, since she evidently fears an untimely end from her gaolers, who are in the pay of this infernal scoundrel."

"And you, my own dearest Edmund, what may not befall you in attempting her rescue? We have never yet been separated since our marriage. Oh, Edmund! should you not return, your Edith could not survive you."

"Edith, my own darling Edith, do not unman me now," he replied, pressing her to his breast. "I will not, must not leave you, if you wish me not to go; but that Almighty God, in whom we both trust, will of his goodness restore me to you again. I go, dearest Edith, where my sense of duty calls me; I go to bring back the penitent to her father's house—to restore an only child, mourned and lamented as dead, to a parent's arms, to gladden once more the heart of the dear, kind-hearted old Earl, my second father. Should I not go, my own precious girl, on such an errand of mercy and charity as this even for a stranger? much more for the loved friend of our early days?"

"Yes, Edmund, indeed you ought. No selfish feelings shall again rise to my lips, in such a case as this Go, my own dearly beloved husband, do as your generous nature prompts you, and I will pray and put my trust in God's mercy to restore you to me again in safety, as well as poor Agnes."

"Then, dear Edith, it is best to go at once—every hour may be of consequence! but you must not tell the Earl or Mrs. Errington the errand on which I am going. It may be a fruitless one—poor Agnes, may, indeed, be no more; and this would cause my dear old friend a renewal of grief, re-open the wound now nearly healed. Let me secure his child first, if still living, and I doubt not this can easily be effected. Her heartless husband there is of course no chance of meeting. He is too much occupied with his new victim to venture near the château, and I will obtain sufficient assistance from the authorities of the nearest town to obtain her release without much trouble. You have no danger to dread on my account, and I shall take my faithful servant with me; so now, my beloved Edith, let me prepare for my journey."

That same afternoon Edmund left home with the stalwart Thomas, now his valet and confidential servant, both well provided with arms and ammunition in case of meeting with resistance, using all dispatch in travelling day and night to the place of their destination, the town of A——, within twelve miles of the old château in which Lady Agnes was now kept a prisoner. Here Edmund had an interview with the Prefect of Police, briefly telling his story, and explaining his object, when, after a short delay, he was accompanied by that functionary and two of his assistants.

As the carriage drove up the long avenue through which the approach led to this gloomy old mansion, embowered among lofty trees, the cracking of the postilions' whips caused every inmate to rush to the windows.

"It is my lor' Colville," exclaimed Pierre Dupont, hurrying to unfasten the hall door, at which he stood bareheaded, ready to receive his expected master. But great was his surprise and consternation when the Prefect of Police, springing from the carriage, the blinds of which had been partly let down, to screen him and Edmund from view, told him he was his prisoner. Resistance being out of the question, he was ordered instantly to conduct them to the apartments of Lady Agnes. But she, hearing Edmund's voice, sprang like lightning down the stairs, and fell senseless in his arms; and Edmund, as he held the once blooming and beautifully rounded, but now pale, attenuated form of her he had so fondly loved, overcome by the sad contrast, could not suppress his tears.

A little French girl, now her sole attendant, ran quickly to the assistance of her mistress with eau-de-Cologne and water, by which she was soon revived, having been carried by Edmund to a sofa in an adjoining room.

"Oh, Edmund!" she exclaimed; "dear kind Edmund, you have come to save your undeserving, unhappy Agnes. I feared I should never again behold any one dear to me, or revisit my native land. But God in his mercy has heard my prayers, and sent you to my relief. But oh! is my dear kind father still alive?"

"And well, dear Agnes," taking her thin, trembling hand in his. "All your friends were well when I left home."

"Thank Heaven!" she ejaculated, fervently, "for this unmerited blessing. Oh, how far, far above my deserts!"

"You have not much time to spare now, dear Agnes," Edmund said, gently; "and when sufficiently composed, we will go. Thomas can assist your servant in packing up your things; but take only your own, and what you absolutely require, for the carriage will not contain many packages."

"Oh, let us go directly," Agnes said, impatiently, her thoughts brought back to the object of Edmund's journey; "let us go, or he may return and prevent me."

"No, Agnes, you need not fear your husband; he will not interfere."

"Is he dead, then?" she asked, anxiously.

"No, dear Agnes; though for your sake I wish he had been; he is too much occupied with his pleasures to come here now—but we can talk of these things on our journey."

"Yes, dear Edmund, I will not ask you any more questions; for oh! how I long to leave this gloomy, dreaded place."

Within an hour, Edmund, with Lady Agnes and her little French servant girl, who would not leave her mistress, were seated in the carriage on their return home. From the weak state of his companion, Edmund wished to remain at the old town of A—— the first night, but Lady Agnes entreated him to proceed further, as long as daylight lasted, in dread of being followed by her husband, of whom she could not conceal her great apprehension, by keeping the blinds down on her side of the carriage, lest she might by any chance meet him on the road.

"My dear Agnes," Edmund said, seeing her continued agitation and excitement on this account, "I shall be seriously offended if you give way any longer to these useless fears and anxieties. Your husband is, to my certain knowledge, in Lancashire, at a friend's house, and I will vouch for his not appearing to obstruct you. I will answer also that, if you met him, he would only recognise you, if he did at all, by one of his polite bows."

"Is he lost, then, to all sense of feeling and honour?"

"No, he has not lost what he never possessed; he is the same heartless villain he ever was; but pray do not allude to him again. The mention of that man, and his infamous, murderous conduct towards you, renders me quite savage. Forgive me, dear Agnes," he said, observing her deep sorrow, and taking her hand in his, "if I have inflicted upon you any unnecessary pain—but until we reach home let us dismiss this unpleasant subject—only, on my honour, you are safe from him; so draw up the blind and let down the window, to admit this fresh balmy air, of which you stand so much in need."

Relieved of needless apprehensions by Edmund's positive and repeated assurances, Lady Agnes began soon to recover some degree of composure. The rapid motion of the carriage—the new scenery through which they passed—the variety of objects on and near the road, all these conspired to cheat her of her melancholy thoughts, and inspire her with fresh spirits. The heavy, crushing weight of hopeless despair had been removed from her mind, and freedom from those gloomy prison walls of the old château—from which she had feared never to escape with life—made her feel light and even cheerful, if not happy. Still she was very weak in body; and Edmund, now secure of his prize, would not permit her to be hurried unnecessarily through the remaining part of their journey.

"We will now take things more quietly," Edmund said, gaily, on the evening of their second day's travelling; "there is no need to hurry, and, to confess the truth, I feel nearly knocked up myself; so we will rest here to-night, and I will send Edith a few lines, to which you can add a postscript if you like; but don't write to your father or Mrs. Errington, as I wish to give them a joyful surprise, since neither know of my having gone to bring you home, and Edith is not to divulge the secret until our return."

From the heat of the weather, Edmund deemed it prudent, on account of his companion's weak state, to travel by easier stages; and the change of air and scene had effected considerable improvement in her health and looks, when they reached their last resting-place on French soil, before setting sail for the white cliffs of Old England. Their passage across the channel was quick and easy; the sea being unusually calm, with just sufficient breeze to waft them over; and, on reaching Dover, Edmund immediately set forward with four English posters, to travel with all speed to London.

They were within five miles of the metropolis, when a travelling chariot passed them at a furious rate, drawn also by four horses, the blinds being down; but as it was whirled by, a puff of wind blowing the silken curtain aside, the features of Sir Digby Colville, reading a letter, were revealed to Edmund, who was sitting forward on the right side of the carriage, Lady Agnes leaning back upon the cushion.

"Ah!" thought Edmund, "thou false villain, thou art now too late; thy victim has escaped—we are on British ground—and I have that paper with me which shall consign thee to a gaol, if thou dare follow here; still, to avoid a scene, I will hasten on with all speed; he may hear at Dover of our arrival there, but he cannot overtake us then, even if he make the attempt.

As they stopped to change horses at the first stage out of London, on the Great Northern road, where the day coach had just drawn up, Edmund heard a well-known voice at the carriage window.

"Ah, Edmund! how do, old fellow? Boxed up pretty close, I see; but let down the window, my boy—I've a word for your ear."

Refusal being out of the question, Edmund did as desired, when the Major, catching sight of Lady Agnes, reeled back as if shot.

"Eh! 'pon my life—is it—can it be? or am I dreaming? No, by gad, sir, it is really Lady Agnes—come to life again, by gad!" But before the last words had passed his lips, Edmund shouted out, leaning from the window, "Forward, my lads, as fast as you can go; good-bye Townsend—keep this secret until we meet again."

But the secret was too great—too marvellous to be confined within his own breast, and being engaged to dine that evening with a large country party at Lord Dunkerton's, out it came at the dinner-table, thus:

"Well, Townsend," the Marquis asked, "what news from the provinces?"

"That, by gad, my lord, which will make your hair stand on end, as it did mine to day."

"Indeed! Something more strange than usual, I suppose. Your stories are always wonderful."

"All I have ever told, Dunkerton, are as milk-and-water to this. Now, whom do you think I saw this very day, travelling post haste with Edmund Knightley down to Woodborough?"

"Well, it would be nothing wonderful for him to be seen travelling with his wife, for they are always together, in public and private; although it would be a wonder to see some husbands I could mention anywhere with their wives; but I am a bad hand at guesses, so let us know, without further parley, who this wonderful companion was?"

"Lady Agnes Colville!"

"Good God, sir!" exclaimed the Marquis, dropping his knife and fork on his plate, and springing back from the table in violent agitation, as if he had seen her ghost. "Come, come, Townsend"—his face as pale as the table cloth—"this won't do; joking on such a serious matter."

"Joking, my Lord! I am *not* joking; but I swear, as surely as I see your face at this moment, so surely did I behold that of Lady Agnes this very day, with Edmund Knightley, in his travelling carriage, as we stopped to change horses at Barnet. Edmund let down the window to speak to me, and I had a full opportunity of scanning her features; she is greatly changed—thin, pale, and haggard; but I will swear to her identity."

"Saw double, I suspect, Townsend," the Captain said, observing the Marquis's consternation.

"I saw single and clear enough, Duncombe. At first I thought myself under a delusion, and I rubbed my eyes well to be sure it was not from defect of vision; but to settle that matter, I will bet you and every man at table fifty pounds round that I saw Lady Agnes, as I state, this very day. By gad, sir! I'll take my solemn oath it is as true as that I am sitting at this table."

"Good heavens!" exclaimed the Marchioness, "are you not deceived yourself, Major Townsend, by somebody resembling Lady Agnes?"

"On my honour, I assure your ladyship, I have not been deceived; I had sufficient time to examine her features thoroughly, although she leaned back to screen them from me—and as I live, so is that unfortunate, ill-used woman amongst the living souls of this villanous world; and God knows I speak the truth."

There was a dead silence as the Major pronounced these last words, in a solemn, serious tone; not even a knife and fork was moving—amazement being depicted upon the face of every guest, who sat almost breathless with anxiety to hear more of this extraordinary story.

"Oh! what a Bluebeard!" exclaimed Lady Gertrude Shuttleworth; "what will become of that poor, pale little thing, Miss Aubrey, whom he has so lately married?"

"What a monster of depravity!" added the Countess of C——. "What an escape my poor Charlotte has had!"

But amid all the varied exclamations of this kind from his guests, the Marquis maintained unusual gravity, merely muttering to himself, "What a confounded fool!"

It is almost needless to state that the news of this extraordinary event spread like wildfire through the west end of London during that night and the following day; and, as a matter of course, quickly found its way into the newspapers.

CHAPTER XLI.

We must now follow our travellers to the end of their journey, St. Austin's, where they were rapturously received by Edith who had been watching day by day in restless anxiety for their return. At last the carriage was seen approaching by the lower drive from the drawing-room window, at which she had sat for hours together lately, to catch the first sight of her beloved husband; and without waiting for bonnet or shawl, Edith rushed to the hall door, and was once more clasped in Edmund's arms.

Her reception, also, of Agnes, was little less affectionate; for she had heard of her deep dejection and contrition, and could now welcome her as a friend indeed, with whom she could have some community of feeling; since Agnes had become not less changed in ideas than in personal appearance.

As yet Edmund Knightley had carefully concealed from her knowledge the infamous conduct of her husband with regard to her supposed death, or his second marriage with another, fearing the effect such heartlessness might produce upon her debilitated constitution ; but intending by degrees to break this distressing intelligence, when she should become more strong in body and mind, and feel once more at home in her father's house.

It was his first business now to acquaint the Earl with the astounding information of his long mourned child being still in existence, and he felt the difficulty of the task he had to perform ; but it could not well be delayed beyond the first night of her reaching St. Austin's. We find him, accordingly, early the next morning, on his road to Woodborough, and need not say how joyfully he was received by the old peer.

"Well, Edmund," he said, "I suppose I must not be angry with you for leaving your old uncle so suddenly, without a word of explanation ; and Edith, during your mysterious disappearance, has been equally uncommunicative ; in short, all that she would tell me amounted to this, that you had been sent for most unexpectedly to visit a very dear friend in France, on very particular business, and that I must await your return to know more of this unlooked-for call."

"You have heard the truth, my dear uncle, from Edith's lips, but the person I went to see is equally dear to her as to myself; and I am happy to say this friend returned with me last night to St. Austin's. She is about Edith's own age, and having married early in life one of the greatest reprobates that ever existed, was deserted by him some months ago, and left in a foreign land, at an obscure and lonely place, far removed from friends and acquaintances, and without a shilling to find her way home. To me, as the friend of her youth and dear Edith's husband, she wrote an imploring letter, for succour and assistance, and you may suppose our mutual surprise on receiving it, not having seen or heard from her for nearly two years—so that we believed that she had been consigned to an untimely grave, and even her own husband reported her as dead."

"Oh, Edmund!" exclaimed the old man, "how merciless, how more than heartless, must that man be who could desert a young and unsuspecting wife in this cruel manner! How like, I fear, to the fate of my poor, lost child! We know not what miseries, what deprivations she underwent, and died perhaps at last from a broken heart."

The bereaved father groaned heavily as he spoke these words, and the tears rolled down his furrowed cheeks."

"Might not poor Agnes, my dear uncle," Edmund said gently, "have been misrepresented as dead, like Edith's young friend, by her villanous husband, to get possession of her money? Might not this scoundrel have fabricated the story solely for this purpose?"

"Oh, no, Edmund!" the Earl said, mournfully—"the funeral—the coffin—alas! alas! it is all too true! Will the grave give up its dead? None but God can restore to life the inanimate corpse, and the time for such miracles has passed away. Why harrow up my agonised feelings afresh by a reference to that melancholy scene? Why re-open the wound in my still aching heart? Oh, no, Edmund, I shall go to her, but she will not return to me."

"Are we quite sure, my dear uncle, that your lamented child has ever been the tenant of that grave? God is very merciful: He brings to light the hidden things of darkness, and makes manifest the secret machinations of the wicked. 'His way is in the sea, His paths in the great waters, and His footsteps are not known.' The sons of Jacob showed to their father the blood-stained vestments of his favourite child, Joseph, whom he mourned and lamented as slain by wild beasts; but many years afterwards, we read of that father exclaiming, 'It is enough—Joseph, my son, is yet alive.'"

"Oh, Edmund," the Earl exclaimed wildly, as his lips quivered, and his aged frame shook from excessive agitation—"you speak in mysteries—what am I to think?—what believe? Relieve me from this agony of suspense. You would not deceive me—to what does all this tend?"

"To prepare you, my dear uncle, to adore the merciful dispensations of the Almighty, in the restoration of your only child!"

The Earl, falling upon Edmund's neck, burst into tears. They flowed fast and long before he could give utterance to these words: "How good is God! How much more merciful than I deserve!"

"Yes, my dear uncle, indeed He is good! Dear Agnes still lives—and, oh! how thankful am I to have been the instrument in God's hands of restoring her to you again! But she is much changed, my dear friend; sorrow has humbled her spirit, and care has blanched her cheek. Her nerves have been dreadfully shattered by all she has undergone, so you must not tell her what has happened here, or of her worthless husband's second marriage. The shock would be too much in her weak and nervous state; but when stronger, Mrs. Errington can break it to her by degrees."

"Yes, my dear Edmund, we will be very careful—but now let me hasten to bring back my poor suffering child to her father's house."

"Come, then, my dear uncle, will you order the carriage, whilst I see Mrs. Errington?"

To Edmund's surprise, his communication did not excite so much astonishment as he had imagined it would, for Mrs. Errington had gleaned sufficient from Edith during his absence to surmise the truth, although she had carefully concealed it from the Earl.

"You bring joyful news, dear Edmund," she said, as he entered the drawing-room, "which your guileless, warm-hearted Edith has led me to anticipate, although she would not betray your secret. You have returned, with my poor, ill-used, unfortunate child; and oh! how earnestly have I prayed, since I guessed the object of your journey, that you might both return in safety. Poor dear Agnes is sadly changed, I fear; yet better —far better, if God so wills—to die in peace at home than as a deserted stranger in a foreign land."

"With your kind, tender care, dear Mrs. Errington, I trust she will soon recover; but let no allusion be made in her presence to the villany of her husband. You must fortify her mind to endure this sore trial, when strong enough to bear its disclosure; for I fear she still entertains some lingering regard for the heartless destroyer of her peace and happiness. His depravity is only equalled by his plausibility; and, I confess, at that mock funeral, notwithstanding my previous impressions, his conduct induced me to form a more favourable opinion of him; but now that the mask is completely removed, one cannot conceive a more hideous, horrible character. This mock funeral was got up solely for the purpose of obtaining the money belonging to his wife, which he claimed immediately after her supposed death, and spent in paying his debts, to be again let loose upon society; and my firm impression is, that, believing poor Agnes to be in a declining state of health, he intended she should end her days in that old château, whether naturally or unnaturally I will not now say, but may tell you more another day, as the Earl must of course be very impatient to set out for St. Alban's."

The meeting of a father and child, under such circumstances as we have related, may be supposed most affecting, and there is a silence more expressive than words, when the heart is too overcharged with deep feelings of sorrow or joy to give utterance to its strong emotions. Lady Agnes fell tottering into her father's out-stretched arms: and as the old man held her attenuated form to his heart, his tears fell fast over the neck of his almost insensible daughter.

There were no witnesses to this affecting scene, for Edmund and Edith having silently withdrawn from the room, father and child remained alone—no third person could intermeddle with their grief, no eye, save One, beheld their tears, or heard, when utterance was given her, the outpourings of the stricken, repentant child in her father's ears.

"Oh, my too kind father!" she murmured, "can you forgive your wilful, disobedient daughter all the misery and sorrow she has caused you?"

"Hush, my poor deluded child," he said, gently, "talk not of the past—all is forgotten, all forgiven. Let us now grieve no more for what cannot be recalled, but praise God for His unexpected mercy in restoring you to me again. Come, my own Agnes, dry your tears, my sorrow is now turned into joy."

"Oh! that the Almighty may spare me a little longer, my dear father, to prove the sincerity of my repentance, and that I may be some comfort to you in your declining years."

"May God grant your prayer, my dear child; but now, as you love me, dearest Agnes, repress your tears and sobs, which go to my heart; and dear, good Mrs. Errington is waiting anxiously to clasp you in her arms."

The dreaded ordeal had passed, and Lady Agnes, now assured of her father's perfect forgiveness, felt relieved of a heavy weight of care and anxiety, which had been pressing her already humbled spirit to the earth. She was once more at home in her father's house, so changed in mind, feelings, and disposition, that none would have recognised the once haughty, wilful Lady Agnes Gerard of former days.

CHAPTER XLII.

WE must now take a short retrospect of Sir Digby Colville's conduct anterior to, and subsequent on, the mock funeral of Lady Agnes.

To a man of his pursuits and ideas, retirement in an old château was as banishment to a solitary island, for the society of his unhappy wife proved almost as bad as no company at all. There was an uncomplaining, though upbraiding, look in those tearful eyes, which sometimes struck him to the heart, as the wilful destroyer of all her happiness. He felt uncomfortable in her presence—restless, nervous, anxious, painfully anxious to drown his cares once more in dissipation.

In the absence of other women to flirt with, Sir Digby commenced a *liaison* with his wife's lady's-maid, who was quite as handsome as her mistress ever had been, and now of course far more attractive. All the other English servants having been previously dismissed, upon the plea of poverty, and the necessity of retrenchment in every department, her carriage and horses had also been sold, and in the place of butlcr and footman an old French soldier, with his wife and a little girl, had been substituted, who, between them, did all the household work.

The amour with the pretty lady's-maid terminated as such things usually do, and in an evil hour the unfortunate girl, to avoid detection, was prevailed upon by her master to use remedies which in a few days caused her death. Nowise disconcerted by this appalling event, her heartless seducer and murderer almost immediately after devised the plan of turning the death of his victim to account, in furtherance of the project which had now gained possession of his mind. His wife's money would fall to him after her decease, which, from her increasing debility and low spirits, he calculated upon taking place within a twelvemonth at farthest, if not earlier. He was dreadfully short of money, and felt it impossible to remain in the château much longer, when everything reminded him of his guilt. He thought he might safely anticipate in such a case, and by conveying the remains of this wretched girl to England as those of Lady Agnes, claim the long-coveted possession of her fortune. Under thc pretence of paying a secret visit to Ireland to collect some rents, Sir Digby left home the day after the coffin had been removed from the château, and conveyed to the nearest town *en route* for England, Pierre being told by his master that the friends of the deceased girl, who were highly respectable, had requested him, in case of her dying abroad, to have her remains consigned, if possible, to her native soil.

We have elsewhere related the success of this infamous scheme, and Sir Digby Colville's return to London subsequent to the supposed funeral of Lady Agnes, whence, after a short stay, for the purpose of proving her death, and obtaining possession of her property, he again set out for the old château in France, where he was received with joy by his deluded and yet too attached wife. Lady Agnes had few correspondents, save Edith and Mrs. Errington, and it having struck her with surprise that no letters had reached her lately from home, Sir Digby assigned as the cause her father's extreme displeasure at her third application for pecuniary assistance, in which feeling, he said, no doubt Edmund Knightley participated, and had forbidden his wife to continue their correspondence.

This proved the heaviest blow poor Lady Agnes had yet received; to be deserted by the only true friends she had ever possessed—to be neglected and scorned by them in poverty and banishment—almost broke her heart. She wept long and bitterly in the retirement of her own room, and at last, thoroughly overcome by these painful reflections, she fell upon her knees, praying earnestly for grace and strength of mind to support her in this sore trial; and it is thus, when all other sources of earthly comfort and consolation seem dried up, that we apply to that fountain of living waters which ever flows to the relief of the broken-hearted and contrite sinner. From her Bible Lady Agnes now derived support, many passages of which seemed peculiarly applicable to her own case; and it was her only pleasure to sit alone, reading those beautiful and life-giving pages she had never seriously studied until now, when affliction and sorrow had humbled her once proud spirit in the dust.

Sir Digby had passed the winter with her, on his return from England, but as the spring approached he again spoke of going to London, in the hope of ultimately arranging his affairs; that at present his wife could not accompany him, it being necessary that he should remain incognito until these matters were settled. At these words, hope revived in her heart—the hope ever uttermost in her thoughts, of throwing herself at the feet of her once loved, honoured father, and imploring his forgiveness for her undutiful conduct.

Before leaving his wife the second time, Sir Digby gave certain strict instructions to Pierre Dupont about the safe custody of his lady, whom he wished until his return to remain in perfect seclusion. That no visitors were to be admitted to the château, and that he was to keep the strictest watch over her day and night, lest she might endeavour to follow him to England, where, for particular reasons, it would be most impolitic for her at present to appear; and these orders being backed by a round sum of money, with the promise of a larger one if strict attention were paid to his instructions, Pierre Dupont, beginning to comprehend how the matter stood, promised implicit obedience to his master's commands.

Now, the fact was, Pierre was no stranger to Sir Digby's true character, having been his servant some years previously when in Paris for one entire season, and Sir Digby, having again met with him before the dismissal of his other servants, engaged his services with his wife, knowing he was just the person to suit him, as willing to execute any orders, however villanous, he might require at his hands.

"You understand, Pierre," his master said, with a meaning look, "that I wish, for very particular reasons, which I will explain when we meet again, that Lady Agnes is neither to be visited by any one, nor are any letters to be received or sent by her during my absence. You will take charge of them for me."

"Je comprends, monsieur," was the reply, with a diabolical grin.

"Any she may choose to write you will of course undertake to forward to their proper destination."

"Ah! oui; je comprends, monsieur."

"Your little relative, Louise, will attend upon her ladyship. You will not, however, inform her of anything I tell you."

"Certainement non, monsieur—she varra young—me no trust her."

"There is another thing, Pierre, to be strictly observed. Her ladyship must be watched and followed by yourself, at a certain distance, during her walks and rambles, and should she attempt to make her escape, or go beyond the grounds, you will restrain and bring her back. Such are my orders."

"Je comprends," was again the short reply, and after these few directions, Sir Digby left his unfortunate wife the next morning, assuring her of his intention to return as soon as possible, and then accompany her once more to their native land; but that she must not write to him in the mean time, lest her letters might lead to the discovery of his abode in London before his business had been settled, and thus overturn all his plans.

The now subdued and miserable wife reluctantly consented to observe these hard commands of her base, worthless husband, believing implicitly in his assertions, and accepting as true his plausible reasonings. Still, however, there was some light, although gleaming in the distance, which broke in upon her to prevent despondency and despair. "He might be absent a month or two, perhaps not so long; it might be, however, longer. Lawyers were proverbially dilatory—but she might depend upon his return immediately it was possible to do so;" and with these assurances, Lady Agnes consented without remonstrance to await patiently his return.

It was the first week in March when Sir Digby set out on his second visit to London, nearly twelve months after the supposed death of his ill-used wife, the greater portion of her money having been already spent in arranging with his creditors, so that he appeared once more a free and reported rich man in the gay circles of the metropolis. For the last eighteen months Lady Agnes had been suffering from great debility, accompanied with constant cough and severe pains in the chest; and as day by day she had become thinner, Sir Digby gathered from these symptoms that she was gradually sinking by slow degrees from consumption, and that in all probability he should never again behold her alive. To his confidential agent, Pierre Dupont, instructions were given to write him regular bulletins of her health, and to procure for her any medicines she might require, but on no account to send for a physician, lest he might betray her place of residence.

For a month after her husband's departure, buoyed up by the hope of his speedy return, and the genial spring weather, which revives even the most drooping plants, Lady Agnes appeared improving in health; but as "hope deferred maketh the heart sick," she again relapsed into her usually low state of mind, and her nervous anxiety increased so much, that her appetite completely failed her; her cough also returned with increased violence, and she made complaints to the little Louise of the severity of the pain in her chest, which prevented her sleeping. Pierre's wife became very assiduous in her attentions to her unfortunate lady, prescribing various little remedies, decoctions of herbs, and warm cordials at night, which afforded some relief. But the impression made upon this worthy couple was that her days were numbered, and thus about the end of May Pierre wrote his master, advising his immediate return.

This pleasing intelligence reaching Sir Digby at the period when his addresses were being paid to Miss Aubrey, put him into the highest spirits, since he now believed the chief obstacle to his contemplated marriage with a second victim would speedily be removed, and subsequent letters tended to confirm him in this opinion, Lady Agnes having expressed to her little waiting-maid her belief that she could not live through another winter.

Four months had now passed since Sir Digby's departure from France, and Lady Agnes, becoming both excited and alarmed by her husband's long absence, wrote both to Edith and a friend in London to inquire about him. To these letters of course there was no answer. Again she addressed other former acquaintances, with the like result. Another tedious month dragged its slow length along—her suspense and anxiety could no longer be endured, and her suspicions became at last aroused. She questioned Pierre about the non-delivery of any letter from England, saying she had written to several friends, but not one answer had been received by her. Pierre merely shrugged his shoulders, declaring none had arrived; but his evasive replies to other questions roused her naturally warm temper, and she desired him to procure her a conveyance to the nearest post town, to make inquiries herself into the matter.

Pierre again had recourse to objections and evasions, which Lady Agnes, now thoroughly excited, refused to listen to. She insisted upon a carriage being sent for immediately, or she would walk. The weather was fine, she would take Louise with her, and she would hire a carriage to return. Pierre saw by her determined manner and words that the crisis had arrived for informing her of, and enforcing his master's orders, and he firmly, though quietly, told her Sir Digby's directions were that she was not to leave the château during his lord's absence.

Lady Agnes stood for a moment speechless at this information, then, turning abruptly away, burst into tears. The truth flashed across her mind, that she was, for some mysterious purpose, a prisoner in her own house, and all correspondence with her friends cut off. She retired to her bedroom, where, unperceived, little Louise sat silently working in a corner, and falling into a chair, gave way to a violent outbreak of grief, covering her face with her hands and sobbing aloud. The young girl became touched with her mistress's distress, and falling upon her knees before her, took one of her hands and raised it to her lips.

"Oh, do not cry so, my dear lady," the girl said, in soft, pitying tones; "it will make you so very ill again. Oh! say what Louise can do to stop those tears?"

"Do, Louise?" as a sudden thought struck her; "what would you do to save my life?"

"Anything—everything, to save so kind a mistress; but," she added, in a whisper, "we must not talk here," and then in a louder tone, "Milady will take a walk; I will fetch her bonnet."

Lady Agnes understood her meaning, and believing now she had gained a friend, dried her tears and set out for a walk, accompanied, as she often was, by her little attendant. They had proceeded some short way from the house, Louise keeping at a respectful distance behind her mistress, when the young girl, looking back, perceived Pierre watching their movements; and suggested, it being a very warm day, that her lady had better rest on an old rustic seat in the pleasure ground until the heat had abated. The hint was taken by Lady Agnes, who accordingly sought the chair, and Louise, as usual, sat upon the ground at her feet.

"Louise," her mistress said, "we are now alone; will you assist me? I have no friend here but you, and if you will do as I bid you, I will reward you handsomely for your services, and will provide for you as long as you live, so that, should anything befall your unhappy mistress, you shall never be obliged to enter the service of another, or work for your bread."

"Indeed, dear lady, I will do anything I can, but Pierre is very watchful."

"Listen then, Louise, to my proposal. I know my letters have never been sent by him, for I have written many, to which I have received no replies, and I fear your master has met with some accident, or perhaps he no longer lives."

"He is not dead, dear lady; Pierre heard from him only yesterday."

Lady Agnes, starting with surprise, asked, "How know you this, Louise?"

"I overheard him and Madame Dupont talking about it last night as I listened at the door before going into the room.

They said it was strange my lord did not come, when he had written him so often about your being so very ill."

Lady Agnes sat lost in thought for some few moments, when the exclamation escaped her: "It is even thus, then: I am deserted by my husband; he has left me to perish here alone, a prisoner, uncared for, in a foreign land! Oh, could I have believed him so cruel, so heartless! He for whom I have sacrificed all, and every other friend in the world;" and the tears again chased each other down her pallid, care-worn cheeks.

"Oh! don't weep so bitterly, dear lady," again interposed Louise, raising her glistening eyes to her mistress's face; "Louise will do anything you desire."

"Will you promise faithfully to do what I ask you?"

"Indeed, indeed I will, dear lady, if it be at all possible."

"Then you will take a letter for me to the nearest post town, and place it yourself in the letter-box? You have asked me to go to-morrow to the village *fête*, three miles off; you are young and active, but I will give you money to obtain some conveyance there and back, if you think it is too far for you to walk."

"Pierre is so very suspicious," the girl remarked, thoughtfully, "he may search my pockets and find the letter; yet," she added, with childish quickness, "the lining of my bonnet, he would never think of looking there. Dearest lady, I will run the risk, and by going very early to-morrow morning I shall have time to reach the town and return to the village *fête* before the afternoon. My uncle lives only a mile beyond, and I can get his little cart to convey me there and back, telling him I want to buy some things for you."

"Thank you, dear Louise; your plan is very good; you shall have money to buy yourself anything you wish, and to bring me a few *bon-bons* from the fair; but now we will continue our walk under the shade of the trees."

That same evening Lady Agnes, now persuaded that her husband intended to keep her a prisoner there, for some mysterious reasons, while Pierre and his wife were engaged at supper, wrote the letter we have elsewhere alluded to, praying and entreating Edmund Knightley to rescue her. The more she dwelt upon her husband's conduct, the more heartless and suspicious it became. He could write to Pierre many letters, but not one line, not even a message, had ever been conveyed to her since his departure, now nearly five months ago. She was watched, too, and not permitted to leave the grounds. What could this mean? why this surveillance over her? Strange misgivings seized upon her mind. She had read, in some of the old books the library contained, dark, mysterious tales connected with these old, sequestered mansions; of unhappy wives immured for years within their dismal walls, of murders perpetrated, which were not discovered until many years afterwards; and this was a place sequestered and remote enough to raise up suspicions and conjure horrors in her mind, that the fate of others might be realised by herself. The fact, too, occurred to her with unpleasant reflections, that her husband had induced her to make her will in his favour before leaving England. Horror of horrors! could he meditate her death to obtain her money? She had been reading only the week before of a dreadful tragedy like this, which made her shudder; and under these fearful apprehensions, her resolution was taken, to implore Edmund Knightley to come to her rescue.

The letter was hastily written, and given the following morning to Louise, with very particular instructions to post it herself, being sewn up, at her suggestion, within the lining of her bonnet. The precaution proved most fortunate, for Pierre searched both her pockets before she was permitted to leave the house. The faithful girl, now only fifteen years of age, executed her mission with fidelity and quickness—her cousin, a lad two years older than herself, to whom she was greatly attached, driving her to the town of A——, where they delivered the letter into the hands of the postmaster, paying the postage, and obtaining from him a memorandum in writing to that effect, after which the two cousins returned to the village to enjoy the *fête*, and then in the evening to the old château, where, when alone with Lady Agnes, Louise related what she had done, producing the paper signed by the postmaster as a proof of her faith.

It was enough; Lady Agnes, charmed by her ingenuity and fidelity, caught her to her heart, and shed for the first time tears of joy at the now certain prospect of deliverance from that man whom she had so blindly and madly loved.

CHAPTER XLIII.

THE last view we had of Sir Digby Colville was in his travelling chariot, going as fast as four horses could convey him towards Dover, where he purposed embarking directly for the Continent. Pierre's letter had been received by him a few days previously in Lancashire, where he had been passing the honeymoon with his new bride, when seeing at a glance, from the description of his wife's liberator, that he could be no other than Edmund Knightley, and that consequently the exposure of his conduct could not be concealed beyond a very brief period, his resolution was immediately taken, to collect together all the money he could from his victim, Miss Aubrey, and fly the country. With a plausibility and coolness peculiar to his character, he informed her that urgent business required his immediate presence in Ireland for a few days, and under pretence of having spent all his ready money, his unsuspecting and fond bride offered all the cash she possessed at his disposal, and that same night his arrangements were made for leaving early the next morning for London.

Arrived there, he obtained possession of Miss Aubrey's diamonds, which had been left by her, at his suggestion, and in his company, at her jeweller's, to be re-set before their marriage, drawing also a considerable sum from his bankers, on his note of hand, which was advanced in anticipation of a portion of his reputed wife's fortune, to which he was entitled; for it being now clear to Sir Digby that he could not show his face in London, for some few years at least, if ever again, he had prudently calculated upon the contingencies which might arise, and provided himself with a sufficient sum of money, and the diamonds of great value, to enable him to travel comfortably in foreign lands until the storm now gathering over his head should have abated its violence.

Sir Digby, although exceedingly cautious in most transactions, had acted far too hastily with regard to his second marriage, having taken it as granted from Pierre's last dispatches, that Lady Agnes could not live much longer, being, as he concluded, in the last stage of consumption, and that in her weak state it was next to an impossibility she ever could reach her native shores, even should she escape Pierre's vigilance, without money or friends to assist her on the journey. It never entered into his calculation, after all the precautions he had taken, that she ever again could hold any communication with, or receive any succour from home, where all believed her to be long since numbered among the dead. Pierre had also informed him of the intercepted letters, so that he saw no possibility, under his supervision, of her receiving any communication whatever from any of her relatives or friends in England.

It appearing, therefore, to him self-evident that treachery had been practised by Pierre, he set out with the intention of wreaking his vengeance upon him as the subverter of his plans, to whom his disgrace and discomfiture could only be attributed. It is ever thus that the worldly-minded and depraved look to second causes, instead of the First Great Cause, by whom their machinations and evil intentions are defeated. They forget or despise that all-seeing Almighty Being, without whose permission "not a sparrow falleth to the ground."

Upon reaching Dover, Sir Digby learnt that a lady and gentleman, answering the description of his wife and Edmund Knightley, had arrived that morning from Calais, and had immediately set out again with four post horses for London.

"A day too late," he muttered, savagely. "I might have stopped them on French soil, and had my revenge upon that meddling fool Knightley. Had we met, his life should have been the forfeit for this daring enterprise. We may meet again," he continued, thinking aloud; "and when we do, this insult shall be wiped out with his blood. Had Dunkerton not interfered, he would have been prevented doing me this mischief now."

Thus meditated Sir Digby, regardless of those gross irreparable injuries and insults he had heaped upon the heads of two unsuspecting, confiding women; and there are many worldlings like him, who sacrifice without compunction their wretched dupes—led astray by false protestations of love—to their own selfish, unhallowed passion. To women, honour is the most precious heritage—that jewel of great value for the loss of which nothing can compensate, no penitence redeem, no tears reclaim; and yet with what cool indifference, what heartless carelessness, will men rob them of this inestimable treasure, and cast them like worthless toys away! Jealous enough of their own miscalled honour, they will at the same time treat that of woman with indifference and even contempt, boasting of the treachery by which they have accomplished the ruin of some young, artless girl! Such a man was Sir Digby

Colville, who, now defeated in his vile schemes, was obliged to fly his country to avoid prosecution for bigamy.

Upon reaching the old château, he vented his wrath upon Pierre, accusing him of perfidious dealings, and receiving a bribe to liberate his wife. Pierre retorted angrily, being in this case unjustly accused. Fierce altercations and threats followed on both sides, when Sir Digby, unable to restrain his passion, caught him by the throat, shaking him as a dog would a rat, by which the Frenchman's tiger-like disposition being roused to the utmost, he drew a knife from his pocket, and stabbed his master in the side, who fell with a deep groan upon the floor, where he lay motionless, without any signs of life.

Pierre stood for a few moments contemplating the bloody work of his hands, then, shrugging his shoulders, exclaimed, "Ah! I am revenged, and his lady too!" Then hastening to his wife, he told her what had occurred, and how he had been provoked beyond endurance to resent the insulting treatment of his late master.

"Perhaps he is not dead," she said; "let us go and see."

"It is useless," Pierre replied; "he never moved after falling. No, no, bolt the doors, we must escape, as soon as it grows dark."

It was already evening, Sir Digby having arrived late in the day.

Pierre and his wife were at once busily occupied in collecting all the money and valuables they could find about Sir Digby, and in his portmanteau, where Miss Aubrey's diamonds had been deposited; Pierre's eyes glistening with delight on discovering these precious stones, the value of which he well understood.

"Ha! ha!" he exclaimed, exultingly. "Milor Anglais pay well for keeping his secret."

Having ransacked every vestment and box likely to contain money or jewellery, Pierre desired his wife to dress herself in one of his suits of clothes, and as the shades of evening began to fall, they were leaving the house, when the thought struck him, that, by setting fire to the curtains of the room in which the body of Sir Digby lay, the old panels would soon be in a blaze, and all traces of the murder obliterated, before assistance could arrive from the village, about three miles distant. This thought was acted upon without delay, and Picrre and his wife escaped by the back door, the key of which they took with them.

The fierce heat of the room, and crackling of the flames,

roused Sir Digby from the long and fearful stupor in which he lay, for life was not extinct, and by a last effort to escape the horrible fate with which he was now threatened, the wounded man crawled to the window, the framework of which had been destroyed by the flames; and dragging himself forward, as far as his strength would permit, sank again, fainting from loss of blood, upon the lawn, about a hundred yards from the old château, every part of which was now enveloped in one vast blaze of light.

The extraordinary illumination was at length perceived by some of the villagers, who, rousing their neighbours, a cry of fire was raised, men, women, and children quickly gathering together, and with the curé at their head, all who were able set out directly for the château.

The first object presenting itself to their view was the body of Sir Digby Colville, lying apparently lifeless upon the lawn, from which it became evident to the village doctor, upon examination, that the vital spark had not yet fled. The flames were now issuing from every window of the house, Pierre having too effectually done his work, so that the prospect of saving anything from the ruins becoming hopeless, the old château was abandoned to its fate, none daring to venture within its doors.

By the direction of the doctor and curé of the parish, the body of Sir Digby was conveyed in a litter, by four men, to the village, where he was taken to the house of the latter, and by the aid of stimulants, restored to consciousness, though for some hours incapable of speaking.

"It is a hopeless case," the doctor remarked; "he must sink, but we may rouse him sufficiently by powerful stimulants to obtain the information we desire, as to the perpetrator of this fearful catastrophe."

That night, however, nothing could be elicited, from the heavy stupor into which he again relapsed; but on the following day, Sir Digby recovered sufficiently to give a short account of what had occurred; and from this, to him great exertion, he fell once more into a state of insensibility for some hours. Upon being awakened by the pain he was now enduring, and being told by the doctor that he must make the best use of the little time he had to live, he shrieked out with horror, "Am I dying, then?"

"I fear so," replied the doctor; "although a few hours more may be allotted to you—perhaps a day."

"Oh! God of mercy," he cried, "spare me! oh! spare me, that I may repent the grievous sins I have committed! No, no, it cannot be! I am dreaming—not dying. Save me, doctor," he cried frantically, "save me from everlasting perdition! I cannot, must not die!"

"My friend the curé will assist you there," the doctor said; "he will give you absolution from your sins; my art can avail you no longer."

"Do not leave me—do not go," Sir Digby continued, imploringly.

"I will see you again in the evening; but now I must go. I have other patients to attend."

And now the dreaded, terrible reality broke for the first time on the mind of the dying man. He had scoffed at and despised religion as a well-devised system, but suitable only to weak-minded, credulous people—women and children. He had never looked into or wished to study the Book of God. This world had been his only world. He had never given himself the trouble to inquire about that which lay beyond it; and when listening perchance to a sermon—a rare occurrence, for he seldom went to church—the description given by the preacher of the joys of heaven was at direct variance with his ideas of happiness and pleasure; there was nothing to allure a worldly, or gratify a carnal mind—not one sensual pleasure could be found in it—no gay, frivolous society—no trifling amusements—no song or dance, such as worldlings love, to enliven the borders of heaven. It was when about to approach the confines of that other unknown world—when about to appear before an insulted and despised God—that the horrors of his situation burst with overwhelming force upon his affrighted soul.

Thousands and millions like him have lived the life, but rare are the instances, when time for reflection has been allowed them, of any dying the death of the Deist. It is when this world is fast receding from their view—when its frivolous amusements and pleasures can be enjoyed no longer—when friends are powerless to render assistance—when they must pass alone through that dark unknown valley of the shadow of death, that the ungodly look for comfort and support from the only arm which can now succour or befriend them; and were *remorse* repentance, few would die impenitent. But would we die the death, we must live the life of the righteous.

Is it the fear of punishment, or the love of God, which

deters us from the commission of sins? for by this test the truth of our religion can alone be ascertained. If the love of God is not shed abroad in our hearts—if we do not detest sin, because it is the accursed thing which God abhors—we have not vital religion. And why do we not love God? Have we not, every soul of us, to consider him our nearest, dearest friend—one who will never desert us, when all others run away? It was he who watched our helpless infancy—directed by him, our guardian angel hovered around our cradle—it is his almighty arm which has been stretched out to protect us through all the dangers and trials of youth and manhood, and which has led us hitherto safely and securely through the vast, howling wilderness of the world. Have we not reason to be grateful, more than thankful, to our Great Deliverer, through all the trials and troubles of this mortal life? And when we contemplate the price paid for our immortal souls—when we seriously reflect upon that vast, astounding love which began in the manger at Bethlehem and ended upon the cross, does not a mere *professing* Christian appear to us a wonder in the universe?

Whoever you may be—young or old—blessed with this world's goods or bereft of them—heed my words, follow my advice: Make God your friend, who has done such great things for you; believe in him—trust in him—confide in him. Yes, tell him every secret of your heart. Don't look upon him as afar off, an unconcerned spectator of man's ways and thoughts—believe him to be, as he ever is, about your bed by night, and your path by day. Make God's presence the reality it is, and you will seldom commit any great sins. Make heaven also a reality. Look forward to it as your only safe and happy home—as your inheritance. Always be thinking of that house provided for you, not made with hands, eternal in the kingdom of God.

It was now the province of the Catholic priest to soothe the troubled spirit, and pour consolation into the sinking heart of Sir Digby Colville, by the promise of forgiveness, upon a confession of his sins, who, to his great joy, he found, had lately become a convert to his creed. The last religious rites had been administered to the dying man, when an English gentleman, travelling through that part of the country on his return to England, obtained admission to his room. This was Chetwynd, who, hearing of the extraordinary circumstances which had taken place, came to see Sir Digby in his last hours, and offer any assistance he might require.

His charitable visit revived for a few fleeting moments the flickering lamp, which was now quickly burning out, and appeared to animate him with returning life. Sir Digby expressed his thanks to Chetwynd, intrusting him with some brief directions, and to apprise his nephew of his death, who was the heir to his titles and estates; and begging that his remains might be conveyed to Ireland. A message also was sent by him to Lord Dunkerton.

"I dare not ask forgiveness," he said, "of my ill-used, neglected wife, who still lives, although reported dead."

Chetwynd started in surprise.

"Lives—you say!"

"Yes, Chetwynd—you must loathe me for my crimes—but you will soon learn all—more I have not power to tell you; but I entreat you to see her, and assure her I died in just abhorrence of the cruel treatment she has received at my hands—and—one other—oh! ask them to forgive, and pray for my guilty soul."

He could not say more; and sinking back upon his bed, fell into a heavy slumber, from which he never more awoke: thus perishing, unwept, unmourned, in a foreign land, and meeting that fate he had prepared for his unoffending and ill-used wife.

CHAPTER XLIV.

To account for Chetwynd's appearance, we must relate what became of him after his mad attempt to perish with, rather than live without, the woman he had loved so desperately. From irritability of the brain, some excuse may be made for this fearful outrage; it was not premeditated; he never had for a moment contemplated self-destruction, or that greater crime, taking the life of another. Chetwynd possessed a warm heart and generous disposition, but he was like a lucifer match, composed of igneous materials, which, upon the first hard rub, burst out into a flame. He was irritable and impetuous, sometimes to an alarming degree: giving way at the moment to the impulse of those fierce passions which lay latent in his breast until evoked by some sudden excitement. By such men as these murder is committed; for few are so utterly depraved, so hardened, as to shed the blood of their fellow-men without provocation or insult. In a moment of uncontrolled anger, the fatal blow is dealt which consigns the injured to an untimely grave, and the injurer to a living death. It is under the influence of unbridled lust or passion that those fearful crimes are committed which bring quick repentance, and long, never-ending remorse. There is, no doubt, a passing gratification in such indulgences. It is like the outpouring of pent-up waters. The dam is burst, the stream rushes forth in its first irresistible force, carrying all before it; but soon does the swelling, foaming torrent subside into its usual quiet, sullen channel.

Chetwynd, under the promptings of wild, ungovernable passion, tinctured with a little resentment, would, in that moment of frenzied excitement, have consigned himself and Edith Maxwell to a watery grave; for, however we may attempt to disguise the fact, there is in man's nature, even of the best kind, much passion mixed up with his love for woman. We may talk of pure, disinterested affection, and this, no doubt, is felt by many of chaste minds in the first dawning of their youthful love-dreams; but this becomes gradually alloyed with more earthly dross and selfish desires.

Chetwynd was not one of refined ideas on this subject. He was passionately in love with Edith, and her dazzling beauty had now entirely engrossed his whole thoughts and feelings. He had given way to them without the least restraint or reservation. There was no rival in his path to cause him fear or doubt, and he had her father's full sanction to his suit. The first rejection of his proposal he attributed solely to maiden coyness; but, since her illness, she had received him with those soft, beaming looks which he had mistaken for love. There is a sympathetic feeling in woman for the man who loves her in vain, because she loves another—a compassionate expression in her pitying eye, which is too often attributed to a very different cause; and thus Chetwynd, relying upon these outward signs, had deluded himself into the conviction that Edith reciprocated his own feelings. He also entertained the idea, very prevalent with those who have seen the world, that by patience and persevering attentions the love of any woman may be obtained, provided the suitor is tolerably good-looking and agreeable. Some go a point beyond this, by asserting that even the plainest man may win the heart of the most beautiful and accomplished of the softer sex, if he will take the time and trouble requisite for this purpose. Every-day facts appear to confirm this opinion; and as a general rule, it must be admitted that we see much more often handsome women married to plain, even ill-looking men, without the semblance of one external interesting feature to recommend them, than handsome men with plain wives.

Chetwynd, when assured of the Colonel's entire approval of his addresses to his daughter, felt fully satisfied as to the ultimate attainment of his object; and, blinded by infatuation, construed all Edith's blushes and little exhibitions of uneasiness and restraint in his presence as certain proofs of her growing preference. In such a nature as his, however, passion had now obtained so complete an ascendancy, that he could submit to no further delay, and, supported by her father, he never anticipated any serious opposition to his proposal. There might be a little tiresome timidity, or bashful reluctance, on her part, to confess her true feelings; but he never expected anything approaching to resolution or decision from such a gentle, loving, and affectionate girl as Edith Maxwell. The event was already settled in his own mind, that she must become his wife, if now pressed by her father's recommendation, and his own passionate pleading. He never had given Edith credit for the firmness she exhibited, never thought her capable (if influenced by any deep regard for himself) of disputing her parent's wishes; but the meeting in the grotto had at once opened his eyes to her true character, when, giving way to mixed feelings of passion and resentment, he attempted the rash act from which he had been saved by Edmund Knightley; and maddened by his interposition, the fiercest passions of his tigrine disposition, increased by the struggle between them, would have hurried himself and his opponent into eternal destruction.

Defeated in his purpose, the fiend of hatred and revenge still held dominion over him, as he walked hurriedly away, until, feeling faint from this sudden exertion, he leaned against a tree for support, his limbs trembling with agitation, and his heart throbbing with violent pulsations. Reaction followed. His pulse ceased its throbbings, and remorse quickly succeeded, when he began to reflect upon the monstrous crime he had so nearly committed, and the gross outrage he had offered to the daughter of Colonel Maxwell, by whom he had ever been treated in the most friendly manner. His mind was filled with horror, when contemplating the fearful tragedy in which he had so nearly involved the woman he loved with all the intensity of his passionate nature. We have seen the result of these reflections in the letter he addressed that night to Colonel Maxwell; and the day following, Chetwynd left Dropmore.

We need not accompany him in his wanderings by many strange waters, for a period of four years; at the end of which, having heard of Edith's marriage with Edmund Knightley, thoughts of home again took possession of his mind, and, in returning, he passed through Florence, where he met with his old schoolfellow, John Egerton, whom he had not seen for many years. An invitation followed to his house, where Chetwynd was introduced to his sister Lucy—their father having died a few months previously.

There was nothing particularly attractive in the features of Lucy. She was neither handsome nor pretty, neither could she be called plain. She had brilliant eyes, and a fine intellectual forehead, full pouting lips, between which, when she smiled, was displayed a beautiful set of pearly teeth; but the whole contour of her face, although not irregular, possessed no definite character except when, animated by conversation, her eyes became lit up with great brilliancy, betraying all the emotions of her soul. Lucy was of a very affectionate and amiable disposition, but she possessed at the same time great firmness of mind; and some might have called her rather masculine in manners and ideas; there was, however, nothing bold, or positive, or pedantic in her conversation, although well read in general literature, as well as the classics, in which she had been assisted by her brother, himself a good scholar. She was also mistress of the French, Italian, and German languages, exceedingly fond of music, and inheriting superior talents in this respect, both vocal and instrumental, nowise inferior to the first public performers of the day. Chetwynd was not only passionately but even painfully fond of music also. He was excited almost to frenzy by its soul-stirring strains, and lulled like an infant by its soothing melody.

The two old schoolfellows soon became great friends, although there existed not one point of resemblance between them, either in form, disposition, or mind; and John Egerton, although his junior by some few years, looked older than Chetwynd. Cares and troubles had left their mark upon the brow of the former, who was serious and thoughtful; whilst the latter, save at times, when memory brought back the scene of his last parting with Edith Maxwell, seemed as light of heart as in his schoolboy days. They were, however, drawn together by early associations, and that tie which on foreign soil attracts Englishmen to each other—partnership in the place of their nativity. They talked of the olden time, when they first met in the hunting field upon their ponies, with Squire Knightley's hounds; of their first hunt ball, and the partners they danced with; of friends old and young, through whom they felt connected by the interest each felt in these mutual relationships.

Thus a month passed rapidly away, a day seldom elapsing without Chetwynd seeing Egerton, for whom he now felt an increasing regard the more he became acquainted with his sterling good qualities. Lucy also had cast a spell of fascination over him by her musical talents and sprightly, though sensible, conversation; and Chetwynd had never felt himself so much at home as in the society of this brother and sister, who appeared all in all to each other. Both had heard of Chetwynd's mad attempt to drown himself with Edith Maxwell, which produced of course an unfavourable impression of him in Lucy's mind; and although ever ready to receive and entertain him to the best of her ability as her brother's friend, Chetwynd saw clearly that he had made little progress in her good opinion. She welcomed him with a smile, as a common acquaintance, but there was no cordiality in her manner, and at times he detected her inquiring glances towards him, when conversing with her brother upon any exciting subject.

They were alone one morning, when Chetwynd said, in his abrupt way, "You do not like me, Miss Egerton; and as you are candour itself, pray tell me the cause why you cannot regard me, like your brother, as a friend?"

"You look so exceedingly fierce sometimes," Lucy replied, with a laugh, "that I am afraid of you; and I have heard you express opinions so entirely at variance with my own, upon a most important subject, that we can have no community of ideas, thoughts, or feeling, without which true and steadfast friendship cannot exist."

"Upon what subject, may I ask, Miss Egerton?"

"Religion," Lucy said, very gravely. "I fear you are a Deist."

"I may answer you in the words of Pope:—

> 'For modes of faith let senseless zealots fight,
> *His* can't be wrong whose heart is in the right.'"

"I believe you possess a good heart and most kind disposition, Mr. Chetwynd: a heathen may possess the same—excuse me for the observation—but that is not enough to satisfy me.

What is your idea of Christianity? You have asked me to speak candidly, I do so at your request."

"I have never bestowed much time upon the study of either the Old or New Testament, for since my school days I have been chiefly occupied in travel."

"But you have seen your favourite poet's prayer realised in every nation you have visited—

'Father of all, in every age,
In every clime adored,
By saint, by savage, and by sage,
Jehovah, Jove, or Lord!'"

"Yes, Miss Egerton, I have witnessed every kind of idolatry and superstition, from the banks of the Ganges to the wilds of America; but of all creeds the Turkish or Mahometan struck me as the most comfortable."

"And under that conviction, Mr. Chetwynd, I suppose you intended Edith Maxwell to accompany you into the Mahometan paradise."

Chetwynd smarted under the lash of this sharp reproof; but after a short silence, said, "You are very severe upon me, Miss Egerton."

"The surgeon is obliged to use sharp remedies to save a patient's life; these are merciful in the end, when they effect his cure; but I have no desire to carry on this conversation further, Mr. Chetwynd, since, if I speak at all upon this subject, I must express what I feel firmly and candidly."

"Pray proceed, Miss Egerton—I am your willing subject—spare not the knife."

"Well, then, you could not be a Christian to attempt the destruction of yourself as well as another."

"No, Miss Egerton, I must admit I am not a Christian. I cannot comprehend the mysteries of the Christian faith. I cannot understand how Christ could be God and man."

"Can you comprehend, Mr. Chetwynd, how body and soul can be one man? It is past your comprehension and mine how these two, the spiritual and carnal nature, are combined in one frame; yet there can be no doubt of the fact. Will you believe nothing you cannot see and understand? You behold a tree grown, but cannot discern any movement as it grows; you feel the wind blow, yet cannot tell whence it cometh or whither it goeth. You know and perceive the wonderful works of the creation, and must confess that by infinite wisdom and power

God has made them all. Have you no wish, Mr. Chetwynd, no laudable ambition, no worthy thirst after nobler knowledge than that which concerns this lower world? Would you be satisfied, like thousands and millions of grovelling mankind, to live and die as the beasts of the field, enslaved by degrading passions and irrational pursuits? Have you a soul, Mr. Chetwynd, so debased and earthly as this? Are your ideas so circumscribed, your mind so obtuse, your intellect so narrow, that you can think of no other world than this? Have you no desire to look into futurity, no longing after a more exalted and happy state, no wish to enter into those blissful regions inhabited by God and his holy angels? Oh! Mr. Chetwynd, do you possess so poor and spiritless a nature, which a dark-minded Indian would blush to confess? How, with such ideas and feelings as you possess, could we be friends? Yours confined to earth, my thoughts soaring to the world above the skies, where I expect to meet those I esteem here, to live together in boundless eternity, as boundless as our love. Surely you must feel, upon reflection, that you have a far nobler birthright—a higher aim than the attainment of those earthly bubbles, which so quickly burst into liquid air."

Lucy ceased speaking, and Chetwynd sat motionless, his whole attention absorbed in the contemplation of the soul-lit features of her whom he had hitherto regarded with comparative indifference. There was an earnestness in her manner, and a transcendent animation in her sparkling eyes, which struck him with admiration, even with awe; and the thought crossed him, "She has a soul and mind above the generality of her sex."

"Thank you, Miss Egerton," he at last said, "for your candour. I hope we may yet be friends, joined in such friendship as you have described. Will you be my guide in search of these sacred truths, hitherto withholden from my sight?"

"Not withholden, Mr. Chetwynd; you have not begun to search after them. You have contented yourself with earthly objects—earthly pleasures. The pages of that book which brings life and immortality to light, you have never perused. But if you are really desirous of such knowledge, I will lend you this work, 'Paley's Evidences of Christianity'"—taking it down from the book-case —"which will assist you in obtaining that wisdom which cometh from above."

Accepting with many thanks the proffered loan of the work, Chetwynd soon after took leave of his now interesting instructress, and remained the whole of that evening engrossed with his new study.

However good in themselves, edifying and instructive, there is nothing like effective, enthusiastic preaching to enforce the truth of the very best sermons; and Chetwynd felt more convinced by Lucy Egerton's persuasive, impassioned eloquence than by the clear expositions of the theologian whose work he was perusing; and he found himself continually sitting at the feet of the female Gamaliel, listening as an obedient little child to her instructions. There was a sublimity in her ideas, a poetical oratory in her words, an animated enthusiasm in her manner and looks, which sent conviction to his mind that every word she spoke came from her heart; and his wild thoughts and feelings were gradually, although imperceptibly, yielding to an influence he could no longer resist.

Within three months from his first introduction to Lucy Egerton, Chetwynd had become an entirely changed man; his restless, tigrine disposition ameliorated, if not subdued; and from keeping a constant watch over his thoughts and feelings, they could no longer break out into fierce rebellion against his now awakened convictions. There had been a sharp conflict in his heart between natural and spiritual impulses, and fortunately in his case the spirit proved stronger than the flesh. Chetwynd had become infected with the enthusiasm of Lucy Egerton in the right cause, into which he now entered with heart and soul; for with a man of his sanguine temperament of mind, there was no middle course.

The result may be divined. He pleaded before her the necessity of her constant care and supervision, to keep him in the path she had taught him to pursue, even unto the end.

"Dearest Lucy," he said one day, taking her hand, "you have begun a good work; oh! do not leave it half done. I may relapse into my former evil ways and errors, from which you have reclaimed me. You have saved me from destruction. We may now be friends, and something more than friends, in this world and eternity. Oh! let me hope that you will henceforth deign to be my guardian angel. By your sweet counsel I have become an altered being. The dayspring from on high has shone into my heart. I have now a nobler purpose than that of living for self, and worldly pleasures; and, in the words of the beloved disciple, dearest Lucy, I beseech you, 'let us love one another.'"

"I will not deny," Lucy said, calmly, "that I feel a deep

interest in your future welfare, and I trust, under Providence, I may have been the humble instrument of converting you from the error of your way; yet marriage is a solemn obligation, too solemn to be hastily contracted. I must have time for reflection. I would see that the seed has fallen on good ground. I will not give you my final answer now, but six months hence, should you continue in the same faith and mind, perhaps," she said, with a deep blush, "I may not be inexorable."

And she kept her word, as Chetwynd preserved his faith and love.

CHAPTER XLV

FROM the death-bed of Sir Digby, we will now turn to her upon whom he had inflicted almost a living death—a sense of shame and dishonour which could cease only with her existence. Two days after the departure of Sir Digby from Pennington Hall, Mrs. Aubrey returned there on a visit to her daughter during her supposed husband's absence in Ireland; and as day after day passed without a line from him, Miss Aubrey began to express her surprise and alarm at his silence.

"It is very strange," she remarked to her mother on the sixth morning, when they were at breakfast, "that there is still no letter from Sir Digby: what can have become of him? I shall write to-day to know if he has reached his place."

"Perhaps he has had a tedious passage, my dear," Mrs. Aubrey said, scarcely raising her eyes from the *Morning Post*, which she was attentively perusing. "Husbands soon forget the time when they were lovers—but, good heavens!" she exclaimed, suddenly, "what is this?" as the following paragraph struck her eye, under the heading of—

EXTRAORDINARY DISCLOSURES IN HIGH LIFE.—We are informed, upon unquestionable authority, that Lady Agnes Colville, whose death was reported in our columns some fifteen months since, is still actually amongst the living, and that she has now returned to her paternal seat, Woodborough Park. It appears, by the statement we have received, from a gentleman of undoubted veracity, and well acquainted with her ladyship and family, that she was left by her husband in a sequestered place in the South of France, and that, in anticipation of her death by rapid decline, he had, before that event occurred, married another wealthy heiress.

"Impossible!" exclaimed Mrs. Aubrey, in excessive agitation; "and yet Lady Agnes was the name of Sir Digby Colville's first wife, and her father the Earl of Woodborough. Oh! my child—my poor ill-used, deceived child! can this be true? can you have married such a monster?"

"Oh, no, dearest mamma, it cannot be true; this is some ridiculous story. Sir Digby is honour and truth itself. He is incapable of such base, horrid conduct. I do not believe a word of it."

"Then, my dear, I will write directly to the editor of the paper for his authority in propagating such scandalous news."

Mrs. Aubrey, however, had her misgivings upon the subject, from remarks she had heard in London about Sir Digby since her daughter's marriage, which kept her in a restless state of anxiety until the answer came from the editor, in these words:—

MADAM,—We beg to inform you that the paragraph to which you have called our attention is strictly true, and although we must decline giving our authority, you will find, upon inquiry, that Lady Agnes Colville is now with her father, the Earl of Woodborough, to whom she returned about a week ago.

"Alas! my poor dear child," cried Mrs. Aubrey, bursting into tears on reading this confirmation of her fears; "it must be true. You have been deceived and ruined by that false, heartless man! His first wife still lives! Oh, what a villain to treat us thus!"

Miss Aubrey sat motionless and speechless in her chair, stunned by this overwhelming intelligence. The shock was too great for tears or lamentations. Her mind became utterly bewildered, and with a deep sigh she fell back in her chair. Mrs. Aubrey attempted in vain to rouse her, and ringing the bell hastily for assistance, her senseless daughter was carried to her room by herself and lady's-maid, and placed on her bed. Miss Aubrey remained in a state of delirium and high fever for several days, her medical attendant anticipating the worst; but at length, youth and a strong constitution prevailing, she became restored to a consciousness of the degraded position in which she was now placed. This feeling caused her tears to flow apace, to the great relief of her overburdened heart; and, by her mother's soothing words and unremitting attentions, she became gradually restored to a more resigned state of mind.

During her illness a letter had been opened by Mrs. Aubrey, from the jeweller, who, having heard these strange reports, wrote to inform her that Sir Digby had called and taken away her diamonds.

"Monster of depravity!" exclaimed Mrs. Aubrey, indignantly. "Of what crimes has not that man been guilty!"

A month had now elapsed since Miss Aubrey's first attack of illness, when Captain Duncombe, who had been well known to Mrs. Aubrey and her daughter for some years, claiming relationship with their family on his mother's side, arrived unexpectedly at Pennington Hall.

"I come, my dear madam," he said, on shaking hands with Mrs. Aubrey, "to sympathise with you in your affliction, and I am also the bearer of a message from Mr. Chetwynd, who witnessed the last hours of Sir Digby Colville, whose death must give you more cause for rejoicing than mourning."

"Dead! is he really dead then?" asked Mrs. Aubrey, in unfeigned astonishment.

"Yes, my dear madam, of that there can be no doubt. Chetwynd saw him die. He was stabbed by his French servant, and left in the old château to be consumed amongst its ruins, where he had intended his unfortunate first wife should have perished; and being rescued from his dreadful fate by the villagers, he lingered two days in great agony of body and mind, until released by death from further suffering."

"I cannot feel for him, Captain Duncombe; he has brought my poor child to the brink of the grave by his wicked, base conduct, and ruined her prospects in life for ever."

"We ought not to speak ill of the dead, my dear Mrs. Aubrey, but he was indeed an unmitigated monster of depravity."

"You may truly say so," Mrs. Aubrey replied, "for he has also robbed my daughter of our family diamonds."

"Of which it seems he was in turn robbed by the Frenchman, from whose hand he received his death blow; but," the Captain added, "these, Mr. Chetwynd thinks, may possibly be recovered, by sending a description of the jewels and the man, which he has given me, to the French police."

"They were of great value," Mrs. Aubrey said, "and the attempt to recover them shall be made through a friend of mine in Paris; but of Sir Digby's death, or the jewels, pray do not say a word to my poor child, who is still too weak to bear any fresh cause of agitation."

Captain Duncombe remained with Mrs. Aubrey three days, by her desire, during which she broke by slow degrees to her daughter the news of Sir Digby Colville's death, which was received with more composure than she expected—in fact, Miss

Aubrey had never been seriously in love with him, but as is the case with many women, her self-love had been gratified by his deferential attention to her wishes and plausible adoption of her opinions. She had never experienced for him that deep, devoted affection of the heart by which a first true love is distinguished; and the infamy he had now brought upon her name and family roused her feelings of just indignation for such an audacious insult offered to her honour.

Duncombe had always been a great favourite both with herself and mother, and his cheerful conversation tended in some measure to relieve the gloomy thoughts by which she had been hitherto oppressed; and at his departure he was again invited by Mrs. Aubrey to spend a few days more with them before their leaving home for Italy, where it was their intention to winter.

CHAPTER XLVI.

At Woodborough Park we find Lady Agnes restored once more to her father's arms, yet apparently to him and Mrs. Errington in the last stage of decline; and, in consequence of their fears, Dr. Bateman, the clever physician of Waterton, who had before attended her, was immediately sent for. After a close examination of his patient, the learned doctor returned to the Earl, who was anxiously awaiting his opinion, and with a cheering smile said, "Your apprehensions are groundless, my lord, I am happy to tell you. Your daughter's lungs are as sound as my own; she is suffering from nervous affections and great debility; her pains in chest and side, although so acute, are merely nervous; it is all upon the nerves, my lord, nothing more."

"Are you quite certain, doctor?" asked the Earl. "May you not have mistaken her case?"

"No, my lord, upon that point there can be no doubt, and I may assure you that in a few weeks your daughter will be restored to health. She requires tonics, good living, and cheerful society; but avoid all excitement. She must be kept in the dark as to certain events which have happened, for the present, and all will be well."

"Thank God!" ejaculated the Earl, "for this unexpected mercy, for I feared my poor child had only come home to die."

"To live, my dear lord, I hope," was the cheerful reply, "to be a comfort to you in your declining years. So now, to begin the cure I have in hand, I will do myself the honour of dining with your lordship this evening, to see what effect a little cheerful conversation will produce upon Lady Agnes, and an extra glass or two of your excellent old port wine. Tonics, my dear lord, porter and port wine are the chief medicines she requires."

"I wish you could dine with us every day in the week," the Earl said, cheerfully.

"I feel flattered by your compliment, my lord; this is rather a leisure time with me just now—fine, clear, beautiful weather, and few cases on hand. Your lordship may have reason to repent your hospitable invitation."

"I shall be the gainer, my dear sir, by your agreeable company and amusing anecdotes; and I really do hope you will dine here as often as you can give us that pleasure."

"The day after to-morrow, then, my lord, you may expect me again, and if our young friend, Edmund Knightley, with his charming wife and children, could be prevailed upon to meet me, and spend a few days at Woodborough, they will help me effectually in my case."

"Yes, yes, doctor, I understand; they shall be invited directly."

Dr. Bateman was what is called a character—that is, an odd character. He was exceedingly clever in his profession, and a man of superior abilities in other respects, and he possessed a large stock of quaint, amusing stories, which he told in a manner peculiarly his own. It was surprising to see with what eagerness ladies would gather round him after dinner, when he began some of these quaint relations, with features calm and demure, whilst his hearers were almost convulsed with laughter.

Dr. Bateman was a fine, portly personage, with a strikingly handsome and intellectual countenance, expressive of great good humour and kindly feelings, exceedingly courteous in manner, and consequently a great favourite with the softer sex, although equally well received by the gentlemen of the county, whose families he attended, his strict secresy when consulted gaining for him universal esteem and confidence; for he was never known to divulge anything about his patients, or talk about family matters. That evening he endeavoured to rouse Lady Agnes from her despondency, relating such stories as he thought would enliven and amuse her, and so far succeeded in raising an occasional smile upon her face.

"Come, my dear young lady, you must take a glass of wine with your old doctor."

"I am sure you will excuse me," she replied, "for papa has given me two already."

"Of sherry," he added, "which I do not approve in your case; so now you must take a glass of champagne with me, two of which you are to drink every day at dinner, and a glass of port wine with your dessert."

"You intend to make me tipsy, doctor," she replied, more cheerfully.

"Oh! no, my dear; champagne is peculiarly a lady's wine, light and cheering; a bottle would do you no harm, and I am sure you will not abuse your doctor for prescribing such agreeable medicine. I must bring back the roses, my dear young friend; you have been starving and frightening yourself to death nearly, on account of the pain in your side, which we must drive away by generous living; and mind, my dear madam," he added, turning to Mrs. Errington, "the porter at night—not a bad composing draught."

Dr. Bateman continued with this lively, cheerful conversation to make his patient feel more at ease with herself, and dispel the fears she entertained that she was fast hurrying to her grave; and his sparkling sallies of wit and good humour produced the desired effect, Lady Agnes being rallied out of her gloomy anticipations.

A fortnight had now passed since Dr. Bateman's first visit to Lady Agnes, who under his treatment, and with Edith now as her constant companion in all her drives and walks, began slowly but perceptibly to improve in health and spirits, although still nervous and anxious about her husband.

"Can you tell me, dear Edith," she asked one day, as they were walking together, "what has become of Sir Digby? Mrs. Errington assures me she does not know, but perhaps Edmund has heard something."

"Why agitate yourself, dearest Agnes, about one who never cared for you, and left you to perish, as he believed and hoped, amongst strangers?"

"Perhaps business detained him longer than he expected, and he might have intended, as he said, returning to bring me home."

"Pleasure, not business, dear Agnes, kept him in London, and he denied you even the pleasure and comfort of hearing from your friends. For fifteen months not a letter of yours has ever reached Mrs. Errington or myself—you tell me you wrote several—and you confess you were kept quite a prisoner in that old château, by the man who had vowed to love, honour, and cherish you as his wife! How can you, my dear Agnes, bestow another thought or care upon such a heartless monster in human shape?"

"He is my husband still," she said, mournfully.

"He has cast you away, Agnes, and cancelled all obligations you owed to him."

"How so? Dearest Edith, in mercy tell me what more he has done; I know and feel there is something you conceal from me; I can bear it now, indeed I can; anything is better than this dreadful suspense. It wears me all day, and prevents me sleeping at night."

"I fear I should be doing wrong to say more now, dear Agnes; but, believe me, you ought no longer to disturb yourself about so worthless a character."

"Tell me all, Edith—I implore, I entreat you, if you really love me; my mind is fully prepared for the worst. You have told me already too much or too little. Let me sit down in this garden chair, let me hear all now; it is indeed better so."

Edith, seeing her excessive agitation, thought it better to comply with her request.

"Well, my dear Agnes, you know how he deserted and left you in the power of his French servants, cutting off all communication with your friends; but you did *not* know the reason he had for treating you thus cruelly. Believing you to be in a rapid consumption, he represented you as already dead. Yes, dearest Agnes, long and deeply were you mourned by us all; and he obtained your money from your trustees, which he spent in paying his debts, and living in his old style of extravagance, and then—oh! I cannot tell you more."

"Yes, yes, you must, dearest Edith," grasping her arm, and becoming deadly pale—"all, everything, you *must* tell me."

"Then, my poor Agnes, that heartless man married another deluded victim, like yourself—young, and an heiress!"

"Married her! did you say?" gasped Agnes. "Oh, no! no! this could not be, whilst he knew I still lived! You have wronged him. He is incapable of such horrible depravity and wickedness as this!"

"He is, believe me, capable of anything, dear Agnes—anything and everything dishonourable and treacherous. Our opinion of him has never changed. We warned you of his true character, although then ignorant of half his villany: but you would not hear a word against him; you would invest him with virtues foreign to his nature; you loved an ideal character, raised by your own impulsive mind and overwrought imagination. All save yourself foresaw the consequences of your rash marriage, as far as regarded your happiness with such a man; and now you would screen his vices, and take the part of one who never loved you, but, despising your weakness, has trampled under foot the laws of Gód and man! There exists not the slightest doubt, my dear Agnes, of his having married another; your own death was announced fifteen months since in all the papers, as was his marriage a short time after to Miss Aubrey—that was her name—an only child, and heiress like yourself. She has a fine place in Lancashire, where that man was living with her, when Edmund went to rescue you from your prison walls in France, and he has now, it appears, deserted also this wretched girl; fearing the punishment due to his detestable crimes."

"Oh, dear Edith! this is indeed dreadful. I could not have believed any one capable of such wickedness, although Edmund had partly prepared me to expect something very bad." And covering her face with her hands, she burst into tears, sobbing hysterically.

"My dearest Agnes, I fear I have done very wrong in yielding to your entreaties."

"Oh, no! dear Edith, the blow must have fallen; but it is hard to bear. It has crushed every latent hope of happiness in this world; for I loved him once, Edith—loved him passionately, and we cannot forget our first love. It is a vision of the past, which will still recur again and again, and hold its place in our memories and affections, which time is powerless to efface. Do you not feel this in your love for Edmund?"

"It is indeed too true, dearest; but had Edmund thus treated me, I could forgive and pray for him, although I could never see or live with him again."

Lady Agnes, feeling it impossible to extenuate or defend the conduct of her husband, relapsed into silence; and although mourning in secret his many crimes and ill treatment of herself, she became, after the first bitterness of her grief had passed away, more calm and resigned to her unhappy fate. Lady

Agnes had loved him with all the strength of her first young ardent affections, and what woman ever forgets the husband of her youth, although stained with the darkest crimes, or guilty of the most base conduct towards herself? In the retirement of her room she offered up prayers that he might be led to repentance and a new course of life; but, alas! for him those prayers had become unavailing; he had gone to appear before a higher tribunal; and when the intelligence of his death was cautiously made known to his sorrowing wife, a few weeks later, by Mrs. Errington, she bowed her head in meek submission to the decree of Heaven, exclaiming, with unfeigned humility, "God's will be done!"

CHAPTER XLVII.

SOON after Chetwynd's return with his bride to the home of his forefathers, John Egerton arrived in London from the Continent, *en route* to the same place, and having a leisure day there, he was sauntering through Lincoln's Inn Fields, when a gentleman accosted him, of whom he had some indistinct recollection, although he could not call his name to remembrance.

"I think, sir," he said, "I have the pleasure of addressing Mr. John Egerton?"

"My name is Egerton," was the reply; "may I beg the favour of knowing yours?"

"Misterton, my dear sir; the son of your old family solicitor."

"Ah! your features struck me as not unfamiliar; but some few years have passed since we last met, when you were quite a youth; but I hope your father is well?"

"I am grieved to tell you, Mr. Egerton, that he has been dead more than twelve months; and when looking over his numerous deeds and papers, one has turned up, relative to your father's affairs, which is of great consequence, and how it became detached from the other papers connected with this property, I am at a loss to conceive; but it is most probable that, when looking over these documents, my father was called away on pressing business, and the deeds being tied up, this was left out for more careful perusal, and by a mistake of his clerk, I conclude, placed among deeds belonging to another property. We held the mortgage upon Hardington, as I believe you are aware, for many years, but upon further advances being required, we were unwilling to exceed the sum already borrowed, and consequently all the deeds, save this lost one, were handed over to the solicitors for the new mortgagees, Messrs. Barker and Grinder, of Bedford Row, whose harsh dealings with your father you, of course, know, and their hasty sale of his property to Mr. Shuttleworth, for a sum considerably below its real value; the costs claimed by these sharp practitioners being quite enormous. Your poor father, however, being threatened with arrest also by these people was obliged to fly the country, and his estates being seized, were completely sacrificed by Barker and Grinder, to cover their mortgages and costs; in fact, it appears they were aware that some deed was missing to complete the title, and accepted the first offer made by Mr. Shuttleworth, who was too eager to close so good a bargain, although himself a retired solicitor, and not ignorant of the hitch in the title.

"No doubt, my dear sir," continued Mr. Misterton, "he reckoned on your father's reduced circumstances, thinking it impossible for him to find the means to dispute the sale, even should the missing deed come to light."

"Then what course do you advise me to adopt, Mr. Misterton?"

"With your permission, I will first take the best counsel's opinion, although I have no doubt whatever myself upon the subject; and if that is in your favour, and you can raise sufficient money amongst your friends to pay the law expenses, we will proceed at once against Mr. Shuttleworth by ejectment; no tedious Chancery suit, my dear sir, which would not suit our finances—but try it at the next assizes. The impression was that the entail ended with your father; but it is evident, from this deed, that he had only a life-interest in the estate, to which you were entitled after his decease; and if, as I say, *you* can find sufficient funds to try the case, *I* can find the money on mortgage to pay off the sum claimed on his behalf as a life-tenant only, and leave you a handsome income from the property besides."

"Well, Mr. Misterton, I am delighted to hear such welcome news; and as my sister is now married to Mr. Chetwynd, to whom I am going on a visit for a few weeks, I will first consult him upon the matter, and perhaps he may assist me to recover my rights."

"No doubt of it, my dear sir; Mr. Chetwynd is a client of

ours, and being exceedingly wealthy, a few hundreds would be nothing to him, and if he will send me instructions to proceed, we will lose no time in commencing operations, and the opinion of counsel shall be forwarded to you at Dropmore without delay."

We need scarcely say with what a light heart and joyful anticipations John Egerton left London after his interview with Mr. Misterton; and it will be readily understood how Chetwynd, with his generous feelings, offered at once to assist his brother-in-law with any sum he might require to reinstate him in his property. Mr. Misterton's views being confirmed by counsel, proceedings were commenced forthwith against the illegal possessor of Hardington, Misterton coming down himself to serve him and the tenants with the proper notices on such occasions.

The dismay of the Shuttleworths was surpassed only by the joy of Egerton's friends, and the neighbouring gentry, to whom this money-made man had rendered himself most obnoxious and disagreeable. Mr. Shuttleworth, however, lost no time in retaining two of the leading counsel to defend his cause, although from his opponent's strict silence, he remained to the day of trial ignorant of the point upon which he was to be assailed, Barker and Grinder, the solicitors for the mortgagees, being the only witnesses on his side, to prove the transfer of the property into his possession.

The court was densely crowded—the cause exciting great interest in the county—when John Egerton's counsel, without any forensic display, quietly stated his client's case :—That the Hardington estate had been strictly entailed by the grandfather of the present John Egerton, but that his father had been persuaded he could cut off this entail by suffering a recovery; but supposing this had been done, as asserted by the opposite party, still he was prepared to prove that deed of no avail.

"Perhaps," he said, "my learned friend on the other side, to save the time of the court, will not object to state whether they attach any importance to that deed said to have been executed by the plaintiff's father?"

Shuttleworth's counsel, fearing to compromise his client's case, demurring to this question, the other continued :—

"My learned friend, of course, is aware that he has no such document to produce, although reference has been made to it in other papers connected with the mortgage; but although he is unwilling to oblige me in this matter, I will produce this deed, which has never been properly executed, and I have also certificates of the baptism of my client six months prior to this date, and his nurse, with two other witnesses, in court to substantiate this fact; so that, another heir having been born to the estate, all the proceedings connected with the sale of the Hardington property have been illegal."

The deed and certificate being handed to the judge, he perused them attentively, and then asked Shuttleworth's counsel what course they intended to pursue. A brief consultation was held between them, after which the leader said that if the plaintiff would agree to repay Mr. Shuttleworth the purchase money and costs of the new house he had erected upon the property, he would advise the defendant to proceed no further in the case.

Egerton's counsel replied that his client was willing to do anything that might fairly be required of him; that he would pay the mortgage money raised upon the property by his father, but not one shilling of those costs claimed by Messrs. Barker and Grinder, for illegal acts against him and his property; and, as to the house built by Mr. Shuttleworth, his client had felt too greatly annoyed and aggrieved by the demolition of the old mansion, with which old associations were connected, to think of paying a farthing for this fantastical erection.

Another consultation was held, for a few minutes, between his leading counsel and Mr. Shuttleworth, which was terminated by the former, who, addressing the judge, said they must consent to a verdict for the plaintiff.

This announcement was received by a cheer throughout the court, which sent the defeated cotton-spinner, or, as he was now styled "The Railway King," reeling out of it; when, another case being called, the large concourse of people began quietly to disperse, many of whom accompanied John Egerton and his friends to their hotel, loudly cheering and hurrahing through the streets.

This was the first check to the ambitious views of this hitherto successful parvenu or money-made man, against whom the tide of fortune had now turned. The news of his defeat reaching London, some depositors became a little nervous about the banking business, and applied for their money; others soon followed their example, and a general run immediately commenced, which on the third day cleared the coffers of Shuttleworth and Co. of every sovereign they contained. In fact, this great speculator had been dealing so extensively in railway projects and other schemes, that his capital was nearly all afloat on paper and scrip, which it was impossible upon such an unexpected crisis to convert into gold ; and a smash was the inevitable result, which ended in his being declared a bankrupt.

Had he been content with railway transactions, he might probably have realised a very large fortune ; but the banking concern caused his ruin, by affording so many more opportunities for trafficking in other people's money as well as his own. By offering six per cent. upon deposits, he drew immensely upon the public credulity, and, of course, used the money showered in upon him for the last three years in every project likely to pay. His purchases of land had been also very extensive. Some of his schemes had failed, some paid him well ; and others again required time for their development, whether they would pay or not. But his creditors would not wait. The affairs of the bank must be wound up, in which about a million of money was involved.

Fortunately for our friend Jack, Grimston Hall had been properly secured to himself and his children, where he was now content to live in a very *humdrum* way, as the Captain termed it, the greater portion of his time being occupied in drinking beer and smoking cigars, until he became as round as one of his favourite casks.

John Egerton had now become reinstated in his ancient patrimonial estates, and the mystery was soon after explained why Emmeline Knightley had refused so many overtures of marriage, and her constant attachment to the once poor, but now wealthy proprietor of Hardington received its well-merited reward.

"We must call upon the Chetwynds, I suppose?" Edmund said to his wife one evening when they were enjoying a *tête-à-tête* after dinner.

"Yes, I suppose so."

"The first meeting with him, I fear, will be very disagreeable to you, my dear girl."

"Oh ! no, Edmund ; not disagreeable, although perhaps rather awkward ; but I hear he has become quite a new creature since his marriage with Lucy."

"Ah ! she is just the person to suit *him*—not *me*, dearest, as you were once led to believe. She was not the sort of person I should have ever fallen in love with—no, not even supposing I had never met Edith Maxwell."

"And why not, Edmund? She is very amiable and affectionate, I think I may add good-looking, highly talented, and nearly as well acquainted with the classics as yourself."

"Just so, my love; but the last qualification is by no means a recommendation to men. Defend me from a classical scholar in petticoats, or a masculine woman! The idea of a blue-stocking seems to dispossess your sex of half their feminancy, those softer, gentler qualities we so admire. You have just sufficient spirit and courage, my love, to make a heroine—*videlicet* your last parting scene with Chetwynd."

A cold shudder passed through Edith's frame at these words, which Edmund observing, he rose from his chair, and, placing his hand upon her shoulder, said almost in a whisper—

"Forgive me, my own precious one! I know a recurrence to that scene must call up painful thoughts."

"And grateful ones, too, my beloved Edmund; for where had I been now, had not the Father of all mercies sent you to my rescue?"

"And I? my greatest, dearest of all earthly treasures! I thank my God daily, hourly—nay, every moment my eyes rest upon those sweet, lovely features—that so undeserved a blessing has been bestowed upon me, for which I can never feel sufficiently grateful. Yes, dear Edith," he continued, lowering himself upon his knees, with his head resting in her lap, "I sometimes think my happiness too great to last—too much for any mortal. Since that day you confessed your love, all with us has been one unclouded sky—unbroken sunshine; no sorrow has for a moment darkened our ever bright days of happiness, no unkind look or reproachful word has passed between us; and I think I may say truly, we have one heart and one soul only, so entirely are our thoughts, ideas, and feelings blended together."

"Yes, my own dearest husband, it is indeed as you say, and the source of my great happiness is that your Edith has made you so happy."

"Ah! my dear child, you are too good, too beautiful for me, and a coronet would have been graced by that fair brow, save for my meddling interference."

"Never, Edmund," she said, firmly; "I have never loved but one, and that one is Edmund Knightley."

"And a most lucky fellow has been that same Edmund, my precious girl, to have obtained this coveted possession."

"How fortunate for me you are satisfied. But now," she

said, with a laugh, "you must rise, my true knight, from your suppliant posture, or Thomas may think you have been behaving very ill, and fallen on your knees to ask forgiveness, if he sees you at my feet when he brings in coffee."

It has been said that "marriages are made in heaven." Some are, undoubtedly—very few—perhaps one in a thousand; the other nine hundred and ninety-nine being mere worldly compacts, matter of business bargains; passion on one side, expediency on the other—perhaps deception on both. How little unity is there of heart and spirit in those thus united! How slight and frail the bond by which two such persons are held together in this unblest, unholy contract! But oh! what a withered heart is hers who has married the man she loves, and, when thus united, finds he has no love to give her in return for her devotion! Ah! that is the canker-worm which eats away the bloom from many a young, confiding wife's cheek—hopeless, helpless, unrequited affection. Such has been the lot of thousands—such was the lot of Lady Agnes. Love on one side only. Such fatal mistakes are of every day occurrence. Why is it so? it may be asked in return. How can girls, or women even, better versed in the mysteries of human nature, ascertain the true feelings of any man's heart? How can they discern between professions and realities? By careful, unprejudiced observation. They must not fall in love with a man first, and then expect to see his imperfections, when a veil has been drawn before their eyes by their own hands, through which they have little inclination to penetrate. This is the old story of trying to believe what you wish to believe. Women are naturally more clear-sighted in these affairs than men, if they will only follow the bias of their own sound judgment, without suffering themselves to be led astray by vanity and foolish fancies.

Men's dispositions are often betrayed by the merest trifles. A look, a word, a gesture, if narrowly watched, reveals their true feelings. Their opinions also upon important subjects may be easily ascertained. Hasty marriages generally turn out badly; and they ought to do so, if they do not. Women have no right to complain of bad tempers and bad treatment, if they despise the most common rules of prudence in the choice of their husbands.

CHAPTER XLVIII.

We are now in the middle of October. The equinoctial gale have been strewing the earth with the bronzed foliage of th trees, now nearly stripped of their faded honours; and many stately elm in Wychwood Park has bowed its head before th hurtling fury of the blast. The six years that have elapsed hav now completely silvered the head of the worthy master of th hounds, although in health and spirits he has suffered little b the lapse of time. He is sitting after dinner in his old arm chair, his only unmarried child, Reginald, occupying a *vis-à-vi* position. Since the marriage of Edmund, and his daughte Emmeline with John Egerton, father and son appear to hav been drawn rather more closely together, for there existed n longer any cause of jealousy between the brothers, when Edmun had his separate establishment.

"Well, Reginald, what sport to-day?" asked the old squire

"Very little, sir."

"No scent, I suppose, with these blustering winds?"

"Rude Boreas did not interfere with us in that respect, sir We had a capital scent."

"What did, then, Reginald?"

"The old story; Will cannot ride up to his hounds."

"Poor follow! he suffers dreadfully sometimes from thos fractured ribs; some six years ago, one was not properly set and at times he can scarcely sit in his saddle over a fence."

"He cannot go on, sir, through the season."

"What's to be done, then, Reginald? Charley will neve make a huntsman."

"I am quite of your opinion, now. Once he gave a promis of better things; but he made a sad hash of it to-day when Wil was not up, and lost our fox for us in a trice by one of his fool hardy casts."

"Why did not Edmund take the hounds in hand, then?"

"Simply, sir, I conclude, because he declines to interfer with Lane's prerogative and our *ménage*. He has always bee a great stickler for orderly conduct in the field, as when hunts man he would admit of no one meddling with him, he in tur will not meddle with Will Lane; in short, Edmund seems no to take very little interest in our proceedings."

"Because he thinks rather, Reginald, he might be considere inclined to usurp your place."

"Scarcely from that motive, sir, since he knows I never pretend to handle hounds."

"Well, what is to be done, as you are the only person to be considered, now Edmund takes so little interest in the pack.'"

"Let him have more, then, sir."

"How so?"

"I have no ambition to be a master of fox-hounds, having no fancy for kennel work, neither is the odour from the boiler, from which even our drawing-room is not free when the wind sets in from the north, particularly agreeable to my olfactory organs. Some out-and-out fox-hunters may delight in such balmy, aromatic breezes, and would persuade you their wives relish them also—*credat Judæus, non ego.* So I vote, rather than give Will a retiring pension for life, and engage another huntsman, which would be paying for two in place of one, that we hand over the whole concern as it stands—men, horses, and hounds—to my sapient brother Edmund, and let him clear off the lot, boilers, kennels, &c., to St. Austin's as soon as he pleases. That is my advice, sir, in these depressed times. Edmund can do things cheaper than we can—hunt the hounds again himself, and keep on old Will as his kennel huntsman—and he has more money to spend than we have."

"Well, Reginald, not a bad suggestion, if Edmund is so inclined. But he is a married man now, and has a wife to consult. Edith may object to his keeping hounds, although not to hunting with them."

"Edith object, sir, to anything Edmund wished to do! Why, the very idea is, begging your pardon, almost too ridiculous. Whatever Edmund does or thinks, is in her opinion right, and I am not quite sure, if he proposed keeping half a dozen other wives, like the patriarchs of old, that she would say nay."

"There, Reginald, you are mistaken in Edith's character; she will not tolerate anything or any one coming between her and her husband's love. That is the point of objection I had more particularly in view; she might fancy Edmund's affection for her would be divided with his hounds, for he is very fond of animals."

"So is she, sir; and I'll bet a trifle she will soon make pets of every handsome hound in the pack."

"Well, Reginald, as they both dine with us to-morrow, we will talk the matter over; but if he consents, I must make him a present of the pack, and the servants' horses also."

"*Volontiers, mon père*—I quite agree in that proposition, and so the hounds will still be in the family."

"More wine, Reginald?"

"No, sir, thank you; let us join the ladies."

Reginald was in high spirits that evening, from the contemplated addition to his income when the hounds should be transferred to his brother, and he was glad to see his father entering so quietly and unsuspiciously into his scheme. Reginald's views as to marriage had undergone no change since his first introduetion to our readers, but were rather more confirmed than heretofore. He was becoming a decided bachelor in ideas and habits, but he wanted more money to spend in London, to which he resorted every season for amusement and gaiety. Reginald loved his liberty and himself. As a single man he was petted by the old ladies, and well received by the young. He was the sole heir to large landed property, although somewhat eneumbered, and might have married well if so inclined. But, to do Reginald justice, he possessed too much pride to make marriage a moneyed investment. He would not have sold himself to a Semiramis for the wealth of Babylon, had he not felt a preferenee for her above other women. He had never yet been truly in love with any of the fairer sex. The sentiment was ineonsistent with his nature. One he had loved to a certain extent, and one only, and she was now his brother's wife. But even for Edith's sake he could not bring himself to tolerate the idea of marriage, when in connection with other drawbacks of limited ineome, and the prospect of a family of ehildren. His stock of love was too small to submit to sueh saerifices of comforts; for Reginald disliked squalling brats, and entertained a great dread of the *res angusta domi.*

Notwithstanding, however, his aversion to children generally, his little niece Edith had worked her way into a corner of her uncle's heart; his former love for her mother, such as it was, being apparently transferred to her little blue-eyed daughter, now four years old. This beautiful child Reginald loved as much as he could love any human being; and his cold sarcastic nature was melted into tenderness by her innocent prattle and sweet, cherub-like features, when sitting on his knee, with her little dimpled fingers twisted about his handsome curly hair, or diving into his waistcoat pockets for hidden treasures. Little Edith had been the means of healing the breach of the two brothers, and his once bitter taunts against her father had given way to the softening influence of his child's sweet smile and gentle, loving manner towards her uncle.

Young Edmund was the favourite of the old squire, but there was no approach on the boy's part to share with his sister the caresses of Reginald. Children are quick in perceiving how far they may go, discovering, as by instinct, who are kindly disposed towards them; and the boy Edmund, having seen no inviting look in his uncle's eye, confined himself to his grandfather's society, with which he felt perfectly satisfied.

The following evening a rather large party had been invited to dine at Wychwood, although it might almost be called a family circle, consisting of the aged peer and Lady Agnes, the Chetwynds, Egertons, and Maxwells, with old Squire White; the only one on the list in no way connected with the other guests. Lady Agnes had now laid aside her widow's weeds, and amongst her friends and acquaintances the name of Colville had been entirely dropped, as if by mutual agreement or tacit consent. This name had long been hateful to her father's ears, and no servant of his whole household ever uttered that forbidden name in his presence. The past was to be buried in oblivion—at least no allusion was ever made by the Earl in any way to his daughter's ill-fated marriage.

Lady Agnes had now entirely recovered her health, but not her good looks. Care and suffering had fretted away the bloom of her youthful beauty, although she had scarcely reached her twenty-fifth year. Her features preserved their natural well-defined outline, but there was a mournful expression in those once dark brilliant eyes, betokening the pressure of some heavy load still lying hard upon her heart. People of course began, as they always will do, to hazard opinions about her marrying again, but no such thought had crossed her own mind. Bitter, indeed, had been her experience of wedded life—bitter, ever bitter the reflection of having bestowed her young, warm affections upon one who had never given her a single token of reciprocal love. All had passed away now, as a horrid vision, rather than a hardly tried reality, and at the name of marriage the blood seemed to grow cold at her heart. She had made her first willing cast in the lottery of life, and it had come forth a blank; by that issue she was inclined to be content, she had no wish to make a second venture. Her thoughts were now devoted to other objects. Her attentions to her aged father were unremitting, in the hope of making some amends for her wilful and unkind behaviour; and her spare time was devoted to alleviate the distress and wants of the poor. Still, however, at her father's request she was prevailed upon to accompany him in his visits to their nearest neighbours and dearest friends, amongst whom the family of the Knightleys stood the first.

Upon this occasion Edmund and Edith reached Wychwood Court early in the afternoon, bringing with them, as usual, their two children, who remained the night whenever they dined there, so that Mr. Knightley and his son had full time to discuss the hunting business before the dinner hour.

"Well, my dear boy," the old squire asked, when he had laid before him Reginald's proposal, "what do you think of it? Your brother, as you perceive, will never keep on the hounds when he may become owner of this place; and I must confess it would give me pleasure to see my old favourites under your care, provided they will not lead you into greater expenses than you can afford. But I shall, of course, expect and insist upon allowing you a certain sum to assist in maintaining the establishment during my lifetime; and if necessary no doubt a very fair subscription might be raised amongst our friends and the members of the hunt to bear you quite harmless. The Earl will help you; Chetwynd, who has now become one of us, is very rich, and a liberal fellow also. Welford, Addleby, and others would willingly lend you a helping hand."

"Enough, my dear father; I will gladly take the hounds off your hands, and will not refuse some little assistance from yourself, if you insist upon giving it; but I will ask of others none at all. Having a large farm in hand, I shall not feel much the loss of hay and corn eaten by the horses—in fact, like fatting cattle, they will return me the only profit I obtain sometimes, in the manure, the extra good quality of which will give me an extra number of sacks or bushels of corn, or double weight nearly in my root crops, so that on that score we shall be nearly even; and I am now keeping a stud of brood mares, whose produce will supply the places of the old worn-out hunters. So there again there will be no drawing on my pocket. And as to servants and the hounds, I shall keep no more cats than will kill mice; so, my dear father, I think I can manage to hold on the old pack in the family without in the least incommoding myself or asking for contributions from others."

"You have not yet consulted Edith or the Colonel; perhaps one or both may object to your embarking in the undertaking."

"Not the first, my dear father; her consent will, I know, be instantly accorded; and I rather think the Colonel will feel pleased than otherwise at my promotion to the honourable post of commander-in-chief in the field, as his daughter, my own darling Edith, will thereby be raised to greater distinction amongst the ladies of the county."

We need scarcely add, that Edith's consent was most readily given to her husband's proposal, since from his prudence in money matters, and his attention to proper economy in the management of his property, as well as establishment, she believed him incapable of undertaking anything he was unable to accomplish, without injuring his income, which far exceeded their expenditure, neither of them having expensive ideas or habits.

"Anything and everything, my own dear Edmund," she replied, "which can afford you pleasure or gratification, will, as you well know, contribute to my own; and to confess the truth, I think a little more horse exercise will be of benefit to your health, for you are beginning to grow rather stout, and I do not wish to see you like my quondam admirer, who may now be fairly called Alphonso the Great."

"Ah, my darling, you are ever trying to find excuses for gratifying my fancies; and now, with a kiss for your kindness, I will just step down to the kennels and pour some balm of Gilead into poor old Will's heart, for Reginald, it seems, told him this morning of his being superseded in his office, which would very nearly break his heart. Poor fellow! he has his darlings like myself;" and straining Edith to his heart, Edmund walked quickly down to the kennel.

Will Lane was not there; but walking the hounds out in the park, with Jack only, the under whipper-in. The old man was moving slowly along, with his favourites around him, his eyes being cast upon the ground, and his mind engaged in painful reflections, when Edmund's light tap upon his shoulder roused him from his reverie.

"Ah! Mr. Edmund," he exelaimed, turning quickly round, "you did frighten me, and that's true; but I'm a-thinking, sir; my thoughts were all wool-gathering just a while ago."

"Well, Will, speak the truth; about what were your thoughts so busy?"

"About them, Mr. Edmund," pointing with his whip to two old favourite hounds; "Mr. Reginald said something this morning about their changing masters. I am old, sir, and handy broke down now with this pain in my side; but it's hard to part, Mr. Edmund, with old friends, although they be but poor dumb critters; they seem to know, poor things, by looking up so sorrowful-like into my face, that we sha'n't be much longer together;" and he turned aside, to brush away with his coat-sleeve the falling tears.

"Will Lane," Edmund said, impressively, as he witnessed his old friend's deep emotion, "have you ever known me break my promise to any one?"

"Oh, no! Mr. Edmund, never."

"Well, then, this promise I make you; you and your favourites shall never part, so long as life is spared you both. *I* am the new master, *you* are their huntsman still, and ever shall be, as long as you can toddle about the kennel yard; does that satisfy you?"

"Oh, dear! Mr. Edmund, indeed it do; it's put life and joy into my old heart."

"Give me your hand, Will; that promise I thus ratify to my father's old faithful servant, and his son's respected master in woodcraft; will that make you happy?"

"Happy, Mr. Edmund! happier than a king. Then Master Charley ain't to be handling them, as I feared?"

"Charley will be handling some other hounds before long, Will, unless he completely alters his tactics. I shall put Jack forward in his place, if he takes any more liberties in the field, and that you may tell him; we can do without him."

"And far better, I'm thinking, Mr. Edmund, since you can help us again."

"Well, Will, now you understand that, as long as you can hunt the hounds, you are to do so; but don't worry yourself about riding up to them, or riding at all, when your side gives you pain. I can do that part of the business, and handle them when you are not at head; but go out you shall, as long as you can sit in your saddle."

"Well, Mr. Edmund, I shall do as you please, but I'm a-thinking you had better take 'em in hand yourself, and I can stay at home."

"No, Will, that shall not be; I shall not be pleased with your staying at home, unless you are really too ill to go out. Two heads are better than one, and we shall play old gooseberry with the foxes—you as huntsman, and I as head whipper-in."

"Ah! Mr. Edmund, you means it kindly, I know; and I shall do as you tell me, but——"

"Another word, Will, and I'll hang up old Solomon before your eyes. Now take the hounds home to the kennel, and as I dine and sleep here to-night, you must come after dinner to drink your new master's health, and hear what your old one has to tell you."

"Ay, sir! may God bless him and you too, and all belonging to you—dear Miss Edith—ah! I'm an old fool, always a-thinking of old times—my dear young mistress, I means, Mr. Edmund."

"She will keep you in order, as well as her husband, Will."

"Ay, ay! God be praised you've got such an angel as that for your wife; it does one good to look upon her sweet face."

"Then come up and tell her that yourself to-night;" with which Edmund turned away, resuming his walk back to the house.

There was a peculiarity in the temperament of Edmund Knightley's mind which unfitted him for worldly life. He would have been considered a fool or idiot amongst worldly men, for he happened to be one of those eccentric beings whose highest pleasure it is to give pleasure and comfort to others. He also possessed a delicacy of touch in rendering such services, which greatly enhanced their value; and happier far did he feel now, when retracing his steps to his father's house, than even the old faithful servant he had left so happy in the kennel, patting the heads of his favourites with cheerful looks and words, although the tear still stood in his eye.

"Ah! Jack," he exclaimed, "God be praised! Mr. Edmund is our new master, and I'm a-thinking you'll soon be in Charley's place, for he won't stand no more of his nonsense. You see Mr. Reginald and the Captain, and some of the fast ones, have set his head all agog, by saying he ought to be hunting hounds instead of whipping-in; but Mr. Edmund says he may handle other people's hounds if he likes, and that pretty soon too; the pack belongs to Mr. Edmund now. Old master has made him a present of them."

"You bain't in earnest, Mr. Lane?"

"Yes, I be, Jack; it's all settled, and he's a-going to build new kennels directly at St. Austin's, and a nice new comfortable house for your old huntsman to end his days in, God bless him! and you're to have another, Jack, when you chooses to marry Betsy Green."

"Hurroar! Mr. Lane," cried Jack, throwing his cap up into the air, which, alighting on old Solomon's back, caused that individual's hackles to rise with a sudden sharp growl and spring of defiance towards his assailant.

"No offence intended, old fellow," Jack said, smoothing down his bristles, "you and I never falls out. Well, Mr. Lane, this is summut to put us both in spirits, and if you don't want me now, I'll just step across to Tom Springfield's, to give him the news, and be back again by bedding-up time."

Tom Springfield was sitting smoking his pipe after dinner, with a jug of two-year-old October before him, on a little round table near the fire—his old father snoozing opposite, in his rickety arm-chair—when Jack's voice was heard at the door, asking if he was at home.

"Yes, he is," cried Tom; "come in, Jack! Anything the matter?"

"Well, sir, there is a little matter I thought you'd like to know about."

"Nothing wrong—eh?"

"No, sir, just the contrary."

"Then fetch a chair and sit down. Now Jack, wet your whistle first—clear the cobwebs from your throat—that will do it," handing him the jug.

"Thank'ee, sir," said Jack, taking a draught; "that be something like liquor."

"Well, now for the matter—what is it?"

"Old master have gi'ed up the hounds."

"What?" cried Tom, springing upon his legs in consternation, "d'ye call that good news?"

"Then this is, sir; Mr. Edmund has got 'em."

"Quite sure of that, Jack?"

"Sartain, sir."

"Holloa, Molly!" cried Tom.

"What is it you wants, please?" asked a round, florid-complexioned lass, appearing at the summons.

"Three beakers, and a jug of hot water, Molly. There, Jack, finish off the ale, and you shall have a taste of this," taking down a long-necked bottle from the cupboard.

"What's happened?" asked the old man, awakened from his nap by his son's loud voice.

"You shall hear, father. Now Jack, out with it, all you know."

"Well, sir, Master Edmund has just been down to the kennel, and told Mr. Lane that the old squire have made over to him the hounds, hosses, and all on us—the whole consarn; and he begins as master to-morrow."

"So far so good, Jack; but what's the cause of it?"

"There, you see, Mr. Springfield, Master Reginald has been long a-talking about having a new huntsman, and wanted to put Mr. Lane aside; but the old squire wouldn't have it. So Mr. Reginald says he'd better give up the hounds to Mr. Edmund at once, for he would not keep 'em on, when it comes to his turn to do it. So old master cuts it short, and hands 'em over directly. There, sir, that's the long and short of the matter—the job's settled."

"And a capital good job too, Jack. The right man is in the right place now, anyways. But what about poor old Will?"

"Just this. Mr. Edmund says he shall hunt the hounds as long as he can sit in the saddle, and he'll ride up to 'em when he can't, and put 'em right for him; but that he shall never have another huntsman put over his head as long as he lives."

The smack of Tom Springfield's large open palm upon his knee rang through the house at these words. "That's him, father—him all over. Master Edmund has got a heart as big as our four-year-old bullock!"

"Yes, Tom, you know he were always my favourite, and I wishes—— well, 'tain't no good a-wishing."

"No, 'tain't, father; wishing won't alter things, but things may come about as many of us wishes, one of these days; so now, father, we will drink to the health and success of our new master, and may long life and happiness be in store for our old one!"

CHAPTER XLIX.

THAT same evening, when the ladies had left the dining-room, Mr. Knightley, turning to Abel White, said: "My old friend, I have perhaps some unwelcome news to tell you—but it is a fact—that I have resigned the mastership of the hounds."

So unexpected and startling a piece of intelligence struck the old squire dumb, who looked as he felt, all amazement for a few seconds.

"You are joking, Knightley," he at last said.

"Indeed I am not. Reginald and I agreed last night it was the best thing we could do, under the circumstances. I am getting too old to see much of hounds now in the field, and Reginald does not feel disposed to carry them on when I am gone; so we settled the matter by appointing a successor at once."

"Ah!" muttered the old man, setting down his glass upon the table and looking hard into the fire, as if there was something there between the bars of the grate which had entirely absorbed his whole thoughts and attention; but this monosyllable alone escaped his lips.

"Don't you wish to hear the name of the new master, White?"

"No, sir," was the short, indignant reply. "I have seen my last day with fox-hounds."

"Come, come, my old friend, you and I must go out to see how they are managed."

"No, Knightley; I've done with it altogether, when you throw up the pack——"

"Unless—you must allow me to finish your sentence—unless you approve our choice of a successor."

"Who is he then, Knightley? Not that coxcomb, Welford, I hope."

"No, no, nor Addleby, who's mad enough to undertake anything. No, White, the new master sits at this table."

"The deuce he does! Perhaps Mr. Chetwynd?" looking hard at that gentleman, with anything but a pleased expression.

"I can relieve you of all anxiety on my account, Mr. White," Chetwynd said, with a good-humoured smile; "I am not the fortunate individual selected for this honour."

The old man's gaze then falling on Edmund's face, he said, "What a blockhead I am! You are the man. I read confirmation in your eyes. It is so, my boy?"

"I believe it is, sir," he replied, "and I hope you will approve my father's and brother's choice."

"They have done well, Edmund; the old pack is still in the family, and I am satisfied. Pass the bottle, I can now drink a glass of wine in comfort."

"Or a bottle," insinuated John Egerton, slily.

"Yes, Mr. Egerton, it may be a bottle. The first words of my friend Knightley knocked me down at once. I did not know how to take them; my heart seemed sinking within me;

and I think, as you say, it will take a few extra glasses to set me right again."

"Well, then, White," Mr. Knightley said, "we must of course drink the health of the new master, and have in Will Lane to join in the bumper."

"Assuredly, Knightley; I second the proposal with all my heart."

The bell being rung—the summons issued—Will Lane soon made his *entrée* a few paces into the room, where he stood, cap in hand. And as he thus stands we will complete the hasty sketch of the man we had before commenced with our pencil—for we rarely use the pen.

Will Lane, as we recorded elsewhere, possessed a very spare frame, well knit together, and what it wanted in robustness was fully compensated for by great muscular power. His height was one inch only short of six feet. His features, if not exactly regular, were not deficient in intelligent expression; and there was a meaning in his full, dark eye and closely compressed lips which a physiognomist could not mistake. His hair had now assumed a very silvery grey appearance, and, save for an occasional twitch about his mouth, expressive of a pang within, he stood almost as erect, and looked as well, as when he was first introduced to my readers, some six or seven years since.

"Come, Will," Mr. Knightley said, "sit down; I have something to tell you."

"I had rather stand, sir, if you please."

"You had better take that chair, Will."

"If it's all the same to you, sir, I'd rather remain as I am."

Abel White rose, without uttering a word, and approaching him, took his cap from his hand and threw it quickly into a corner, then, holding his arm, led him to the table, placing a chair next his own, in which he made him sit down. He then put a piece of cake on a plate before him, and filled a glass with wine. This was done in silence; Will Lane looking all the while like a little obedient boy, by the side of the gigantic form of the Father of the Hunt.

"You don't mind," he then said, "eating off the same plate and drinking from the same glass as your favourite, Miss Edith?"

"God bless her, squire, no. The wine will taste all the sweeter."

"There, gentlemen," Abel White said, "could any of you have turned a prettier compliment to a lady than that? Who will dispute my friend Will Lane's courtier-like demeanour to the fair sex? Egad, sirs! he sadly mistook his vocation when he preferred the pigskin to the woolsack; he might have been Lord Chancellor, or a Bishop, by this time. Well, well, Will, it will very soon be all the same to you and me whether we have eaten our dinners with a steel or a silver fork. The only difference between us then will be, which has done his duty best in that sphere of life to which it has pleased God to call us, and many that are first here may be last in the world to come. An honest and true-hearted man is God's noblest work; and as our Great Master was not above sitting down with a few lowly fishermen, neither should I be. Drink your wine, Will, and munch your cake, or I'll tell Miss Edith you wouldn't eat off her plate."

"No, no, squire, don't tell her what's not true. I'm getting on very comfortably; but I'm a-thinking, sir, I've no business to be sitting down in the company of my lord and the gentlemen."

"I'm a-thinking the contrary, Will. We like your company in the field, and we like it here too, so shut your mouth on that subject. And now your old master is going to give us the health of the young one."

"My dear Edmund," said Mr. Knightley, "in resigning the mastership of the hounds and country into your hands, I feel assured I shall meet with the most cordial approbation of every member of our hunt, and the gentlemen of the county generally. In fact, from your partiality to the sport since a boy, and the talents you have exhibited as a huntsman in the field, you are particularly suited to succeed me in the position I have so long held, as master of the fox-hounds; and I need scarcely add my sincere wishes for your success in this, not very enviable, undertaking. Our friends here are witnesses that I now make you a present of the pack, servants, and horses, which are yours from this hour; and may you have health, strength, and long life to enjoy your favourite amusement!"

The toast was received with warm congratulations to Edmund from every one present, although with no applauding acclamations, not even from Abel White, who, although well pleased with his successor, could not repress a feeling of deep regret at the severance of his old tried friend from the pack which had been so many years established at Wychwood Court.

Edmund Knightley, rightly conjecturing what might be passing through his father's mind, merely said—

"I feel most grateful, my dear father, for your flattering

speech and generous present of the hounds and horses, and hope my friends present will believe I fully appreciate their kind congratulations when drinking my health. I will only say this much more, that if you or Reginald should at any time require back the hounds and horses, they shall be as freely returned as they have been freely given."

"Thank you, my dear boy; but as I never have been much addicted to kennel work, and now care little about hunting, save as the means of meeting my friends in the field, the pack will fare much better with your superintendence."

"That is exactly my case too," Reginald said. "I hate kennel business, and confess to hunting more for the sake of the riding than the hounds. You are just cut out for a master, Edmund, and I wish you joy of your bargain; for, by Jove! I would as soon be prime minister as be at the head of a fox-hunting establishment. Don't think for a moment that I would deprive you of your darlings. They are all your own, and I never wish the *odora canum vis* to assail my nostrils again, as it has done for the last twenty years, when I first throw up my bedroom window in the morning. The scent from the kitchen is bad enough sometimes; but, by Jove! horse-leg soup beats ox-tail hollow! No, no, Edmund, keep them all to yourself, my dear fellow; your stomach can stand this sort of thing, mine never would."

"It is fortunate for society, Reginald," Abel White remarked, "that some of us have stronger heads, frames, and stomachs than others, or the world would never go on as it does. You have always been a bit of a dandy since the days when I used to dandle you on my knees, and a little squeamish too about things which other lads did not regard; but, as we learnt at school—*sit sua cuique voluntas*—you have your tastes, we have ours, so we shall not fall out about differences of opinion. As you don't fancy keeping hounds, it is fortunate for us Edmund does; for I at least should regret exceedingly to see them go out of the family."

"I have only one more observation to make," Mr. Knightley said, "upon this subject, which may as well then be dismissed, and that more immediately concerns my old esteemed servant Will Lane. It is my intention to requite you in some measure for your faithful and laborious services, by a pension of a hundred per annum for your life, with the house and premises you now occupy, and the keep of a horse also, giving you the choice of any you now ride."

"Oh, my dear, good master!" Will Lane said, in a husky, choking voice, "I don't want that, sir, indeed I don't; for I've saved up a little money to make me comfortable in my old age, if life is spared me."

"You have never disputed my will yet, Lane, and you must not now. I am resolved on making you this allowance—it is little enough—but that you shall have, so not another word, for that point is settled and done with; and although I would not permit you to enter the service of any other, the exception, of course, is made in favour of my son Edmund, who will most likely be too glad to have you to assist him still; for, except when suffering from pain in your side, you can handle your hounds in the field as well as ever."

"Yes, yes, my dear father, Will and I have already settled that part of the business."

"Oh! my dear master," cried Will, "you have been too kind to me. I can't thank you as I would. I don't deserve all this."

"Yes, you do, you blubbering old fool," said Abel White; "no more of that now, Will; the thing's done and settled, so drink your wine. How does old Solomon's son go on in his work?"

"He's just like his sire; and I'm a-thinking, squire, he will make just as good a hound."

"That's all right, Will; those Solomons generally turn out well."

"The best in the kennel, Squire; nothing can beat them."

"Well, gentlemen," Chetwynd said, "these matters having been adjusted to the satisfaction of all parties concerned, I hope you will not consider me out of order in making a proposition, which, as a member of the Hunt, I am partly justified in doing. We must feel all grateful to my friend, Edmund, for undertaking the responsibilities and trouble of this arduous office; but I do not think he ought to bear all the expenses too; and as I must say that I am most desirous to share this burden with him, I trust he will do me the favour—for I shall consider it a favour—to accept an annual draft from me, on the first of November, for five hundred pounds."

"Bravo! Chetwynd," exclaimed Abel White; "you are not the kind of man to do things by halves—that is a noble, generous offer; and although the rest of us cannot follow you in such large figures, there are, I believe, amongst us those most willing to lend our young friend a helping hand—with heart and purse also."

"I thank you most heartily, Chetwynd," Edmund said, "for

the kindly feelings towards me which prompted that proposal; but you will perceive my motives for declining it, lest by refusing similar offers from other friends I might be accused of undue partiality or caprice; and at present it is my father's wish, and my own, that ours should not be called a subscription pack. Should, however, the expenses prove more onerous than I expect, I will then, with pleasure, avail myself of the kind assistance of my friends."

"Well, gentlemen," exclaimed Reginald, "as I think we have done quite enough kennel work for one night, my proposal is to join the ladies."

"Ah, Edith," he asked, upon entering the drawing-room, "where is my little pet?"

"Where all the children ought to be at ten o'clock, Reginald; in bed."

"Is it so late, then?"

"Yes, that hour has just struck."

"Ah! that's always the case, Edith, when we get upon that interminable topic, fox-hunting. Old Abel would have held on till midnight; and whom do you think we have had, as an addition to our party, after you deserted us?"

"I think I can guess; Will Lane."

"Just the person, Edith; and I have my suspicions that Abel intended to introduce him into the drawing-room also."

"You know, Reginald, he is a great favourite with me and Emmy; quite a lady's man," she added, with a smile.

"You will have plenty of his society soon, then, my fair sister, when Edmund takes the hounds to St. Austin's, and I rather suspect a little too much of it. But as you are such an obedient, passive wife, I conclude you will put up with that and other greater nuisances."

"Willing and cheerful acquiescence can scarcely be called obedience, and I shall be as glad as Edmund to have the hounds at St. Austin's—they are such noble-looking, handsome animals."

"Oh! of course; but if Edmund fancied some lions and tigers, they would also become pets of yours; you are too passive by half, Edith, always giving in to your husband's fancies. I once thought you a girl of spirit."

"Then, would you like me to convince you that spirit is not lost, by telling you I will not hear a word more against your brother?"

"My dear Edith, you know I meant nothing against him; but, seriously, I should not like my wife to be so tame and easy as to say 'yes' to everything I proposed; a little spice is very necessary to vary the flavour of an every-day dish. I do not fancy plain boiled chickens."

"Neither do I like them, Reginald, with vinegar and pepper; but you are inclined to be impertinent, sir."

"My dear, sweet, charming sister, pray give me a thorough good box on the ear, if you really believe what you say. Impertinent to you, my dear girl! nothing could be further from my thoughts. Well, my dear Edith, there is one great comfort to me, marriage has made you look neither dumpy or dowdy. Edith Knightley will suffer a comparison with Edith Maxwell; in fact, had you been as beautiful then as you are now, I rather fancy I should have popped the question before Edmund."

"It is fortunate you did not, for two reasons."

"What are those, my pet?"

"One, that I am much too tame, you know, to suit a gentleman of your high spirit; and the other I shall leave you to guess."

"I suppose that is not very difficult to surmise; you would not have accepted me? That I suspected long ago. But did you ever behold such a metamorphosis as in your quondam passionate admirer? The wand of Circe could not have effected a greater change than that wrought by Lucy. By Jove! he is as meek as a lamb. But here comes your old beau, Abel White, in whose august presence I always feel like a mouse before a lion, so *addio, carissima mia.*"

The old squire did look very imposing that evening, quite colossal to men of moderate frames; and he was also a dandy after his old fashion, although disapproving of dandyism in others. Abel always dressed well, albeit *more antiquo*—that is, he showed an abundance of cambric frill—not within, but without—the largest white waistcoat in which the human frame had ever been encased. Abel's was a waistcoat, indeed! sufficiently capacious, the Captain averred, to make him an entire summer suit for the cricket ground. His neckcloth might have contained as much muslin as there is damask in a small table-cloth. His upper garment, a large high-collared blue coat, with brass buttons; short continuations, with buckles at the knees, succeeded by silk stockings, displaying a leg which, save for its fine regularity of shape, would have been supposed to be produced by elephantiasis; a neat, highly polished shoe, with buckles, finished Abel's costume. *Ingenti sub hoc corpore*, however, lay one of the most kind and gentle hearts—for his was a meek and lowly mind, condescending to notice the meanest things on earth.

"You have heard, of course, from Reginald," he said, advancing to Edith, and sitting down on the ottoman by her side, "the cause of our rather long detention in the dining-room; but as here this subject is forbidden, I would merely relieve you from any apprehensions as to Edmund's being led into expenses he cannot afford, and say that his father purposes making him a very handsome allowance to help to maintain the establishment; and should that prove insufficient, Chetwynd has generously offered to add five hundred a year, which Edmund, as I anticipated, declined; but it will be my business to raise amongst his friends, whenever necessary, a sum sufficient to cover every expense, and I think you can trust your old friend Abel White to hold him harmless in this matter."

"Indeed I can, Mr. White, and I feel most grateful for the very kind interest you take in Edmund's welfare, who, I am sure, will manage everything as carefully as possible."

"Yes, my dear, he has ever been a prudent lad, with no expensive habits or nonsensical fancies, and he will do things well, although economically. The Colonel, I thought, might oppose us a little; but seeing the general disposition to aid and assist with heart and purse, he is rather proud now of his son-in-law's preferment to one of the first posts of honour in the county, and I suspect will volunteer his assistance also; for, between ourselves, my dear, your papa—notwithstanding his usual complaints about scarcity of money and hard times—has much more of the former than he can spend. Well, all the better one of these days, for my little god-child, who, if it please God to spare her life, will be an heiress.

"Not a very rich one, Mr. White."

"Rich enough, my dear. It is a great drawback to a woman's happiness having too much worldly pelf, which every worldling is trying to pilfer. Heiresses are more to be pitied than envied. Had not your poor friend Agnes been represented as passing wealthy, she had not attracted the attention of that greatest of all villains, some of whose class are always lying in wait to entrap unwary girls when first introduced to the world. Well, I suppose, now that Mrs. Chetwynd has taken her seat at the piano, we must all become listeners instead of talkers. But those Italian bravuras are not at all to my taste. She has a splendid voice truly, and yet the tones want that soft silvery melody which wins and engages our deepest attention by going at once to the heart."

CHAPTER L.

"My dear," Chetwynd said to his wife, the morning after their dinner party at Wychwood Court, "it is our turn now, I think, to have a housewarming, which I propose giving some time next month, and I will ask Edmund to bring the hounds here the next day. We have ample room to accommodate many of our more distant acquaintances, and your brother John will no doubt assist us in this respect. I vote for doing the thing well, with a ball and supper."

"It will be very expensive, Edward."

"Of course, my dear Lucy, it will cost money, but we can well afford it, once in our lives at least, if not oftener, and this is a fitting time for dispensing our hospitality; so you and Emmeline can make out a list of all we know, far and near, rich and poor, lay and clerical, within a certain distance."

"Lady Gertrude and Mr. Shuttleworth, Edward?"

"Yes, my dear, of course. Poor fellow! he is more an object of pity than dislike. We must not visit the sin of the father upon the son; irrespective of which, his wife's relationship to Dunkerton is sufficient reason for our inviting them."

"Is Captain Duncombe to be included?"

"Certainly, Lucy; his mother and sisters also. That Captain is not a bad sort of fellow, and extensively patronised by the ladies."

"So I have heard, Edward; and that Edith Maxwell could scarcely resist his persuasive eloquence to become Mrs. Duncombe."

"There you have been decidedly misinformed, my dear. She had no eyes or ears for any one but Edmund Knightley, since her first introduction to society, although her attachment remained for some time locked up in her own breast. And now, my dear Lucy, having business to attend to this morning, you can drive over after luncheon and consult Emmeline, who knows every one we ought to ask."

A few days after the cards were issued, the Captain dined with his old *protégé* at Grimston Hall, where, from being greatly patronised by Lady Gertrude Shuttleworth, he had become thoroughly domesticated—as much, or even more, than he had been at Hardington during the short reign of Shuttleworth *Père*."

"Well, Jack," he exclaimed, when they were discussing the one bottle of port, after Lady Gertrude had retired, "'you are doing very nicely, my dear,' as the butcher said to the fattening calf; 'and you'll only want a little blood-letting to turn you out into very pretty veal.' What with sitting half the day smoking and drinking beer, and the other half snoozing in that luxurious chair, you are becoming an object, Jack—yes, a veritable, undeniable object of amazement to your friends—a *monstrum horrendum informe*, and I may add the remainder, *cui lumen ademptum;* for as to eyes, you are beginning to resemble a mole, or that fat pig of yours in the sty, upon which you bestow so much attention. By Jove! one can scarcely tell whether he has any eyes at all in his head. But, seriously speaking, you must take to hunting again. Lady Gertrude agrees with me on this point, and I will make you a present of my old hunter, Doncaster, to begin work with on the fifth of November, when all the world will be at St. Austin's, to greet the young master."

"I don't like him, Duncombe, and shall not go out with his hounds."

"Then you are an *asinus*, Jack; for Edmund Knightley is well disposed towards you, although you thought once to rob him of his lady love."

"And you too, Duncombe, I suspect tried the same game."

"After you, my boy, if I did at all—*quod est demonstrandum*, which requires proof; but at any rate, you had your first innings."

"That don't signify; I'm booked now, and laid upon the shelf, with the prospect of running a dead heat with the Patriarch Jacob. By Jove, Duncombe! if they go on multiplying in this fashion annually, there will be a famine at Grimston Hall, and I must cut away into Egypt or France, where food is cheaper than hereabouts."

"Never mind, old fellow, large families always get on better in the world than small ones, and you will be able to put your dog puppies out to walk, with little trouble, if you play your cards well. Dunkerton has friends at court and the horse-guards—get you commissions for two or three, no doubt; and Edmund Knightley can help you with the East India Company, one of the chief directors heing related to him; so to keep well with all, you must don the bit of pink again. You will be forgotten if you sit up here all day, like an owl in a barn. Come out, Jack, into the sunshine—let people see you are alive."

"Well, Duncombe, but, after that unlucky go of the governor's, I am almost ashamed to show my face."

"A pack of stuff! What had you to do with it? You

were settled and off his hands long before that event took place; and I hear that people say—you are to be pitied, not blamed. By-the-bye, who do you think stumbled up against me in Manchester, last week?"

"My governor, most likely."

"Just the man; looking as well as ever—asked me to dine at his shop—everything very quiet of course; but he is creeping up again, my boy; has made a good spec or two already, and gave me a hint he should be able to hold his head up again in a few years, perhaps, nearly as high as ever. Yes, there's the mystery with men in trade, which I can't understand. Down they come—crash, all at once—get into the *Gazette*—through the court—haven't a stiver left—goods and everything sold off; and within a few months there they are again, set up in business, with stock in hand, and credit to any amount. But if a poor devil of a gentleman, like myself, were to get into trouble and lose his money, his dearest friends would not help him with the loan of a five-pound note. I don't mean to accuse your governor, Jack, of dishonest practices, for I believe he intended to act fairly by all; but he had so many irons in the fire, at the same time going the whole hog with his town and country establishments, that I felt sure he would burn his fingers at last. Lucky for you Grimston Hall was settled upon yourself and family."

"Well, Duncombe, what did the governor say more?"

"That he was too deeply engaged at present to pay you a visit just yet, perhaps not for some time; but you were to keep up your spirits, and not stick so closely to the beer barrel, and that in a few days he would send you a pipe of sherry, instead of swallowing such a quantity of malt liquor."

"That governor of mine is not a bad sort of fellow, Duncombe."

"Certainly not, but a long way from it. He helped Dunkerton and myself to some pretty little pickings; in short, to confess the truth, he made a man of me, with those few hundreds I invested in railway scrip—sold them again, nearly cent. per cent., and here I am now at my little crib on the hill, just as jolly a dog as either of your wealthy bachelors—Welford or Addleby—as comfortable as any man need be."

"Without a wife, Duncombe, you should have added."

"I'm not quite sure, Jack, that a wife would add much, if anything, to the comfort of my little hunting-box, which is on a small scale, neat and cosy—room enough for one only. A wife and children would spoil the snugness of the thing entirely."

"You were always such a lady fancier, I thought you could not live without them."

"I may just exist—barely exist, Jack—without one of these dear creatures; but the beauty of the most lovely picture seems to fade when you have brought it home, and look on it daily. What do you think?"

"More than I must say;" and Jack turned a wistful look towards the door; "things can't be undone now, Duncombe."

"Not without a deal of trouble; and you are not worse off than scores of other fellows. Got a good manager, Jack, any way."

"Ah! yes—very; keeps everything in order, and"—

"You too—no denying it, old fellow."

"Fought hard at first for the head place, but it wouldn't do; anything for a quiet life—you understand—quick temper, fretful, &c.—fighting made things worse."

"Just so: the best part of valour is discretion; you are a prudent fellow, Jack. Go to Chetwynd's, of course?"

"My lady will, but I had rather not; poor work looking on when a fellow is booked, with a family of six small children. No woman would dance with me now."

"Ask your old flame, Edith; she is the belle of the lot yet, and she won't say you nay; she is far too kind-hearted to remember the past."

"Then if you think so, Duncombe, by Jove! I'll go. That governor of mine made a sad hash of the job, or she might have suited me."

"Not unlikely, Jack, if you had suited her; but she did not belong to the class of marrying women, that very common class who will marry any man for a good settlement. There you and some others made a great mistake; she was not the girl to have accepted a prince, unless she loved him with all her heart. Edmund Knightley was the man; and a lucky fish he is—we minnows must put up with smaller flies."

"Tea is taken into the drawing-room, sir," interrupted the friends' further discussion upon this subject. The announcement acting as an electric shock upon our hero, by rousing him up from his chair instanter.

"Take any more wine, Duncombe?" he asked.

"We may as well finish the bottle of sherry, not above a couple of glasses in it."

"My lady wife takes two always at luncheon."

"Ah! I see—just the quantum left: don't like a fresh cork drawn for herself, I suppose?"

"You are not far out, Duncombe."

"She has got an eye to business—quick and sharp. Sit down again, Jack, and hand me the bottle;"—upon taking hold of which, he filled his friend's glass, and then his own.

"Who pays your wine-merchant's bill?"

"I do, of course, Duncombe."

"Then you have the best right to drink the wine. Now economy is all right and proper, to a certain extent, but a wife has no business in her husband's cellar; that's your department, and I advise you to keep the key yourself. You have your four thousand a-year, and if you cannot afford to give a friend a few extra glasses of wine when he dines with you, I think that a very hard case indeed; and, by Jove! sir, circumstanced as you are—all the money on your side, and little enough on hers—you are a confounded fool to be kept in this straight order by your wife! You are an easy-going, contented fellow, Master Jack; but you are not to be made a cipher in your own house. A woman has no right to rule her husband, whom she has sworn to obey, and, by gad! if ever I should be fool enough to marry, no wife shall ever govern me. Pull the bell, and let's have another bottle, not to finish, but to broach—and show your butler your determination not to knock under any longer."

"Perhaps we had better not, Duncombe—there will be a row if we do, when you are gone."

"So much the better; have it out, and let her know who's who. I'll do it for you, as you are so shilly shallying;" and rising, Duncombe gave the bell a rattling pull, which brought the butler directly.

"I want another glass of sherry, Plimmer."

The gentleman in black bowed and withdrew, without another word about tea, for there was an expressive look about the Captain's mouth which meant mischief.

The fresh bottle was soon introduced, from which the Captain, having helped himself, pushed it across to his companion, with the remark, "Not a bad tap, Jack, and a decided improvement upon the last, which had been decantered too long; wanted finishing, old fellow—all the better for my lady to-morrow. You are not in spirits to-night; toss it off, I will stand the racket."

"Your tea is quite cold," were the words addressed to the Captain, as he entered the drawing-room, by Lady Gertrude, who was sitting near the fire reading the newspapers of the day.

"Of no consequence to me, I assure your ladyship, as I seldom take tea after wine."

"Mr. Shuttleworth has detained you so long," she continued, "that I was just going to have it removed."

"*I* detained him, Lady Gertrude, not he me; and as to the length of time," taking his watch from his waistcoat pocket, "it is hardly half-an-hour since you deserted us; but the fact was, that knowing your ladyship takes sherry only, I persisted in finishing off the remnants of the stale bottle, and asked for a fresh one for your ladyship's benefit at luncheon to-morrow."

"I think Mr. Shuttleworth takes too much wine, he is becoming so very stout."

"More wine and less stout would prevent him becoming so very stout, Lady Gertrude, and I have been advising him to resume his horse exercise. He must take to hunting again, or he will soon become a waggon-load instead of a cart-load."

"We cannot afford to keep hunters now, Captain Duncombe; we can barely manage as we live to keep out of difficulties."

"One month less in town would give your husband six months' hunting in the country."

"Oh! I cannot give up dear London, it is the only opportunity I have of seeing my relations, and keeping up my connections. To oblige Mr. Shuttleworth, seven months of the year are spent in this dull country place, where one is devoured by ennui, and distracted by the children."

"Well, Lady Gertrude, I think you will have plenty of gay doings here this winter, and I conclude you patronise Mrs. Chetwynd's ball."

"Perhaps I may; but do you think it will be worth a new dress?"

"Worth attending, certainly; for Chetwynd has invited half the county; and he has the most splendid suite of rooms for such a purpose in all Huntingshire. Moreover, Mrs. Chetwynd and himself are sure to do the thing well."

We will only say that the Captain's prognostications in respect of this grand *réunion* at Dropmore were more than realised. It was a splendid affair; and strange to relate, everybody was pleased; even the pettish Lady Gertrude, who, having a new dress for the occasion, displayed it to the full, by joining in nearly every dance, and flirting outrageously with a German cousin, the Baron Sternheim, greatly to Jack's disgust; but as both conversed in the German language, our hero could not collect, save from looks and gestures, the purport of their discourse.

"Who's your friend, Jack?" asked the Captain, "staying at Grimston?"

"Can't say, upon my life, Duncombe. Lady Gertrude calls him Cousin Adolphus; may be so, for anything I know to the contrary; for he's an uncommon cool hand: rings the bell for everything he wants without consulting me; can't drink port, but does his two bottles of claret easy after dinner, and not long about it either. Then off to the drawing-room *squallini bellini* with my lady till midnight, long before which time I'm obliged to go to roost."

"Fashionable looking fellow, Jack, and I dare say well-bred; but I never heard Dunkerton say anything about German connections."

"Suppose it's all right though, Duncombe, eh?"

"Or *vice versâ;* all t'other way; but you had better take a snooze in your arm chair, my boy, and not go to roost quite so early, whilst the Baron remains at Grimston."

"Egad, Duncombe, from what my lady said yesterday, he is booked for an inside place there during the winter. He wants to see English country life, it seems, and foxhunting, so Dunkerton is to be asked to mount him two days a week; and for to-morrow you are to lend him a hunter."

A prolonged "wh-e-e-w!" escaped the Captain at this information, who seemed for a moment occupied with his own thoughts, but after a pause he added—

"Yes, Jack, I'll lend him a horse if asked, and much good may it do him. You shall have old Doncaster though, and come out and see the fun. Now go and ask Mrs. Edmund Knightley to dance with you; she will, if not engaged, I know."

Edith was engaged for that and the succeeding dance; but pitying our crest-fallen hero, who was looking that night the picture of misery, she made him quite happy by accepting him for the third; for since his father's downfall, Jack had become exceedingly meek and humble, and he expressed, as well as he could, his sense of Edith's condescension in conferring a favour almost unexpected.

"I am so much obliged," he said, "for the honour you have done me—for it is an honour I value above all others—and that you do not look coldly upon me, like so many, since my father's unfortunate failure; Lady Gertrude even does not spare me."

"I am sorry to hear this, Mr. Shuttleworth; you are not liable for the faults of others."

"Although punished for them, Mrs. Knightley."

"By the worldly-minded, not by those of Christian feelings, Mr. Shuttleworth. We shall see you I hope, at St. Austin's, on the opening day there, as you have heard, no doubt, of Edmund's taking the hounds."

"Many thanks for your kind invitation, which, although I had given up hunting, I will certainly accept."

"Oh! Captain Duncombe," exclaimed Lady Gertrude, "you are the very person I have been seeking. I wish to introduce you to my cousin, Baron Sternheim."

Bows being exchanged, she added, "Could you let the Baron have a horse for to-morrow? He is a grand chasseur in his own country, and wishes to see how hunting is done in ours."

"*I will lend* a hunter with pleasure, Lady Gertrude; but although accused of being a gentleman horse-dealer, I have not yet put up the notice over my stable door, 'Horses to let on hire.'"

"You misunderstood me, indeed, Captain Duncombe; I never supposed you let horses out by the day or week."

"Then, if your ladyship will do me the favour of calling at my crib to-morrow, on your road to Dropmore, your cousin shall have the choice of the only two horses I have fit for use that day."

"I am exceedingly obliged by your kindness. Have you seen Mr. Shuttleworth? as we purpose leaving now, very soon."

"He was dancing, when last I saw him, in the large saloon, with Mrs. Edmund Knightley."

"Indeed!" was the only word uttered, in a surprised tone, which reached the Captain's ear, as with a bow he passed on.

CHAPTER LI.

THE gathering together of foxhunters, the morning succeeding the ball at Dropmore, was fixed for twelve o'clock; and as every house in the neighbourhood was filled with guests for the last night's entertainment, a very large meeting was expected. Carriages and horses were seen approaching from every quarter, and by the hour named some three hundred horsemen appeared in hunting costume upon the lawn at the western approach, which was separated from the pack by a single chain fence only.

Will Lane, with his pack of eighteen couples selected for that day's hunting, looked the *beau ideal* of a hunstman of the olden time, on his favourite old grey, with his two attendants, Charley and Jack, all in their new uniform, and dressed with scrupulous neatness. Their demeanour also was that of servants belonging to a true English gentleman, somewhat stately, although most respectful; feeling a pride in imitating their master's courteous manner to all.

"Ah! Will," exclaimed the old squire, Abel White, "you look more like yourself this morning than I have seen you this month past."

"Yes, sir, I feels well and happy; it's here, squire," pointing to his breast; "Mr. Edmund's kind words have made me feel as light as a bird. No heart-burning now, squire. That young gentleman yonder," meaning Charley, "don't show us any more of his airs now, since Mr. Edmund gave him a bit of advice."

"Glad to hear it, Will. But we have a large attendance this morning!"

"Yes, squire; I'm a-thinking I never see quite so many afore in this place. Mr. Chetwynd's ball have done it, sir."

"No doubt, Will. There are men from all quarters here to-day, and a German Baron, they say, to see how we do these things; but come from where they may, they can't pick a hole in our turn-out—men, horses, and hounds; and I trust we shall find a traveller to show them the country."

The stranger had selected, as the Captain anticipated, the finest animal of the two offered him, a big, slashing, chestnut horse, called Firebrand, which he bestrode after the fashion of the German school, with a seat and hand more like a cavalry officer of his own nation than an English foxhunter; and it was evident, from the horse's fidgeting and curveting against a too tightened curb, that the Baron was intent on displaying his horsemanship to the ladies, a large number of whom were gazing upon the scene, some from the windows of the house, and others from their carriages. The Captain and his chum, Jack, having taken their glass of jumping powder, were sitting on their horses watching the Baron's proceedings, when the former remarked:—

"Keep your eyes upon him, Jack, on account of my horse. Old Doncaster won't pull an ounce, so take things quietly; ride in your friend's wake, and I've a notion you will see some fun, for that arrant fool knows no more about handling a hunter than a rhinoceros—jamming and cramming him against the bit as if he were on parade."

"What am I to do, Duncombe, if he gets spilt?"

"Take care of my horse, Jack, and let that chap take care of himself; but don't let him have the old one you are riding. Ah! there it is, just as I thought: Firebrand won't stand it any longer; he has reared bolt upright, but the fellow don't come off; that seems a lesson he has often practised before. He smiles and bows to the Marchioness and Lady Gertrude with a *vos plaudite* air. But look! that dig of his spur has made Firebrand mad—he's away, by Jove!" and with a bound, catching the bit on his teeth, Firebrand dashed furiously for the chain fence, over which he sprang high in the air, taking it sideways, and throwing his tormentor clean out of the saddle.

"Ah!" cried the Captain, "he is down on his knowledge box; pick up your friend, Jack, whilst I go for my horse."

Save the crumpling of a new beaver into something like an opera hat, the Baron sustained little or no damage to *propria persona*, or to his other vestments, the turf being soft and clean. He picked himself up without waiting for Jack's assistance, for which he might have waited some time, since our hero did not exhibit the slightest appearance of alacrity in rendering aid to the discomfited Baron, who looked exceedingly disgusted with the result of his grand display of equestrianism in the presence of this large phalanx of female beauty.

Firebrand, having been captured by a groom, was led back by the Captain to his rider, who had remained stationary on the spot where he fell, apparently wholly intent on restoring his hat to its former shape, but in reality dreading to appear on foot before the ladies.

"I tank you, sare," he said, addressing the Captain, "for de troble you take in catching mine horse; but he want de *manége*, sare; he no half taught de use of de bit in his moth."

"We don't break our hunters, sir, in riding-schools," the Captain replied, rather testily; "this horse will not stand what you call the *manége*—holding him tight by the head, and cramming the spurs into his side at the same time. In our hunting fields we ride with a slack rein, Baron."

"Vare well, sare; I much oblige for de loan of your horse, and de advice."

"I dont like the look of that fellow, Will," remarked Edmund to his huntsman.

"Nor I, sir," was the reply; "and I'm a-thinking he will be in a-top of the hounds, if they get in his way."

There was a short dialogue between master and man, after which the former, riding up to his first whipper-in, said something in a low tone, to which the only response audible was, "Yes, sir," with a hand raised respectfully to his cap.

"Now, Will," cried Edmund, "we are ready, move off."

On the signal to advance being given, the master and Charley put themselves at the head of the pack to clear the way, Tom Springfield and Jack acting as rear-guard. The laurels on the pleasure ground were to be first drawn, and the day being fine, many ladies were walking about the lawn facing the south-west, to which there was no admission for horsemen, Will Lane and Charley attending the hounds on foot. Within five minutes after a crash was heard through the evergreens, which sent the pheasants whirling up in the air, with their beautiful plumage glittering in the sunbeams; like so many skyrockets, and the hares scurrying and scuttling about the lawn in frenzied bewilderment, running against each other and the ladies, like a lot of rats bundled out of an old corn-stack. Every hound is at him—every tongue let loose—as the fox breaks from the centre belt of laurels across the open green-sward in view of the whole pack.

"Oh, how charming! what a beautiful sight!" burst simultaneously from a hundred pair of rosy lips, the owners of which think little in that moment of excitement of the quivering heart, beating with suffocating sensations, in the body of that little scared animal, flying in terror from his ruthless pursuers, all frantic for his blood. How little do those fair ones consider what their own feelings would be if chased by a body of Red Indians, and obliged to run for their lives!

Roused by the echoing cry of the hounds, every horse is set in motion, prancing, plunging, curveting—all champing their bits with eager impetuosity to join in the fray. The fox makes for the lower bed of evergreens, near the wicket gate leading into the park, towards which a rush is made by the whole cavalcade, the foremost of whom arrived there just in time to head him before he had emerged five yards from the fence. He turns short, nearly into the mouths of his pursuers, but eludes their fangs. Again wood, hill, and dale resound with the merry cry of hounds as they race him up the narrow plantation under the boundary wall; again he breaks in view before them across the long terrace-walk, at the extreme end of which stands an old-fashioned rustic summer house, then unfortunately occupied by a nursery maid and two children, by whom the fox is again headed, and, dashing into a bed of rhododendrons, is lost to sight—for a moment only; he reaches the large middle belt once more, is whirled round and round by his maddened foes.

A lady meets him with her parasol, as he makes an effort to escape their jaws; he turns short to the right towards the house; he is outflanked by the wide-spreading pack, some of which dashing from the covert meet him at right angles, and roll him over on the lawn.

"Oh! how horrid!" is now the exclamation from all the fair lookers-on. "Poor thing! what a dreadful death!"

"Dat de ladies' vox, I suppose," the Baron remarked to Captain Duncombe; "de scene very good, and de music of de dogs—but no gallop for de *cavaliers*."

"That is to come now, I hope," was the reply; "the ladies first, gentlemen next; that's the order of things in our country, Baron."

"You manage dis ting very well, Capitain—von *grand spectacle*, we see it all—de hunting, de dogs, and de vox killed."

"Now then, Baron, we shall find a gentleman's fox in yonder wood," as Will Lane was trotting away across the park in close converse with his young master.

The hounds were thrown into covert very quitely, and Charley went trotting briskly down the drive to the gate at the further end, through which he speedily disappeared.

"Where dat hunter go? I follow," the Baron said, about to start after him.

"No, no, Baron, stop—that won't do; he is only the whipper-in, sent forward to view the fox away; we must wait for, and follow the hounds."

"Vary well, sare; but hark! I hear de dog bark; he find de fox now."

"Presently, Baron; all in good time; that's only old Solomon speaking on the drag."

"Dat Solomon grand dog, I suppose; he got fine name."

"He's a wise old fellow, like his Jewish namesake; he tells us the fox has been here; but as the other hounds don't join, I fear he has given us the slip.

The Captain was not wrong in his conjecture. An old fox, hearing the clatter on the lawn, had quitted his quarters long before the hounds entered the wood; but old Solomon, with a few others, kept working on his line, until they marked it away in the field below.

"That's the fox we want to-day, Will," Edmund said, as the hounds kept feathering on.

"Well, sir, then we can let 'em try a bit what they can do; they seems to like it better, sir, as they push on under the hedge, and if we can get up to him he is the right sort to show us some sport."

In this manner the hounds had traversed four large pasture fields, although with little improvement as to pace, when Will Lane said, "Perhaps, sir, we had better hold on at once to Moor Copse; that's his point, sir—and get out of the crowd of gentlemen who keep pressing forward."

"Not yet, Will—an old cunning fox, when not found by hounds, will lie up in a hedge-row sometimes. Give them a few minutes more; and look! the young ones are getting on now. Work of this kind will do them good."

"Dis vara slow," the Baron remarked; "mine horse, he pull so to get on."

"It will be fast enough presently," the Captain replied; "this is what we call walking up to our fox."

"Ah! vara good! we walk truly; dis no grand vox chasse."

The words had scarcely passed his lips when, on the other side of a thick sedgy hedge-row, a sudden chorus burst forth from the whole pack, which sent every man's heart bounding to his throat. The fox had sprung out just before the hounds reached it.

"Come on!" screamed the Captain, as he sent his horse at the double fence, getting in and out of the opposing quickset very cleverly, on the other side, over a drop leap into a dark peaty meadow. "Now, gentlemen," he said, looking back, "take your places," as men and horses came floundering down, many of the former showing the way, headforemost, to their astonished steeds. Firebrand would have it now all his own way, and the Baron, remembering his owner's advice, and thinking it most prudent not to dispute the point with him, gave him his head.

"Mine ——, what a leap," he muttered, as he was thrown forward upon the pommel of his saddle, by Firebrand's coming down upon his knees; "dis horse, he jump *terrible;* but where de dogs—me no see them—how me follow?"

"Go along, sir!" roared a first-flight man, dashing past him; and along he *was* carried, amidst a shower of peat mud dotting him all over like a cameleopard. The fox had skirted the corner of Moor Copse, through which the hounds dashed like lightning, and were now streaming away across the second meadow at a terrific pace, with Edmund, Will Lane, and Charley only in their wake.

"Come along, sir," shouted the leader, whom Firebrand

seemed determined to follow, "come along!" as he sprang over the fence into the thicket; "we shall see them the other side."

"Oh! mine head! mine hat," cried the luckless Baron, being torn through the stiff blackthorns at the mercy of Firebrand, held only by one hand, the other being raised to defend his face from the sharp prickles. "Dis place *terrible*."

"Never mind, sir; come along!" again reached his ear, and the Baron showed on the other side a figure to behold; without his hat, his long hair hanging in wild disorder over his scratched and bleeding forehead.

Some dozen pink jackets were now added to his company, who all boldly encountered the stiff fences and deep ditches of some half score rough pasture fields. Firebrand carrying his rider cleverly over all without a stumble.

"The river, by Jove!" exclaimed his leader, "and not a bridge in sight: have it we must."

"Me no swim, sare," cried the Baron in consternation at the wide, rapid stream, within one field of them.

"Your horse can—so come along!" and splash went horse and rider into the bed of the foaming torrent.

"Oh! mine got," exclaimed the now terrified Baron, as Firebrand sprang high in the air, to clear it at a bound. Oh! dis is *terrible* work; dis gentleman vox, he der Freiscühtz, de red *diable*." Further words were stopped, by the spouting and splashing of water about his ears, from which, when emerging, the only visible sign of Firebrand was his head above the eddying current.

"Give him his head to follow me, and don't pull the reins," was again shouted forth from the bit of pink cloth, now sailing rapidly down the stream, which in a few minutes was seen to elongate up the bank, at a place where cattle came down to drink. "All right again—here we are on terra firma once, more—now for it, to catch them!" and away sped the first-flight man like an arrow from a bow, renovated by his shower-bath for fresh exertions. "Hark! I hear them; hark!—they have reached Hazlewood. Oh! for two turns there in my favour and we shall be up with you, my young master. Ah! how they rattle him round the covert—every hound seems to have him in view. Ay! there's Charley's holloa: hark back! he has been headed!"

A moment's pause——the pack have swung a few yards outside the wood hedge.

"Hark back!" again cried Charley, with a rate and crack

of his whip. They turn like lightning to the well-known tongue of Old Solomon, who has met the fox, and in a second the wood re-echoes with the full chorus of the pack, crashing and dashing through the stuff, which bends before them like reeds to a flood of outbursting waters. "Twang—twang—twang" goes the horn: "Forward, away!" screams the master; "yonder he flies, up the side of the hedge-row to the right."

"Ay, ay! a bit of luck for me now," exclaims the leader of the Baron; "they are turning our way; but, hang it all, that double post and rails, with a blown horse! Must do it steady in and out—come along!"

Our leader on his made hunter bounds in and over cleverly the opposing bars; but hearing a crash behind him turns his head, and there lies the Baron on his back, and Firebrand disentangling himself from the splintered timbers.

"Hurt, sir?" asks one of the dozen, now pressing on.

"Oh! mine vriend—mine arm."

"Ah! nasty fall, very," replied the other, passing on; "can't stop; doctor behind."

"Come along, sir!" roared another voice, "your horse is caught for you, and they are at check."

The Baron, thus roused, discovered he had only strained his wrist, and by running across one field, found his horse tied tightly to the gate post. He had only, however, just time to re-mount when "Forward!" again rang in his ears.

"Ah! dis chasse," he muttered, "de cry, it always be de same—vorward, vorward; vere to dis gentleman vox go?" he inquired of his leading friend.

"Ten miles more, perhaps," was the quick reply, "come along."

"Oh! dat man, he alway say 'Come along——' vare to, I wish to know?"

They had now reached a small thick covert on the crown of a hill, in which the gallant old fox hung for a few minutes, with the vain hope of shaking off his pursuers.

"Ah! there they come," exclaimed his conductor, looking back upon the vale they had just traversed; "the bridge and road have let in the ruck to that line of gates—see how they hustle and bustle along through them. By Jove! they will catch us up now. Confound this wood! yet listen! do you hear the hounds?"

"No, not one dog barks."

"Then they are away—the master and the huntsman have

given us the slip—come along!" and setting spurs to his horse, the leader rounded the crest of the hill. "Ah! yonder they go, all clustering together like a flock of pigeons, and as mute as mice, heads up and sterns down, running as if they had him in view: come along," and crash went the speaker through a thick bullfinch, leaving one skirt of his coat fluttering on a blackthorn bough.

"Stop, monsieur! you lose your coat and pocket-handkerchief."

"Never mind; come along."

"Ah! dat man—dat 'Come along!' he leave his leg behind, and still say 'Come along!' Dis English chasseur, he de bery *diable*," and rush went Firebrand through the fence, and with another fearful scratch across the Baron's face, he was landed in the field below like a trapped frog, with arms extended round his horse's neck.

"A near go," was whispered almost in his ear by a well-known voice. "Pick him up, and come along."

"Aha, Capitain, dat you?"

"I hardly know; Dick Highflyer said he should not have known me, save for the colour of my horse's mane."

"Where you been, Capitain?"

"Pitched head foremost into a bog—left one boot there, and my hat: ride al Turco, now, with my bandana round my head; but never mind, come along;" and away went the Captain on his Arab, switching his tail from the prick of the one spur, with Firebrand and the Baron in close companionship.

"Ven dis *grand chasse* end, Capitain? I am vara fatigue."

"Keep up your pluck, Baron, we haven't half done yet; now for a fly," as a five-barred gate stood in their way. Over went the Captain like a bird; but the Baron, remembering his last mishap at timber, pulled Firebrand with a jerk on taking off, which threw him across the top bar; but being old it gave way, saving the Baron from a rattling fall.

"Just missed a broken neck, or smashed ribs, Baron," cried the Captain, hearing the crash. "Give him his head, sir, or he will give you something to remember presently."

For four miles further the hounds held on their course with little variation in speed, and each man was obliged to be content with the position he held; the edge had been taken off their horses' mettle, which now took their fences more deliberately, and their riders began to see the necessity of husbanding their strength for prolonged exertions.

"Well, Baron," asked the Captain, "what think you now of our foxhunting?"

"Vara grand, mine vriend—ride, ride, ride; jomp, jomp, jomp; but me not see von dog, or dat gentleman vox; dat leetle animal he go *terrible* fast vor dog not to catch him."

"Look out, Baron," cried the Captain, as they were galloping side by side towards a gentleman's seat, "there's a drop t'other side, sit back."

"Ha! Ha! mine vriend, dat jomp take me by surprise."

"Just so, Baron; we call it—ha! ha! Hark! by Jove, there's a holloa the other side of the house, and there they go; you see the hounds now, Baron, running up that ploughed field yonder to the right?"

"Ah! me see de dogs—look vara leetle now."

"They will look less presently, if we do not mend our pace; the ground goes lighter, so come along," when switch went the Captain at a stone wall, over which, touching the top of it with his hind legs, his horse sprang cleverly.

"Dis vorse and vorse," muttered the Baron, "Virebrand not go drow dem. Mine heart! vot a clatter!" as a cart-load of stones followed his descent into the next field: "ah, dere bigger von to come."

"The gate in the corner," cried the Captain, looking back; "follow me."

"Ah, de choice of de two evils; but Virebrand, he break de gate." Firebrand, however, did not effect this so cleverly as the last, the bars being new and stiff, and the result was a roll over of biped and quadruped into a road, biped going first, to make a cushion for the other to fall upon.

"Hurt?" asked a familiar voice, as horse and rider staggered to their legs.

"Oh! oh!" gasped the poor Baron, beginning to recover his breath.

"Here, old fellow, have a pull at my flask," said our friend Jack; "pumped the breath out of your body, that's all; queerish about the stomach, Baron, eh?"

"Vara uncomfortable here," putting his hand on his chest.

"Never mind, soon go off—all right again. Here's a road, no more fencing yet, so come along."

"Ah! mine vat host, he wheeze out, too, 'Come along!' Dat seem de war-cry of dese English vox hontsmen."

For a mile and more Jack took the lead of his German cousin along the road, bespattering him all over with mud and mire, when, to his inexpressible delight, the fox crossed over some three hundred yards before him.

"There he goes, by jingo!" cried Jack, slackening his rein.

"Vat go, mine vriend?"

"The fox, by all that's lucky! There, Baron, you see him going over that field to our left?"

"Ah! me see; but vare de dogs and de hontsmen? Me vish dey catch dat *terrible* vox."

"Hurrah! here they come, helter-skelter over the wall; they'll have him now, Baron; we are first at last; come along."

Jack and his friend now took up the running at their best speed, going down the hill to meet the hounds, which were bending towards them, when the highest of all the stone walls they had yet seen—the boundary of an old park—stopped them short in their career.

"You not jomp dat, Shuttlevorth?"

"No, hang it," cried Jack; "but hold my horse, whilst I make a way through," and down came the stones on both sides, until a breach was effected, through which old Doncaster scrambled to his cautious rider on the right side.

"Now," cried Jack, safe in his pigskin, "come along, there go the hounds over the opposite hill; that confounded wall has spoilt our start; but see, here is another road all in their line."

The hounds, as Jack had said, were now climbing the opposite hill, having passed through a small covert in the narrow though deep valley below, which offering considerable obstruction to those unacquainted with the only narrow track-way leading out of this thicket, Edmund and Charley were the only two with the hounds, Will Lane being unable any longer to keep his place.

"By Jove, my Lord," cried the Captain to the first-flight man, as they were toiling up the opposite bank together, "they have slipped us again; but there's the huntsman just before us; where are the hounds, Will?"

"Right ahead, sir; I can't go much farther; but young master is with 'em."

"Where's his point now, Will?"

"Conholt Woods, Captain, I'm a thinking if he can reach 'em."

"What! five miles further still! By Jove! my Lord, this *is* a run."

"Just the thing I like, sir; so come along."

The pace begins to slacken as some arable fields are crossed, and at last the hounds threw up on a piece of fallow, where the fox had been headed by a plough team.

"Turn them to me Charley," cried Edmund; "he must be to the right; see those magpies flying and chattering above that hedge-row yonder; that's his line; look how they dart down now—they view him if we don't. Here, here, here," cried Edmund, lifting his hounds over the fallows; "forward, my lads!" and with heads up and sterns down, away went the pack with fresh energy.

"Now we shall have him ere he reaches that big wood."

"Tallyho!" shouts Charley; "there he is in view, across that grass field." Foreman and Fleecer are racing for his brush; he makes one last effort, eludes Fleecer's fangs, and bundles through the wood hedge. Foreman springs over.

"Beat us, sir," says Charley, "at last."

"Not so, they have him!" exclaims the delighted master; "that sound of almost stifled tongues, none can mistake."

"Whoo-whoop!" shouts Charley, jumping from his horse and tearing through the black thorns, "they *have* got him, whoo-whoop!"

Captain Duncombe and the Earl of Waterton—Edith's former suitor—were toiling up the furrows of a heavily ploughed field, their horses scarcely able to make a trot, when the former exclaimed, "Hark! my Lord, that's Edmund Knightley's whoo-whoop—ay, they have him—I hear now the baying of hounds. By Jove! that's a rare piece of luck, before he could reach those thundering big woods; we may take it quietly now."

"I am for keeping my place, Duncombe, from find to finish. There are some half-dozen pinks behind us straggling along here and there, so come along."

Our friend Alphonso, meanwhile, had, with his German cousin, fortunately fallen into the wake of Will Lane, who knew a by-lane leading up to the covert.

"Now, gentlemen," cried Will, seeing them at a loss what to do, "follow me; I'm a-thinking we shall get up in time to see him afore he is thrown to the hounds."

"What, have they killed him?" asked Alphonso.

"Ay, sir, sure enough. I hear Mr. Edmund's scream, there's no mistaking what that means."

"De dogs got dat gentleman vox at last, eh, mine vriend?"

"Yes, Baron, it's all right."

"Me so tankful dis *terrible* chasse is done."

"Come along then, there will be other chaps getting in before us; let us ride on as quickly as we can."

Edmund Knightley, with the desire to please the select few whom he could perceive struggling up in awkward plight, on their distressed horses, had thrown the fox over the bough of a tree standing in the centre of the field, around which the hounds were baying, their deep tones mingling with the shrill notes of his horn, when the Earl of Waterton made his appearance first on the scene, being soon followed by the Captain and Reginald Knightley.

"Capital wind up, Knightley," he exclaimed; "I congratulate you upon so satisfactory a result: a very near thing though?"

"Rather; but they would have had him three fields back, save for a plough team; and yet so beaten was he that these big woods could scarce have saved his life."

"Well done, Edmund!" cried Reginald, now walking his horse leisurely in; "that old gentleman has tried the nags to-day, and mine has had more than *quantum suff.* Not quite in trim yet; too early in the season for a splitting run like this. By gad, there's a fellow in every field between this and Moore Copse; but, by all that's ludicrous, who's that coming up with old Will, tattered and torn, and all forlorn, without his hat?"

"Baron Sternheim," the Captain said, "to whom you were introduced last night by Lady Gertrude."

"By gad!" Duncombe, I should scarcely recognise him in this disguise."

"Ah! mine vriend has been in de wars to-day. I vonder how he relishes dat vox *chasse* now. By gad, sir, his face is cut to ribbons."

"He does not want pluck, Reginald," Lord Waterton observed; "for I can answer to his having had some rattling falls; and he took the river like a duck, where he got a precious ducking with myself."

"A *nolens-volens* sort of venture that, I suspect," the Captain remarked; "Firebrand *would* have it, whether the Baron would let him or no. 'Heigho! says Roley,' like the frog who went out courting against his mamma's wishes."

"Better offer him the brush, Reginald," Edmund said, "if Waterton does not want it—he was first up."

"Let the Baron have it by all means," Lord Waterton replied.

"Ah! mine leetle vriend," the Baron said, now approaching the tree, "I am so glad to see you dare; you give de great trouble to catch you."

"I hope you enjoyed your gallop?" Edmund said.

"Vell, tank you; de *chasse* vara grand; but dat jomp, jomp, jomp, *terrible* work; and dat river! ah, but vor mine vriend dere in de half coat, me veed de vishes at de bottome. I tank you kindly, sar, now, vor your good adviee, and leading me out de foaming stream. Aceept mine obligations and mine card," he continued, tendering his bit of pasteboard to Lord Waterton, who expressed his pleasure at having been able to render the Baron that little service, and offered his own card in return.

"Ah!" he exclaimed, glaneing at the name, "you noble rider as well as nobleman. You grand nation of vox hontsmen."

"My brother has desired me to offer you the brush, Baron Sternheim," Reginald said, "we eonsider it the trophy of war."

"I tank your broder moeh, he vara good; but me no take it from me Lord Waterton, he eome first."

"No, no, Baron, thank you. It is your first appearanee in the hunting field, and we must all beg your aeeeptanee of it for having ridden so gallantly, without your hat, through this severe run. Your friend Shuttleworth will have it properly preserved for you."

"Tank you, me lord. I shall prize it vara moeh, as a memento of my first *introduction* to your grand English *chasse*."

A ring having been formed by the horsemen round the tree, Edmund Knightley held the fox for a moment above his head, and then with a short shrill view holloa, threw it to the expeetant pack, jumping and baying around him.

"Ah, dat shriek!" eried the Baron, "it go drough mine ear," putting his hands to his head; "but dat leetle vox, he soon devoured by dose grand dogs; dey eat him up, skin and all."

"Now, gentlemen," said Edmund, remounting his horse, when the last ceremony had been performed, "having done our best to eater for your amusement, we hope you are satisfied with 'Our Finish.'"

THE END.

CPSIA information can be obtained
at www.ICGtesting.com
Printed in the USA
LVHW022012120422
716028LV00006B/219

9 783752 590043